The Dawlish Chronicles

Britannia's Innocent
February – May 1864

Britannia's Guile
January – August 1877

Britannia's Wolf
September 1877 - February 1878

Britannia's Reach
November 1879 - April 1880

Britannia's Shark
April – September 1881

Britannia's Spartan
June 1859 and April - August 1882

Britannia's Amazon
April – August 1882
(Includes bonus short story *Britannia's Eye*)

Britannia's Mission
August 1883 – February 1884

Britannia's Gamble
March 1884 – February 1885

Britannia's Morass
September – December 1884
(Includes bonus short story *Britannia's Collector*)

Britannia's Rule
September 1886 – April 1888

Being events in the lives of:

Nicholas Dawlish R.N.
Born: Shrewsbury 16.12.1845
Died: Zeebrugge 23.04.1918

and

Florence Dawlish, née Morton
Born: Northampton 17.06.1855
Died: Portsmouth 12.05.1946

Britannia's Rule

The Dawlish Chronicles
September 1886 – April 1888

By

Antoine Vanner

Britannia's Rule - Copyright © 2022 by Antoine Vanner

The right of Antoine Vanner to be identified as the author of this work has been asserted by him in accordance with the British Copyright, Design and Patents Act 1988.

All rights reserved. No part of this book may be reproduced or transmitted in any form or by any means, electronic or mechanical, including photocopying, recording or by any information storage and retrieval system, without written permission from the author, except for the inclusion of brief quotations in a review.

Library of Congress Cataloguing-in-Publication Data:

Antoine Vanner 1945 -

Britannia's Rule / Antoine Vanner.

Paperback ISBN: 978-1-943404-44-5

Kindle: ISBN: 978-1-943404-42-1

Cover design by Sara Lee Paterson

This is a work of historical fiction. Certain characters and their actions may have been inspired by historical individuals and events. The characters in the novel, however, represent the work of the author's imagination. Any resemblance to actual persons, living or dead, is entirely coincidental.

Published by Old Salt Press

Old Salt Press, LLC is based in Jersey City, New Jersey with an affiliate in New Zealand

For more information about our titles go to: www.oldsaltpress.com

To learn more about the Dawlish Chronicles go to: www.dawlishchronicles.com

Britannia's Rule

The Dawlish Chronicles
September 1886 – April 1888

By

Antoine Vanner

Britannia's Rule - Copyright © 2022 by Antoine Vanner

The right of Antoine Vanner to be identified as the author of this work has been asserted by him in accordance with the British Copyright, Design and Patents Act 1988.

All rights reserved. No part of this book may be reproduced or transmitted in any form or by any means, electronic or mechanical, including photocopying, recording or by any information storage and retrieval system, without written permission from the author, except for the inclusion of brief quotations in a review.

Library of Congress Cataloguing-in-Publication Data:

Antoine Vanner 1945 -

Britannia's Rule / Antoine Vanner.

Paperback ISBN: 978-1-943404-44-5

Kindle: ISBN: 978-1-943404-42-1

Cover design by Sara Lee Paterson

This is a work of historical fiction. Certain characters and their actions may have been inspired by historical individuals and events. The characters in the novel, however, represent the work of the author's imagination. Any resemblance to actual persons, living or dead, is entirely coincidental.

Published by Old Salt Press

Old Salt Press, LLC is based in Jersey City, New Jersey with an affiliate in New Zealand

For more information about our titles go to: www.oldsaltpress.com

To learn more about the Dawlish Chronicles go to: www.dawlishchronicles.com

Britannia's Rule

Prologue

La Cluse-et-Mijoux, Eastern France, February 1st, 1871

The two forts to the right of Pelletier's position had fired only intermittently in the last hour, just enough to drive back each tentative enemy advance through the narrow pass. Now the French guns had fallen silent and some grim Prussian commander was probably counting the hushed minutes and deciding whether it was time to push forward again.

The guns in the forts must be down to their last rounds now, Pelletier thought, shells conserved for one last storm of death in the gorge cut by the Doubs river. Their geysers of flame and snow-streaked mud had made it impassable for the enemy's main body for a full day and night. The shelling had bought time for tens of thousands from General Bourbaki's trapped and shattered army – France's last, squandered, hope – to limp eastwards up the single narrow road from La Cluse towards the Swiss frontier. Most had crossed by now into that haven, eight kilometres distant. For many it might just as well be eight hundred. Snow, frozen mud, abandoned guns and wagons, discarded rifles and haversacks, dead and dying men and horses, deep drifts to either side, all had reduced progress to a crawl.

There was but one objective now for Pelletier and for those gunners in the forts. Not to stop the Prussian advance, but to delay it just long enough for the last Frenchman to drag himself across the border. And Pelletier hoped that that he would be that Frenchman. The honourable but disarmed internment that the government of neutral Switzerland had offered, or death here on French soil, would be preferable to capitulation to the Prussians. He had a family tradition to uphold.

Light snow was falling and the leaden clouds promised even heavier to come. Even in full daylight, the temperature had been well below freezing. Now, in mid-afternoon, it was dropping yet further. Pelletier focussed his field glasses with numb fingers on the gorge's mouth. It emerged there into a widening valley that narrowed again towards the hamlet of La Cluse. The tail of the French column had passed through during the night, leaving the road strewn with the litter of retreat. Once the Prussians spilled from the gorge, all that would lie between them and the rear of the defeated French army was La Cluse itself. Nestling within another, though wider, defile and flanked by the forts on the slopes above, the village's barricaded streets and loopholed houses might still hold for a few hours after the forts were abandoned for lack of shells. Pelletier's smaller force was positioned westwards of the southern fort, well hidden among the trees and rocks on the lower slope, well placed to menace a Prussian advance.

"Do you believe the rumour, sir?" Major Gustave Desmarais was crouched with Pelletier behind a rock outcrop.

"Even if it's true, it makes no difference to us," Pelletier said. "We'll hold as long as we can, no matter who's in command."

But it did matter, he knew. The rumour that Bourbaki had tried to shoot himself the previous night, and had failed even in that, sapped hope from troops already close to despair, close to breaking.

Two weeks before, Colonel Fernand Pelletier had commanded a full brigade – a battalion of chasseurs-a-pied, two of line infantry, three batteries of light artillery, a company of engineers and supporting transport. Part of an army of eighty thousand men, it had battered itself to near extinction in a three-day attack against the Prussian defences along the Lisaine river. Few brigades had fared much better than his. In the retreat that followed, all but surrounded by the enemy, cold and snow and freezing rain had killed many of the survivors.

Tempted, like Bourbaki, to put a pistol to his head, Pelletier kept reminding himself that his grandfather had survived worse on the road from Moscow. He forced himself to radiate confidence that he did not feel and something of that resolution had passed to his surviving troops. Scarcely half of his original brigade had reached La Cluse but its units, depleted though they were, had somehow maintained cohesion. He had selected those best fit to fight and kept them with him. The sick, wounded and frostbitten he sent towards Switzerland with the retreating column. Now his chosen remnant, less than six hundred men, a mix of line infantry and chasseurs divided into five ad-hoc companies, was strung out, concealed, on a three-hundred metre front. The single mitrailleuse – a multi-barrel weapon – was in place at the centre, the only piece saved from his artillery so reluctantly, but necessarily, ordered to be spiked and abandoned on the retreat.

Desmarais cupped his hand to his ear and frowned in concentration. "Do you hear that, sir?"

It was distant, westwards, from beyond the gorge, faint, but unmistakable. They had heard it from behind the Prussian defences they had hurled themselves against on the Lisaine. A military band was blaring into life, was then engulfed by thousands of voices rising into a slow, solemn anthem.

The Prussians were coming.

"Hold fire until you hear the mitrailleuse," Pelletier told Desmarais.

He pointed to the road leading from the gorge towards La Cluse. It bowed slightly to the north but for most of its length it ran straight towards his position until the shoulder of the slope to his right blocked it from his line of fire. Over those five or six hundred metres, the Prussian advance would be shielded from direct fire from the village but he himself could direct all he had on the head of the enemy thrust.

He felt reassured that he had Desmarais, an experienced career officer, to command the three companies on the right of his line. There had been no time for trenches and the men had sought what cover they could behind rocks and bushes. Wet, cold and famished, they had spent the night here without fires and he wondered how much longer they could endure. Many were reservists, recalled six months before. Some had seen prior service in Algeria, Italy, China or Mexico. Stiffened by regular officers and sergeants, their presence had steadied the more recent, half-trained, recruits from the Garde Mobile.

Time now to pass back down the line. The troops could also hear the distant singing. No need to enjoin silence. They knew already what was coming, knew also that the war was lost, and the wait would be an agony of fear and regret. Pelletier stopped here and there with a word of encouragement, emphasised to the officers the need to maintain volleys rather than individual fire, satisfied himself that whatever ammunition remained had been distributed. Had time allowed, he would have passed on through the two companies on the left. No help for that. Dubois, the major in command there, could be relied on.

"Loaded?" Pelletier asked the lieutenant, Dallaire, whose four gunners manned the mitrailleuse.

"Loaded, sir." Dallaire pointed to three metal plates laid out on empty ammunition boxes. "Those also. And enough to fill one more."

The breeches of the weapon's twenty-five rifle tubes, clustered to look like a single barrel, would be closed by one of those magazine plates, cartridges loaded in the holes bored in them. Mounted like a small cannon on a two-wheel carriage, it could deliver a lethal concentrated volley at ranges longer than the eight hundred metres of deep snow that now lay between it and the gorge. Dragged to this position by manpower alone, for its starving horses had been incapable of moving it off the road, a shallow pit had been scraped for it with bayonets.

The first Prussians, infantry all, were just visible through the falling snow, surging in a dark mass through the gorge. No response yet from the forts' guns. Hemmed in by the steep cliffs to either side, unable to deploy in open line, the Prussians were bunched in individual companies. They were running with bayonets fixed but the last night's snow lay deep, slowing the leaders.

"They're in range, sir." Eagerness in Dallaire's voice. The mitrailleuse could do fearful execution there.

Pelletier shook his head. "Not yet."

The first Prussians were through. The greater mass was thrusting up the road behind them. Other units, company size, were fanning out into the ground on either side and deploying in more open order. They floundered forward through deep snow, left behind by the main thrust. More troops were bursting from the gorge and –

A deep boom from Pelletier's right, and then another, and another, as the fortress artillery spoke. They must be firing at maximum depression for the shells ripped lanes through the packed Prussian mass still in the gorge before exploding. Flame-shot smoke and snow boiled up from the defile, blotting the troops beyond from view, shocking those before it into a floundering run forward.

Five shells, five only, for the fort-gunners were being frugal, but enough to dam, however briefly, the flow through the gorge. The onward Prussian rush along the road, the plodding advance to either side, slowed. Men there were glancing backwards in horror. The gorge was blocked for now, and they were isolated, with no support pouring through to reinforce them. Pelletier saw officers, swords in hand, shouting to their troops to follow, sergeants hurrying back and forth along the ranks to urge advance. So too had his own officers – and he himself, on horseback before the beast was shot from under him – rallied breaking troops on the Lisaine. The only hope for those Prussians exposed on open ground was to press forward toward the shelter offered by the slopes ahead.

All unaware of Pelletier's concealed line.

The snow was falling more thickly now and the Prussian advance was half-hidden in its swirls. They were lumbering forward, the units on the road far-outstripping those in the fields to left and right and heading towards Major Desmarais's hidden riflemen. The range was five hundred metres, and closing. France's breechloading Chassepot rifle was deadly in the hands of elite chasseurs-de-pied, and Desmarais still had a scattering of them in his companies. At three hundred metres, the veteran reservists would likely be effective and even the rawest recruits might sometimes be lucky.

"There. A full plate, but wait for my order." Pelletier pointed towards the head of the column.

Dallaire sighted the mitrailleuse himself, edging the barrel across on its limited traverse, adjusting the elevation a little above horizontal. The range was close to three hundred now, and the exhausted Prussians, their run slowed by the snow to a fast plod.

"Ready, sir." Dallaire stood back.

A gunner was crouched now behind the weapon, squinting along its axis, hand on the firing crank.

Five more rounds blasting from the fort, well timed, ten seconds between each. The shells ploughed through the Prussians now pressing across the site of earlier devastation in the gorge, hurling fountains of fire and smoke and snow and hot metal fragments. The troops there were falling back and there would be no reinforcements for the doomed men advancing up the road.

Pelletier's glasses were fixed on the Prussian leading ranks. He saw an older officer, red-faced, exhausted, winded, close to collapse, yet still trudging on out in front with sword upraised. A regimental standard bearer followed close behind, flanked by two younger men, captains or lieutenants perhaps. Despite the cold, they had cast off their greatcoats for ease of movement and their austere dark-blue uniforms were caked with snow. Men to respect, men like himself, Pelletier thought, and he felt no hatred. But no pity either.

"Now," he said to Dallier.

The mitrailleuse rippled into life, twenty-five rounds, each screaming a half-second apart as the gunner ground his crank. Pelletier saw a gash gouged along the axis of the Prussian column, that gallant old officer smashed down, the standard bearer too, men behind them falling, three or four in succession felled by bullets over half as heavy again as a Chassepot's. To his right Pelletier could hear Desmarais shouting the command to open fire, an instant later the crashes of the first aimed volleys, split seconds separating those of his three companies from each other. Stunned by the mitrailleuse's savage lash, bewildered, the column was already halting as the fully fury of Desmarais's hail ripped through them. Gaps were appearing in the column, men falling, others dashing from the road for some illusory cover in the fields alongside. Now the two companies to Pelletier's left were opening fire, and Desmarais called for his second volley. They were concentrating on the Prussians further back, mowing gaps there also.

Acrid gunsmoke wreathed between the trees along Pelletier's line and rose to lie like a grey blanket above. It unmasked the French position and already fast-thinking Prussian officers must be realising that rushing it was their only, desperate, hope. Retreat towards the gorge would mean minutes more of exposure to this deadly fire. Even as the next volleys crashed into them, Prussian troops were being urged off the road to form line in the fields alongside. Many were already crouched, some prone, possibly directed to remain so until some order could be imposed. Several were returning fire, shooting wildly towards their unseen enemy until some sergeant strode between them, demanding that they halt and quelling panic.

But Pelletier's immediate concern was not for the isolated Prussian infantry ahead – it would take long minutes for the officers to organise any concerted attack. And when it came, exhausted troops stumbling forward through the drifts and tripping over snow-covered furrows, Desmarais' merciless fire would halt it, drive it back.

Unless . . .

Unless enemy artillery could blast this position, sending shells screaming over the heads of the advancing infantry and into the tree-clad slopes where the French riflemen crouched. Even a dozen rounds bursting among his companies in fast succession – and Prussian gunners were superbly capable of rapid fire – could disrupt Desmarais's volleys enough to cover a desperate enemy surge.

Pelletier swung his glasses towards the gorge's mouth. It was from there the threat would come, where some death-or-glory battery commander would race out to bring his cannon into play. He saw movement there, mere shadows in the white swirls, and then two booms told of one of the French forts opening again. An instant later the snow billows in the defile flashed yellow as the shells exploded. Grey smoke rolled through the white there but, as it dispersed, Pelletier saw that the shadows had faded back, Prussian movement through it was once more deterred.

"Dallier!" he called and pointed to the gorge. "Shift your aim there. But hold your fire. Wait for my command."

No need to strain on the wheel-spokes of the mitrailleuse's mounting, for its barrel-stack could traverse the necessary twelve degrees on its cross beam. Dallier made the final adjustments himself, then raised the elevation for greater range. He stood back, let the gunner – a proven, trusted man, expert with this weapon – take the firing crank, and nodded to Pelletier.

Then the waiting.

The Prussian infantry on the open ground ahead were forming two ragged lines, the second fifty metres behind the first. Officers and sergeants were hurrying stooped men into position, to cower for now in the shelter of the slightest undulation or leafless bush. A hush had fallen, broken only by distant cries from the wounded further back. Desmarais was holding fire, avid for the moment when the Prussians would rise again and drive forward in a forlorn hope.

Now came what Pelletier had expected, what he would have ordered himself, what could be the only salvation for the Prussian infantry who could neither advance nor retreat without fearful loss. A six-horse team was bursting through the murk at the gorge's mouth, whipped by the riders on their backs, other gunners crouched on the bouncing limber behind them and on the gun – a nine-pounder, Pelletier guessed – at the rear. Great clods of snow and frozen mud flew from beneath the horses' hooves as they slewed and weaved between the craters and debris left by the earlier shelling.

Instants more would carry the gun-team into the mitrailleuse's sights. No option now but to rely on the gunner's judgement of the exact moment

"Fire!"

Two long seconds, the gunner's hand grasping the firing crank, his whole being concentrated on sighting towards the gorge.

Then the first burst, four, five rounds only.

A miss.

The frantic animals forged on unscathed, limber and gun slewing in their wake. Another burst, no more successful. It was impossible at this range, and through the falling snow, to judge if the mitrailleuse's elevation had been too high or too low, even to know if the Prussian riders had noticed the fall of its shot. But now the team, even the gun at the rear, had passed the line of fire, was clear of the gorge mouth, was wheeling over to the left into more open ground, as far as possible from French small-arms fire.

Dallier, ashen with failure, was looking to Pelletier, his expression posing the inevitable question. To shift aim or —

"No! Only the gorge!" Pelletier forestalled him. "Raise elevation one degree! Nothing more!" It was a guess, but ranges were more often estimated to be shorter than they actually were. "There'll be more following."

Now was the time when the forts should have blasted what shells remained to them into the gorge but their guns were silent, perhaps forever. All depended now on the mitrailleuse.

The gun-team that had come through had skidded to a halt in a spray of mud and snow three hundred yards behind the still-forming lines of Prussian infantry. The riders had sprung from their mounts, were unhitching them, leading them back, and the gunners were straining on wheel spokes to align the cannon while others were pulling shells and charges from the limber.

"Here they come!" Dallier yelled.

Two more Prussian gun-teams were charging down the gorge, threading at breakneck speed between the craters. The limbers and guns leaped like demented animals over the broken ground, crews clutching to them like limpets.

Now the mitrailleuse stuttering into life again, five, six rounds.

Dear God! Let the elevation be correct!

A horse was crashing down, the first behind the leader, hooves thrashing, body twisting, rider thrown. For a second more the team dragged the beast's flailing body with it, then slowed, was suddenly a pile of plunging, kicking, animals. Limber and gun ploughed into the chaos.

"Finish the plate!" Dallier shouted to the gunner. The crank swept on, continuously this time, the dozen remaining rounds tearing into the mass of equine and human flesh, beating chunks of wood from limber and guncarriage.

The mitrailleuse fell silent, but already the gunner's assistant was pulling the empty ammunition plate from its breech, thrusting in another and locking it in place.

The second Prussian team had been close behind the first but now the rider on the lead-horse was pulling it across to the right to shear past the wreckage.

"Full plate!" Dallier called.

The hail of heavy rounds lashed this team no less mercilessly than the other, hurling it down beside it, both together all but blocking the gorge mouth.

The mitrailleuse fell silent and a deeper sound, a boom, washed from across the open fields ahead. Pelletier, gaze fixed on the carnage at the gorge, had missed the flash but, when he swung about, he saw clearing smoke. The Prussian gun team that had run the gauntlet successfully had brought their nine-pounder into action. At this instant its shell was speeding towards the trees where Desmarais's gunsmoke had revealed his companies' position.

It did no damage. The elevation was too high, the detonation way up on the ridge behind, but that would be corrected for the second shot. The gunners must already be feeding shell and charge into the smoking breech.

"There!"

No need for Pelletier to point. Dallier already had his men heaving on the wheel spokes, edging his weapon round to bear on this new target.

A flash at the Prussian muzzle, the boom arriving an instant later, and then an explosion among the trees and rocks somewhere along Desmarais' line. It might have killed or it might not, but it was encouragement enough for the line of Prussian infantry in the fields to lurch to their feet and stumble forwards, officers thrusting ahead with swords upraised.

Again the mitrailleuse, a short burst, unsuccessful, towards the cannon, a pause for aim correction, failure again, more adjustment, bearing at least correct as the rounds threw up running plumes of snow just short of the Prussian weapon. Elevation up another fraction. Now the long burst that emptied the plate was smashing into the cannon and its crew. The terrified horses held to one side were breaking free and the gunners were falling or throwing themselves down.

And all the while the Prussian lines were advancing. Men tripped, fell, struggled to their feet again to blunder on through sometimes thigh-deep snow. The lines undulated as some sections pushed ahead on easier going underfoot and others slowed on obstacles hidden by the white blanket. Through his glasses Pelletier saw exhaustion, rasping breath, and fear, on their faces, but stolid resolution too. In minutes, maybe less, many would be dead or dying and, even if he felt no pity, he felt respect.

Desmarais was still holding his companies' fire, so too Dubois on the left, both relieved that the threat of Prussian artillery was lifted. At well under three hundred metres range now, individual marksmen would have chosen-targets, officers most of all, in their sights.

The snowfall was thickening again and dusk was close. Through the failing light the oncoming Prussians were little more than shadows. The closest were two hundred metres distant. Shouts from officers were failing to raise cheers but their men were still plodding resolutely ahead.

A hundred metres, and the leading Prussians were breaking into a stumbling run.

Five score Chassepots crashed as one from the furthest right of Desmarais' companies. Instants later, the others followed, and then on the left, Dubois's two companies were beating fire into the flank of the foremost Prussians.

The slaughter had started and darkness was a half-hour away.

Pelletier was giving France her last victory, a small one, at the close of a war that had been lost even before it began.

*

The sky was reddening in the east. Pelletier was standing a few metres west of the raised frontier barrier and still on French soil. He was unsteady from exhaustion, his feet were numb, and he was shivering because he had given his greatcoat to a cover a delirious man in a wagon bed. The cold dawn light cast long shadows as the tail of the retreating column trudged past, limping men supporting others in worse states, wretched horses at their last extremity dragging the final few carts of wounded through slush and mud.

Just across the invisible border that stretched between the red and white stripe-painted posts at either side of the track, Swiss troops were directing the defeated French to cast their weapons and ammunition on growing heaps. A dozen or more fires blazed beyond, freezing and famished men clustering around them for meagre warmth. The Swiss has set up field kitchens and long lines of disarmed men were shuffling through them, grateful for warm soup and hunks of bread. The barns and sheds of this insignificant village of Les Verrières were already full of wounded. Tents, a few with red crosses, were scattered in the surrounding fields. This was internment, not imprisonment, and Switzerland was rising nobly to the challenge of feeding and sheltering unexpected thousands.

"We never thought it would end like this," Desmarais said.

He was standing by Pelletier, no less exhausted after the nightmare eight kilometres retreat through the darkness from Le Cluse. Their ammunition depleted, they had fallen back first on the village after the repulse of the hopeless enemy attack across the snow-shrouded fields.

They had joined the defenders in the hamlet's loopholed houses and waited for an attack that did not come. Perhaps the Prussians wanted no further casualties in a war already won and lost. In the early hours the last French troops, the garrisons of the forts and Pelletier's force included, had slipped eastwards into the night. The track had been a quagmire churned by thousands of boots, furrowed by countless wagons, littered with abandoned equipment. Each step had been an agony, the pace dictated by the slowest, hobbling and supporting each other up the steady incline towards the border.

Now the final remnants, chasseurs who had formed the rear-guard, limping and shambling but still with a hint of defiance about them. It pleased Pelletier that they were still carrying their Chassepots. He stepped forward, raised his hand in salute, and they recognised him, and returned it. They plodded on and then passed between the striped posts. Swiss soldiers came forward to meet them, gestured to them to cast their arms aside and move on towards the field kitchens.

Pelletier and Desmarais were alone on the French side now. They looked back down the debris-strewn track that snaked down to Le Cluse. Pelletier fancied that he saw flags flying above the abandoned forts but he resisted the urge to scan them through his glasses. It was painful enough to know that they must be Prussian.

They moved towards the border. Two Swiss officers – senior, by their uniforms – were waiting for them just beyond, ready for the formalities of salutes and handshakes.

Pelletier stopped just short.

"You first, my friend," he said to Desmarais.

France had been broken and humiliated and he would be the last to leave French soil.

It wasn't an end, he told himself.

For him it would be a beginning.

The West Indies 1886
Lesser Antilles Chain

The island of Roscal, at the North-East, comprises the British
Crown Colony of Roscal (West) and the Republic of Guimbi (East)

Chapter 1

Port of Spain, Trinidad, September 9th, 1886

The coaling had finished and the crews on all three ships were sluicing the black residue of dust from every surface.

Dawlish would ask no more of the begrimed men this day. The sun was already dropping in the west and they deserved the time to wash and rest before the never-ending holystoning and painting would begin again next morning. *Scipio* and *Clyde* and *Navigator* would be immaculate when they departed from the roadstead of Port of Spain three days from now, hulls and upperworks gleaming white again, funnels and masts and yards bright ochre, brasswork glinting.

This was hurricane season but if none was encountered then in two weeks' time all three ships would steam past the Square Tower at the narrow entrance to Portsmouth Harbour. Alerted to sighting of the white hulls off the Isle of Wight, Florence would be standing there with wives of officers and seamen alike. And she would have Jessica in her arms, pointing to *Scipio*, explaining who was on board. Love washed through him while he tried to supress the memory of the dreadful way the precious child had come to them. She was making her first faltering steps when he had left some six months before. By now, she might be starting to speak.

He was sitting at a folding writing desk on *Scipio's* stern-walk, a captain's most-envied perquisite, his own most private place onboard. The light land breeze cooled him pleasantly as he wrote up his personal journal for today. He completed a paragraph – a record of awakened memories of this island when he had been here as a midshipman – and looked up and towards shore. A steam pinnace was pulling away from the jetty there, the sun's last rays reflected on her polished brass funnel. She was *Scipio's*, sent a half-hour before for routine collection of mail. Now she had a bone in her teeth, was making all the speed she could. A similar craft was casting off also and following in her wake. Slower, more elegant, than *Scipio's* pinnace, the Union Flag, rather than the While Ensign, flapping at her stern identified her as the governor's. This was the craft that had borne His Excellency, his wife and his staff to dinner with Dawlish and his officers two nights since. She had approached at a more leisurely pace then and she was not expected now.

He returned to his journal. Clavering, third lieutenant and officer of the watch, would alert him if the pinnaces' arrival signified anything that demanded his attention. That was unlikely. The small flotilla, with Dawlish as commodore as well as *Scipio's* captain, was here only to recoal.

Brannigan, captain's steward, stepped out on the stern-walk.

"Mr. Clavering's compliments, sir. An' there's another gentleman with him. He says it's urgent."

"I'll see them in my salon."

It was large but furnished, by Dawlish's choice, with the same Spartan severity as on his previous command, the cruiser *Leonidas*. His sleeping berth and washing facilities were located just forward on the starboard side, a steward's pantry similarly placed to port. This salon was his office, his library, his dining room and his home, isolated from officers and lower deck alike. A captain should be a man apart. His powers of decision and command must take no account of familiarities or friendships.

He met them standing, did not invite them to sit. The young civilian accompanying Clavering had been at a reception at Government House a few nights since. Dawlish could not recall his name but he introduced himself as Geoffrey Mapperton, aide to the governor.

"You have a message from His Excellency?"

Before Mapperton could answer, Clavering said, "I think you might want to read this first, sir." He reached out a manila envelope, the name of the telegraph company on it almost obliterated by a red URGENT stamp.

Dawlish scanned the words on the six strips pasted on the form. Uncyphered, from the Admiralty, London. Clear orders, action with all despatch, but in support of, and in cooperation with, the civil authority.

Not unexpected war, not a show of force off some island colony in revolt nor landing of a naval brigade to protect British lives. Something Dawlish had never foreseen, something no naval commander had ever prepared for. And a name, an island he knew only by name and had never visited when serving on the North America and West Indies Station two decades before.

Roscal.

North-east of Antigua.

And a word he had never expected.

Volcano.

"His Excellency has also received a telegram, captain. He knows about your instructions," Mapperton said. "He thinks he may be of help. There are sensitivities you should know about, he says. He suggests that you might want to meet him tonight."

"In a half-hour," Dawlish said, then turned to the steward who was hovering behind. "My compliments to Commander Hammond. I wish to see him here."

His mind was racing. Distances, speed, coal. And items and stores other than what a warship carried normally. Clavering was navigating officer and could be put to immediate essential work. Dawlish told him the destination, said he needed a course, sent him away. Hammond arrived, a little dishevelled, as if aroused from a nap. He was older than Dawlish but had demonstrated no resentment at serving as his executive officer. His last service had been command of a gunvessel on the China Station and he had come well recommended. His quiet efficiency and meticulous attention to detail had confirmed that evaluation.

"With all despatch? Full speed?" Hammond sounded incredulous when he saw the Admiralty signal. "It can't be less than seven-hundred miles. Two and a half days at the fastest."

Scipio, had made just over sixteen knots over the measured mile during acceptance trials but had never sustained such a speed for more than two or three hours. Doing so demanded a prohibitive rate of coal consumption. Sixteen knots required over twice as much fuel as the normal cruising speed of ten. The demands on the bunkerage of the squadron's two other ships, the cruiser *Clyde* and the gunvessel *Navigator*, would be just as severe. It was impossible to know how long this service might take, no confidence that adequate freshwater supplies might be available at Roscal. Distillation, if needed, would devour coal.

"Get a message to the bunkering company," Dawlish made a quick decision. "All the coal that can be safely carried in sacks on deck. Signal *Clyde* and *Navigator* that they'll do the same. Loading to have started before midnight."

"The company will want a premium for that, sir. It's Saturday today. Workers, tugs, lighters, nothing's ready at this hour."

"Send Stockley. He'll beat the price down." The paymaster had a reputation. "Coaling complete by first light. There may be other stores needed too. It may take longer to find them." Dawlish turned to Mapperton, the civilian. "We'll need medical supplies, as much as can be spared here from the hospitals, more even. I trust His Excellency will assist and authorise the funds?"

"I believe you can rely on that, captain."

"Our surgeon will come ashore with you to help find what's needed. But we must have it by dawn. Food too, as much as possible." All three ships were fully provisioned, but for their own complements only. There would certainly be more needed. "And as many picks, shovels and axes as can be found."

Dawlish flicked his watch open. Ten minutes to seven.

"We'll depart in twelve hours," he said. "Kindly see to it, Commander Hammond."

Exhausted by the day's coaling through they might be, the three vessels' crews would have no rest this night.

*

Scipio's pinnace chugged shorewards. Dawlish was standing in the stern cockpit with Mapperton, Stockley the paymaster and Waller the surgeon

A faint afterglow hung in the western sky. The three warships stood against it as black silhouettes.

The sight made Dawlish feel proud. Command of the massive *Scipio,* his for the last thirteen months, was the reward for his service in the Sudan. Admiral Richard Topcliffe, even if seldom seen in uniform, or at the Admiralty, had seen to that, over-riding the claims of more senior captains. *Scipio's* two turrets amidships were staggered to allow cross-deck firing. A single funnel between them, rising through the flying bridge above them to link the superstructure fore and aft. Two masts, for lookout and signalling only, no sailing rig. Steam had finally triumphed.

Scipio, and her sisters *Colossus* and *Edinburgh*, might be the Navy's ugliest ships, but they were the most powerful and modern too, steel-built, mounting four breech-loading twelve-inch rifles. But for what lay ahead these would be worthless. Only the discipline and resourcefulness of the squadron's crews would count, *Scipio's* four hundred, the three hundred from *Clyde*, the hundred and twenty from *Navigator*.

Detached from service in the Channel Fleet, each vessel the most modern of their type, the squadron was returning from a voyage that had brought them to Buenos Aires, Montevideo and Rio de Janeiro. There had been more to it than showing the flag. Dawlish knew – because Topcliffe had confided in him – that British shipbuilding interests had urged the venture and the government had consented. South American states, not least the Argentine Republic and the Empire of Brazil, were ready to spend money their people could not afford on naval might. If British yards did not deliver, then French ones would instead. There had been nothing overt, but each vessel – even little Uruguay would value a craft such as *Navigator* – had been admired by those who mattered. Emperor Pedro II of Brazil himself had trod *Scipio's* deck and had marvelled at the hydraulics that rotated her turrets and rammed her guns. There had been no obligation for Dawlish to mention orders, costs or contracts. That could be left to the embassies and the representatives of building yards after the squadron had departed.

The pinnace was drawing alongside the jetty now.

The time for courtesies and diplomatic niceties was past. What lay ahead might have something of Hell itself about it.

*

London had authorised funds.

His Excellency, Governor of Trinidad, an iron-haired but vital man of sixty, seemed to enjoy the challenge of assisting. Dawlish had liked him for the sense of pragmatism that underlay his intelligent conversation when he had joined him in an excursion to Trinidad's Pitch Lake. Now the governor had sent Mapperton to assist *Scipio's* surgeon to gather – it sounded better than commandeer, but it meant the same – medical supplies from Port of Spain's two hospitals. Another aide would rouse merchants and empty the town's warehouses of picks, shovels and axes. Food was perishable and the markets would hardly have opened when the vessels departed but the governor's chief clerk, a black Trinidadian who impressed Darwish as capable, had family contacts who might supply a minimum. Stockley would need no help in prodding a reluctant coal supplier to find labour and begin moving sacks to the ships. Glancing out from the balcony of Government House, Dawlish saw arc-lights blazing icy illumination over the three vessels. Preparations were well underway.

"You might wish to join me in my study, Captain Dawlish," His Excellency said. "It'll be more convenient there."

The Colonial Office's cable was longer than the Admiralty's signal. The eruption had occurred three days before.

"Roscal has no telegraph connection, captain. Antigua does, so the governor sent a schooner there – it took almost two days, due to bad weather – to alert London. There was a lot of confusion when she left, so there's little concrete information. Just that there's been an eruption, a town damaged and threatened to be isolated by lava flows. Panic and some looting."

"Deaths?"

"Probably, but numbers are impossible to estimate."

A map lay on a library-table in the corner. A moth was flapping around the globe of the kerosene lamp above it.

"I thought you might find this of use, captain. It's the only map of the island we have here. It's twenty years out of date, but the main features won't have changed. At least not until three days ago. And it may have changed even more in the meantime."

Navigation charts on *Scipio* had shown Dawlish the outline of the island but nothing of the interior. This map showed the western half in considerable detail, a labour of love for some army topographer, but the east was largely blank.

Dawlish studied it. Elongated, tapering at its eastern end, blunt at the west, its central axis ran south-of-east to north-of-west. The scale indicated it as about thirty miles long and half that at its widest. Contour lines indicated a ragged belt of high ground across its centre from the north coast to the southern. Concentric rings rose to identify Mont Henri and Mont Sully in that belt. Another, Mont Condé, rose close to the island's eastern tip. The heights were indicated as approximate, about 3000-feet, and the single word 'dormant' identified all three as sleeping volcanos.

The governor had been following Dawlish's gaze.

"They're not the problem." He stabbed his finger at the map. "It's this one here. Mont Colbert."

On the north-western coast. Another rough circle of close contours, rising above the low-lying flat plain to its east and south. Approximate height 3500-feet. A town, identified as Saint Gérons, lay between the volcano and the sea. It didn't seem large, but it had a small harbour and it might have grown in the two decades since the map was made.

"There's a torrent of lava running into the sea to the east. There was fear of another to the west. If there is, then Saint Gérons will be cut off, maybe inundated, the report said. It's smothered with ash, and more was falling when a boat got away to Escource – here, it's the capital. The governor relayed what he knew then. It could be worse by now."

Saint Gérons might no longer exist, Dawlish thought. He remembered reading Bulwer-Lytton's *Last Days of Pompeii*. That was all he knew about volcanos and it was terrifying. Scant preparation for what must lie ahead.

"Was there any warning?"

"None. There'd been no eruption for two centuries. Nobody expected it."

Silence. A shared sense of foreboding.

And for Dawlish, awareness that he had no idea what measures would be needed. He must depend on his imagination, visualise the situation there, and make best use of the two-day passage to put preparations in hand. Preparations that might prove wholly inappropriate.

"Have you ever visited Roscal, captain?"

Dawlish shook his head. All he knew was the island's location and that sovereignty was split. Only the western half, the Crown Colony of Roscal, was under British rule. A dashed line north to south through the central highlands marked the border. The Republic of Guimbi lay east of it.

"I never visited myself either," His Excellency said. "It's an anomaly. French originally, valuable for its sugar. Britain took it in the Seven Years' War but ceded the eastern half back to France in 1763, part of the price for keeping Canada. The slaves rose up in 1791. They'd had bad masters and now they butchered them and their families without mercy. The French tried to retake the place – a savage business that lasted on and off for years. Britain invaded in 1806. By that time the slaves had set up a republic they called Guimbi. They worked with us to see off the French finally."

"And sovereignty remained divided?" It was coming back to Dawlish now, history once read but long forgotten.

"That was the price for the slaves' cooperation. There was no desire to commit more British troops there. So now there's Her Majesty's Colony of Roscal in the west and the Republic of Guimbi in the east.

They're about equal in area. But Guimbi's a wretched place, probably the poorest in the Caribbean. Its presence is resented internationally. One Haiti is enough. Nobody wants to see a second black republic succeed, even if it's a tiny one."

"Is this important at this moment?" Dawlish didn't need a history lesson. He wanted to know about the present crisis.

"It might be. There'll be unrest, maybe worse, in the Roscal colony if the current business isn't handled well. Its population remained slaves long after Guimbi was established and recognised. Emancipation came forty years ago but, de facto, white still rules black in Roscal. It's resented. The blacks look east, ignore the poverty in Guimbi, see only black ruling black. They want the same."

What His Excellency had described as 'current business' seemed straightforward to Dawlish. Saving a town's population from appalling death, perhaps diverting lava with dams and demolished houses, evacuating families, treating injuries, organising food supplies, burying dead, maintaining order. Not easy, not simple – and he knew that he probably hadn't even imagined the worst of it – but straightforward.

"Why wouldn't this business be handled well?" Dawlish felt affronted. "We'll find solutions, do our damnedst." The Navy always did. And often more. Sometimes the impossible.

His Excellency recognised his irritation but did not rise to it. "This is confidential, captain. It won't go further." His voice had a note of caution. "Your instructions are to cooperate with the civil authority."

"Yes?" It sounded obvious.

"That means the governor, Sir Clifford Belton. I know him since Oxford. And we were secretaries together in the Madrid embassy in the fifties." He paused as if reconsidering what had he intended to say.

Dawlish prompted him. "A competent man, no doubt?" He was wondering how competent a man needed to be for assignment to govern so insignificant a Caribbean island. He'd heard the name before, from Florence. It had been used without Sir Clifford's knowledge in a cruel hoax in London, one he was probably still unaware of.

"A clever man." His Excellency hesitated. "This is in confidence, captain. You'll understand that. Sir Clifford's a diplomat to his fingertips even if he's often called the dullest man in England. Slow, methodical, endlessly patient, never threatening, a born conciliator. That's his strength. Roscal's small, but sensitive, and there's always unrest simmering. That's why he was sent there. To square the circle. To balance the interests of the plantation owners – many of them are of French descent – against the demands of Roscal's blacks. And keep on good terms with Guimbi and ensure that it doesn't inspire sedition west of the border. I understand that he does all that well."

"But not a man of action?" Dawlish said.

"He's never needed to be. He's never faced anything like this eruption before. He'll be slow in his decisions, hesitant to commit. He'll need your urging, Captain Dawlish. I advise you to be firm. Firm but diplomatic."

"And if I'm not?" Already Dawlish could foresee the need for fast decisions, perhaps independently of Sir Clifford.

A long silence, and then His Excellency said, "I wouldn't advise that, captain. Quiet as he is, he's not a man to cross. He's got friends in high places. Probably higher than any of yours."

It was time to get back to the ships. Dawlish declined the offer of a glass of wine. A long night lay ahead, visits to all three vessels and brief speeches to the crews, explaining the need, asking for their best. He'd have it, he knew. Rough, ill-educated, often violent and drunken ashore, as many were, British seamen had a strong streak of compassion when confronted with suffering. And he must visit the engine rooms also, emphasise his trust in the engineers, artificers, stokers and trimmers who would labour in a hell of heat and humidity as the ships raced north.

They would be the real heroes of the next two days.

HMS *Scipio* – *Colossus* Class Battleship

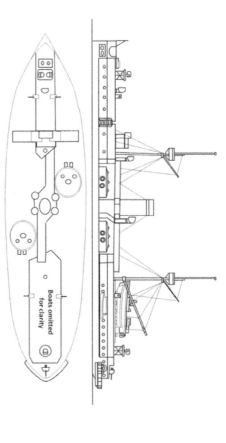

Builder: Chatham Dockyard, 1883 - 1885
Construction: Steel
Displacement: 9420 tons
Length: 325 feet overall
Beam: 68 feet
Draught: 26 feet
Armour: Compound
   Citadel: 14" to 18"
   Deck: 2.52 to 3"
   Turrets: 14" to 16"

Machinery: 2 Engines and Screws
   7500 Horsepower
Speed: 16.5 Knots (Max.)
   8 Knots (Cruising)
Armament: 4 X 12" breechloaders
   5 X 6" breechloaders
   4 X 6-pounders
   4 X 14" torpedo tubes
Complement: 396

Motto:
Nil Intentatum
(Nothing unattempted)

Chapter 2

The passage was fast, the sea calm, no gathering of dark clouds on the horizon to herald onset of a hurricane. *Scipio* maintained just under sixteen knots on the first day, one less on the second due to leaking steam glands.

Dawlish sent *Clyde* ahead – she could manage a knot more. Even a few hours gained in arriving at Saint Gérons might make a difference. Whatever Faulkner, *Clyde's* captain, would find there, he could be trusted to take appropriate action. The small *Navigator*, single screwed and designed for endurance rather than speed, could only trail behind, pistons flailing and single screw thrashing, striving to deliver her maximum eleven knots. The auxiliary sailing rig had been set to complement her engine but the light airs could do little more than flap the canvas. Yet at Roscal she might prove invaluable, her small size and shallow draught allowing approach close inshore.

Departure from Trinidad was delayed until well after midday by securing supplies. It was Sunday and it proved difficult to find workers ashore when church-services represented entertainment as well as spiritual sustenance. Being at sea brought no respite from labour. The stores brought on board must be positioned on deck for fast off-loading. Davits and hoisting gear must operate flawlessly, boats and their equipment must be readied for continuous use. A possible demand for clean water to those who had been driven from their homes necessitated running piping from the engine room to delivery points along the deck-edge. Coal could not yet be spared for distillation, but the evaporator and condenser must ready to start it fast on arrival. The scale of injuries at Saint Gérons might well overwhelm the ships' sick berths and so the wardrooms must be converted. Furnishings, carpets and decorations disappeared, replaced by trestle tables, cabinets of instruments, racks of bottles, crates of bandages and dressings, scrubbed steel decks and the smell of carbolic. *Scipio's* sailmakers, on board only for sewing and maintenance of awnings, were now making stretchers, their poles shaved down from planking stores.

Dawlish ordered adjustment of watch-keeping through the daylight hours, allowing brief sleep only, with reversion to normal during darkness only. Many on *Scipio*, officers as well as men, had served only on large ships in the Channel or Mediterranean Fleets. Inured to unbending routine, without exposure to the surprises, uncertainties and improvisations encountered by small vessels on distant stations, they would be tried to their limits. But, so far, they were doing well, had caught Dawlish's own sense of urgency and something too of the apprehension that he disguised in himself. He tried to visualise the situation in the threatened town, the needs of its inhabitants, what more preparations he could put in hand during these two days of passage.

He hoped they would be enough.

*

"I thought you would want to see this, sir," Lieutenant Clavering, officer of the Morning Watch, said when Dawlish came to the bridge. He had been roused from the long, deep sleep he had allowed himself on this second night at sea. It might be the last he could have for some time.

Sunrise was still an hour away, the sea smooth, the air cool. The sky's dome was clear and star-studded but it was towards the northern horizon that Clavering was gesturing. A great dark mass lay just above it, shot through with intermittent but rapid flashes of red as if a vast thunderstorm was raging there.

Mont Colbert's anger had not subsided.

"It's at least fifty miles, sir," Clavering said.

It had to be. Arrival had been estimated for three hours from now. Dawlish took the prism-binoculars the young officer offered. He focussed, could see little detail, but had an impression of a maelstrom of churning smoke, a long billowing streak above which an ever-taller column rose and writhed. He felt a thrill of fear and awe, sensed the same in Clavering and the helmsman, in the two midshipmen and the seamen standing close. He had tried to visualise it before but, now seen, its immensity oppressed his spirit. Whatever mortal man might accomplish against such might could be but puny.

But he would contend.

He and his three crews.

Nobody must sense his doubts and fears. He must be seen to be taking this in his stride. He turned to Clavering, forced calm into his voice.

"A memorable sight, lieutenant. Inform Commander Hammond. He'll want to see it too. And tell him I'll be on the bridge again at six. I'll sleep 'til then."

He knew he wouldn't, but it didn't matter. The word would go about. The captain wasn't daunted, would slumber in confidence that *Scipio* and her men were prepared.

For anything.

*

Roscal's south-western shore lay close off the starboard bow. Long beaches extended north and east, backed by steep bluffs in places, level green-clad land beyond. That land stretched towards the chain of hills across the island's centre, the steep masses of Mont Sully and Mont Henri rising above at south and north and marking the boundary with the Republic of Guimbi. But it was the mountain that rose at the island's north-western tip that Dawlish's gaze, like that of every other man on deck, was locked.

He had imagined the volcano as conical but Mont Colbert was a jumble of steep-sided peaks with gullies gashed in their sides. Fans of bare rock, frozen evidence of earlier eruptions, ran downwards, their edges bordered by vegetation that was now blanketed in grey. Even at this distance, some ten miles, spasms of rumbling were audible, each accompanied by a vent of steam and smoke gushing from some new fissure. There was no single point of eruption. It was rather a string of clefts and small craters, each belching its own addition to the cloud above and sending rolling walls of murk, thinning as they went, down the lower slopes. Scarlet flashes deep inside the dark churn told of yet fiercer venting further north. There was no sign however of the glowing stream of lava that had been reported. That must be on the far side of the mountain.

Scipio was still driving due north, past the headland on her starboard beam that hid Escource, Roscal's capital. Then the bay on which it stood revealed itself, small vessels clustered before the town, boats stroking between, people milling on the foreshore, an impression of chaos there.

The large white villa on the slope above must be the governor's residence. Sir Clifford Belton might even now be holding *Scipio* in a telescope lens, relief flooding through him that assistance was at hand. Meeting him would have to wait. Dawlish wanted to be moored as soon as possible off the stricken town of Saint Gérons. He would see the situation there for himself, receive the report of *Clyde's* Captain Faulkner, establish priorities, decide a plan, initiate action. Only afterwards, when all in danger had been evacuated, would he meet the man whom he'd been warned was slow in his decisions and hesitant to commit. He would present a *fait accompli*, avoid arguing over a plan of action with the governor.

A schooner was leaving Escource and heading north, making slow going in the light airs, only a few crewmen visible on board. A few minutes later an almost identical craft was seen sailing southwards, her deck packed with people. Apparent sisters, they could only be shuttling between Saint Gérons and Escource with evacuees.

The western coast was slipping past, Escource now far behind. Grey ash was dropping like snow from the dark clouds above, feathery flakes that tasted acrid when Dawlish touched one to his tongue. As quickly as a seaman swept the bridge clean, the ash soon lay deep enough again to show footprints. It lay heavy on the land also, dull grey on ground and trees alike, as if gripped by a winter frost. The few small settlements on this western coast looked no less blanketed.

"Deck there! Off the starboard bow!" A call from the lookout at the foretop.

A tiny steamer, white hulled, smoke spilling from her funnel, was recognisable as a naval pinnace. It must be *Clyde's*. As *Scipio* advanced, the foreshortening decreased and a string of five smaller craft revealed themselves, on tow, astern. The sight gave hope. *Clyde's* arrival at Saint Gérons had been of benefit already. Faulkner must have decided to send survivors from there to Escource. The fact that he was moving them by sea might well mean that the town was by now fully isolated.

Scipio held course. The pinnace would pass between her and the shoreline at a mile's separation. Through his glasses Dawlish saw that the string was making slow headway. The pinnace's boiler must be straining to its limits. He could see only three men on board her but the sight of sennet hats in the bows of the boats on tow indicated at least one seaman in each to maintain order. The craft were deep laden – men, women, children packed together, buried beneath bundles of whatever pathetic belongings they had rescued. White skinned or black, all looked ghostly under a film of ash. Even at this distance there was an impression of dazed exhaustion after terror, of the reality of deliverance, and of the uncertainty of the future, not yet comprehended.

Dawlish turned to Hammond, beside him on the bridge.

"I think they deserve a cheer," he said. It was all he could do for them. Whoever was in charge of the pinnace was doing well and recognition was always valued.

A hundred men or more lined atop the superstructure and stood and cheered three times as *Scipio* swept past the pinnace and her tow. *Clyde's* men waved back. In one of the towed boats a seaman was urging the occupants to respond also. They caught something of his spirit. Women were pulling off head-ties and waving them. Men were holding up children and pointing to the great white vessel ploughing north. The cheers and waves were being picked up in other boats too, rocking them as occupants struggled to their feet. Dawlish found himself moved. These people were not beaten. Those remaining in Saint Gérons might not be either.

The towed string dropped astern. The land to starboard was level, fertile-seeming, farms or plantations, scattered huts, clumps of trees. A village with a stone church lay on what must be the road from Escource to Saint Gérons that paralleled the coastline. Dawlish could see thatch or corrugated-iron roofs of shacks and large buildings too, probably planter's residences, barns or mills, what must count here as a large community.

Mont Colbert was off the starboard beam now. Soon *Scipio* would swing eastwards around the island's north-western cape. In places on the bare, growth-free slopes the ground was heaving, boulders tumbling down, small landslides between long fractures and small craters. Steam and smoke rolled from them and, at intervals, brief blasts of flame, showering gales of sparks and embers. It reminded Dawlish of a Bessemer converter he had seen purifying molten steel at a Sheffield mill. But there had been only a single mouth in that industrial hell. Now, at any one time, a dozen larger were vomiting. Higher up the mountain, flashes barely seen in the heart of the dense smoke indicated yet greater fury there.

The low rumble was continuous, broken at intervals by sharper cracks. The sun was hidden by the dark layers above and ash was falling from them ever more thickly. It lay like a dull scum on the waters, pocked in places by lumps of floating pumice. The air was foul with a stench of sulphur stronger than any from a cannon's discharge.

Scipio's bows were swinging over, rounding the cape and steadying on an eastwards course. Now Dawlish saw flowing lava, a broad stream down the mountainside, broad in places, narrowing as it funnelled into a deep gully that ran a jagged course towards the sea. Dark streaks and patches moved with the orange flow that slowed as the ravine broadened between steep bluffs, twenty or thirty-feet high. A wooden trestle bridge must have stood here, supported by a central column that had been swept away by the torrent, for half-burned sections had dropped down against the bluffs. Huts on either side indicated that this was where the road to Saint Gérons had crossed the gulley. Now an impassable barrier blocked that road. The ravine broadened as it reached the sea, the lava split into a half-dozen torrents that quenched themselves in boiling cauldrons that threw up great billows of steam.

Saint Gérons could be seen two miles off the starboard bow. It was a jumble of one and two-story buildings and with huts strung along the beach to either side, others straggling up the still-green slopes behind. Higher up, bare rocky inclines ran up towards the smoke-enveloped peaks. As yet there was no greater eruption there than a few small vents of steam. In the broad bay before the town a jetty reached out from a quay into deeper water, several of *Clyde's* boats moored alongside. Three large warehouses stood just beyond its landward end. The cruiser herself lay anchored further out.

Whatever might be happening to the east, the town was wholly cut off by land from the west. That Faulkner had decided to evacuate residents by sea boded ill. Dawlish wanted to see for himself. He ordered maintenance of course, but at half-revolutions now. The town slipped past. A long, steep sloping shoulder ran down to level ground a mile beyond. At its highest point the most violent eruption of all was in progress, flame and smoke bursting from a half-dozen points. Thin rivulets of lava were snaking down the slopes, losing themselves in some unseen valley.

Scipio was crawling now past the ridge's end and, as she advanced, its eastern side came into view. If there had been vegetation here, then it had been scorched away. It looked as if two or three craters had merged into one, a jagged gap at one side. Three long gullies ran down from it, fanning out to a quarter-mile or more's separation where they reached the plain below. Streams of lava ran from them and across the half-mile gap between the slope and the beach. The largest stream, pouring in a torrent fifty or sixty-yards wide, was spilling molten rock over a cliff edge into the sea. Fed by the glowing flood, a black shelf of cooled lava was extending out from the shore, steam boiling from the seething water.

Saint Gérons was cut off on the east as well as on the west. It was not immediately threatened by lava flow but the rumbling and groaning of the tortured mountain indicated that the situation could change in minutes. There was one way out of the town, and that was by sea.

Scipio swept abut in a sixteen-point turn, back towards Saint Gérons.

There must be no new Pompeii, no modern Herculaneum.

The evacuation must be fast.

And total.

*

Clyde's captain, Faulkner, was waiting for Dawlish when his gig arrived at the jetty. It had been the first boat dropped. The anchor-party was still active on *Scipio's* bows but her steam pinnace was already being swung out by the main boom. The smaller steam-launch, the barge and two cutters on chocks on the after superstructure would follow. The four whalers were dropping from their davits at the deck-edges.

"My apologies, sir. I would have come out to *Scipio* but –" Faulkner half-turned, gestured to the crowd further back along the quay that was being held back by a line of marines and bluejackets.

Dawlish brushed the apology aside. Faulkner was where he was most needed. Red-rimmed eyes in a grey-dusted face told of tireless work since arrival.

"I saw your pinnace and her tow," Dawlish said. "Damn well done."

"A start," Faulkner's voice was hoarse. The ash was not feathery flakes alone but fine powder that drifted like mist and caught in nose and throat. "A hundred and seventy in those boats. There's at least another eighteen hundred more in the town."

"We sighted two schooners too."

"They're a local businessman's. A decent chap called d'Erlanger. The *Eponine* and the *Cosette*. They're doing damn good work but they can't carry more than eighty on each trip."

Dawlish's mind raced. *Scipio's* pinnace could manage perhaps two hundred on a single tow. Her smaller steam launch might be capable of a third of that. Ten miles at least to Escource. Four knots at most with heavy tows. An hour to discharge the human cargo, the pinnace re-coaling the while. Then ten miles back, faster with the lightened boats. Five and a half, say six hours, another two to pack the next string of boats. Three round trips possible in twenty-four hours. Calm seas, as at present, would permit that. With *Clyde's* craft managing the same, and the two schooners trying their best, it would take two days at the least to get all St Gerons' residents to Escource. And that assumed that pinnace and launch engines, not designed for such continuous labour, would not break down.

He looked up to the smoke-engulfed mountain above. His eyes locked in the lava streams that were emptying into the unseen valley to the east. Faulkner followed his gaze.

"There's a bowl there," he said. "I've sent a middy and two men to watch it. It's filling up and there's no abatement of the flow into it. If it overflows then…"

Faulkner's words tailed off. Dawlish could see for himself what he feared, the low, gully-gouged slope that ran down towards the town's eastern side. A ridge high above the houses hid the bowl from sight.

If there was to be an overflow, worse still if a breach… Dawlish's mind recoiled from the thought.

A shudder ran through the jetty planking under his feet. Fear coursed through him for an instant and he hoped it did not show.

"They're intermittent, these tremors," Faulkner said. "Some are much worse, enough to collapse houses. I've set a hundred men to help dig out survivors." He paused. "They're not finding many. It's bad, sir. Very bad. Women and children too…"

Dawlish would see it for himself but that could wait a little. One action mattered above all else.

Get everybody out of the town. But evacuation to Escource by boats would take too long, was not a solution.

The crowd milling beyond the line of bluejackets and marines was restive. Dawlish felt mixed pity and respect for the men in ragged clothing there, the women with head-ties, the children barefoot and half-naked, the black faces dusted white by ash. Their forebears had survived slavery. They themselves had little more than their lives. Even that modest boon might now be wrenched from them. He had seen and admired people like them on other Caribbean islands when he'd been a midshipman. And once, for a few short weeks in Cuba, a subterfuge had made him live like them himself, despised and abused beasts of burden that had somehow kept their courage, their dignity and their hope.

He pushed the memory aside.

A few, men mainly, were jostling forward, were being driven back by threats from the line of guards, were complying with sullenness. Women behind were urging them on. Somebody who looked like a clergyman was trying, without much success, to calm them. No bayonets had been fixed but it might come to that if the fear was to turn to anger and anger to panic.

Tremors, lighter than before were rippling from the shore and out along the jetty. Each new one brought a collective moan of terror from the crowd, single shrieks rising above. This could be mob within minutes, and then a riot, warning shots, order lost, death, wounding, trampling and –

Dawlish made his decision. There was no alternative.

"We'll have to move them to the ships," he said. "All of 'em. First the women and children. The men will have to wait."

It would be difficult, but it must be done.

Within this day.

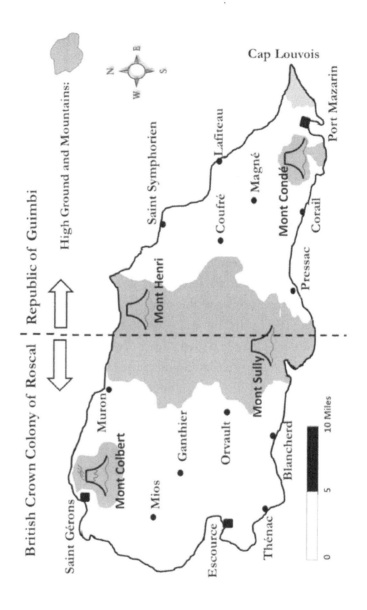

Chapter 3

Late afternoon, the sinking sun casting long shadows.

Dawlish was standing on *Scipio's* bridge and watching the boatloads of townspeople moving out to the warships. Seamen were hauling terrified women and children up ladders to the deck-edge and, hoisting the infirm on bosun's chairs or stretchers. Even though they would be accommodated on the open decks, it had taken longer than hoped to ready the ships to receive them. Large canvas awnings had been rigged to shield them from the ash. The galleys alone could not furnish even the minimum of food for so many and makeshift stoves on deck must supplement them. It would be hours yet before *Scipio's* distillation plant was delivering sufficient fresh water. The ships' carpenters had improvised rough canvas-screened latrines that now jutted from the vessels' flanks, men to starboard, women and children to port. The converted wardroom and the sick bays were already treating casualties – thankfully few burns, but many crush-injuries in survivors rescued from under rubble. Three had died already, two more were likely to follow and many of the remainder would be crippled for life. A baby had been born on *Clyde* and another was imminent on *Scipio*.

Dazed women were settling children on the sections of deck allocated to them. Some had brought a few prized items but most had not even a cloth to lie on. *Scipio's* boats had been joined by those from *Clyde* which had arrived back from Escource after landing survivors there. Dawlish had the midshipman who had commanded the steam pinnace and her tow brought across to *Scipio*. He seemed about seventeen and his name was Winterton. He looked, and was, angry.

"Nobody knows what to do with them in Escource, sir," he said. "Some jack-in-office – pardon the term, sir, some official – tried to stop me landing them. He said had no instructions, no authority to permit it. And when I got 'em ashore –"

"You took no notice of the fellow?" Dawlish liked this lad's spirit.

Winterton smiled for the first time. "He changed his mind. I think he didn't like the look of my coxswain."

No need to enquire further. Dawlish had handled similar situations in his youth.

"What happened to them then?"

"Nothing, sir. They were just left to join a mob that was in Escource already, people who'd got out from Saint Gérons in recent days."

"And nobody in charge?" Some aide of the governor's should be there, the chief of police too, the harbour master at the least.

"Not a soul, sir. But in the end, I rooted out somebody who seemed to have some sense, even though he wouldn't actually do anything. I scribbled a message to the governor and told this chap to get it to him. It was all I could think of. I knew I needed to get the boats back here sharpish."

"You did right." This young man might be worth watching.

But his news was worrying. It was five days since the first eruption. It should have been time enough to get essential measures in place in Escource. Accommodation in churches, schools and warehouses. A hospital readied, feeding provisions also. As much and more than was already in hand on the two warships. Dawlish remembered what he had heard of Sir Clifford Belton. Slow in his decisions, hesitant to commit, Roscal's governor was not a man of action. He'd need stiffening.

Dawlish dismissed the midshipman, then turned to Commander Hammond, who had been listening also.

"We need an officer in Escource. A man with drive, an air of authority, damned if he'll be said 'No' to. Somebody who'll see what's needed, will convince the governor of it and make sure it's done."

"I thought you were going there yourself, sir?"

"Not now." Dawlish pointed shorewards.

The thin lava streams cascading down into the hidden valley had widened. More vents had opened on the slopes, steam gushing from them. The sky above was dark, the air thick with falling ash. Tremors, some very violent, had continued through the afternoon. Bodies, some still living, were being dug from beneath tumbled houses. The crowd waiting to be taken off the quay was more belligerent now. Hungry, thirsty, worried about wives and children already evacuated, men predominated in the throng. There had been several violent incidents, and bayonets had been fixed. Approaching darkness, lit by the flames belching high above and by the fearful lava glow, might urge yet worse unrest.

"I'd send you, Commander Hammond," Dawlish said. "You'd be ideal. But you're needed here. What do you think of Stockley?"

"He'd be ideal. A good organiser." The executive officer hesitated. "But –".

"But he's abrasive," Dawlish said. Soon after taking command, he had told *Scipio's* paymaster that he'd noticed it and didn't like it. It had been an uncomfortable man-to-man interview. Stockley had moderated his behaviour since.

"I don't advise it, sir," Hammond said. "He'll have to deal with the governor. He's well capable of antagonising him."

From what Dawlish had heard of Sir Clifford Belton, that seemed all too likely. By not having gone to meet him as soon as he had arrival, he himself might have offended him already. With instructions to cooperate with the civil authority, Dawlish could not afford a breach.

And there was only one solution, unpalatable for depriving *Scipio* of another competent officer. But unavoidable.

"We'll send Clavering with him. After Stockley has introduced himself to Sir Clifford he'll deal with him through Clavering." Dawlish had not warmed to his navigating officer. Smooth as an eel and a toady to boot when it suited him. But capable. He'd sense advancement if this task went well. "He's the second son of the Earl of Greybrook. That'll count for something with Sir Clifford Belton."

Hammond looked reluctant to lose him, but that didn't matter.

"The pinnace can get them to Escource in three hours," Dawlish said. "I'll write a note for Sir Clifford and send it with them. I'll talk to

Stockley and Clavering once it's ready and leave them in no doubt of what's needed."

And afterwards he'd go ashore again.

A long night lay ahead.

*

One of the warehouses, half-full of great puncheons of lime-juice, had been opened by its owner to shelter women, children, the old and the infirm while they waited. Unlike the truculent menfolk held back by the cordon of bluejackets and marines, they looked stunned beyond comprehension and feeling. A few lamps cast long shadows. The only sounds were of babies wailing, women sobbing, old people racked by coughing, a small group in a corner led in prayer by a black clergyman. But here, at least, was shelter from the falling ash.

Dawlish supressed the pity he felt. These people needed action, not sympathy. He was satisfied that transportation to the warships was proceeding as fast as possible. But even that might not be enough if…

He thrust the thought away, shook ash from the cloth that had protected his mouth and nose, wrapped it in place again. He motioned to his escort – a *Scipio* midshipman and two seamen – to follow him into the town.

Saint Gérons' most senior policeman, a white Roscallan, had left with his entire family before the road westwards was cut by lava flow. Dawlish was impressed by the sergeant left behind in command of some two dozen constables, all black like himself. Without instruction, Sergeant Samuel Dorsette had set his men to searching, street by street, for residents too terrified to leave their houses and to shepherd them towards the quayside. Now Dawlish encountered him again, this time with four constables. They were driving a half-dozen bound men, roped in file, towards the harbour. All looked cowed. Two had swollen and bleeding faces, red patches soaking the ash on them.

"We found them robbing houses, sir. Bad men, thieves, looters." Sergeant Dorsette spoke with the lilting West-Indian accent that Dawlish had come to like twenty years before. He paused. "And two of them were bothering a woman, sir."

"Any more like them?"

"There's four in the station cells." The sergeant looked up towards the flame-shot billows high above. A tremor had just passed. "They could die there, sir, if …"

"Go there, bring them also," Dawlish said. He turned to the midshipman escorting him. "Go with this gentleman. Bring him to the jetty. My compliments to Sub-Lieutenant Walton there. Prisoners to be put to work. He's to take no nonsense from them. They'll be the last we'll bring on board. Then rejoin me."

"God will thank you for this, sir." The police sergeant snapped a salute. For all that he was grey-caked and red-eyed, he emanated resolution no less than humanity.

Worth a dozen like his superior who had fled.

The ash was falling ever more thickly now, the great feathery flakes glowing orange as they caught the light of some new geyser of flame. It lay ankle-deep on the street and walking through it raised eye-stinging clouds. For all that his mouth and nose were covered, Dawlish could feel it gritty on his tongue. At intervals, some new shudder far above sent small hot pebbles showering down, driving anybody caught in the open into whatever cover they could find.

Dawlish headed for the southernmost edge of the town. Here boulders had come crashing down the slopes to crush huts and humble wooden houses with thatched or rusted corrugated roofs. Already weakened by the tremors, some half-consumed already by fires ignited by incandescent embers, many had collapsed. Some hundred and thirty of *Scipio's* crew, and another hundred from *Clyde,* were labouring here, assisted by many men from the town. Together they had lifted beams and rubble, had listened for feeble calls for help, had dug with hope that was all too often disappointed. They had pulled out survivors, had stretchered injured to the jetty, had laid the dead in rows, faces covered with whatever shreds of fabric could be found amid the wreckage.

But the dead must await their turn for the burial that yet more violent eruptions might make impossible. All effort was concentred now on the ruins of what must have been a large three-storied building. Part still stood, brick-built at the ground level and that above, the highest of wood, the roof of tiles. It must have been a row of tradesmen's stores – a half-burned sign identified one as a tailor – with living quarters in the floors above. Two shops had collapsed and the remainder looked likely to follow. As Dawlish arrived another powerful tremor struck. Bricks and planking, rafters and beams, pieces of modest furniture, shook loose in a cloud of ash from the standing remnant. A scream, piercing, prolonged, unforgettable, rose from somewhere deep beneath the piled debris and then abruptly ceased.

Through the settling ash-cloud Dawlish could see the tripods that his seamen had erected earlier, jury-rigged from spare spars. Three stood on the hummocked rubble, one at a crazy angle, all with blocks and tackles suspended from their apexes. The tremor had collapsed a fourth tripod and voluble swearing indicated that some seaman had been injured. The work was beginning again, tugging on splintered beams beneath which men were burrowing with picks and spades, passing loose fragments to their mates above. A brief cheer arose as a limp body was handed up, was then cut off by recognition that rescue had been futile

To one side of the ruin, two of *Scipio's* sick-berth stewards and a civilian were crouched over the body of a child. A steward stood up and stepped back, shaking his head. So did the civilian, his slumped shoulders telling more of despair than of exhaustion. Then he picked up the body, not ungently, and laid it as last on a row of eleven. He saw Dawlish as he rose and approached.

"You're the captain of that big warship?" The voice hoarse and with only the slightest hint of the local accent. He swept his hand clean of ash, showing sun-bronzed white skin, and held it out. "I'm Edmond d'Erlanger."

Dawlish had heard the name already but he had not expected to see the owner of the *Cosette* and *Eponine* and of the lime-juice warehouses labouring here. The handshake was firm and brown eyes met Dawlish's with the confident assurance of an equal. It was impossible to guess his age since his face and beard, like Dawlish's own must be, were grey with ash.

"You're an Englishman?"

"A Roscallan. Proud of it. We've been here two centuries. And not English either, when we came. French."

Dawlish thanked him for making the warehouses available

d'Erlanger shrugged. "Nobody's going to steal the juice. What's it worth anyway, compared to that?" He gestured towards the collapsed building. "Eight of my employees lived there. All with families. Shops rented from me too, little businesses and –"

"You owned it?"

"I own a quarter of the town. Not that it may matter by morning." He gestured towards the low ridge that hid the valley into which lava still flooded. Small steam vents had opened at several places along it. "If that breaches, there'll be no Saint Gérons. Let's pray that everybody will be on your ships by then."

Dawlish sensed a regret that embraced more than loss of fortune.

"We're doing our damnedst," he said, "And –"

A cheer was rising over at the heaped rubble and then the voices of officers calling for silence, for work to go on. A seaman came hurrying to Dawlish.

"Mr. Wheeler's compliments, sir. He says you –"

Dawlish didn't hear the rest, was already hurrying over with d'Erlanger following. He stumbled up the heaped rubble towards the tripod at the top. The seamen surrounding it stood back to let him through. He sensed elation, new energy, hope. He saw Sub-Lieutenant Wheeler grasping the cable that led down from the block to hoist out debris. He was leaning out, staring down into an irregular shaft, almost blocked eight or ten feet down by fallen beams.

"There are people down there, sir. We can hear 'em. Two at least. Listen, sir."

A petty officer shouted to silence chatter among the men.

Now Dawlish could hear a voice, a woman's, weak and pleading, and a crying child. Then a man, shouting, his words indistinguishable.

d'Erlanger pushed past, crouched listening at the shaft edge. He called back down, his words also hard to follow for he was using a local dialect and in an accent stronger than when he had spoken earlier to Dawlish. Further calls from below, then the man's voice rising above the child's wails, d'Erlanger answering, his voice loud but calm. At last, he turned and looked up to Dawlish.

"Five alive. Alcide Chapelle, one of my foremen. He thinks his wife's leg is broken. His mother's down there too, but she's dead. He can feel her hand but the rest is buried. The children are bruised, nothing worse, himself also."

Dawlish was staring down at the beams that extended across the shaft that Wheeler's men had dug. Ten or twelve-inch solid wood, anchored by the rubble to either side. The dark gap between them, through which the voices could be heard, was scarcely a foot across. A baby might be pulled through it, but nothing bigger.

"How large is the space they're in? Dawlish said.

"Just big enough for them all, but they're cramped. And too low even to kneel up in."

"How far down?"

"They were sheltering in his wife's shop when the tremor struck. Street level."

Ten or twelve feet beneath the beams. Impossible to know how broad the air-passage. Cutting through the beams too soon might well collapse the shaft. It would be essential prior to removing the beams to enlarge it into something like a crater. And then the shaft below must be excavated with infinite care and if another violent tremor…

A fleeting mental image of the entombed family crushed, of debris showering on the digging seamen, of the shaft collapsing. And worst of all, a breach in the ridge above and lava spilling down and…

Dawlish recognised the same fear on the faces of the men around him. But resolution too. The child's persistent crying ensured that. They would not hang back. He was about to speak but d'Erlanger was ahead of him.

"A hundred guineas between you if you get them out in two hours." He spoke directly to the men. "A hundred more if it's in an hour."

And Dawlish did not object.

*

Dawlish was climbing up the ridge with d'Erlanger, keeping the steaming fissures to their right. Their boots scrabbled on the slope's warm, dark gravel and progress was slow. The smell of sulphur was strong, the ash-fall heavy and a ghastly red glow shimmered above the crest. Two seamen followed, one with a lantern for signalling. If a breach occurred here now there might still be time for some two hundred men labouring below to flee for safety.

And abandon that family, Father. Mother. Three children. Dear God, don't let it come to that!

And that was why Dawlish was making the climb, so that the responsibility for giving the order to flee would be his alone. Fear of his own annihilation was strong but it was nothing by comparison with his terror of such a decision.

The midshipman whom Faulkner had posted on the ridge as an observer came down to meet and guide them.

"There's greater flow now, sir." His voice a croak. "The level's still rising."

A solid wall of heat met them at the crest. Some forty feet below lay the lava lake, sluggish crimson currents eddying across it and carrying darker streaks. It was eighty yards, and more, across and twice as long, with fingers reaching into gashes in the slope. The steep gradient above it rose five or six hundred feet until lost in a churn of smoke. Five streams were cascading, one larger, broader than the others, spilling like an incandescent waterfall over a jutting outcrop.

The midshipman pointed to it.

"That burst out ten minutes ago," he said. "And there, sir," he pointed to a thin trickle further to the right "That's just started."

It was impossible to know if the ridge they stood on could contain the flow. At this very moment small fissures might be creeping through it, joining each other, gathering strength for one great rupture. And even if they didn't, the lava must eventually overtop the ridge, roll across, gouge a course towards the town beneath. The volume of the inflow could not be guessed, nor how many hours remained.

d'Erlanger must be thinking the same. He had turned, was looking down towards the rooftops far below.

"It was a happy place." He was talking as much to himself as to Dawlish. A man taking leave. "Not a paradise, but better than it ever had been before. It could have been better still."

"You loved it?" Dawlish liked this man, admired the nobility of his pity and his desolation.

"Not just the town. The people. I gave them work, fair wages, hope." A dying man might speak with such sad pride. "A school. A hospital. They valued it all. You can't see my lime plantations from here, they're there beyond the hills and they'll survive. But Saint Gérons will be gone. My wife had hoped for more."

"Has she left yet?"

"She left eleven years ago. She died."

But melancholy would not serve and Dawlish was looking northwards. An idea had sparked, was struggling for life within his brain. It was daring, crazy even, probably impossible, but still too vague, too unformed, to merit outright dismissal.

"Join me," he said.

He did not look back to see if d'Erlanger followed. He walked along the crest, arms raised across his face to shield it from the lake's radiance, following the curve to the left that led across the northern end of the filling valley. He could see straight out to sea, a mile distant. A scattering of huts lay at the eastmost outskirts of the town. The slope that rose from close to the shoreline to the point on the crest on which he now stood was gashed half-way down by a ravine. It was in shadow, and impossible to see how deep, but it widened as it plunged down towards the sea.

"Do many live there?" he pointed to the huts.

"Few," d'Erlanger said. "Mainly menders for the road to the east."

The road that's already cut.

Dawlish could see *Scipio* and *Clyde*. Their white hulls were reddened by the glare and their arc searchlights were illuminating paths for the boats shuttling between them and the town. The harbour's jetty was visible, so too the three warehouses at its land-end, but a steep ridge hid the rest of the town from sight.

The ground shuddered. Above the lake's southern end, a small avalanche was plunging down and splashing orange fountains. High above, another fissure had opened and a glowing stream, still narrow, was seeking a course downwards.

Time stopped.

Terror.

Another tremor, weaker.

Slow waves were rippling across the lava's surface, lapping up the sides, falling back.

And then they died, the lake smooth again, the crest unbreached.

A respite, not a deliverance.

But the idea in Dawlish's brain was no longer a spark, but a flame that grew brighter as he looked again seawards. d'Erlanger was looking there also, perhaps the same inspiration dawning.

A chance. A desperate chance.

Then a long, piercing scream from the west, unmistakable as a steam whistle, answered by more powerful blasts from *Scipio* and *Clyde*. Out in the far darkness navigation lights were forging closer.

HMS *Navigator*.

An omen of hope, perhaps.

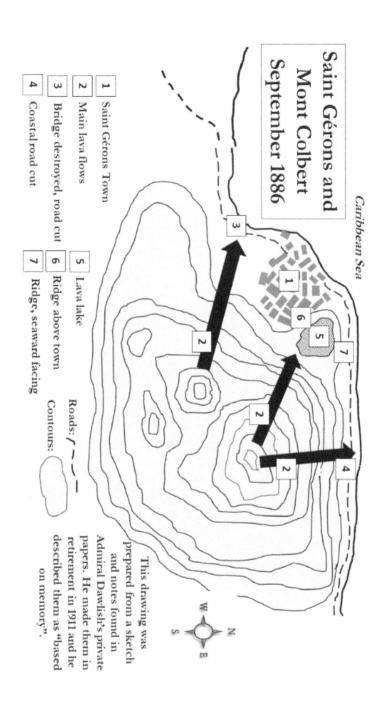

Chapter 4

The tremors had lessened in strength and frequency though the night. Smoke still churned from the ruptures high above, blotting the sky, and steam blasted from smaller fissures. Neither the lava flows nor the rain of ash had diminished. But the glowing lake had not broken its banks even though its level was still rising.

A narrow shaft had reached the trapped family, though not within the time for which d'Erlanger had offered a reward. He'd pay anyway, he told the seamen as the mother and the dazed children, all past even whimpering now, were loaded on stretchers. The father, last out, insisted on walking as they were hurried towards the jetty. No more sounds came from beneath the rubble and it had been time to send the exhausted work parties back to their ships.

Three groups of marines, guided by Police Sergeant Dorsette and his two most trusted men, had combed the streets, house by house. They had hammered on doors, rooted out residents reluctant to leave, arrested a half-dozen more looters, brought sick and infirm to the warehouses. The deposits and ledgers of the town's single bank had been taken there too, accompanied by the manager and two clerks who had remained until they could be given armed escort. Now they were part of the handful still waiting at the jetty for transport to *Navigator*. Her arrival meant less crowding on the decks of the other vessels. In company with *Clyde,* she would depart by mid-morning for Escource. Having landed their human freight, both would steam back immediately to take off the nine hundred camped on *Scipio's* decks.

For *Scipio* was not leaving. Not yet.

And Dawlish needed her decks to be cleared.

Dawn was breaking when he accompanied the last patrol through Saint Gérons' deserted streets and alleyways. d'Erlanger strode beside him, but neither spoke, oppressed less by personal fear than by the silent desolation of a town still intact, but on the verge of destruction. The only signs of life were dogs that came to them, tails wagging, great soulful eyes offering loyalty that could not be accepted, or stray cats that scurried away in flurries of ash. There was pathos in the sight of empty market stalls, shuttered shops, locked doors, humble homes abandoned with their contents. A small chapel with a corrugated roof called itself the Ark of Zion, another like it a little further on, the Bethel Tabernacle. A stone-built church with stained glass windows, Catholic, d'Erlanger said, confronted an Anglican competitor across the central square. The police station, the bank, the customs office, d'Erlanger's lime-press yard were closed, the footsteps leaving from them almost obliterated by the deepening ash.

There had been life here, joy and sorrow, love and nurture, hope and sometimes despair, ambition and greed, strength and weakness, all that human life encompassed.

Not a paradise, but better than it ever had been before. It could have been better still if...

This town was on the cusp of death, its dark shroud already cast over it, the lava lake seething above and Mont Colbert rumbling its slow tocsin. It was waiting for the coup-de-grace that a breach on the slope above could bring at any moment.

But once chance to save it remained, a desperate one.

And Dawlish had decided.

He would risk it.

*

Even with *Scipio's* decks still crowded, preparations could be put in hand. Dawlish explained his intentions to Hammond. A model executive officer, he could be relied upon for meticulous organisation and execution. Dawlish went to his quarters, was grateful for Brannigan, his steward, taking his clothes to beat the ash from them and laying out fresh attire. Then Brannigan must have breakfast ready in a half-hour's time, with d'Erlanger invited to share it. Dawlish had offered him accommodation on board in Clavering's vacated cabin It was not just because he liked this white Roscallan but because he was the most senior figure of authority, albeit informal, left in Saint Gérons. Then Dawlish sponge-bathed – he valued the luxury of his own bathroom as much as the privacy of his stern-walk – and felt reborn as he washed the grey powder from his beard, hair and skin.

d'Erlanger was no less transformed. He was an iron-haired man of fifty now, an air of dignity about him despite the misfitting, but clean, borrowed clothing.

As they ate, Dawlish told what he intended.

"I can't guarantee that it'll be successful," he said. "It may make things worse if it doesn't. It's a gamble. And I don't know the odds."

d'Erlanger sat in silence, toying with his fork. At last, he said, "It's worth trying. The town's doomed anyway. That ridge above it won't hold forever."

"You've met Sir Clifford, the governor?" Dawlish asked.

"Several times. And once as a guest at my plantation."

"He'll respect your opinion?"

"He'll respect the d'Erlanger name. There are only half-a-dozen on the island that he does. All old families."

Dawlish paused. He had known this man for less than a day but he had sensed a strong core of decency. Practical, compassionate, honourable and generous. A man to trust. He reminded him of a Frenchman he had known in Paraguay. Whom he'd liked and admired. And whom he'd killed.

"Would Sir Clifford support my decision?"

"He might. But he'd need a week at the least to evaluate every argument pro and con. Then he'd refer the decision to London for confirmation."

"If I proceed with this, Mr. d'Erlanger, and if the town's destroyed, and so much of your wealth with it, it may end my career."

His promotions, however dearly bought, had roused envy. The higher he advanced, the greater the glee with which others would seize upon his failures. And Topcliffe was not a sentimental man. His patronage had rewarded success but could be lost by a single fiasco.

"You'd want me to confirm to Sir Clifford that I'd assented?" d'Erlanger said. "You don't need to ask me that, captain. You know I will. You can have it in writing if you wish."

"Your word's enough." Dawlish regretted already that he might have implied doubt of it.

They finished breakfast in silence, then returned to their cabins. Dawlish instructed Brannigan to call him in four hours.

Then he slept.

*

Clyde returned from Escource in mid-afternoon, *Navigator* an hour later. Stockley had appointed himself harbourmaster and Clavering had secured Sir Clifford's approval for it after the fact. Two requisitioned warehouses were now sheltering the neediest and every boat in the harbour, however small, had been commandeered to bring the Saint Gérons refugees ashore. *Clyde* also brought a message for Dawlish from the governor. The four pages of copperplate script began with a florid greeting and thanked for the rapid arrival of the warships. But Sir Clifford also regretted that Captain Dawlish had not visited him for consultation before undertaking action at Saint Gérons. He looked forward to meeting him soon to formalise arrangements. The remainder of the letter consisted of eleven points of which Captain Dawlish must take cognisance in the meantime. Eight of them referenced sub-sections and paragraphs of various Acts of Parliament.

Dawlish scanned them and decided to ignore them. Observance to the letter would not save him in the event of failure.

As many as possible of those remaining on *Scipio's* deck had been loaded into *Clyde* and *Navigator*. The evacuees were transferred to *Clyde* by boats as soon as she moored but *Navigator* drew alongside *Scipio's* port side, a delicate operation, well manged. Fendered and secured, gangways allowed transfer of all *Scipio's* remaining guests except d'Erlanger. Even before the gunvessel drew away again, every rail and stanchion along *Scipio's* starboard deck-edge was being lowered. Mast and funnel stays were checked, loose items sent aft, ventilator cowls turned to port. In the wardroom and galley, crockery was removed from shelves and packed in boxes. Fresh in Dawlish's memory was the damage *Scipio* had wreaked upon herself by blast and shock during gunnery trials. Now she was clearing for action as if with an enemy battlefleet.

And still the mountain was unquiet, smoke and flame belching on its upper slopes, the air sulphurous, ash falling. But the tremors had weakened further even though the lava streams still flowed into the cauldron above Saint Gérons. It must be close to the crest now and a breach might just be imminent.

Dawlish sent a sub-lieutenant and a half-dozen men ashore, not to the deserted town but to the few huts beyond its eastern edge which d'Erlanger had indicated as the homes of roadmenders. It was essential to know that they were unoccupied. They returned with one poor addled wretch who had resisted his neighbour's urges to leave with them. His wits might have deserted him long before but now the volcano's fury had driven him into an abyss of terror and madness. Bringing him to *Clyde* removed the last obstacle to action.

But Dawlish's attention was fixed now on *Scipio's* guns, the four twelve-inch breech-loaders that had been fired just five times before, all in the course of single exercise. Encased in circular turrets with armoured walls sixteen-inches thick, trained, elevated and loaded by hydraulic power, they were of the most potent type afloat. Unseen below, artificers were greasing slides and tightening glands. A deck deeper still, shells and silk-bagged propellent charges were being readied for raising to the guns above.

It was early afternoon. Dawlish watched each turret make three full and smooth rotations. He timed each at fifty-seven seconds. The sight awakened memories of the brutal manual labour needed to rotate a turret on an ironclad in Danish service some twenty years before. He had been in command of that open-topped cylinder then and the two nine-inch muzzle-loaders it sheltered had been puny by comparison with *Scipio's* weapons. But they had done execution, had inflicted slaughter on waves of troops attacking defensive positions ashore. The remembrance chilled him still. Naïve ambition had led him to mercenary service in a war that was not his and he had killed men with whom he had no quarrel. In retrospect, he was glad that it had brought him no reward. But tonight there would be no human target, something vaster, perhaps invincible, and the battle would be in defence of life rather than its destruction.

He went below. The guns could be loaded in one turret-position only, muzzles laid on the beam, the barrels elevated, breeches opened, shells and charges already laid in troughs behind to be driven in by hydraulic rams. This process too was smooth, controlled by valves and levers, a contrast to the block-and-tackle manhandling into muzzles on that Danish warship he could not forget. He felt pride as he watched. *Scipio* was the embodiment of the navy of steam and steel that he had helped bring about, however much others still bewailed the twilight of wood and sail. And this was just the beginning.

Satisfied, Dawlish left with a word of commendation to Tyrell, the gunnery lieutenant, his gun-captains and his crews. It was from the bridge perched above the armoured conning-tower on the forward superstructure, that he would command.

Command for battle.

*

Scipio raised her anchor an hour before sunset and crept forward a half-mile. A kedge dropped from her stern, the cable paying out as she glided forward, past the road-mender's huts on the land a half-mile distant. The steep slope on the shoreward side of the hidden valley, into which the lava streams still flowed, lay on her starboard beam. Screws churning at dead-slow, she glided on, the anchoring party at the bow ready to knock the chain-stopper pins free. The slope was off the starboard quarter when Dawlish gave the word. The anchor splashed, caught as the engines slipped into dead-slow astern, and a full six shackles rattled through the hawse pipe. A capstan party aft – no steam-driven winch there – was drawing in the kedge cable.

Anchored fore and aft, *Scipio* lay beam-on to the slope. The calm sea was scummed with ash and pumice, sickly pink in the light of the sinking sun and the burning mountain. *Clyde* and *Navigator* lay a mile astern. *Scipio's* own boats were moored to them, safe from the coming blast of their parent's wrath.

Britain was at peace with the nations of the world and so the magazines carried a mere ten rounds for each twelve-inch gun. But half were solid shot, designed and proven to punch though ten inches and more of solid armour, unsuited for what lay ahead. It was the remainder, the bursting shells, that would be of use and it was impossible to know how effective – if at all – they might be against this unimagined target. If not, what followed would be a spectacular and ignominious failure, visible to hundreds.

Darkness had fallen. Dawlish, silent, standing on the starboard bridgewing, could sense mixed apprehension and excitement in Hammond and d'Erlanger just behind him, in the yeoman of signals by his side. He felt the same himself as he focussed his glasses. The slope's crest lay like a black curtain that blocked view of the bases of the lava steams flowing into the hidden valley. He turned to Hammond.

"Searchlights."

A half-minute later the arc-light on the foredeck burst into icy life. Its counterpart at the stern followed. Dawlish's instructions to the sub-lieutenants stationed with the operators had been clear. Now, in conformance, the ellipses of light first thrown on the water moved landward, found the roadmenders' shacks, shifted leftwards, elevated slightly, reached the base of the slope, climbed it. They found the crest, swept back and forth across it, then dropped, one stacked above the other, sweeping slowly across the slope's incline. Dropped further, they swept across again.

Now the lower of the two beams had caught the apex of the ravine that Dawlish had seen below him when he had stood on that crest the previous night. The beam halted, held the apex and the higher beam dropped below it. The upper reaches of the inverted vee-shaped gash were illuminated now by two stacked ellipses of light.

If the seaward slope that dammed the hidden valley had a weakness, it must be here.

Dawlish had once employed smaller guns than *Scipio's* to tumble down a massive bastion weakened by an earthquake centuries before. But that had been hard masonry, his memory reminded him, vulnerable to collapse. The sloped ridge that was the target now was thicker, composed of loose debris deposited there by earlier eruptions. *Scipio's* shells might just bury themselves in it before blasting innocuous craters.

"Order to Mr. Tyrell. One round. At his convenience."

A system of electric bells transmitted instructions from the bridge to the turrets. Tyrell, the gunnery lieutenant, was positioned beneath the sighting hood in the starboard turret, eye to the fixed telescope, hand on the lever that controlled rotation. The great cylinder inched over a few degrees, stopped, came back a little, rested. The barrel of the righthand gun elevated to the angle specified on the manufacturer's tables following testing on the proving range.

"Protect your ears." Dawlish lifted his hands to demonstrate, dropped them as d'Erlanger complied. Pride would keep him and the other officers from such a measure. The convention was a stupid one that led to so much deafness in old age, but he would not be seen to disregard it.

The wait seemed endless.

And then the long streak of flame, the simultaneous crash, the churning yellow billow that seared the eyes and rasped the throat, the ash-clouds whipped from *Scipio's* decks, the barrel sliding back against its recoil piston. Dawlish's glasses were locked on the illuminated ravine and for an instant he saw a dark circle punched in the slope what might be twenty or thirty feet to the right of the gash's edge. The flash came a second later, throwing up a dark fountain as the sound of the detonation washed over the ship.

Nothing.

The blast had triggered no landslide, no small earthquake, had left only a small crater. The slope still held and above and beyond it the glowing streams still cascaded down into the brimming valley.

"Another round from Mr. Tyrell. At his discretion." Dawlish hoped that he sounded unperturbed.

Again the shrilling bell and moments later the turret edged leftwards perhaps a half-degree as Tyrell corrected the aim in azimuth. *Scipio* had heeled slightly with the previous discharge but the weak rolls that followed had died by now and she was again on an even keel.

Seconds, aeons, passed.

Then the stabbing flame, this time from the turret's lefthand gun, the smoke, the crash, the recoiling barrel, the vessel's heel …

… and the shell's impact in the very centre of the ravine, the bright orange detonation, the flying gouts of shattered rock, the rain of debris.

Breath inheld, unspoken hope – no, longing – for the first trembling of the slope, for the slightest slide of rocks or scree.

But nothing.

"Two rounds. Simultaneous."

Dawlish could feel the uneasiness around him, d'Erlanger's most of all. It was essential that he himself conveyed no sign of doubt or irresolution. He did not lower his glasses, held them fixed on the ravine, wondered if the aim should be corrected to strike lower down, decided against it. The closer to the apex of the ravine's inverted vee, the better.

The starboard turret was rotating two or three degrees to lie directly on the beam. That was essential for loading but the perfect aim of the last shot might be hard to regain.

He forced himself not to look at his watch. A reloading time of a minute fifty-seven seconds had been achieved on exercises. It might be no different now, but it felt like centuries before the gun-barrels, raised to maximum elevation for reloading, dropped again and the turret crept back to its previous heading. Another half-minute as Tyrell adjusted the elevation, a half-degree lower than before, for both barrels were warm from the last discharges.

They blasted as one. The shells' detonations showed that one had buried itself in the ravine while the second gouged a half-crater along its rightward edge. Dawlish's spirit soared as the searchlights' cold beams illuminated a small cascade of loose rock to the right.

More interminable minutes to reload and re-aim. Then the next salvo, landing close, very close, to the previous point of impact.

Again nothing. But hope would die hard.

Over half of the bursting rounds in the starboard weapons' magazine had been expended. No option now but the expedient Dawlish had dreaded – use of the port turret meant firing across the deck. The diagonal disposition, each turret positioned off the centreline, looked practical on paper. The vessel's narrow superstructure allowed – in theory – all four twelve-inchers to bear directly fore or aft. Two on either side could cover the full sixteen-points bow to stern. Over a narrow broadside arc amidships all four could be brought into action on either beam.

The solution had an elegance that must have delighted a geometrician, but it had ignored the blast effects of cross-deck fire. Live-firing exercises had proved it. The paint scoured by flame from the unplanked deck amidships could be easily replaced, but not so the damage to the flying bridge above, the protection of the funnel uptake, the ventilators clustered around it. Clearing *Scipio* for action had prepared her for employment of the port as well as the starboard turret but Dawlish had hoped there would be no necessity for it. Now he could not avoid it.

He gave the order.

The port turret was already manned, its guns loaded. It swung across, creeping the last degrees to bear on the target ravine. Tyrell had gone across to supervise the aiming, leaving his deputy in charge of the starboard turret. Given dwindling shell stocks, Dawlish had decided against single sighting shots. He would rely on Tyrell's experience with the earlier salvos to guarantee close hits.

Now the electric bells ringing in both turrets, the port's weapons blasting an instant before the starboard's, four long spears of flame flinging seven-hundred pound shells shorewards. Two smashed into the ravine, the others a fraction to its left, their detonation a single fiery sheet.

This time, movement on the slope to the right, and above, the point of impact. A small avalanche was opening a long rent, the cascade strengthening as rolled, more boulders, more scree, promise of landslide.

But a promise unfilled.

The fall continued for another minute, weakened, died. The dark line of the crest above showed no sign of subsidence. It still dammed the lava streams flowing from the angry heights above. If this seaward slope was not to be ruptured, then the fiery lake would soon be overtopping at the slope above the town.

"Another broadside."

Firing would be at longer intervals now since the port turret would need to turn almost a half-circle to line up its guns for loading before swinging back to aim across the deck.

"This time. It must be this time." d'Erlanger yielded to the tension, spoke what all felt, was silenced by a nod from Hammond towards Dawlish. The burden of success or failure was his alone this moment.

An agony of waiting. Then the broadside.

The impact was close to the previous. Again there was movement, more rockfall from the same point as before. A broad, flattened inverted vee was creeping upwards from the fall, fast at first, then weakening but not dying.

All bursting shells in the starboard turret's magazine had been used and it was now firing solid shot. The urge to aim the next broadside at that fall was strong, but Dawlish resisted it. Some complex network of fissures on that slope were transmitting the impacts within the ravine to some point of weakness above it to the right.

Another broadside. Four good square impacts and –

The slope was moving again, an avalanche heaving from that flattened inverted vee, strengthening as it roared down and rippling further out on either flank.

"The crest! Look at the crest!" d'Erlanger grabbed Dawlish's arm.

There, to the right of the crest's centre, was subsidence. No break, no breach, but a stretch of forty or fifty yards that had sagged relative to the height on either side. And below it the avalanche still rolled. One searchlight swept across to show that the slide, its base obscured by clouds of dust, was still widening. The other light held steady on the ravine.

Dawlish felt joy surge through him but his only words were "Another broadside."

It was the last, none further needed. A long overhang above the landslide was collapsing into it and then a widening vee was rising from it, up the slope towards the crest itself.

Then the breach.

A tiny notch at first, a glimpse of bright lava within, but then a glowing flow bursting from it, tearing at its sides. That notch was broadening, ripping deeper, and then it was a notch no more but a long weir across which lava was pouring seaward in a deluge. New fissures were spreading, new landslides commencing at a half-dozen other places.

Then the collapse, the slope beneath the crest moving as a single mass, heaving free, roaring down, the lava flood surging over it, draining what had been the hidden valley.

Silence on the bridgewing now, not just relief but awe of what *Scipio* had unleashed. The lava had separated into six separate streams that weaved between the tumbled rocks to find their easiest courses. The great landslide was weakening and settling as it reached the flat ground towards the coast. The nearest fingers of lava were still a half-mile from the water's edge but they would creep on towards it, engulfing the roadmenders' shacks and the ground east of them. But that didn't matter.

Mont Colbert was not dead and might have yet more fury to wreak. But for now, Saint Gérons had been delivered from the menace of the lava lake above it.

It might yet live.

Chapter 5

Clyde and *Navigator* sailed for Escource soon after daybreak but *Scipio's* boats had to be hoisted aboard before departure. Dawlish sensed the same pride among her crew as in himself, awareness that they had shared in an unprecedented victory. He had gone to the turrets and magazines to thank the crews before they were stood down, had congratulated Tyrell and his deputy on their gunnery.

And d'Erlanger had thanked him.

"My wife would have been grateful too," he said. There was something deeper than sadness in his voice.

When *Scipio* departed soon after noon, the lava flow that her guns had triggered had reached the sea and was quenching itself in clouds of steam. Dawlish invited d'Erlanger to the bridge to view the town as it slid past, blanketed as if by a grey snowfall, intact but deserted. They watched in silence, the thought unspoken that this might just be a stay of execution, not a reprieve. Mont Colbert might remain active for weeks or months or years.

At Escource, *Clyde* and *Navigator* had already sent their passengers ashore. *Scipio's* anchor was no sooner dropped than Lieutenant Stockley, acting harbourmaster, came aboard to report. He had done well. Burn and scald victims had been the first to land and be carried to the local hospital. The ships' surgeons and their helpers had been working there since arrival. They were overwhelmed by numbers now.

"It's the ash," Stockley said. "A lot who've breathed it in are coughing their hearts out. Old folks and children most of all. It's pitiful."

The most vulnerable of the refugees had shelter in scant comfort in the warehouses that Stockley had commandeered. The ships' cooks were dispensing soup from cauldrons brought across from the galleys. The black clergyman whom Dawlish had seen leading prayers back in Saint Gérons was acting as interpreter. Stockley introduced him. The Reverend Elijah Gagneux, sixty at the least, looked close to collapse but he made no complaint. He was thankful for deliverance but concerned about what would follow.

But the majority of the men landed were slumped anywhere they could find along the quayside, penned much as they had been at Saint Gérons by bluejackets and marines.

"Why?" Dawlish said.

"The governor hasn't decided what to do with 'em. He won't have them loose in the town until he's made his mind up."

Sir Clifford has had three days to do that, Dawlish thought, though he did not say it.

"It's damn lucky we've Sergeant Dorsette and his constables with us," Stockley said. "These people trust him, like they trust Reverend Elijah. They listen when they tell them to be patient, that something will be done. Without them, it wouldn't be so quiet."

Then Stockley said what Dawlish was already thinking.

"It can't go on like this, sir. Do what we can, there's little enough food. There're no latrines. They can't even wash the ash from their clothes or from themselves. There's no cover for most of 'em if it rains and God knows it's bad enough for them already in the sun. They're not cattle. They're worn out, exhausted, don't know what will become of them. They've no fight in them now but by the morning they'll be restive."

That was the nightmare now.

Time for Dawlish to meet His Excellency, Sir Clifford Belton.

*

d'Erlanger had a house in the town, a small one, he said, because he had business interests here. He would however be going directly to his plantations south of Mont Colbert.

"I can't accommodate everybody for Saint Gérons there," he told Dawlish. "I'll see what can be done though. Tell Sir Clifford that."

And more. d'Erlanger kept four horses here, two to draw a carriage, which he'd take to his plantation, two for riding. Dawlish was welcome to a mount while he was here. He accepted d'Erlanger's offer and joined him in the landau that had come to collect him at the quayside. The surly crowd gathered there opened to let them through. The mood changed when they saw d'Erlanger and called appeals for help. A few pushed forward and reached for his hand. There was no mistaking the mood of desperation but Dawlish recognised respect, even affection, for d'Erlanger.

His small house turned out to be a large villa on the gentle slope above the town. Of the two riding horses, Dawlish selected a dapple-grey gelding called Bayard. A black groom, introduced as Hippolyte, would accompany him on the other mount, a mare, Marianne.

Government House stood a half-mile further up the slope in a landscaped and well-tended garden. It was a long, white two-storied building with bougainvillea climbing up to wreathe the balcony on the upper floor. Impressive as it was, it must seem a comedown from the embassies where Sir Clifford had spent most of his career.

Alerted by the police guard, Lieutenant Clavering emerged on the front steps as Dawlish swung himself from his saddle and passed the reins to Hippolyte. He felt sudden anger. Clavering should have reported to him on *Scipio*, as Stockley had.

"His Excellency will see you in about an hour, sir," Clavering said. "He's still in consultation with his Advisory Council. He instructed me to see you have refreshments in the meantime. I'll let him know that you're here. If you'll come this —"

"You can go back to Sir Clifford and tell him that I too am a busy man. You're here to represent me, Lieutenant Clavering. Remember that." Dawlish's temper was rising, and he knew he could not let it. He had to work with the governor.

Friends in high places. Not a man to cross. The more so because a riot is perhaps brewing down in the harbour at this very moment.

Clavering was stammering what might be an evasion, but Dawlish was not listening.

"Present my compliments to His Excellency, lieutenant." He had softened his tone. "And my apologies for asking him to leave his council meeting. Tell him the matter's urgent."

A black major-domo in an exotic livery of the previous century conducted Dawlish to what must be a waiting room. It was comfortably furnished and a footman arrived to light the kerosene lamps, for it was sundown now. Another appeared with iced lemonade – the cost of bringing ice here must have been enormous – or anything stronger, if desired. Dawlish disliked their subservience, their bobbing heads, their unctuous smiles. He had seen too often that such servility had disguised resentment, even hatred.

The open French windows opened on to a terrace. He stepped outside. Night had fallen, the sky above clear and moonlit, but to the north, eight or ten miles distant, the profile of Mont Colbert was black against it. A great cloud rolled above it and drifted westwards. The flame belching from three different points cast a dreadful crimson hue on the bottom of the smoke blanket. But no glow of lava streams. Hidden from sight here by the mountain's bulk, the flow was all northwards, seawards.

"Captain Dawlish?"

He turned to see a tall but stooped man in dark clothing, white-haired and clean shaven, face set in what might be a permanent frown of concentration. He extended his hand. Sir Clifford's grasp was limp. He looked as if he had never been any age but sixty through his entire life.

"I had hoped to see you earlier, captain." The voice was tired, so too the watery blue eyes behind a pince-nez.

Dawlish had decided that he would make no apology for his decision to go straight to Saint Gérons. He was about to speak but the governor forestalled him.

"My apologies for not meeting you at the harbour, captain. My most heartfelt apologies in view of what I'm told that you've already achieved But the Advisory Council can't be ignored, especially not in the present circumstances. Gentlemen who're never easy to deal with and impossible to hurry. You'll understand, captain." He smiled. A thin, bleak weary smile, inviting sympathy.

It was disarming. Dawlish found himself drawn to him. And then he heard a small internal voice.

He made his career this way. He's here because of it.

"I understand, Your Excellency." No other answer possible.

"It's sufficient to address me as 'Sir Clifford', captain. You'll perhaps join me in my study? It's better to talk there and it offers a good view of the harbour."

It did. *Navigator* lay close in, *Clyde* and *Scipio*, further out in deeper water, their lights pinpoints, their white hulls ghostly.

"A magnificent sight, captain," the governor said. "A magnificent achievement too, I've heard, saving Saint Gérons from destruction. Only the scantest details, mind you. I'd welcome knowing more."

Go slowly with this man. Build trust

"Have you a map here, sir? Good. Thank you."

It was a copy of the same out-of-date map that Dawlish had seen in Trinidad, its scale too small for what he needed.

"May I trouble you for a sheet of paper, Sir Clifford? And a pencil. Some things are better conveyed that way."

In a silence that the governor did not interrupt, Dawlish sketched in quick strokes the coast, the mountain ridges, the eruptions, the rising lava lake above the town. He pointed to it.

"You can see that a breach in the ridge here, Your Excellency, would have engulfed the town." The memory of looking down from the crest, the glowing sheet to one side, the buildings far below on the other, seemed even more terrible now than on that night.

The governor was nodding. There was an impression that it was for politeness only, as a minor royal personage might feign interest when shown a prize heifer at a country-show.

"And this is what we did about it, Sir Clifford…"

He felt proud when he told it, the efficiency of his crew, the accuracy of the gunnery, the persistence in the face of possible failure. But words could not convey his elation when the slope slid at last, when the glowing flood raged through the widening breach, when he felt the thrill of triumphant assurance that Saint Gérons would be spared.

"Well done, captain. A notable achievement. But –"

"But, Sir Clifford?"

"An expensive decision, captain. Taken independently and without consultation. I assume that the cost of the munitions expended was high? Yes? An expense, I fear that nobody in London anticipated. But we'll leave it to the Admiralty and the Colonial Office to decide who pays."

"I trust you'll support my decision, sir?"

"That'll require consideration captain. Full consideration, of course. You can be assured of that."

"You might wish to discuss it with Mr. d'Erlanger, sir. He can better explain the threat to the town than I can."

"Aah, Mr. d'Erlanger." A pause. The bleak smile had long since faded. "That gentleman must be approached with caution. He's not popular with his fellow planters. We need to tread carefully around him."

"There's an urgent matter, Your Excellency," Dawlish said. "The people we brought from Saint Gérons. There's unrest and –"

Sir Clifford cut in. His tone was sharper now. "Have you any idea of the problems you've caused here, captain? You assumed a lot by evacuating Saint Gérons, landing so many people here without my approval. And what are we to do with them now?"

"Feed them. Shelter them."

"Easily said, captain. You took too much on yourself. There are procedures regarding such matters. Evaluations, consultations, approvals. And you may be underestimating the necessity for the support – support, not just assent, mind you – of my Advisory Council. Some of the most influential men here, men who matter, plantation owners, men of business. And they're not happy about the mob you've transported here. What's to become of these unfortunates? There's unrest enough in the town already, in all Roscal indeed."

"And there's unrest on this quayside this minute, Sir Clifford. The mood's ugly. There could be a riot by morning if nothing's done. Reassurance of temporary shelter, of further food distribution might be enough to deter it. But reassurance tonight and –"

"I understand that you've men enough to control any riot, captain."

"Not without violence." A fleeting mental image of stones thrown, tempers lost, scuffles, warning shots, rifle butts, men down, kicked and trampled. At worst, bloodied bayonets. "The Saint Gérons people have suffered enough."

Sir Clifford remained silent and gave the impression of a man almost overwhelmed but striving to hide it.

"Perhaps there's some waste ground outside the town," Dawlish said. "I've stores of canvas, rope too. Picks and shovels and axes taken on board in Trinidad. Officers and petty officers who can organise. I've men who're handy in any emergency, carpenters, sailmakers, artificers, who can direct others too. And there's no shortage of labour down on the quayside."

Something of relief on Sir Clifford's face. A burden lifting.

"Canvas shelters," Dawlish said. "Shacks if there's wood enough, mud brick and palm thatch if there isn't." He remembered German monks who'd worked wonders with such materials in Africa. Men dead now, massacred. "And latrines. There'll be sickness without them. But they're easily dug. Wells too, if we have to."

An eternity before Sir Clifford answered.

"How much ground, captain?"

Dawlish had no idea. "Ten acres at the least," he said. A wild guess, but he hoped it sounded authoritative. "Open if possible. If there's a stream nearby, then so much the better."

Again silence. After a minute Sir Clifford said, "Could you oversee the business, captain?"

"Yes. We could begin tomorrow, if you can nominate a place. But we'd need to let those people who're restive at the quay know about it tonight. It'll offer some hope and quieten them."

"And food, captain?"

"I can supply enough for another day, maybe two, from the stores we brought. But after that you'd need to see to it, Sir Clifford."

Silence once more, longer. Dawlish looked away, unwilling to see the older man's look of tortured concentration.

"There's one possibility, captain." The words hesitant.

The governor stood, moved to a framed map on the wall. Escource, a surveyor's hand-drawn, hand-coloured work. He pointed to an irregular polygon on the south side of the bay, bounded on one side by the water's edge. What looked like a house and three separate fields. And much less than ten acres.

"Le Marigot. A small manor, gone to rack and ruin," Sir Clifford said. "My predecessor ordered it possessed in consequence of taxes unpaid for years."

"Is it occupied?"

"No. There's been opposition to its sale. The owner might have been a drunkard but he was from an old French family. That counts here. The Advisory Council refused to support disposal."

"You can't override them?"

"In law, yes, captain. In practice, no. I must carry them with me on so many other things. There's too much at stake to offend them."

"The council's meeting here tonight? Waiting for you to return to the session?"

"Yes, captain."

The telegram received in Post of Spain had been unambiguous. Action with all despatch. In cooperation with the civil authority.

The civil authority lacked resolution, but Sir Clifford would know how ensure that blame was shared, perhaps completely shifted.

To Dawlish.

A riot, especially if blood was shed, would cancel the success bought by *Scipio's* guns, could end his career.

"What exactly is the council, Sir Clifford? I had assumed that as governor you have supreme authority here."

"It's not that simple." The voice, though weary, was patronising. Dozens of lesser mortals must have heard the same words before from these lips. "The council's advisory only, but that doesn't mean it can be ignored. Its members, especially the planters, know this place and they're powerful within it."

"Who appoints them?"

"The governor. Not that I've done so myself. Changing appointments made by my predecessors would have been provocative. With the risk of unrest being fomented here from Guimbi – that's what matters most here, captain – I need these men's support to keep their workers quiet, if not necessarily loyal."

This man is frightened. Hovering between Scylla and Charybdis, he's indecisive. Only an ultimatum can break this impasse.

"Do I understand, Sir Clifford, that you won't authorise setting up shelters in this place – what do you call it? Yes, Le Marigot."

"I'll need time to convince the council and –"

"I regret that I must record this conversation in writing, sir." Dawlish said. He was playing high stakes, he knew, and this was coercion, not cooperation. "And my warning about a possible riot tomorrow. My recommendation for a decision tonight. My protest against delay."

"There's no need to dramatise, captain." Sir Clifford's tone soothing, but forced. "You surely have men enough to contain any disturbance until –"

"I'm damned if I'll take the blame for any bloodshed." Dawlish felt his temper flaring. That was dangerous. Better to be quiet, let his words sink in.

And they did, though the wait for them to do so was agonising.

"Le Marigot's a good solution," Sir Clifford said. "A temporary one, of course. I'll stress that to the councillors. And agreed jointly by you and me. My secretary, Mr. Blackford, will draw up the authorisation. I'll send the Commissioner of Police to assist you do it."

"Thank you, Sir Clifford."

"Thank you, captain. And now," the bleak smile was back, "I must return to the council. Not easy men, and they won't like it. A long night ahead to convince them, captain, a long night."

But Dawlish didn't care.

He had what he had come for.

*

A long night indeed.

Dawlish rode back to the quay, Hippolyte leading to show the way in the darkness. In addition to the Roscallan patois, the groom had reasonable English. He could be invaluable in the coming days. He led Dawlish's gelding back to d'Erlanger's stables. He would return with it next morning.

"They're quiet enough now, sir." The marine lieutenant in command of the quay-guard there gestured to the men muttering in small, crouched clusters and the sleeping bodies slumped against walls and bollards.

Stockley appeared.

"I'm returning to *Scipio*," Dawlish said. "I'll see you there in a half-hour. Bring the Reverend Elijah and Sergeant Dorsette with you."

After food had been distributed next morning, both men would be invaluable in explaining to the refugees what was planned and helping form work parties.

Dawlish must see *Scipio's* officers too, and the captains of *Clyde* and *Navigator*. A plan and organisation must be hammered out tonight and tasks assigned to the crews of all three warships. An officer – *Scipio's* marine major, Gormley, would be ideal – must survey the Le Marigot site, decide locations for shelters, field kitchens and latrines. Others must organise distribution of tools and appoint petty officers to oversee digging and construction. The tents kept on board each ship for use by landing parties would provide models for the sailmakers to copy.

The potential for unrest and riot would remain, especially if the food supply was not addressed soon, for little remained of what had been so hastily loaded at Trinidad. That would be a matter for Sir Clifford, one which would probably afford him every opportunity for delay and indecision. The danger of clashes between the refugees and Escource's population could not be discounted, for desperate fathers of families would not hesitate to loot or steal. Bluejackets and marines must be a constant, if unobtrusive, presence, escorting supplies and guarding the worksites. Coordination with the governor's staff and subordinates would be essential and obstruction might well be expected from the Advisory Council that concerned Sir Clifford so much.

And on, and on.

It would be impossible to think of all necessities tonight and get measures in place to address them.

But there would be a start.

Chapter 6

The first work party, four dozen men with picks and shovels, all young and able-bodied, plodded under bluejacket guard to Le Marigot just after noon. The Reverend Elijah and Sergeant Dorsette had recruited them and were now busy cajoling others to enlist. Their patient explanations of the plans, and timely delivery of provisions from the ships, had scotched the threat of riot, for now at least.

Dawlish himself had joined both men in the first hour of their task. The French that had been his second tongue since youth provided some ability to comprehend the patois and allowed him to answer questions and add assurances. The mood had been sullen at first but was changing with awareness that something was being done. Moving among them without a side-arm, he shook innumerable hands, clapped shoulders, joined laughter when somebody's incomprehensible joke or query raised it. He sensed an indomitability in them, resolution and courage that they might not recognise in themselves. In Cuba, six years before, he had lived as a labourer among others like them. Their forebears too had survived slavery. Here, as there, was the strength of the humble who endured.

During the midnight planning conference in Dawlish's quarters on *Scipio,* Sir Clifford's secretary Blackford, a young Englishman, arrived with authorisation for occupying Le Marigot. He looked as taken aback as several officers had when they saw the black clergyman and sergeant present, even if reticent until called upon. Nobody had dared voice an objection in Dawlish's presence. By mid-morning however, several of the ships' officers had commented that, black or not, both men were doing a good job.

Dawlish rode out to Le Marigot. It lay a mile beyond the last straggling limits of the town and what he saw disappointed. One field was overgrown with waist-high grass, the others with scrub that ran into a swamp close at the bay's shore. Mosquitoes droned in clouds above it. The house, though large, was roofless, doors and windows long-since pillaged, shrubs growing out through the gaps. And only a single well, with part of its surrounding wall collapsed.

"We can't bring anybody here until we've cleared ground." Major Gormley of *Scipio's* marines gestured towards the grass. "This is where we'll start."

He had already made his survey and showed a sketch – locations for tents, latrines, a makeshift kitchen and a store – and asked for Dawlish's approval. The house might serve as refuge for the most vulnerable if new rafters were positioned and a tarpaulin laid over them. There was standing timber enough to lay a narrow walkway of logs across the swamp and construct a short jetty for landing necessities from the ships. A half-mile distant, a stream cascaded down a gentle slope towards the bay. If dammed at a higher level, canvas hoses from the ships could carry fresh water from it. Nothing of it all was impossible, though it would take time, two, three days before the first residents could be moved here.

"How many?"

"A hundred or so if we've the first tents ready."

"And in total?" Dawlish had already feared the answer.

"Not everybody. Four or five hundred, and maybe even that may be too much. It looks as if this place floods in rain and if the latrines overflow – well, you can imagine it, sir. It could be a death trap. Even if they're only here for a few weeks then…"

All too easy to visualise dysentery and worse ripping through here, as deadly as the lava that had threated Saint Gérons.

"Keep the work party here tonight," Dawlish said. "I'll have food sent, canvas for shelters too. I don't want them back at the quay."

No official had appeared from the municipality to offer advice or support. No news of food supplies. The promised Commissioner of Police had made no appearance, not during the night, not by now in mid-afternoon. There had been signs of resentment among the town's existing residents against the newcomers, not surprising in view of the existing poverty that Dawlish had seen as he had ridden through. Insults, and a few stones, had been hurled at the work-party on its way here but the presence of the bluejacket escort had deterred anything worse. He disliked the idea of using of naval personnel to suppress wider unrest. That should be the governor's business.

That, and a larger site than Le Marigot.

*

Dawlish would look back on these days as among the most frustrating of his life. What had to be done was obvious and difficult, but not impossible. The skills, the enthusiasm of the warships' crews for this novel task, the willing labour that the Reverend Elijah mobilised, much of the materials needed, all were at hand. But the governor proved endlessly patient at each encounter when he explained reasons for delaying decisions.

Food was available for purchase in the markets in Escource and elsewhere and, in principle, Sir Clifford decided that he could justify releasing funds. But for a week only. Beyond that, he would need the authorisation of the Colonial Office in London.

"How much to request?" he told Dawlish. "It's a thorny matter. Who deserves assistance? Many from Saint Gérons will have brought money with them. They can afford to pay."

"And if they can't?"

"The truly indigent merit feeding, no doubt of that, captain. Sustenance but not luxury. But how can their poverty be proved? And those labouring at Le Marigot – better they be remunerated with food rather than money. But with how much? For the worker alone, or for his whole family? And these people are prolific, their families large."

"They can't be let starve." It seemed obvious.

"Principles of political economy are involved, captain, remember that." Said with a trace of condescension. "The Poll Tax brings in little. Since beet cultivation has expanded in Europe, the price of sugar cane has fallen, and the colony's tax revenues in consequence. Other than Mr. d'Erlanger, few planters invested in lime-growing. Half of them teether on bankruptcy. They were critical of the taxation rates on their lands and activities even before this wretched eruption started. They'll resent further levies and –"

"And there's too much at stake to offend them." Dawlish had heard Sir Clifford say that a dozen times already.

"Precisely, captain."

It took two days more for the governor to decide before *Navigator* could bring his secretary to Antigua to despatch a telegram to the Colonial Office. *Navigator's* captain carried a signal from Dawlish to the Admiralty, his actions summarised in a few truncated and enciphered sentences. He also sent a letter for Florence, to be forwarded by mail packet. At the age that Jessica now was, when every day brought new development, he begrudged the delay in returning to Britain. He loved her even more than when she had first touched his heart.

Work was progressing on the ships and at Le Marigot. The first tents, tarpaulin shelters, storm ditches and latrines were in place and more were completing by the day. The log walkway reached steadily across the swamp and the jetty had been commenced by a detachment from *Clyde*. Work parties slept under quarterdeck-awnings stretched between poles and families were moving in. There was a sense of a community establishing itself, informal hierarchies emerging, leaders not just like the Reverend Elijah but others too, women among them. The distant rumbling of Mont Colbert and the smoke still spilling from it – on some days, depending on wind, ash drifted as far as here – were constant reminders of loss of homes, but the initial shock was past.

The number of evacuees remaining at the quayside had been reduced, for d'Erlanger had arrived back to announce that he could accommodate some three hundred on his own properties beyond Mios, south of Mont Colbert. The new arrivals would have to construct their own shacks with the aid of his plantation workers but food would be no problem. He sent carts to carry the weakest but the remainder must walk the eight miles.

Dawlish reluctantly approved Sir Clifford's request for a bluejacket escort lest there be problems when they passed through Escource. The town had thrived in the days of sugar-cane dominance but they were now past. Saint Gérons' prosperity, based on d'Erlanger's lime cultivation, pressing and export of lime juice, and his development of its harbour, was resented.

The evacuees' departure still left some seven hundred at the quay, the majority old, infirm or very young. Sir Clifford would not have them in the town and was adamant that they remain penned in. At Dawlish's insistence, a police cordon, black constables commanded by a white Roscallan inspector, replaced that drawn from his own crews. Conditions worsened by the day, the sanitation problem most of all, and Waller, *Scipio's* surgeon feared outbreak of dysentery. Transferring them to another site, ideally larger than Le Marigot, was urgent.

Sir Clifford did not disagree, when Dawlish pressed him yet again, but he explained that landholding was not straightforward here. The Bourbon Crown had made the original grants two centuries before. Slave revolt and attempted French reconquest had seen entire plantations lost, many of their masters massacred. The aftermath of British seizure saw acknowledgement of the rights of returning plantation owners and grudging acceptance of retention by slaves of small family plots on marginal ground. Ownership disputes were running sores, Sir Clifford said, complicated by elements of French law persisting in the statute books. And even a half-century since the abolition of slave holding, old French planter-families were still bitter. Britain had compensated them for loss of their human property, but it had never seemed enough.

Yet for all the condescension, all the hesitancy, all the agonising over matters that seemed straightforward, Dawlish could not dislike the governor. His integrity was absolute, his sense of duty no less. A widower, he had no other interest than his work, labouring long hours on matters better left to subordinates. Now it was the decision on where to relocate the remaining refugees that caused him anguish.

Three sites had been identified, two inland but the third on the coast, outside the village of Thénac, five miles to the east. Dawlish rode out with Major Gormley to see it. Fields that had been devoted to sugar cane lay overgrown and the plantation owner had offered them for rental. A stream flowed along the eastern edge and out across a beach to the sea beyond. Scrubland lay to the west and abandoned cane fields to the east. It appealed to Dawlish, for people and supplies could be brought here by ships' boats, so avoiding passage through the streets of Escource. He went to Sir Clifford on return and pleaded the case. The two alternatives, plantation land untilled and also for rental, were owned by councillors. Selection of either would be preferable, the governor said. Dawlish heard the same reasoning as before – such men could not be antagonised – and his frustration was rising.

"Can't they be ignored for once?" he said. "They don't rule this place, do they?"

A flicker of annoyance on Sir Clifford's face. "You're stepping beyond your role here, captain. There's more at stake here than you need know about. You may leave those matters to me." But his tone softened. "I've a few questions about your proposal. Let's discuss them."

They did, the mood relaxing.

And in the end Sir Clifford agreed.

Thénac if would be.

*

Navigator returned from Antigua with telegraphed authorisation for Sir Clifford to purchase food and with telegraphed instructions from the Admiralty for Dawlish. *Clyde* was to return to Britain but *Scipio* and *Navigator* were to remain at Roscal until further notice. Weekly reports to be sent by wire via Antigua and an evaluation of the performance of the 12-in guns to be forwarded by mail. And a signal addressed to Dawlish personally.

"Well done. T."

Nothing more, but enough.

Topcliffe was taking notice.

*

Four days later, Dawlish was viewing progress at the Thénac site when one of *Scipio's* cutters drew in to the beach under sail. A midshipman plunged over into knee-deep water and came running. His face was flushed.

"Commander Hammond's compliments, sir. There's an emergency, he says, 'an you should know about it."

"What sort of emergency?"

"I don't right know, sir. He said it's sensitive, urgent too. About a gunvessel that's arrived."

"Gunvessel?" Dawlish had not expected any reinforcement. "Where from?"

"From Guimbi, sir."

From then tiny black republic to the east. Impossible to imagine that it possessed a gunvessel. Harder still to imagine why it was here.

It was quicker to return by road. Hippolyte had ridden with Dawlish, had tethered both their mounts in shade. In minutes they were drumming at a smart canter along the packed-earth track to Escource. From the brow of the hill above the town Dawlish saw the gunvessel anchored in the harbour, closer in than *Scipio*. He had expected to see something ancient and decrepit, some surplus craft of Crimean vintage, virtual scrap sold on through increasingly minor navies. But this looked of the last decade, single funnel and barquentine-rigged, like a modern *Forester*-class vessel, though the overall profile suggested something other than British, from some French or Italian yard perhaps. The Royal Navy had dozens of such vessels, the French slightly fewer, all useful for maintaining control or suppressing unrest in distant colonies. Such a vessel was a surprising acquisition for a tiny, impoverished republic like Guimbi.

The quayside was thronged on the town side of the cordon. A line of bluejackets, which had not been there when Dawlish had left, stood ten yards behind the police that formed it. The crowd was making no attempt to break through towards the warehouses and was congregated at the head of the main landing steps. Most there were dressed like labourers he had seen working in the fields and several were carrying spades and, worryingly, machetes. Plantation hands, not townspeople. There seemed to be no sense of aggression, rather of bewilderment that they were here at all. Some were standing in small groups, others sitting with legs dangling over the quay edge as if waiting for direction. They opened a passage to let Dawlish through but he swung from the saddle, handed his reins to Hippolyte and nodded to him to take his mount on through the cordon.

"Bonjour, mes amis." He reached out his hand. First one, then two more, took it. Others were stepping back, avoiding his gaze, not hostile but perhaps embarrassed. Several were looking over their shoulders.

"Passez-vous une agréable visite de la ville?" He smiled as he said it. The words sounded too formal, but they were the closest to the patois that he could manage. He had already learned that the most here spoke only the most rudimentary English.

"Ça va bien, monsieur, ça va bien," one mumbled. He was looking over Dawlish's shoulder, fear in his eyes.

Dawlish turned. He saw two white men approaching. Well-cut seersucker suits, cream waistcoats, thick gold watch chains, bright neckties, broad-brimmed straw hats. Florid, fifty perhaps, they looked like identical twins.

"You're Dawlish. That's what you call yourself, isn't it?" No outstretched hand.

"I haven't had the pleasure so –"

"We're damned if we care about your pleasure," one said. His English was accented like the patois. "You're not welcome here, sir. Not you nor your ships nor what you've brought from Saint Gérons."

The other pointed towards the newly arrived gunvessel. "And we're damned if any Guimbian black sets foot ashore from that ship," he said. "We've brought people here to see they don't. You can tell that to your friend, Sir Clifford Belton."

"Captain Dawlish!"

Commander Hammond and Lieutenant Stockley were coming out through the cordon. Dawlish turned his back on the two men and walked towards his officers. He spoke before they did, voice low.

"What's this bloody nonsense about, commander?"

Shouting made him glance back. One of the whites was gesturing to the labourers they had brought to line up on either side of them. With his cane he struck one who was not fast enough across the shoulders. The man flinched, bowed his head as a beaten dog might, and shambled into place. The other white was urging them to yell and wave their implements. They were complying, though with no obvious fervour. Beyond them a new group, more vocal and led by a few whites, was hurrying along the quay to join them.

"She arrived three hours ago." Hammond nodded towards the gunvessel.

The flag flapping weakly at the stern was a blue, black and red tricolour. Like France's, but with the white replaced.

"A boat pulled across from her to *Scipio*," Hammond said "A fellow in a uniform, a black who called himself a lieutenant, asked if an envoy might come on board to speak to the captain. That mob you see was gathering already. Somebody must have seen the ensign and have guessed that something was afoot. I could see the situation was sensitive I didn't want to receive anybody in your absence and said he'd hear from you on your return. I trust that was appropriate?"

"Correct, commander."

"He handed me what he said was this envoy's credentials so you could decide. Here's the document."

A large envelope of thick cream paper with a crest that showed palm trees on a shield beneath two manacled hands rending a chain apart. A single stiff sheet within, crested also, divided into two columns. Elegant Italianate handwriting, French on the left, English to the right.

To whom it might concern.

That Maître Jacques Badeaux was the accredited representative of the President of the Republic of Guimbi. Assistance requested to arrange a meeting with His Excellency, Sir Clifford Belton, Her Majesty's Governor of Roscal, on a matter of mutual interest.

Dawlish scanned it in both languages. Flawless, if stiff, in English, but the French was courtly and old fashioned. Diplomats wrote like this a century before. A red wax seal confirmed the signature as that of the president.

This was a matter better to be handled by the governor but he must have already seen this vessel from Government House. He was probably still havering over how to act. He must have guessed that it would arouse the ire of the planters who concerned him so much. It might be days before he decided or, worse still, referred the matter to the Colonial Office in London for instructions. In the meantime, this gunvessel would swing at anchor, interpreted by those now inciting the mob as a provocation, possibly even a trigger for a riot. If blood was shed, Dawlish had no doubt as to whom Sir Clifford would shift the blame.

"Did you inform the governor about this mob?" he asked Hammond.

"No, sir. It was growing too big and too threatening. I thought it better not to send somebody through it, just in case. That's why I sent the message to you by cutter rather than by road."

And just as well, Dawlish thought.

"I was concerned by the mob breaking through to the warehouses and the people there," Hammond said. "The police cordon's not worth a damn on its own. So I sent men ashore to back it up."

"You did right," Dawlish said. "Now, where's Clavering?" The liaison officer who shuttled to and fro daily with messages to or from Sir Clifford.

"At Government House."

Dawlish pulled out his notebook and pencil, scribbled on a page and ripped it out. He walked across to Hippolyte, still mounted and still holding Dawlish's gelding.

"You'll put this in Lieutenant Clavering's hands. No other, him alone. You understand? Good. But wait for my word."

The mob had grown, was a solid mass. Except for the whites – and more of them were at the front now – there seemed to be no great enthusiasm. The larger part was here because employers and masters had demanded it. A show of force, the bluejackets brought forward with bayonets fixed and halting just ahead of the police line might well disperse them. But it needn't come to that. Confronting the bluster would be enough.

The white twins who had first insulted Dawlish were close. He walked back towards them and they held their ground.

"It's Badeaux who's out there, isn't it?" one shouted. "We know him of old! You can send him back where he came from. He isn't wanted here."

Dawlish approached.

"Badeaux will turn his guns on this town," the other twin yelled. "A signal for a black revolt, for a massacre of whites! 1791 again!"

"You don't know who we are, do you?" the first called. "We're the Souliers. You hear that? The Souliers, Etienne and Armand Soulier. That matters here. And Armand's a member of the Advisory Council."

The name was familiar. Sir Clifford had let it drop several times in conversation. The brothers were the bane of his life, he'd said, but they could not be offended.

"We've been warning Clifford for months that this could happen. The old fool will have to listen to us now. He'll have to."

Dawlish forced himself to smile, not take offence. "Then all the better that he knows about it. My groom will be carrying word to him. And I trust that your people here will let him through unmolested."

"What about that Guimbian ship? It could open fire at any time."

If it did, it would be suicide.

"Look over there, gentlemen," Dawlish said. "You see that ironclad, HMS *Scipio*? You see her guns? One shell would be enough to blow that Guimbian vessel to matchwood. Whoever's on board her isn't mad enough to risk it."

"You'll give orders for that?"

"I'll give orders to have her watched. And a guard boat will stand by her and circle her in darkness. Nobody comes ashore from her without my consent."

"Nobody's coming ashore from her anyway, Dawlish. We'll see to it that they don't." Soulier turned to his brother. "Won't we, Armand?"

And in that moment Dawlish sensed uncertainty. He smiled again, tried to speak with reasoned calm.

"I wouldn't do that if I were you." He turned towards the cordon, nodded towards the bluejackets beyond it. "Those men will escort anybody I'll bring ashore to see Sir Clifford. It wouldn't be wise to hinder them."

He didn't give them time to reply.

"My groom will be leaving for Government House now. You'll make a path for him, I trust?"

They did.

Hippolyte was on his way.

Time now to meet Maître Jacques Badeaux, envoy of Guimbi.

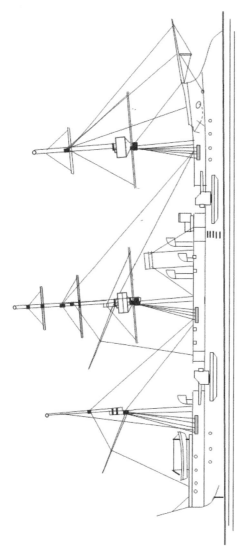

Belette Class Gunboats

Builders:
    La Seyne, Toulon; Claparéde, Le Petit-Quevilly
Five units built, 1882 - 1885
Construction: Composite, wood on iron framing
Displacement: 395 tons
Length: 202 feet overall
Beam (inside sponsons): 29 feet
Draught: 14 feet
Armour: Only on ram

Machinery:
    Compound Engine, Single Screw
    800 Horsepower
Speed: 13 Knot (Max.)
    8 Knots (Cruising)
Armament: 4 X 138mm breech-loaders
    Mounted on Sponsons
Complement: 105

Chapter 7

Lieutenant Clavering brought a carriage from Government House, one previously placed at Dawlish's and his disposal for liaison purposes. It was stouter than the elegant landau that Sir Clifford used in town and better suited for tours over rough roads around the island. It was waiting when Dawlish's gig touched at the harbour steps to bring the Guimbian envoy ashore. The bluejackets and marines brought forward an hour before to keep the half-truculent, half-curious crowd at a distance now formed a half-circle around the landing point. They stamped into a salute as Maître Jacques Badeaux ascended. Dawlish followed, escorted him to the carriage and sat on his right.

He changed into full formal uniform before he'd had himself pulled across to the gunvessel. Unsure what to expect, he met an elderly man in a black frock coat and immaculate white linen whose impeccable manners and dated French reminded him of his youth. He had stayed with his dying uncle in Pau and had learned the language there. There were many retired functionaries in the spa-town – dignified, punctilious and fastidious – who spoke and deported themselves like Badeaux.

The only difference was that he was black.

The bluejackets fell into file on either side of the carriage, rifles shouldered, bayonets scabbarded, as it moved away. The crowd was a mob no longer. The hours spent in shuffling uncertainty in the afternoon sun had drained all menace from the conscripted mass. Even the fury of the Soulier brothers had abated. They stood apart with a half-dozen other whites, glowering in silence as the carriage passed along the quay and into the town.

It was easy to converse with Badeaux, impossible to believe that he had come here to trigger a massacre. Despite his curiosity, Dawlish did not ask him the reason for his visit. That would be Sir Clifford's business.

"And where did you learn such excellent French, captain? So very few of your countrymen speak it well."

Dawlish told him.

"Aah, Pau," Badeaux said. "A beautiful town, I understand. But I lament that I have never visited the south. My years in France were spent mostly in Paris. Happy years of apprenticeship in my profession. We inherited French law in Guimbi and have needed to do only a little to adapt it to our circumstances. It was good to learn it at its source."

He was a lawyer, Dawlish learned, a friend and adviser of Guimbi's president, but he held no ministerial position. It was pleasing, he said, to be asked to represent the republic in these circumstances. They were trundling through the streets now, the seamen and marines in steady step alongside. People were emerging from shops and homes to watch, heads from windows. The sight of a black man riding in a carriage with a white must be a novelty here. A few – all black – shouted Badeaux's name and waved. Fewer still, looking about them first, cheered. He smiled towards them but made no other acknowledgement. Other than from the whites who turned their backs in silence, there was no sign of hostility.

"Have you visited Escource before, maître?" Dawlish said.

"A few times, captain. On public matters. But never on an occasion as sad as this. Alas! The devastation wrought by Mont Colbert's fury has touched the hearts of all on this island. Human borders mean so little at such times."

They had left the town now and had started up the gentle slope towards Government House. Talking with Badeaux was pleasant and Dawlish realised that this was the first time he had done so with a black man as an equal. Badeaux had shifted the conversation towards the naval presence, was complimentary about *Scipio's* bombardment at Saint Gérons. He seemed to know as much about it, and about the refugee resettlement, as Sir Clifford did and he showed rather more interest in the details. Whatever his sources, he was well informed. Dawlish realised that he himself was being probed with apparently innocent curiosity. It was the work of a professional lawyer, one who elicited information but gave nothing significant in return.

Dawlish kept his own answers general. And all the time that he was parrying queries as to how long his ships might remain here, his thoughts kept drifting back to the gunvessel in the harbour. The armoured ram sweeping forward under her bowsprit marked her as of French design, probably of composite construction, wood planking on a steel frame. She looked not unlike vessels of the *Belette* Class with which he had exchanged courtesies in other harbours.

Tarnished gilt lettering at the stern identified her as *Le Déchaîné*. Sponsons, two to a side, extended beyond the bulwarks. The single pivot-mounted guns they carried were covered by tarpaulins but the outlines suggested modern breech-loaders. She had looked well from a distance but, when neared, showed patches where paint was scoured from the hull's flank, a clumsy repair of stove-in planking, sags in the mizzen's standing rigging. The conditions on deck had appalled him. Engrained with dirt, it would take a week of holystoning to make it acceptable. And worse. Brasswork that had never seen polish, iron fixtures dusted with rust, the funnel encrusted with soot, a ventilator with a missing cowl, seamen in uniform remnants whom a no-less slovenly officer had brought to reluctant attention when Dawlish boarded. Badeaux had met him at the entry-port with a speech no less extravagant than if he had been welcoming a full admiral. The captain introduced himself as Maurice Queuille in good French, the accent slightly different to that common in Roscal.

What surprised Dawlish most of all was that the deck was piled five-feet high with bulging sacks. Several had split and beans had spilled from them. Sweet potatoes had dropped from another. Had he not seen the covered guns, he might have thought that this craft had been converted to commercial service.

Badeaux had invited him aft to share a glass of wine, and led him aft along a narrow lane between the sacks to the captain's cabin. It had been well-appointed once but now the wood panelling was warped and stained and the ill-assorted furnishings mildewed and faded. Then wine had appeared, toasts drunk. Badeaux was thankful that arrangements were in hand to bring him to the esteemed Sir Clifford, whom he lamented not meeting before. And no mention of any reason for this visit. It had been a relief afterwards to escape the musty atmosphere.

Government House was in sight now. Dawlish did not know if he would see this man again. He hoped not. International relations – and Guimbi was a sovereign state, even if a negligible one that did not merit even a consul from Britain – were Sir Clifford's responsibility and forte. Dawlish himself now wanted only to be gone. Another week would see the last of the refugees settled. Mont Colbert, smoking weakly now, posed no immediate threat to life. England, home and beauty beckoned as strongly for him as for any man on *Scipio*.

And yet . . .

Why a nation as poverty-stricken as Guimbi possessed a gunvessel not yet a decade old intrigued him. Even if acquired at second or third hand, she would have been an expensive purchase. European powers used others like *Le Déchaîné*, dozens of them, to represent their interests on distant stations. The guns they carried and the armed parties they could land were enough to quell riots or minor uprisings. How long was Guimbi's coastline? Some forty or fifty miles? If there was internal unrest, what could a gunvessel accomplish that forces moving on foot could not?

When he had left the vessel, Dawlish had seen that one of the tarpaulins had slipped enough to show something of the gun beneath. It seemed powerful for a craft of this size, four or five-inch calibre, he guessed. But it looked ill-maintained – paint flaking from the barrel, rust streaks on the mounting, elevation and traversing handwheels missing. An expensive weapon to be left in such a state. If the three other guns were in similar condition, the Souliers had nothing to fear from them.

The carriage was rumbling towards the gates of Government House. A last chance perhaps to satisfy his curiosity. The direct approach was best.

"A professional seaman's query, maître." He tried to sound casual. "Has *Le Déchaîné* proved herself of value?"

No immediate answer. Dawlish sensed that his pose of simple sailor had not convinced. But when Badeaux did speak, his voice was trembling with regret as well as anger.

"You've seen her, captain. Her shame, our shame. I can't deny it. Not just a squalid disgrace, but a warship that we don't need and never will. She was ordered new by a president and two ministers who shared a bribe from a French shipbuilder to build her for twice or more than she would have cost another buyer. The humblest of our people suffered to pay for that ship. A tenth of her price would have funded village schools, a hospital, clean water. And there was more – new cannons for the fort at Port Mazarin that we don't need. Their prices inflated too."

He broke off, held up his hands, as if embarrassed by his outburst.

"The president," Dawlish said. He knew he should not press the matter further but curiosity was too strong. "The man in office today?"

"No. Two before. One who went too far."

"What happened?"

"A mob stormed the place. His guards joined it. He was beaten, dragged outside and hanged from a lamppost." He paused. "More shame, captain. It's not the freedom dreamed of for so long. And the gunvessel has been so neglected that she found no buyers when we tried to sell her. Not even Haiti wanted her. And so *Le Déchaîné* rots."

The carriage halted at the front steps of Government House.

Sit Clifford, well prepared, was at the top in white tunic and trousers, gold-embroidered collar, cuffs and shoulder straps, medals and orders on left breast, a dark stripe down each leg, a Marlborough helmet adorned with swan's feather plumes.

Le Maître Badeaux was being accorded full diplomatic status.

*

Sir Clifford was courtesy incarnate, greeting Badeaux in perfect French, and leading to him to a salon – elegant but shabby, lacking a woman's touch – to which Dawlish had not been invited previously. The envoy responded in kind. Both men regretted not having met previously, though they knew each other by repute. It seemed a ritual, usage of stilted phrases that bought time for each to weigh up the other. Badeaux wished for meeting in a happier time, for it was the recent catastrophe that had occasioned this visit. Sir Clifford paid extravagant compliments to Dawlish and his crews. Without their skill and heroism, the catastrophe would have been greater still. Badeaux expressed his admiration.

Despite their platitudes, Dawlish sensed that Sir Clifford was pleased that Badeaux was here and that he himself was absolved of all responsibility for allowing him to land. The governor had sent no message to the gunvessel, had probably foreseen that Dawlish would take the first step and had done nothing to stop it. But should reception of this envoy of Guimbi's president trigger outrage among his Advisory Council, or if London would not approve, the responsibility for the welcome would be Dawlish's, not his.

Dawlish was included in the invitation to sit. Wine was brought, refreshments offered. The preliminaries were passed.

"You have perhaps brought a message from your esteemed president?" Sir Clifford said.

"With your permission, Your Excellency, it is may be better that you read his own words. Words written from the heart." Badeaux produced a cream, crested envelope, from an inside pocket.

Sir Clifford took it. "In the president's own hand? Yes? Thank you."

He held it with the reverence he might have accorded a missive from the Russian Czar, and not from the president of a pauper state with a population little larger than a London borough's. He walked to a desk, picked up a paper knife, slit it open. A single sheet. He adjusted his pince-nez and began to read. He looked up, smiling.

"A noble gesture, Maître Badeaux. And welcome too." He handed the note to Dawlish. "Generous and magnanimous, captain. I think you'll agree."

The crest, two manacled hands and a broken chain. A single sentence of greeting, free of diplomatic flourishes. Only a half-dozen followed. Sorrow for Mont Colbert's victims, sympathy for the bereaved. Guimbi's citizens were united in grief with their friends in Roscal. The days ahead would be hard for all who had suffered loss. And hope that a small contributor to alleviation of their distress would be welcomed. *Le Déchaîné* was loaded with food.

And below, a spidery signature.

Auguste Ravenel, President.

"This will be welcome, maître, and appreciated" Sir Clifford said. "The need is great." He turned to Dawlish. "I trust you can arrange to have the cargo discharged as soon as possible, captain. It would be best brought directly by your boats to the camp at Thénac."

Construction of that camp was barely started and only a handful of refugees were settled there so far. But the governor's intent was clear. No passage of the food through the town. No need for the Guimbian warship's crew to come ashore. No provocation. No riot. And minimum advertisement of the gift.

If asked, Sir Clifford would find reasons – bad roads, threat of a dysentery epidemic, difficulty in coming ashore – why Maître Badeaux could not meet refugees at Thénac.

"One day will no doubt suffice to transfer the food, captain," the governor said. "Yes? That's excellent. I imagine you'll have preparations to begin tonight. You'll want to return to your ship now. Our guest and I will have a few small matters to discuss. He'll be returning to *Le Déchaîné* in my personal carriage. I trust you'll leave your men as escort."

Dawlish stood up, shook hands with Badeaux, undertook to contact Captain Queuille to arrange discharge. It was dark outside and he found the bluejackets resting behind the house, many with pipes glowing in the soft warm darkness. The lieutenant in charge had arranged food for them, despite reluctance from the governor's major-domo. He was well capable to seeing the Guimbian envoy safely back to port.

The carriage that had brought him carried Dawlish back to the quay. The would-be mob was long dispersed and quiet reigned.

Another long night lay ahead if the gunvessel was to be gone in twenty-four-hours' time.

*

A week passed. The visit of the Guimbian gunvessel was a memory now, one that Sir Clifford never alluded to during his discussions with Dawlish. It was if Maître Badeaux had never visited, as if *Scipio's* boats had never landed the gift of food at Thénac. The last of the refugees had been transferred to the newly constructed camp there by now. With them gone from Escource, the Soulier twins had no occasion to incite outrage or threaten riot. *Navigator* had carried despatches and draft telegrams to Antigua for transmission to London. On her return she had carried the signal from the Admiralty for which Dawlish was hungering.

Scipio and *Navigator* to return to Britain, re-coaling at Bermuda.

But with one unexpected qualification.

Scipio to pay a courtesy visit to Guimbi's capital, Port Mazarin. Captain Dawlish to relay Her Majesty's thanks to President Ravenel for material aid given in the aftermath of Mont Colbert's eruption. A single day and night would suffice.

And Sir Clifford would provide instructions.

*

Dawlish suspected that the visit to Guimbi had been suggested by Sir Clifford himself.

"A most appropriate initiative," he said. "One supported by both the Colonial Office and the Foreign Office. One that will benefit both Guimbi and Roscal."

It seemed a come-down for *Scipio*, Dawlish thought. A few scant weeks before he had welcomed the emperor of Brazil on board. But he held his peace and asked, "Why?"

"A salutary reminder of British power, captain. The whites here in Roscal fear Guimbi as an inspiration for the blacks to rise in insurrection and massacre. They'll see *Scipio's* visit as one serving notice that no Guimbian meddling here will be tolerated."

"Is there really such a threat?" Dawlish said. He had seen poverty here but more of sullen resignation than of hostility.

"An exaggerated fear in my opinion, but convenient for some members of the council and their ilk," the governor said. "But there's some grain of truth in it. The current Guimbian president, this Ravenel fellow, is different to most who preceded him. He's honest and he's done more for the poor there – and that's ninety-five percent of the population – than anyone before. And the better things become in Guimbi, the more likely it is that the blacks here will resent their own subservience."

"And I'm to meet the president. What am I to say?"

"Essentially nothing, captain. Words of appreciation, that sort of thing. Thanks for that gift of food. And I'll draw up a formal document that you'll present. Not on my behalf, mind you, but on Her Majesty's government's. I'll sign as proxy."

The preparations for departure began. Decisions as to what to leave behind and what to take back on board. Stockley, the paymaster, spending endless hours with Sir Clifford's bookkeepers, deciding what was to be charged to the island's accounts. Fresh fruit and vegetables were contracted for, to be delivered on the day prior to sailing. Hands that had spent recent weeks constructing shelters and supervising digging returned to painting, holystoning and polishing. Dawlish was determined that *Scipio* would arrive pristine at Bermuda. Coaling there was a necessity, for water distillation had three-quarters emptied her bunkers.

The camps at Le Marigot and Thénac were now communities, rather than refuges. Anybody with money enough, or had relatives elsewhere who were willing to accommodate them, had left. Many of the men were going out daily to seek casual labour. The women had turned shelters into approximations of homes. Children played happily. Several carpenters had set up businesses making beds and benches. The Reverend Elijah Gagneux and his Catholic counterpart, between whom there seemed no animosity, had set up separate schools in each camp under the shelter of canvas awnings.

With little prompting, residents had set up teams of volunteers to clear drains, empty cess pits, see that old people without families were cared for. Dawlish had objected to the proposal to assign Saint Gérons' police chief to oversee the camps. The man had deserted his post at the first signs of Mont Colbert erupting. Sir Clifford had yielded and Dorsette, now promoted to inspector at Dawlish's request, maintained order with the constables he had brought with him during the final evacuation.

Dawlish felt moved by it all.

Despite the reminder from the thin smoke drifting from the volcano to the north that it was still active, there was an air of optimism, even cheerfulness. He suggested that Sir Clifford might visit, was not surprised that he agreed. There was credit to be claimed for success that he had done little to further.

The governor was at his pro-consular best. Splendid in his white uniform, he inspected bluejackets' and marines' guards of honour, stopped here and there along the ranks to ask questions and to compliment on jobs well done He paced the lines of tents and shelters, admired feeding areas and latrines, shook hands by the dozen, was sympathetic to evacuees' tales of loss and woe. He commented with approval on the storm ditches and water-supplies and listened with apparent rapt attention to a leading seaman who explained the difficulty of digging cess pits in soft soil. He heard the Reverend Elijah detail at length how the schools had been set up and volunteers found to teach in them. He called for encores when the children's choirs sang psalms. He stooped to enter tents that sheltered the infirm old. And he was cheered when he left.

On the following day Dawlish brought him in *Navigator* to view Saint Gérons. That it still stood, unharmed, and that the lava flows that had threatened it had long ceased, was gratifying but the impression of deadness depressed. Sir Clifford assented to Dawlish's proposal to go ashore. The streets were in places shin-deep in ash and pebbles and many roofs had collapsed under the weight. Smashed-in doors and shutters, and footprints, as if in snow, indicated that others had returned before now to loot but no sign was seen of them. They must have come by boat, for the chasm that cut road-access from the west was still unbridged. But the town was habitable and construction of a replacement bridge, Sir Clifford said, would be his priority. Mont Colbert might sleep for centuries more and in the meantime the town could be repopulated.

Dawlish felt gratitude and pride.

Scipio's guns and crew had won a victory here.

*

Commander Hammond was well capable of overseeing *Scipio's* last preparations and on the penultimate day here Dawlish allowed himself his only time of recreation in Roscal. d'Erlanger had invited him to his plantation home north of Mios and now he rode the nine miles there with Hippolyte as guide. Large swathes to either side of a road that was little better than a cart-track must once have been sugar-cane fields, but wild growth was now swallowing them. The few managed plantations he saw were small, and smaller still were the groves of immature lime trees. Vegetable plots surrounded decrepit shacks and the few larger houses seen were little better. It was hard to believe the Britain and France had once squandered so many lives and so much treasure to control this now-impoverished island.

Yet all changed beyond Mios. d'Erlanger must have invested in lime cultivation long before anybody else and his extensive groves looked well established. Work parties, Saint Gérons refugees perhaps, were busy clearing more ground and planting saplings. Small cottages, well maintained like their vegetable plots, were strung out along the track for the last half-mile to the plantation mansion and sounds of children singing came from an open-sided school. d'Erlanger's house looked well over a century old. The interior was shabbily comfortable, walls decorated with accomplished watercolour landscapes. When Dawlish asked, d'Erlanger admitted that he had painted them himself. It was his main recreation. He lived simply otherwise.

d'Erlanger was optimistic about a return to Saint Gérons. He too had gone there, by boat, to view. His juice-presses there were intact, his storage vats too, though what they contained had soured. The warehouses and jetty were undamaged and he expected to be exporting again in the coming year. The refugees lodging on his land were also eager to return and he would contribute to replacement of the lost bridge. He had other plans too. The southward-facing slopes of Mont Colbert, unscarred by lava flow, offered promise for growing coffee. He was importing beans for a trial sowing.

They were sitting on the verandah now, drinks in hand. Before them, a single, red-leafed tree, not tall, rose from a circular bed of luxuriant flowers.

"Roscal needs employment," d'Erlanger said. "Not just to give the people better lives, but to save them. Do you know how many who've left for Panama have died there?"

"Dozens?" Dawlish knew that the French effort to build a canal across the fifty-mile isthmus, had an insatiable demand for labour. He remembered seeing a great dredger departing for there with pomp and pageantry. So much hope then, so much suffering now.

"Hundreds dead already, Captain Dawlish. Yellow fever and malaria, a killing climate and labour as brutal as their ancestors endured as slaves. They know it but they still sign up so they can send a pittance back to their families."

And Dawlish remembered this man's desolation on the night when Saint Gérons had seemed lost. He was speaking now as he had spoken then.

"You love this place, these people. Why so much?"

d'Erlanger paused, as if judging how much to reveal of himself. But that experience on the ridge above the lava lake had built a bond.

"There's bad history here," he said. "Two centuries of it and my family at its heart. Slaves brought from Africa, used up, replaced. Men whipped to death, women violated. Worse." He pointed to the flower bed. "My grandfather's grandfather had two men broken on the wheel there. Another suspended in a cage from a gibbet to starve to death."

Dawlish sensed a spirit in torment.

"Worse things were normal beyond there." d'Erlanger gestured eastwards. There was the line of forest-shrouded peaks that ran south across the island, from the cone of Mont Henri to that of Mont Sully, and separated Roscal from Guimbi. "When the slaves rose up in '91, they had a lot to revenge. They slaughtered entire families of plantation owners. Then the French came to reconquer – more murder, more atrocity – and any slaves who could retreated into those mountains and held out for years. The growth's dense. It's impenetrable in places, with only two passable tracks through to Guimbi. And then the British came back to fight the French. They brought more hell with them until in the end there was peace of a sort. Even after it had gained its independence, Guimbi built forts to guard the tracks in case the British ever decided to invade."

"Forts?"

"An obsession of one of the first presidents. Two stone forts on the French model. He conscripted thousands of labourers to build them. One form of slavery to succeed another. But he was assassinated, and his successor abandoned the work. They're probably well overgrown by now."

They lapsed into silence. Dawlish was feeling a chill coursing through his spirit, the same guilt and remorse that so often returned in nightmares. He too had once brought back enslavement to a people who had risen in revolt. That he had refused payment for his participation in that squalid private war in Paraguay brought no consolation. He had committed to that expedition for motives of selfish ambition, had given his word to serve, and honour had demanded that he see the tragedy to its dreadful end. He was still too ashamed to tell Florence the full story lest she despise him. He had tried to forget it, had tried elsewhere to make amends. But the guilt always returned, would never leave him.

He disguised his discomfort and said to d'Erlanger, "But under British rule, your family prospered?"

"My grandfather and my father were more humane than those before them. They adapted to British rule. They saw no future in bearing grudges like the Souliers and other families who lost plantations in Guimbi even though what they had here in Roscal was restored to them. A few still delude themselves that someday they'll recover what they lost in Guimbi. They pray for the republic there to fall apart, as it's come close to doing several times."

"This is lovely place," Dawlish wanted to break the air of sadness.

d'Erlanger shrugged. "Perhaps. But the memory of what was done here will never leave, nor the debt to be repaid either."

"You've done your best," Dawlish already felt the words inadequate but had to say them. "The limes. Saint Gérons. The people who seem happier here than elsewhere You seem a good employer and –"

"It killed my wife." The tone dead, cold statement of a fact.

"How?" The word slipped out before thinking.

"Our one child died. A boy, three years old. Strong and healthy. Then a fever took him in just three days. The thought haunted her that it was God's retribution for what had happened there." He nodded towards flower bed. "When consumption struck her, she had no will to live."

They sat in silence for ten minutes.

Then it was time to leave. Sir Clifford would be dinner-host to Dawlish and his officers that evening.

And at dawn, departure.

Chapter 8

"Commander Hammond's compliments, sir. He's on the bridge and –"

Dawlish struggled into wakefulness. His steward, Brannigan, was standing by the cot with a lantern and tapping him on the shoulder. He heard no more, realised it must be serious, for Clavering was standing the middle-watch and would have hesitated to summon the executive officer to the bridge without good reason. And serious for the executive officer to alert his captain.

"Turn on the electricity."

Brannigan flipped the switch and harsh light flooded the cabin. He helped Dawlish strip and pull on trousers, tunic and boots. The clock read one-twenty. No motion of the anchored ship. No unexpected weather then, no sound other than the faint hum of the dynamo in the engine room throbbing through the deck.

It took three minutes between the oblivion of deep sleep and pounding out on deck and towards the ladders leading to the bridge. The night was dark, the moon a sickle, the clear sky starlit.

A distant crackle of gunfire, faint but unmistakable, a half-dozen rounds, rifles, Dawlish judged, then silence.

Hammond was bracing himself against the bridge rail and looking south-eastwards through a night-glass. He handed it to Dawlish.

"You can't see much. The rise of land is in the way but five minutes ago flames were rising above it. We think it's the Thénac camp."

And again, a brief crackle.

"It started a quarter-hour ago, sir." Clavering came forward. "Only flames. I thought maybe some house on fire and –"

Dawlish wasn't listening, was focussing, sharpening the wide-lensed night glass's inverted image. The boundary between the dark ground and the slightly lighter sky was just discernible. And yes, beyond the slight hump of land, there was the faintest flickering glow. Just as he moved to lower the glass, a single tongue of flame erupted through it, blazed bright enough to illuminate trees along the skyline, then died back. This was indeed more than a house fire. It might be a cane-field ablaze, for there had been no rain in days.

But . . .

It could be a coincidence. The entire town knew that *Scipio* and *Navigator* were about to depart. And many in it still begrudged the presence of the refugees, had been restrained from anything more dangerous than resentment by the presence of bluejackets and marines at the camps. Sir Clifford had been satisfied that even that antipathy had faded by now, even if Dawlish wasn't.

"You've taken a bearing?" He said to Clavering.

"Yes, sir. And checked it on the chart. It's Thénac. No doubt of it."

The only guards there were a half-dozen of Inspector Dorsette's men. Sir Clifford had yielded to Dawlish's urging that they be armed with Snider-Enfields from *Scipio's* armoury. Even after a week's instruction, the marine sergeant set to training them was still dismissive of their skill.

And if there was riot at Thénac, Sir Clifford would hesitate to order action. Roscal's police were normally unarmed and he'd haver over a decision to issue weapons or despatch a force. Concern about the Advisory Council would weigh upon his mind.

A vision flashed through Dawlish's mind of blazing huts, terrified women and children huddling in imagined cover, men beaten down in hopeless resistance, corpses, horror. He had once seen fury unleashed against the helpless in a riot in Anatolia and would never forget it

If I don't act, there could be serious bloodshed.

Five miles of road between Escource and Thénac, but the chance of opposition on the way. Six or seven by water close inshore, arrival undetected, unexpected. But except for a single whaler moored to the boom extending from *Scipio's* starboard flank, all boats had been lifted on board and secured. The boilers of the steam pinnace and launch were cold and would take an hour to raise steam.

He turned to Hammond. "Major Gormley and ten of his marines into the whaler. Seamen, strongest we have, to pull her. Wearing boots. Rifles and bayonets, twenty rounds, nothing more. Get two cutters in the water, twenty-five men, seamen, marines, an officer in each. You'll remain on *Scipio* to see to it and –"

"You're going to Thénac yourself, sir?" Hammond looked surprised.

"I'll be with the whaler." Dawlish said. The blame should his alone if things went badly, especially with Sir Clifford bypassed. "The cutters to follow with all despatch."

The ship was coming to life as he hurried back to his cabin, to finish dressing and to arm himself.

And ignore the doubts that rose to nag him.

He was committed.

*

Dawlish saw the flames as the whaler stroked around the headland south of Escource. Two blazing fires and smaller glows of others burning out. Individual reports of rifle-fire, no volleys, long breaks in between as if the shots were for warning only. Through his binoculars he could discern figures silhouetted against the flames, flitting in and out of the darkness to either side in frantic efforts to limit the spread.

A mile to go. The sounds of shouting growing with each yard forward, anger, fear, wailing shrieks of women driven beyond despair. Yesterday the Thénac camp had been a community, no longer just a refuge. Now this.

Cold fury washed through Dawlish. There must first be deliverance. And afterwards, retribution.

Silence in the packed whaler as it advanced through wisps of drifting smoke that carried the smell of burning wood. Dawlish turned to Gormley, the marine captain standing with him in the bows.

"Pass the word to the coxswain. Hold position a half-cable off the beach." He needed to see more before landing. As land he must. "You and your people to stay with me when I go ashore," he said to Gormley. "None of the seamen to follow without further orders."

Somebody had seen the craft approach, was on the beach, calling out, words indistinguishable but the terror in them unmistakable. Others joined in. Dawlish ignored them as the pulling crew backed water and held the whaler stationary. Now he could see people in large clusters along the water's edge. Beyond them, one of the larger fires had died but the other was still roaring. It must be at a school, for what had once been a canvas awning on *Scipio* was now a sheet of flame.

"Captain Dawlish!" A voice stronger than the others sounding from the beach.

"Inspector Dorsette!" Dawlish could make out his face, lit on one side by the dancing scarlet light.

"We need help, sir! We can't hold them back much longer."

"We're coming!"

Four seamen leaped overboard as the bows ground on the sand and dragged the whaler forward. Dawlish dropped into knee-high water, advanced to meet Dorsette. Gormley and his men were fanning out to form a protective half-circle around them. Three more single rifle-shots from the darkness beyond.

"How many?" Dawlish said.

"I don't know. Many, many." Dorsette look frightened but his voice was steady. "Some of them have guns, just a few. The rest with machetes and clubs. We had no warning."

"You're holding them back? Good! Show me."

Most of the residents must have already fled to the beach or to the brush bordering the camp to either side. The by-now familiar lines of tents and shelters were deserted as Dorsette led Dawlish on, the marines, with bayonets fixed, as close escort.

Past the burning school. The awning that had protected it had collapsed by now and had transformed the pathetic little desks and benches fashioned by camp-carpenters into a blazing pyre.

"They came this far," Dorsette said. "We had to fire to drive them back. There. That's one." He pointed to a body slumped on the edge of a storm-ditch. A muscular black man, his tattered clothing worse than that worn by most of the refugees.

Some labourer conscripted from a master's plantation. A dupe.

Beyond this point at least a third of the tents and shelters had been burned. Loot abandoned in panic – humble possessions, cooking pots, blankets, clothing – strewed the ground. From the darkness ahead came shouting, taunts, insults.

"Any more dead?" Dawlish asked Dorsette.

"Of our people? Two men and a woman. But many injured."

And now Dawlish saw men, refugees, sheltering in the shadows of still-standing shelters, improvised clubs in hand, machetes, poles. There was desperation on their faces, terror, doubt that they could withstand another onslaught. Yet resolution too, willingness of fathers and sons to sell their lives in defence of their families. A few called out in thanks at the sight of the marines.

Dorsette had positioned his men a little further forward, strung out in the cover of a drainage ditch. For thirty or forty yards ahead, nothing lay but charred or collapsed remnants, some still glowing or smouldering. Beyond was the mob, the numbers impossible to guess, a dark mass illuminated in places by the light of waving torches. There was something more than anger in the shouting, something closer to hate. Even if many there were plantation workers urged here by their masters, and if only hope for easy pillage had driven some, the repulse by Dorsette's men and the bravest of the refugees had aroused a lust for revenge.

"We've been saving ammunition," Dorsette said. "Firing over their heads when they come any closer. But there's not much left."

"No matter now," Dawlish said. He turned to Gormley. "Hold this line. I leave the dispositions to you. Warning shots, but shoot to kill if you must. And give each constable five rounds."

The marines, spreading out in line, went forward with Dorsette towards the ditch at a crouching run and leaped in.

Dawlish remained behind in the shadow of a half-burned shelter, weighing options for next action. There was no further danger of the mob surging into the camp again. Gormley had men enough to deter it. And there were two cutters on the way with another fifty armed men, more than enough to advance and disperse the mob.

But…

Justice demanded more than dispersal. Murder had been done, loss inflicted, families beggared and terrorised. Whoever had organised this – most probably the Soulier twins or others like them – would be the first to make their escape when the mob broke up in terror before an advancing line of bayoneted rifles. The men who should stand trial for this atrocity should be those who incited it, not the ignorant labourers beholden to them. The cutters must be close now. If each were to land the men they carried not at the camp, but a half-mile to either side of it, they could advance through the cover of the abandoned cane-fields to the east, and the scrubland to the west. Wheeling around to meet behind the mob, the pincer movement could surprise it and trap it against Gormley's line.

There was still time to organise it. Decision made, Dawlish doubled forward to tell Gormley his intention, then hurried back towards the beach. A small, frightened crowd had gathered around the whaler, held back by the seamen. He pushed his way though, ignoring the babbled appeals for help.

"All back in the whaler!"

Hands reached out to hoist him in as seamen heaved it off the beach. He fancied he could see a shape to the west, the merest glint of light too, oars dipping, rising, shedding droplets in steady rhythm. He ordered the coxswain to steer for it, heard cries of disappointment, despair at abandonment, from the people at the water's edge.

The whaler gathered speed, met the cutter a mile to the west. Dawlish hailed and they drew together. Clavering was in command, with Sub-Lieutenant Walton, a midshipman and seamen armed with Sniders and cutlasses. The second cutter was following close, Clavering said.

Quick orders.

Proceed two miles east, beach the cutter and leave it under guard. Press inland in silence, using maximum cover, for a mile. Trusted men to scout ahead to determine the location of the mob. Sweep around behind it, still under cover. Hold position then, and be patient.

The second cutter was pulling into sight from behind the headland to the west as Clavering's pulled away. Dawlish's whaler advanced to meet it. The gunnery lieutenant, Tyrell, had brought Sub-Lieutenant Wheeler and two midshipmen in addition to his seamen. Dawlish sensed excitement mixed with apprehension. The closest to combat that most of these men had experienced was the bombardment of the ridge at Saint Gérons. Service only on large warships could mean an entire career spent without seeing a shot fired in anger.

Short consultation, and then the whaler led the cutter on. Both grounded in the shallows at a point Dawlish judged as being a half-mile west of the camp. The scrub came down almost to the water's edge, thick enough to mask movement but not enough as to hinder it. The smell of burning had carried this far and the mob's sustained shouting fury was punctuated by irregular rifle shots. Gormley's marines must have been seen and whoever had brought the rioters must be weighing a decision whether to make one last attempt to charge or to disappear back into the night.

Dawlish sent a petty officer, Dixon, ahead with three veteran seamen to reconnoitre. He followed, Enfield revolver in hand, leading the remainder of his men in two files, their bayonets still scabbarded. He felt the same dryness in his mouth, the same hollowness in his stomach, and the same fear of failure as when he had first seen action as a boy in China. The physical risk was incalculably less now but the threat to reputation and career was absolute. Should this initiative descend into a blood-bath – and the potential for it was great – then Sir Clifford would have no hesitation in repudiating his action. Topcliffe would extend no hand to help. He only supported success.

The distance to be covered through the thicket must be less than a half-mile but it might have been thrice as much as regards speed. Even in clear moonlight it would have been impossible to see more than a few yards ahead but in this soft darkness advance could only be slow. Boots crunched on dry fallen leaves, thorns pulled on sleeves, roots tripped, men swore and were hissed into silence. Twice the petty officer ahead sent men back to warn that the direction of advance must be corrected. Dawlish was cursing himself that he had not brought a pocket compass and the thought haunted him that Clavering's column, advancing a mile to the east, might be wandering in circles in overgrown cane.

"There's a track ahead, sir." One of the scouts returning.

"Any movement along it?

"No, sir. But the P.O. and the others are waiting by it."

"Halt your men here," Dawlish said to Tyrell. "Join me."

They followed the seaman for three minutes of cautious movement. The hubbub to the right told that the mob was close. The seaman led them to where Dixon was hiding in the brush bordering the track. Dawlish knew it, had ridden along it numerous times on visits to the camp. Fortune had smiled in bringing them to this spot, he realised, for the vegetation was dense on either side. A full company could be hidden here without detection.

Then voices.

A half-dozen men were hurrying down the track, laughing, cheering each other on and singing. They were carrying unhandy burdens, clothing bundles, boxes, a cauldron. One had enveloped himself in coils cut from the canvas hose that had brought water to the camp.

"Let them past," Dawlish hissed.

Ragged, a few barefoot, passing a stone rum-jar between them and pausing to swig, they must be labourers who had wearied of riot, were satisfied with their plunder, were heading home in mean triumph.

They disappeared from sight.

"Stay here with half your men," Dawlish said to Tyrell. "Block the track only when you hear me fire three rapid pistol rounds. Until then, keep in cover along the sides. But after you hear my signal, nobody's to pass. Warning shots only to keep them back unless they try to break through."

He brought the remainder of the force with him, flitting one by one across the roadway to the thicket beyond, forming two files in its cover. Another slow advance, this time curving to the right, emerging from the brush into more open ground some two-hundred yards beyond. This must be north of the unseen mob and camp. A pause here in the shadows. With luck, half of Clavering's force should be somewhere ahead by now, the remainder blocking the track east of the camp.

Now a handful of dry grass and twigs fashioned into a torch, a match struck, the flame catching. A midshipman waved it slowly back and forth. It died without receiving a response and another replaced it. Dawlish's anxiety was rising that Clavering might be lost, that he himself must drive towards the mob with only the men he had. A third torch burned out and he was lifting his revolver, about to fire his signal, when a winking dot of flame appeared in the dark ahead. He lowered the pistol again. Better to wait and join forces.

The open ground was some three hundred yards across, cane stubble burned after the last harvest. The two forces met near the centre. Clavering had indeed left men at the track to the east to bar escape that way. The unknowing rioters now had forces about them on all four sides, the strongest, some forty men, with Dawlish to the north.

He ordered two ranks formed, the second five yards behind the first, ten between each man. Bayonets fixed now, a round in every breech, whispered admonitions about firing discipline. When called for, warning shots to be fired into the ground ahead, muzzles just high enough to allow discharges to be seen from a distance but low enough to prevent overshoot into the camp beyond the rioters.

It was towards the rear of that mob that the slow advance now began, Dawlish in the centre of the front rank, Clavering following him in that behind. The clamour ahead had not abated. The ranks undulated as they pressed forward over the charred cane, men stumbling on ruts and hurrying to regain position. Now glimpses of flame, torches, drifting smoke, figures briefly revealed by ghastly light, lost again in the darkness.

Closer, close enough to hear individual cries of hate and anger. A hundred yards separation now, bare ground only, and still no alarm raised.

"Halt!" Dawlish's command was a loud whisper, relayed from man to man along the lines. He turned to Clavering. "One volley, warning only. On my word! My word, mind!"

He raised his pistol, cocked, fired three rounds into the air in immediate succession, the signal for blocking of the track to the east and west.

"Front rank! Warning shots. Warning, I say!" His voice a shout. "Fire!"

The crash of twenty rifles, flame spitting in the darkness, smoke rolling, bullets kicking up dust in the ground ten yards ahead.

Then silence, the mob's cries stilled as rioters spun around in shock towards the unexpected threat behind.

"Second rank forward! Front rank, reload!"

Clavering's people advanced through the gaps in the rank before them, halted, raised their weapons, waited.

Another crash of rifle-fire, this time from beyond the mob. Gormley's and Dorsette's defenders of the camp were now serving the rioters notice that they were trapped between forces to both front and rear.

"Mr. Clavering! Another warning volley!"

Then the blast, and then Dawlish ordering his rank forwards, firing again, soil spurting as rounds ploughed into the ground.

"Reload!"

The mob was breaking, shock turning into panic, surging into chaos, first away from Dawlish's fire, then back towards it again as Gormley lashed another volley from the camp, then halting suddenly at the sight of flame glinting on the now-levelled bayonets. Already some were rushing into the darkness to the sides to seek escape eastwards or west along the track.

No need to advance, not yet. Better to let that bedlam grow, terror reign. A volley from each rank, a half minute apart, each answered by Gormley's men. Urged perhaps by some idea of surrender, of dissociation from the night's crime, a knot of men with arms upraised stumbled towards Dawlish's line, were halted by the levelled bayonets, were driven back by shouted warnings.

Now a single volley from the right. The first fugitives to flee down the track towards Escource was being halted by Tyrell's force. A minute later brought a similar crackle from the left. There too, escape was blocked.

Dawlish ordered his lines forward again, a slow steady advance with bayonets levelled. Some clusters of rioters, braver than the rest, held their ground until another ripple of fire broke their resolve and drove them into flight. Others were throwing down machetes and clubs, babbling surrender, herded forward to be pinned against the line held by Clavering and Dorsette.

It would be time then to separate the sheep from the goats.

*

There might be as many as three hundred prisoners penned inside the circle of bayonets. Cowed and terrified, many bruised and bleeding – for rifle-butts had made short work of any last defiance – the full enormity of their plight had dawned on them. From their better clothing, a small number could be black shopkeepers or tradesmen from Escource but the majority of those detained looked like plantation workers or holders of small plots. It was not they who interested Dawlish.

One by one the prisoners were ordered from the circle and brought before him, torches held up to light their faces. He felt pity mixed with contempt for most of them, was repelled by cringing excuses he did not care to hear. There was time only for quick judgment. An unwillingness to meet his glance, a surly furtiveness, an impression of fear of detection of some enormity, were enough for him to nod to two seamen who would drag the prisoner aside to kneel under guard with hands on head with others like him. There few enough, perhaps one in ten. They would be sent to Escource and the courts could deal with them. A jerk of his head proclaimed release for the remainder and earned cringing gratitude.

The number of prisoners was decreasing and among them were the eleven whites who had protested so loudly at first capture. Rough handling that Dawlish did not care to notice had quietened them. It had not surprise him that Etienne Soulier was among them, though there was no sign of his twin brother. He could wait until last.

Now the first of the whites, a young man, hatless, white suit besmirched, very frightened.

"Name?"

"William Gilman. My father's –"

Dawlish recognised the name, one of the few planter families of English stock.

"I don't give a tuppenny damn who or what your father is. What are you doing here?"

"It was the arms from Guimbi." Gilman's voice was quavering, his hands shaking. "They were in the camp. There'd be a massacre if we didn't –"

"What arms from Guimbi?"

"From that ship that came. It wasn't food it brought, it was guns and ammunition and –"

"You bloody fool," The stupidity of it angered Dawlish. "It was food, and my boats carried it here from that gunvessel. Do you think the Royal Navy would help land firearms to provoke rebellion?"

"But Mr. Soulier said –"

"Aren't you man enough to think for yourself?"

The wretched youth was beginning to weep. A dark stain was soaking one trouser leg. Dawlish jerked his head. This coward could go and he didn't want to hear his stammered thanks.

The next was a shipping agent from Escource who must have harboured a grudge against Saint Gérons as a competitor. The next again was a stout middle-aged planter who claimed that fear of massacre had brought him and two dozen of this workers here. They had come to remonstrate with the refugees, to demand they give up the arms from Guimbi that Soulier had assured them were hidden in the camp. Only concern for their wives' and children's lives had brought them here. They had been met with violence and deplored how the situation had deteriorated. Dawlish let the agent go but detained the plantation owner, for he had brought dupes to do his bidding.

And so the next and the next and next, all dishevelled, several bruised. None had seen murder done, they claimed, most had tried to restore order at the risk of their own lives. A few were truculent or belligerent, a sign perhaps of guilt, and those Dawlish detained together with any who had come here with their labourers.

The last was Etienne Soulier.

There was grim satisfaction in seeing his bloody face and one blackened eye. His once-white suit was ripped and filthy as if he had been trampled on the ground. He was limping so badly that it needed a seaman's assistance to bring him forward.

The protests and excuses came in a torrent, but Dawlish was not listening.

He jerked his head.

"Take him with the others."

It would be a slow and painful march to Escource and they would be Sir Clifford's responsibility then.

The sun was rising. *Scipio* could not now depart today but Dawlish was determined that she would do so on the morrow. One day for the visit to Guimbi's president and then course set for England.

The thought struck him that he would never see Roscal again.

And he regretted it.

Something not unlike d'Erlanger's love for the people and the island had infected him also.

Chapter 9

The last day of November, a miserable one in London, sleet drumming on Dawlish's umbrella as he walked up Pall Mall. Though not yet midday, it was overcast enough for lights to burn in the windows of Topcliffe's club. Dawlish mounted the steps, was conducted inside by a doorman who helped divest him of his mackintosh. And yes, his host had arrived already and was in the library. He declined the need for guidance. He had been here before, would find his way.

Topcliffe was seated, reading, in a wing chair. He looked up as Dawlish entered, rose, extended his hand. He too was in civilian garb. Admiral Sir Richard Topcliffe had not been seen in uniform for years and was an unknown, or forgotten, name for many in the navy. His business was conducted from locations other than the Admiralty. He invited Dawlish to sit opposite him, suggested that coffee would be welcome on this cold morning and beckoned to a waiter who was hovering in the doorway to bring it.

"And Mrs. Dawlish is well?" he said. "Good. My best regards. You're a lucky man. She carried herself like a true heroine in that recent business."

Dawlish had only learned of it after returning from the Sudan the previous year. Florence had put her life and reputation at risk to protect his. She had served Topcliffe in the process, had been used by him as ruthlessly as he used Dawlish himself, as he used others hungry for advancement and prepared to risk everything for it. Topcliffe's patronage had brought Dawlish early promotion and prestigious commands, but it had come at a price.

"And the child is well too?" Topcliffe said.

Dawlish told him. Jessica was walking sturdily, had spoken her first words, had been a joy to him since *Scipio* had docked at Portsmouth. Topcliffe heard him, made the appropriate responses. It was impossible to imagine him having a family himself, children to be proud of, grandchildren to dote on.

The coffee came and the waiter left. The day's newspapers were strewn on the large library table and there were comfortable chairs enough to read or doze in, but nobody else was in the room. There never seemed to be when Dawlish met the admiral here.

"I read your reports," Topcliffe said. "Well done."

Dawlish had written them on the voyage from Bermuda, knowing that he would have little time when *Scipio*, on arrival, would enter a drydock for refit. The work on her was well in hand now and the opportunity for taking leave was getting closer. The report to the Admiralty had been coldly factual, had concentrated on operational matters, had been scrupulous in avoiding comment on issues within Sir Clifford's domain. But it was the separate report that he had prepared for the Colonial and Foreign Offices, of which Topcliffe first spoke.

"They liked it," he said. "They might have liked it less if Sir Clifford hadn't also sent a report supporting your action. Roscal's been quiet since." He paused. "But you took a lot on yourself, Dawlish. You pushed your interpretation of cooperation with the civil authority beyond the boundary. Indeed you made yourself the civil authority, did you not?"

"I did, sir."

Do not excuse or explain. Success justifies everything.

Topcliffe let it pass.

"And Guimbi?" he said. "There's nothing but bare facts in your report. You came, you saw, you delivered a letter. Now tell me your own opinion of the place."

"It's even more of a pauper state than I imagined," Dawlish said. "Roscal's rich by comparison. All I saw of Guimbi was Port Mazarin. It's little more than a village, and a squalid one at that. And yet –" He was searching for words to that could explain the paradox. "Yet there's somehow an air of pride about it, wretched though it is."

The blue, black and red tricolour flag had flown above the crumbling fort of the Vauban era that stood on the eastern headland guarding the approach to Port Mazarin's harbour. It was identified on the chart as Fort Montmorency. It was well placed to dominate the town, the approach to the harbour and the coastlines to either side. The lower slopes of Mont Condé, the islands fourth – and dormant – volcano ran down almost to the western edge of Guimbi's ramshackle capital.

Lying at anchor in the harbour, *Le Déchaîné* had made a pathetic but well-meant attempt to dress ship and fire a salute when *Scipio* entered, for Sir Clifford had already sent ahead notification of her coming. Black soldiers in threadbare uniforms, their lighter-skinned officers hardly better clad, delivered a reasonable effort at a guard of honour. Maître Jacques Badeaux was waiting with the Minister of Defence, a General Aubertin, to welcome Dawlish and carry him by carriage to the palace. The word was a mockery. It must once have been the residence of a French governor, but its facade was now crumbling, its interior little better.

"What surprised me was that they seemed so grateful to welcome the visit," Dawlish said "Sir Clifford spoke of it as something like polite intimidation, a reminder of what we could unleash if Guimbi were to cause problems in Roscal. But I don't think they saw it like that in Port Mazarin. Rather the contrary."

"Did Ravenel gave that impression?" A hint of familiarity in Topcliffe's mention of the president's name.

"I think he was sincere about it. Maybe relieved. Badeaux and the ministers also. I'd been concerned that the message I brought contained little more than empty platitudes –"

"Sir Clifford knows how to do them very well."

The hint of familiarity when mentioning that name did not surprise Dawlish. Topcliffe had used the hoax that had exploited it for his advantage. And almost killed Florence in the process.

"The message went down well regardless," Dawlish said. "It was a first time that Guimbi had received one like it from a European power in fifty years, Badeaux said. One that respected the republic's dignity."

"What did you think of President Ravenel?"

"He seemed in pain all the time. He's almost bent double and he walks with a cane. He apologised for not coming to meet me at the harbour. And he has the same old-fashioned courtesy and elegant French as Maître Badeaux. He'd been a journalist in Paris for fifteen years, apparently. Some of the French accept blacks easily, he said."

"And others there most definitely don't. Did he mention the French loans?"

"No." It was the first Dawlish had heard of them. He would have been surprised if any such topic had been raised. His remit had been narrow. Anchor *Scipio* in the harbour to impress. Deliver a formal letter. Exchange compliments. Depart. He had done all that.

"Badeaux said nothing about the loans either?" Another name that came easily to Topcliffe. "And the Minister of Defence, Aubertin, isn't it? Did he say anything?"

Dawlish remembered him only as a thuggish-looking light-skinned black of about fifty in a gorgeous uniform. "No. Nobody mentioned loans. Aubertin said nothing other than the sort of commonplaces one would expect. But the president was almost deferential to him."

"He should be," Topcliffe said. "He wouldn't last a week without the support of the army. All nine other generals, twenty-seven colonels, uncountable other officers and maybe two hundred NCOs and men. Top heavy, and good for nothing but intimidation and what passes for police work, but they make and break presidents. In essence a Praetorian Guard. *Quis custodiet ipsos custodes?*"

"Why do they support Ravenel? He doesn't appear to be corrupt." Dawlish had not expected Topcliffe to know so much about Guimbi.

"Why? Because just a few of them have some residual integrity. They think that every government since Guimbi's revolution has betrayed it by corruption. Ramshackle as the place is, they're proud of the freedom won against all odds. They resent dependence on foreign loans and know that the rest of the world regards the idea of a black republic as a joke. They have their pride."

"Ravenel radiates that." Dawlish had been touched by it.

"He suffered for it too. He came back from France, started a newspaper, scourged bribery, exposed secret deals like the purchase of that gunvessel. Badeaux helped him. His paper was shut down and he was all but broken in prison. That's why he's crippled. But he won an election by a fluke, and a cabal of generals swung their weight behind him. Like Badeaux, he gives an impression of responsibility to Guimbi's creditors."

"He told me there's not a single plantation in Guimbi, and that he hopes never to see one," Dawlish said "Every family to be prosperous on its own small plot. And education, new roads, hospitals He believes it. If he achieves it all then Sir Clifford's fears of success in Guimbi encouraging unrest in Roscal might be justified. But I can't imagine that happening. Where's the money to come from?".

Topcliffe shrugged. "There are always lenders if the rewards outweigh the risks." He looked at his watch. "It's been valuable talking to you, captain. I'm sure you have other obligations in London. I won't detain you any longer."

When he stepped out again into the now rain-swept street, Dawlish wondered why he had been summoned.

It was the first time that he had left a meeting with Topcliffe in the club library without accepting a task that could cost him his life.

But, if successful, further his career.

*

Scipio was in drydock at Portsmouth, her refit due to last six weeks. Dawlish went to her each day for liaison with the dockyard management but he lived at home in his rented villa in Albert Grove in the suburb of Southsea. These were happy days – perhaps the happiest he had ever known, he realised – not just for reunion with Florence but for the shared joy of Jessica's presence. She was a gift as precious to them both as any child born of themselves could have been. She had recognised him as soon as she saw him, had stretched out her small hands to lock her fingers in his beard as she had first done as a helpless infant when –

His mind always recoiled from the memory.

Even now, some two years since Florence had first taken Jessica in her arms on the quayside at Cairo, he had not confided the exact circumstances in which he had found her. She was a beautiful child now, dark hair, great brown liquid eyes and olive skin proclaiming her Coptic heritage. Florence only knew that he had saved her from the bloody aftermath of the Khartoum siege in which her parents had died and that he had brought her, against all odds, down the Nile to safety. But a day must come when the facts must be revealed, if not to Florence, then to Jessica herself. She would be a woman then, would have the right to know.

And have the right to reject and maybe hate him.

But that day would not come for nineteen years, might never come for him. His own death within that time might be a price worth paying to spare himself the duty of revelation. And if not, there would still be the joy of seeing her formed by Florence's love and example to be a woman of courage, compassion and resolution. For now, there was the pleasure of hearing each new word she learned, of her first sentences, of the delight of playing with her, of leafing through picture books together, of shared admiration of the carved wooden animals he had bought for her in Brazil.

The refit was well underway. Responsibility for *Scipio* could be delegated to Commander Hammond to allow Dawlish to take three weeks' leave.

"We could go next week to Shrewsbury," he told Florence over the breakfast table. It was always a pleasant, if brief, time of the day together. "On Wednesday at the latest."

"Ted will be surprised to see how Jessica has grown," Florence said. "He thought she was a doll before. Now she's big enough that he can play with her."

His half-brother Ted – Edgar – was eight now and already aspiring to enter the navy. Their father, a solicitor, had suffered a minor stroke in recent months. And there was worse.

"You'll be shocked when you see Rowena, Nicholas."

He hadn't seen his stepmother, little older than himself, for over a year. Florence had visited more recently. It pleased him that, during his absence in the Sudan, Florence had visited, mended fences and won over a woman who had once resented her for her servile origins.

"Do you think it's really serious, Florence?"

"She knows it is. It's –" She hesitated to say the word. "It's cancer, Nicholas. The sort that every woman fears."

Death was coming for his father too, he thought, and he himself would be the older generation soon. Ted might become his and Florence's charge long before he could be sent to train in HMS *Britannia* at Dartmouth. Dawlish's nephew, Martin Harkness, his sister Susan's son, was already a cadet there.

"We can visit the farms, too, Nicholas. It'll be a pleasant outing."

He knew what she felt but would never say. That the six farms in Shropshire that he had inherited from his uncle, and were managed for him by an agent, were a millstone. In these days of low agricultural prices, a good year brought just a pittance, most others only a loss. And yet he knew he would never divest himself of them. He was an over-indulgent landlord, his agent had told him, but he was still reluctant to demand prompt payment of rents from tenants already on the verge of poverty. A new owner might not hesitate.

But there was another reason.

They were the last link to his beloved uncle, the naval officer whom consumption had taken in middle age. He had lived with him in Pau in his last sad months. His legacy was more than those farms, for he had arranged for Dawlish's admission to the navy, initiation into a hard and unforgiving – but honourable – profession, an initiation that Nephew Martin was even now enduring.

The maid entered with the morning post, a single letter for Florence. He looked away, reluctant to let her see that he noticed her peering closely at it. She did not want him to know that she wore reading spectacles when he was not present. He pretended ignorance of that need – her touch of vanity was endearing.

"It's from Agatha." She reached the letter to him. "She invites us to come to London. She wants to give a dinner in your honour."

"I don't need a dinner in my honour." The idea appalled him. He was, for now at least, a public figure. Mont Colbert's eruption and *Scipio's* bombardment had provided rich copy for the illustrated papers. Full artistic licence had characterised the drawings that showed him standing steadfast on the vessel's bridge while her turrets blazed defiance at the volcano. He didn't want lionising.

"Agatha's always welcome," he said. "Ask her to come here instead. I'll be delighted to see her."

And it was true. Lady Agatha Kegworth had raised Florence from the status of a servant and both had shared danger and privation together in Thrace a decade before. They both nursed Dawlish when he had lain delirious in a jolting cart on the nightmare winter retreat before a merciless Russian advance. Events then and since, and danger shared again, had made the two women all but sisters.

"Oh Nicholas! You know she wants the best for you!" Florence said. "And she has important friends! Not only politicians like her father knows. People you'd find interesting. Men of Science. Engineers. Doctors. Writers. She mentions a professor of geology who'd like to hear about the volcano."

That was tempting. A mathematician herself, first female fellow of the Royal Society, Agatha knew many such learned people.

"For when does she propose it, Florence?" He didn't want to yield too easily.

"Thursday. Just one night, Nick. We could go up in the afternoon, stay at the Charing Cross Hotel, come back next morning."

The longing in her voice touched him. She wanted to show him off, be proud of him before the sort of people that she too esteemed.

He yielded.

*

The guest list was longer than he had anticipated, the dinner a far grander affair. He appreciated Agatha's choice of Brown's Hotel in Albemarle Street for the occasion, rather than her father's mansion in Piccadilly. She would not subject Florence to the embarrassment of being served by a butler and footmen whom she had known when a housemaid there. He saw that Florence appreciated it too, though she did not allude to it.

Agatha's cousin Neville Eversham was waiting with her when they arrived early at the hotel.

"Mrs. Dawlish," He bowed and took Florence's hand. "And Captain Dawlish, a pleasure to see you again. And to congratulate you."

It had been easy to like this Queen's Counsel, a lawyer at the peak of his profession, since first meeting him after returning from the Sudan. He'd helped Florence save a seaman who had served well under Dawlish from long imprisonment in what had been an act of charity no less than of forensic skill.

"Be warned!" Eversham said. "Agatha asked me to stand up after dinner and press you to say a few words about what happened in Roscal."

"I've prepared nothing." Dawlish had been determined not to be put through his paces.

"You needn't say much about yourself." Eversham had sensed his reticence. "Tell about the people's plight there."

Agatha was nodding. "For a good cause, captain." she said. "You'll hear what I have in mind. And no, I won't say what it is."

Indulging her now would be small recompense for what she had done for him in Thrace and he could not refuse her.

Heavy, plain-faced, great myopic eyes glistening through her pince-nez, Agatha looked dowdy beside Florence as they stood, all three, in a receiving line. One by one, some with wives, the guests were introduced, friends of Agatha's for the most part. A Dr. Pauncefote, a philologist. Sir James Greenway, a chemist. The explorer Jonathan Langdon, recently knighted after returning from another expedition in Borneo. A botanist and a professor of geology, both from Oxford, whose names

Dawlish didn't catch. Another, known for his researches in electricity, with whom he would like to talk.

And others. Others that Dawlish did not expect.

Sir Cathcart Soames of the Colonial Office.

Mr. James Lennox of the Board of Trade.

Lord Leverstoke, an elderly peer, who held no office, but must be a friend of Agatha's father.

A Mr. Hyne and a Sir Matthew Glaisher, both bankers.

People from a different world. People of power, of money.

It was to Sir Cathcart Soames, a ponderous and slow-spoken man of his own age that Agatha steered Dawlish in the half-hour before dinner was served.

"I've read your report, captain," he said. "A difficult business in Roscal. Not just the volcano. The rest of it. Well-handled that. And Guimbi, of course. Always sensitive."

And then he said what Dawlish had not expected.

"Has a mutual acquaintance suggested a certain possibility?" He must have noticed Dawlish's incomprehension. "Aah no, I see, not yet. And there's still time needed to –"

He might have said more if the explorer had not broken in on them. Intrepid, the celebrated Sir Jonathan might be, but a bore too. Sir Cathcart, probably well used to such encounters, disengaged adroitly and left Dawlish to endure ten minutes of anecdotes about head-hunters and long-houses. Across the room he could see Florence holding her own amid a group of admiring men. He caught her eye and nodded. It was enough. She swept across, captured the explorer and bore him off in apparent fascination. Dawlish seized the opportunity to seek out the botanist.

And it was better than he could have hoped. Professor Edwin Moncton's focus was tropical, had travelled in the West Indies, though not Roscal, was interested in development of new edible-crop strains.

Citrus?

No, root crops, tubers. Cassava, breadfruit, yams. And a colleague saw great potential in legumes. They were too often overlooked.

Dawlish had no idea what legumes were but he knew that the other crops mentioned were staples of Roscal's population.

"What do 'new strains' mean?" he said.

"Higher yield per acre. As much as doubling present production, sometimes more," Professor Moncton said. "It's slow work, and needs a lot of field testing, but it has promise."

"I made a friend in Roscal who would be interested," Dawlish said. "A planter, a very progressive one. A man called d'Erlanger. He might be glad to correspond, perhaps cooperate and –"

The dinner gong was sounding.

"May I have your card please, captain?" Moncton was fishing in an inside pocket for one of his own. "And write that gentleman's name on the back of yours."

Time then to endure the dinner, toasts and compliments.

Dawlish spoke only briefly when Eversham called upon him. He gave credit to his crews, was surprised by his own emotion when he talked of the courage and indomitability of the refugees, their losses, their cheerful stoicism. d'Erlanger's love of the islanders had indeed infected him, he realised.

And by the time that a cab carried Florence and himself back to the Charing Cross Hotel to sleep, Agatha had launched a fund for relief of distress at Roscal. Herself and Lord Leverstoke as patrons, Mr. Neville Eversham Q.C. as chairman. Over six thousand pounds pledged. And Sir Jonathan Langdon, would donate the proceeds from a series of lectures on his explorations.

"That was sheer blackmail, Florence," he said. "An ambush! They couldn't refuse in front of each other, could they? You knew about it, didn't you? You and Agatha had set it up between you."

"We might have had a word or two about it, Nick." She was laughing now. "But ladies must have their secrets. You must have learned that by now, you plain blunt old sailorman. And because what you told me about those poor people was heart-breaking."

Outmanoeuvred. And glad of it.

He took her hand, kissed it and held it to his cheek.

But even then, he could not forget what else he had heard.

A certain possibility.

Chapter 10

Dawlish had to cut short his visit to Shrewsbury after two days.

He left Florence and Jessica behind to bring some joy to a household over which the shadow of death hovered. Only laudanum could assuage his stepmother Rowena's pain. Wraithlike, the longing and regret in her eyes when she so often hugged Ted close told that she knew the end was near. The knowledge was killing his father too, Dawlish realised, even as the old man told him each day, without conviction, that she was getting better. Ted must sense what was happening, but never spoke of it, not even to Florence. She had volunteered to remain for another week and was resolved to return, indefinitely, when the situation would deteriorate further. But for now, she would read Rowena to sleep each evening, would listen to endless reminiscences from her father-in-law about long-forgotten contested wills, and bring Ted for afternoon drives in the dog cart she drove with such assurance. A big brother rather than an uncle, he had appointed himself Jessica's guardian and she in turn adored him.

The summons to London brought Dawlish to the Colonial Office, not the Admiralty. A commissionaire led him up a grandiose marble staircase and along a broad corridor to a spacious office looking out on Whitehall. He had not caught the exact title of Sir Cathcart Soames's position when he had met him at the dinner, but he realised now that he must be very senior. He had expected to be questioned about his report about Roscal and Guimbi but Soames surprised him.

"Turkey, Korea, East Africa, captain," he said. "And some activities in the United States and Cuba that we prefer not to admit to. It's been a varied career for a naval officer, is it not?"

"A little unusual, yes."

Better not to say more. Be patient. Soames was touching on matters that Topcliffe held close to himself.

"Better understanding of *Raison d'etat* than most officers, captain," Soames said.

Reasons of State. A favourite phrase of Topcliffe's. A justification for measures, any measures, to attain a goal. Measures which governments chose not to acknowledge, even if successful.

"Tell me about Korea," Soames said. "Queen Min, the Chinese, the Japanese. Why did you take the decisions that you did?"

The mission had seemed straightforward, gaining a signature on a codicil to a treaty. But nothing had been as it had seemed at first, and interests and loyalties had shifted. Events outside his control had demanded immediate responses that were political as much as military. Failure would have killed all hopes of Anglo-Japanese cooperation to counter Russian expansion. Only willingness to make unlikely alliances had brought success and, even then, it had been touch and go.

Soames let him take his time, asked questions for clarification only, made no comment on the wisdom of his decisions. This was a trial, Dawlish realised, an assessment of him for some purpose he could not guess. A single word or phrase might count against him but he must ignore that fear, speak coldly as if about some third party who meant nothing to him.

He wanted to take the initiative, forestall Soames's inevitable further probings. "It was somewhat different in East Africa," he said. "The Germans there –"

"Never mind the Germans, captain. We'll get to them later. Tell me about Turkey instead. Why did you commit yourself so wholeheartedly to the late-lamented Nusret Pasha?"

"Because he was a brave man, and a good one too. Because he had a vision, a pragmatic vision, one that appealed to me." The memory, a pang, was strong within him still. Nusret, and the whole Ottoman Empire, had deserved a better fate. "And more, Sir Cathcart, an end to religious persecution. Constitutional government. Modernity. Roads, railways, sanitation, education, hospitals."

"Rather like President Ravenel of Guimbi?"

"Yes."

"Do you think Ravenel can achieve even the slightest fraction of those fantasies, captain?"

Dawlish disliked Soames at that moment for his smug and condescending smile, the implication that a man of action could not understand what Sir Clifford Belton had called political economy.

"No. But he'll do his damnedst. It may take years but –"

"You don't know about the French loans, I gather, captain. No? I thought not." Soames reached for a manila folder on his desk and pushed it towards Dawlish. "I had this prepared for you. It's a complicated matter but it's summarised here in layman's language."

"Why?"

"You need to know about it. I suggest you study it tonight. The loans may crop up in some discussions tomorrow. You're lodging in London, I trust?"

"As your invitation suggested."

Dawlish would be at the Charing Cross Hotel, booked in for the next two nights.

"Let's talk about Cuba now, captain. Your cooperation with that rebel Machado. Some decisions that came near to souring our relations with Spain. And your wife's willingness to play a role in it."

The plan had been agreed with Topcliffe in full acceptance of disowning and abandonment in case of failure. As it nearly had. Success had been at the cost of a wound to Florence but had also brought command of HMS *Leonidas* and all that followed.

So the questioning – the assessment – began again, continued through a lunch of sandwiches, dragged on until late afternoon. Not just the Germans in East Africa, but that private war in Paraguay that Dawlish wished to forget and earlier service elsewhere. He was surprised that Soames was so well briefed, on failures as well as successes, and referred only occasionally to papers before him. He showed no interest in the practicalities of sailing or fighting a ship, or managing a naval brigade onshore, and he cut Dawlish off with polite condescension each time he touched on such matters. It was about his ability to appreciate the wider political and diplomatic framework, and make decisions and accommodations within them, that Soames probed.

They broke up at last, would meet again in the morning. Soames would send a coach to collect him. Dawlish protested – it was a five - minute walk to this office from the hotel – but Soames was adamant and said that he had his own reasons.

And before then, Dawlish must know about those French loans that Topcliffe too had mentioned.

*

He had never thought much about the intricacies of slave-emancipation. It had occurred in all British territories, including Roscal, a decade before his birth. Compensation of slave owners had not aroused resistance or resentment in Britain and the surrounding political and economic issues were long forgotten. But now, sitting in his hotel room after dinner and working through the folder that Soames had given him, he realised that the situation was different in France.

It still rankled there that a slave army had snatched away a profitable colony after two-centuries' occupation, had defeated successive forces sent against it, had the sophistication to negotiate an alliance with Britain against France. Tiny as it was, the Republic of Guimbi had withstood all that the Revolutionary and Napoleonic regimes had hurled against it.

When the wars had ended, its independence had been guaranteed by the European great powers, a condescending acknowledgement of its role in the titanic conflict. France had consented – grudgingly, and at a price. French planter families had been massacred in the early stages of the insurrection and the survivors despoiled of all they had. France had demanded compensation was for loss of human no less than of agricultural property. Forcing that obligation on the infant black republic had seemed to British, Austrian and Russian chancelleries a small price for France's reluctant acceptance of the new Concert of Europe.

So Guimbi had been born in bankruptcy, its land despoiled, its new rulers lacking experience of governance or finance, even when literate. It had been easy for French financiers to advance loans to pay the compensation, loans repayable over decades at exorbitant rates of interest. Sugar exports had died with the plantation system and the new nation was one of subsistence plots that scarcely kept starvation at bay. What revenues the republic had, and they were miniscule, were eaten up by interest payments. Bribery and naivety had induced successive Guimbian governments, which came and went rapidly and often bloodily, to take further loans to pay them.

None of the great French banks had been involved, Dawlish learned. The sums involved were too small to attract their attention but many lesser and provincial banks had fallen for the chimera of high interest rates. Their confidence had not been entirely misplaced. In the mid-60s, during French intervention in Mexico, France had landed a small force in Guimbi to empty the pathetic contents of the republic's treasury to get something at least to keep the lenders at bay.

And yet the bankers had not learned. The same institutions had advanced loan after loan, many just enough to pay the annual interest on earlier loans. It could not last, must someday come crashing down, destroying dozens of small financial institutions, beggaring French widows and orphans and bourgeois rentiers. But not yet. In the meantime, there were profits to be made by the agile and unscrupulous and votes were to be won in France by any politician who defended the lenders' interests.

Dawlish read a second time through the catalogue of greed, stupidity and corruption. It depressed him. He had liked what he had seen of President Ravenel and Maître Jacques Badeaux. But they were living on a volcano no less deadly than Mont Colbert.

And, sooner or later, it must consume them.

*

The morning was miserable with sleet.

"Mr. Dawlish?"

The hotel commissionaire did not address him as 'Captain' and he did not correct him.

"A gentleman's been asking for you, sir." He gestured towards a coach waiting on the hotel's cobbled forecourt. "That clarence, sir,"

A vehicle of high quality, so too the well-groomed horse. No crest on the door. The man inside was his own age.

"MacQuaid." He extended his left hand. "Excuse this. The other isn't up to shaking." The smooth-stretched leather of the right glove told that the hand was artificial.

Dawlish knew the name, though he had never met him. Topcliffe's man, an ex-army major. Florence had had dealings with him while he himself had been in the Sudan. She had spoken of him with respect but not warmth. Effective, but a cold fish, she'd said.

"I thought I was meeting Sir Cathcart Soames."

"You will, captain. You will. Just at a different venue."

The coach lurched into motion. MacQuaid made no mention of Florence and Dawlish didn't either. They lapsed into guarded silence as the vehicle passed up Pall Mall and St. James Street, then turned westwards toward Knightsbridge and Kensington. Dawlish guessed where they were going. Florence had told him that Topcliffe and a staff occupied a splendid house, to all appearances a private residence, in Queensberry Place. He felt a flush of envy that he had never been brought to Topcliffe's holy-of-holies himself, though she had been, when she had accomplished a mission for the old Lucifer.

It was as she had described it, immaculately clean, the smell of beeswax, closed doors, distant voices, the ringing of an unseen telephone and the faint tapping of a typewriter. Soames had already arrived, was sitting with Topcliffe and another gentleman in the large office at the rear that had once been a dining room. That too was as she had described it, impersonal order and neatness, huge framed maps on two walls, a row of cabinets on the third, a large conference table. Topcliffe introduced the other gentleman, white-haired, bewhiskered and portly, as Mr. Farnsworth of the Foreign Office, with no explanation of his role.

"Major MacQuaid will take notes. Informal notes," Topcliffe said. "I trust you agree?"

All did, and the meeting began without any statement of its purpose.

And, once more, questioning about what had happened on Roscal. *Scipio's* role and evacuation of Saint Gérons quickly disposed of, raised only as if out of courtesy, Soames and Farnsworth demonstrating little understanding of that crisis and less interest. It was of the planters that they wanted to know. They spoke the names of d'Erlanger and the Soulier twins and a half-dozen others with a familiarity that surprised Dawlish. They queried him on every detail of the mob's attack on the Thénac camp and whether greed for loot had been a greater motivation than workers' fear of refusing planters' orders.

"You've perhaps heard that most of those men you arrested were freed?" Soames said.

Dawlish bridled. "Most?"

"All your white prisoners. All charges dismissed. The court accepted that Etienne Soulier and his friends had gone there to restrain the mob after they'd heard of the attack."

"That wasn't what they said that night. Most of them pointed the finger at Soulier for urging them to come," Dawlish said. "They were nearly falling each other to absolve themselves and put the blame on him. But all those I arrested had incited murder."

"That's not what they said in court."

"There were witnesses enough." Dawlish was angry now.

"Black witnesses. Do you think any court in Roscal would give them credence, Captain Dawlish? Would accept the evidence of a black against a white? Especially on such serious charges?"

"Did Soulier speak in his own defence? Did he mention that he'd been concerned about arms being stored in the camp?"

"He didn't need to. The case had been dropped already."

"You said 'most' of those I arrested. Who were the others?"

He could guess the answer already.

"Labourers. Five convicted of affray and sentenced to three years' hard labour, two of attempted murder, eight years each. One of murder. An employee of the Souliers. He received a death sentence. It had to be confirmed in London. When Sir Clifford forwarded the papers, he recommended a reprieve. It was granted. The man's been sent to Antigua to serve his sentence there. Hard labour for life."

Topcliffe had been silent throughout the exchange and now it was Farnsworth who spoke.

"You mentioned arms, captain. Is there any possibility of weapons having entered from Guimbi, as some of these planters claim?"

"I can't imagine that anybody in Guimbi could afford to send them," Dawlish said. "That whole nation's destitute. Sir Cathcart has shown me documentation that attests it."

"Or guns run in from anywhere else, captain?" MacQuaid, speaking for the first time.

"Possible, I suppose, but unlikely. What I've seen of Roscal, other than on Mr. d'Erlanger's estate, people seemed more concerned with surviving day to day than planning any massacre the Souliers say they fear."

"How would you deal with gunrunning, were there such a threat?" Topcliffe was asking the question to enlighten the others. He must know how Dawlish would answer, as any competent naval officer would.

"Constant patrolling of the coast would be a waste of time. Without intelligence about recipients on the island it would be hopeless. Only a small craft would be needed to intercept them and a force onshore to root out the recipients – something like a gendarmerie, which Roscal doesn't have."

"It has police. A small number I admit but –" Soames began.

"All but useless." Dawlish said. "Just one inspector worth a damn, a black called Dorsette, and not another officer worthy of confidence. If you're seriously worried about gunrunning then what's needed is a small armed group, well trained, reliably led. And most of all, with eyes and ears in the community."

The turn the discussion had taken surprised him. Senior people – very senior people – were concerned about a flyspeck island of no strategic or economic importance. The issues discussed could be easily resolved at a much lower level.

"Guimbi's president, Auguste Ravenel," Farnsworth said. "Your report gives a favourable impression." He paused. "Have you not been a little naïve, captain?"

The phrasing was insulting, probably deliberately so, but Dawlish didn't rise to it. "What I know now about the French loans doesn't change my assessment of him," he said. If anything, it had raised his estimation. Ravenel knew that he was facing an impossible task, but it did not daunt him.

"How long will Ravenel last, captain? A third of his predecessors have either fled the country, taking whatever remained in the treasury with them, or were murdered in coups."

"He must know the risks," Dawlish said. "But he was relieved, not just pleased, that *Scipio* visited."

Now the question he had been eager to ask since leaving Roscal.

"I presume that it was the Foreign Office that requested the visit to Guimbi. Sir Clifford's letter contained just platitudes and it didn't need an ironclad to carry it. That choice of *Scipio* as messenger implied something more. And President Ravenel recognises it."

He saw Soames flash a glance towards Farnsworth. *Don't explain that. Better drop the subject.* And Farnsworth nodding slightly.

The questioning shifted, back to Dawlish's services in Turkey and Cuba, Korea and East Africa. Not Russian or Japanese or German ambitions and initiatives, but the manner in which Dawlish himself had evaluated risks, made decisions, taken action. Topcliffe sat impassive, made no comment, added nothing, even though he had initiated those missions, had arranged advancement in payment for success. And had been ready to disown Dawlish had he not delivered it.

He was being weighed in the balance, Dawlish recognised, though why he could not guess. Farnsworth had used the word 'naïve' and that was how he, and probably Soames too, considered him, a man who had risked life, limb and reputation. He could sense the patronising satisfaction of those who built careers in meetings and memoranda, who felt superior to men like him, necessary as they might be on occasion. But at the far end of the table, MacQuaid, his bare left hand, which had been jotting notes without apparent difficulty, paused at intervals to stroke the smooth leather on the other. It was an unconscious mannerism perhaps, a reminder of loss. The slightest hint of contempt in his smile confirmed that he recognised the same as Dawlish had done in these two men.

He, like me, has worked for Topcliffe. And paid a higher price.

The session dragged on, even through a buffet lunch in another room, conversation during it guarded and stilted, until the gaslight had been turned up to illuminate the mid-afternoon gloom. It ended without summary or explanation.

Handshakes, thanks for Dawlish's answers, Soames and Farnsworth departing.

"MacQuaid will take you back to your hotel," Topcliffe said to Dawlish. "But first, I'd like a word or two before you go."

MacQuaid left them.

"You can probably guess what's being considered, captain," Topcliffe said when they were seated again.

"No." An honest answer. The entire day had been bewildering.

"They're considering offering you governorship of Roscal."

Time stopped.

The idea was beyond his imagining, beyond comprehension. And he was frightened.

"To replace Sir Clifford?" He could think of nothing else to say.

"Sir Clifford has asked to be relieved. Health problems, serious ones. For you, the duties would be somewhat broader. I proposed it and it's being taken seriously. No recommendation yet from those two gentlemen and, even they advocate it, approval will be needed at higher level. But I'll be backing your appointment, regardless of their opinion."

"But I'm a naval officer and —"

"Your career wouldn't suffer for it, Dawlish. I'll see to that, provided all goes well. It wouldn't last longer than two years. Maybe less."

Provided.

"Is there something more than was talked about today, sir?"

"A lot more. Serious implications. You'll hear about them if and when it's essential. But before any formal offer is made, I need to know if you'd accept."

My father with but short time to live, my stepmother even less. An appointment that would end present service in home waters and frequent returns to Florence and the growing Jessica.

Dawlish's mind was racing.

The chance of failure, of abandonment by Topcliffe, of a career ending in resignation. But refusal most certainly leading to long years as port captain at some minor foreign station or responsibility for some insignificant dockyard.

Topcliffe sensed his misgivings. "Mrs. Dawlish could accompany you," he said. "It would be desirable in fact. Sir Clifford's lack of a hostess didn't help. And your wife's capable of doing much more than welcoming guests."

"Must I answer now, sir?"

"By the end of the week at the latest. You may discuss it with Mrs. Dawlish. She knows how to keep secrets."

Dawlish stood to go.

"One last point, captain. If it all turns out well there could be a K in it for you. But keep that to yourself."

He had never hankered for a knighthood, but it had another implication.

Lady Florence.

The irresistible temptation.

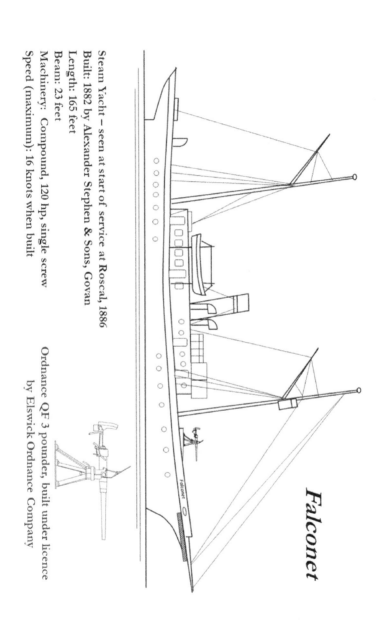

Steam Yacht – seen at start of service at Roscal, 1886
Built: 1882 by Alexander Stephen & Sons, Govan
Length: 165 feet
Beam: 23 feet
Machinery: Compound, 120 hp, single screw
Speed (maximum): 16 knots when built

Ordnance QF 3 pounder, built under licence by Elswick Ordnance Company

Falconet

Chapter 11

Three weeks to work through two trunks full of confidential reports and audited accounts, of legislation, of governance and judicial structures, of assessments, usually pessimistic, of Roscal's prospects.

Three weeks to winnow wheat from chaff, information from data, significant from insignificant.

Three weeks for the mail-ship RMS *Eudoxia* to batter through the fury of the North Atlantic's January storms and on through calmer seas towards Jamaica. From there a smaller vessel, one carrying mail onwards, island by island, as far as Grenada, would bring Dawlish to Roscal.

He welcomed his first-class suite on *Eudoxia* not for its luxury but for its spaciousness, for room to spread out the documentation. Regardless of weather, he allowed himself two hours on deck each day, avoiding anything but brief pleasantries with other passengers. The captain, whom he had requested not to address him as 'Your Excellency', had invited him to visit the bridge at any time. He did so only sparingly. A ship must have but one captain and he needed no comment, advice or approbation from another. But from the captain's table there was no escape and meals shared there with a succession of officials, merchants and planters returning from leave or business in Britain, gave little pleasure. The fawning of some, and the probing of others for some scrap of information that might profit them, irked him. Dawlish had asked for his status to be kept confidential, but some garrulous steward had leaked it. As the new governor of Roscal he had a standing that he had never had as a mere naval officer and he found the reactions it aroused frequently distasteful. He must expect even more of this on the island itself.

It had been a bad time to leave Britain.

Florence and Jessica had stayed behind, not in Southsea, where she had terminated the lease on their villa, but at Shrewsbury. Christmas had ben miserable. Rowena was dying hard, was suffering pain that the laudanum could not check and was aware that death was near. Even Ted understood by now and seldom left her side. The local vicar sat with her twice a week, prayed with her, gave such solace as he could, and she was grateful for it. She was exhibiting a quiet courage that none had ever expected of her.

"I can't leave her," Florence had told Dawlish when he had come there to say goodbye. "She needs me. It's a matter of weeks only. I'll follow you to Roscal as soon as it's over."

His wife's slow agony was killing Dawlish's father too. More hopeless by the day, more plagued by palpitations and faintness, he still refused to admit her nearness to death, avoided even mentioning her condition. He had been self-indulgent all his life, had comforted himself with many low-class women after his first wife's death, was rumoured to have unacknowledged offspring in the town. Dawlish had loved him, but had never much respected him, not as he had his beloved uncle, dead of consumption three decades since in Pau. And now, in the face of coming loss, the old man was maudlin as well as weak.

"I won't see you again, Nick," he had said when Dawlish left. He broke down, began to weep, held him to him. It was the first time he had admitted the reality.

"You'll live to bury me, Father. You'll make old bones. Just you see." Dawlish tried to laugh, make light of it.

"You shouldn't go, Nicholas. I'm an old man and –" He was sobbing now, holding him tighter.

Dawlish felt himself breaking too. Memories of rough kindness, of embarrassing but well-meant boasting of his son's achievements, of clumsy comforting after his own mother, also Jessica, had died when he was four. He had felt the same sharp longing when he had cradled dying men, the rage to share his own vitality with them, to hold them in the world while their spirits were slipping away.

But he had left.

Duty was a hard taskmistress.

*

The official documents, though voluminous and time-consuming, were easy enough to work through on the mail steamer. Commanding major warships had demanded a no-less comprehensive mastery of administration, regulation and technical detail. He would manage well enough, Dawlish decided. But what worried him was his last conversation with Topcliffe, one gravid with threat and uncertainty. The topic had taken him by surprise.

"The French, like the poor, are always with us." Topcliffe pointed to a closed file before him. "Always a damn nuisance too, even when they're not an immediate threat."

Dawlish could not disagree. Centuries had proved it.

"It gnaws into them like a cancer that they've lost two provinces to Germany," Topcliffe said. "They know they're not strong enough to retake them and probably never will be. Even conscription can't give them the numbers needed. But the danger is that they'll be vain and blind enough to try, if they ever can bring in Russia with them. It would trigger a nightmare that we ourselves, and others too, might well be drawn into. Lord knows which side might then best align with our interests."

"They're not building their fleet against anybody but us," Dawlish said. He had seen the French Navy's towering armoured ships, large-calibre guns bristling above tumble-homed sides, long and sinister rams. And, recently, ocean going cruisers designed for commerce raiding and swarms of torpedo boats. France could counter Germany's tiny fleet with a fifth of its present navy. The European balance of power might shift, but the French would always regard Britain as a potential enemy and take measures accordingly.

"France has always been prone to illusions of grandeur." Topcliffe said. "Now they're coming back as colonial expansion's being accomplished by competent officers. Enough to fire deluded confidence when forgetting that it rests on triumphs over weaker enemies. One man, respected for good reasons, who can proclaim himself a new Napoleon and win support across political divides, might well be rash enough to challenge Germany for the lost provinces."

"Is there somebody, sir?"

"There might be. Another potential man of destiny to promise deliverance and glory. We've an informant in the French General Staff who's keeping us abreast. We're beholden to your wife for that contact."

It had almost cost Florence her life. She had only confided the details of the mission to him because Topcliffe had permitted her. Even now, Dawlish did not know the name of the traitor who fed information. His cooperation was secured only because a single hint to the French Ambassador could send him before a firing squad.

"There's a network of officers," Topcliffe said, "an informal one, and all the stronger for that, which extends through the army. It'll act if this would-be man of destiny calls on them. More might well follow them. Not just soldiers either. Journalists too. And the half of the nation that's sick of corrupt politicians. Those angered by inequality. Ordinary people disgusted by the flaunted decadence of the rich. And all, and that's most of France, who can't and won't forget losing Lorraine and Alsace."

"Why does he wait?"

"Until he has struck a single blow, an unexpected one. An act of élan that will cancel a lost defeat, rouse the promise of new glory. One that will prove him to be indeed the man of destiny. One that will galvanise the nation and carry him to power."

Topcliffe paused.

"It could be Guimbi," he said.

A chill run through Dawlish.

"Retake it?"

"Possibly. It's being considered. But it's just one of several possibilities, including Mauritius and Amapá. Maybe not the most likely but –" Topcliffe held up his hands in mock bewilderment. "We want to be prepared."

"Who is it, sir?" Dawlish said.

"You'll know when – or if – you need to know, captain. Rest assured of that. Until then the fewer who know of his network the better."

And so, as the new governor of Roscal worked through the chests of documents on RMS *Eudoxia,* he knew that there was more to his appointment than maintenance of internal peace and promotion of prosperity in the Crown Colony of Roscal.

More, infinitely more, might be at stake.

*

Dawlish had not enjoyed leaving *Scipio*. He had hankered after such a prestigious command for years, one confirming that he was marked for higher things. He had spent little of his career with the great fleets in home waters or in the Mediterranean. For diplomatic reasons, many of the successes that had bought him advancement could never be acknowledged openly. He lacked experience of fleet and squadron manoeuvres and the largest flotilla he had ever commanded had been that which *Scipio* had led to South America. Now he was losing the opportunity of such fleet experience. And even if service as governor of Roscal proved successful, he might be absent from the Navy for two years or more, missing opportunities, his name fading from the list of possible squadron commanders.

And if not successful . . .

Doubt was familiar to him, the old insidious enemy that gnawed the spirit and stifled aspiration. Better to remind himself how Topcliffe had supported him before when other might not have.

His meetings with the admiral before he left had been at the discreet Queensberry Place address, not in the club where they had so often met formerly. It was unspoken recognition that he had been admitted to an inner circle.

"Roscal's not linked by telegraph," Dawlish had said. "The closest British station's at Antigua. So I'll need a vessel – not some local schooner – for fast contact with Antigua. Which means with London."

"The Colonial Office will baulk," Topcliffe said "I doubt if there's a governor anywhere who has an official yacht. That's what they'll see it as. It would set a precedent. An expensive one too."

Ignore that objection. Press on.

"Not just fast either," Dawlish said. "Armed. There's talk of gunrunning, isn't there? Whoever's doing it won't just run up a white flag if they're cornered."

"The C.O. will object."

"But I think you have links to a yet higher level, Sir Richard."

I would never have said this even three years ago. But success buys frankness as well as advancement.

"Go on, Dawlish."

"Let's call it a customs and fisheries protection vessel, sir. One that needs a degree of protection against aggressive smugglers and illegal fishing intrusions into Roscal's coastal waters. I'm sure there must be reports on such incidents. And, if there aren't, I've no doubt that you, sir, can ensure that there are."

"You're learning, Dawlish. You're learning."

It took a week to find the vessel, not through Admiralty channels but by others less official. A mid-sized steam yacht, a plaything that a rich man had tired of, now lying idle and available for charter at Bermuda. A hundred and sixty-five feet, *Falconet* had a compound engine that had driven her at sixteen knots on trial five years before. Boiler and engine would need inspection and overhaul, but that could be arranged. That, and mounting of a quick-firing three-pounder on her foredeck, sourced from the naval dockyard there. She would be slower than Dawlish hoped, but he must settle for it.

"I've somebody in mind who might command her," Topcliffe said.

"A navy-secondee, sir?" Dawlish had assumed it should be some promising young officer. He'd have jumped at such a chance himself when in his twenties.

"An ex-Lieutenant Reginald Sproul. Well regarded until a matter involving a brother-officer's wife. He was invited to resign to spare the unfortunate woman's name. He's seen hard times since and he's been glad to undertake some tasks for me at intervals. He'll suit."

Dawlish recognised the message. No naval involvement.

"As far as possible, it's better that she has a local crew," he said. He'd been impressed by Inspector Dorsette and his men. There must be others of similar calibre among the Roscal's fishermen. "I'd need somebody to lick them into shape. Ex-navy. A bosun, best if already familiar with a three-pounder, with two or three seamen to support him. And an engineer."

One of Topcliffe's clerks already had a list of possibilities and arranged for Dawlish to interview four candidates next day at a civilian marine-employment agency in Wapping. Railway-warrants brought three more thereafter from Cardiff, Newcastle and Liverpool. He had already seen their naval records, none dismal, all time-expired men who had hoped for better prospects in the merchant service or ashore and had been disappointed. One was the worse for drink when he arrived, a second looked in the last stages of consumption and probing revealed that a third was fleeing from what was probably a bigamous marriage. Dawlish selected a fifty-year old ex-Petty Officer, Bradbury, an ex-engineer, Hobson, who had started as an artificer, and three younger ex-seamen, Forbes, Halligan and O'Harney. A tramp steamer that was departing within the week would carry them with Sproul to Bermuda to take over *Falconet*. She should arrive in Roscal two weeks after Dawlish did himself.

Now one man more was needed, one to create and train and command a gendarmerie. Topcliffe already had a candidate but gave Dawlish the right of veto if he thought him unsuitable.

He didn't.

Major Lionel Clemenger, late of the Indian Army's Corps of Guides, one-eyed, limping with a stick – not that that appeared to slow him – impressed when interviewed.

"He made his reputation on the North-West Frontier but he's no less respected as a *shikari*," Topcliffe had said.

"*Shikari?*" Dawlish didn't know the term.

"A hunter. Mainly of tigers, though one of them nearly chewed his leg off before he killed it. I gather that his bag is matched only by a Colonel Moran. They were in less-than-friendly competition for years."

Clemenger had some other business to complete for him, Topcliffe said, but he could arrive in Roscal in five weeks' time.

With these men to rely on, Dawlish knew that his tenure there would be very different to Sir Clifford's.

*

Professor Moncton had been an enthusiastic host when Dawlish travelled to Oxford to meet him.

"Please assume that I know nothing of botany," he had said.

By the end of the two-day visit, he had filled an entire notebook with summaries of explanations by Moncton and his colleagues, all similarly dedicated and enthusiastic. He would remember half or less, he knew, but that would not matter – in the heated greenhouse laboratories he sensed promise of a brighter future. Moncton's colleagues impressed, especially the younger ones who had already conducted field trials in West Africa. They were serious men, driven, even visionary, the sort of men he liked. It was easy to imagine d'Erlanger liking them too, welcoming their cooperation. Moncton had already written to him, introducing himself and his work. He was waiting for an answer.

It was impossible to know what it might lead to, but there was hope.

An unexpected invitation had arrived in a letter for Agatha, just before he left for Roscal. Her father, Lord Kegworth would welcome a short discussion.

At the Carlton Club, he suggested.

The location was a sensitive choice, one that would avoid the embarrassment of meeting in the Piccadilly mansion where Florence had once been in service, where her father and brother were still coachmen.

But there was another reason for discomfort. Kegworth was a director of the Hyperion Consortium. The name of that vast commercial undertaking was enough to stir memories – painful and shameful memories – of Dawlish's unofficial services for it in Paraguay seven years before. Memories that he wished to forget, even though he had refused all remuneration afterwards.

Kegworth's appearance shocked him when they met. He had been florid and hearty when Dawlish had last met him. But that had been before the scandal that had sent his heir into hurried exile ahead of an arrest warrant for gross indecency. Now he was an old man, aged twenty years in four, stooped, unhealthily pale, his handshake weak.

"You're satisfied with your appointment?" he said. "Well deserved, well deserved, Dawlish. The ideal man for it."

He might well have had something to do with it, Dawlish realised. Even if the Liberals were still in government, the influence of a Conservative grandee still counted. And he was a close friend, if anybody could ever be that, of Topcliffe's

"It's about Hyperion" Kegworth said.

Dawlish tensed at mention of the word

"No, nothing to compromise your honour, nothing like that, captain. But Hyperion is looking for investment opportunities. Roscal might well offer some. We'd be glad to hear of any. It would be best if any interested party were to contact us directly."

"I'll bear it in mind, my lord."

"Hyperion's expanding. Not just beef alone."

The canned beef from Paraguay, from far up the Rio San Joaquin at what had once been La Reducción Nueva, Which I helped destroy . . .

Dawlish smothered the memory and forced himself to listen. Kegworth owned half of Northamptonshire but, unlike most of his class, he never feigned contempt of trade, by comparison with land-ownership, as a source of wealth.

"Other foodstuffs, even fruit," Kegworth was saying. "Hyperion has two refrigerated ships in service and experience is promising. And coffee too, not just for the British market. The Germans drink it by the gallon. Great opportunities there too. But we need to secure sources of supply. And loans could be arranged to assist local growers."

"Such as planters on Roscal?"

"Only progressive men, men of vision." Kegworth paused, perhaps sensing Dawlish's caution, then said. "I'm suggesting nothing dishonourable. I know you too well for that. There'd be no question of private profit for yourself."

"Are you acquainted with a Professor Moncton, my lord?" Dawlish said. "A friend of Lady Agatha's?"

Kegworth smiled. "I think I may have heard her mention the name."

The botanist's presence at the dinner had been no coincidence.

Dawlish was due to attend another meeting at the Colonial Office in the next hour. He made his excuses and stood to leave.

Kegworth took him by the arm, walked in silence with him to the front lobby, then suddenly stopped.

"Assure Mrs. Dawlish of my best regards." The words came in a rush, a tremor in his voice. "And my eternal thanks for what she did for my son. And his mother's gratitude too. It was a bad business, it still is, God knows, but without her it would have been so much worse."

From various remarks let slip by Florence and Agatha when they had thought him out of earshot, he had suspected that she had been complicit in Lord Oswald's escape from prosecution. He had not pressed the matter and trusted that Florence had had good reason. Loyalty to the Kegworth family perhaps, gratitude for good treatment through several generations of service. He had never liked Lord Oswald but he would not have wished on him that horsewhipping on the steps of his club and the rumours that had followed. And many other men high in politics and society were widely spoken of as guilty of the same proclivity that had made him a fugitive who moved around Europe in luxurious but disgraced exile

Pity moved him as he saw tears in Kegworth's eyes and felt trembling in the hand he shook.

For all his acres, all his wealth and influence, his lordship's last years were as wretched as those of many paupers.

*

He feared what would await him at Jamaica and though he had tried to prepare himself for it, but it was still shocking when it came.

Three telegrams from Florence.

His stepmother had died two weeks before.

Another, sent five days later. His father had suffered a seizure at the funeral and had not recovered. Ted was devasted.

The last, just two days old, told better news.

That Florence was sailing with Jessica in a week's time, following same route that he had. Ted was coming with her. An agent was arranging rental of the house in Shrewsbury and sending the contents to storage.

A new chapter of his life was beginning. Sir Clifford would remain a week after his arrival in Escource to explain responsibilities and provide advice. Then the full burden would rest on himself alone.

He would be something that he had never anticipated.

His Excellency, Captain Nicholas Dawlish.

Her Majesty's Governor of the Crown Colony of Roscal.

Chapter 12

"The existing militia's a liability," Clemenger said. "No training, damn little discipline, not a single officer worth the name, even if they are volunteers, some of 'em senile and a joke among the people."

The major had been in Roscal for two months, Dawlish for three. Sir Clifford was a fast-fading memory. This meeting with the commander of the newly created Rural Guard was Dawlish's last of the day. The unit's title sounded less French than *gendarmerie*, but that was what it was in practice.

"The militia's just ceremonial now," Dawlish said. "Nothing more. And I'm the only one who can call it out."

"They're armed. That makes them dangerous."

"With a few antiquated Brunswick rifles that haven't been fired in years? And old men who've forgotten how to handle them, if they ever did? But disbanding the militia would raise resentment I can't afford. Senile as they are, there are influential men among its officers." Dawlish realised that he was beginning to talk like Sir Clifford.

Major Clemenger had returned to this point in every meeting since he had arrived. With Inspector Dorsette as his deputy – and recruiter – he had thrown himself into training the Guard in basic military skills, not least mastery of the Snider-Enfield rifles that Topcliffe had arranged to be delivered.

Dawlish steered the discussion away from the militia.

"You're satisfied that the Guard's reliable enough for deployment, major?"

"Just three posts initially. Muron, Orvault and Blancherd," the major said. "A sergeant and twenty constables in each. And Dorsette here in Escource with forty for reserves and rotation."

Dawlish had identified the locations even before Clemenger had arrived, all north to south, just west of the mountain ridges that separated Roscal from Guimbi. He had decided by instinct only, had no sources of intelligence to justify the disposition. Now that would change.

"And recruiting informants?" Dawlish said.

"That can't be rushed. Once the posts are in place, and trust established, people will talk more freely. Schoolteachers or clergymen, field workers, market women. Loose tongues, gossips, a few with grudges. We'll identify them. Most will never think of themselves as informants. The reports will come back to me and I'll seek patterns."

The meeting ended with agreement to commence deployments in the following week. Dawlish saw Clemenger to the front steps himself. He stood there for several minutes, looking beyond the town and harbour below towards the glory of the setting sun and savouring the scent of bougainvillea. To the north, no smoke drifted from Mont Colbert. The last wisps had faded just after he returned. Since then, he had come to love this view. And something more. A growing love for all he saw, a care for the island and its people, a feeling akin to that for *Leonidas* and *Scipio* and their crews when he had commanded them. The concerns that troubled him, and there were many, seemed at a moment like this to be light burdens, well worth the bearing.

He felt a small hand reaching up into his, looked down and saw Jessica. Heart overflowing, he lifted her, kissed her, showed her the sunset, was pleased that she already knew the word. He looked back, saw Florence standing at the door with Ted, and she motioned him to go ahead without her. He lowered the child again and they set off hand-in-hand along the terrace, stopping to pick a few sprigs of bougainvillea. It had become an evening ritual. The door of his study was further on, open to catch the evening breeze. One of the servants would already have placed a vase of fresh water on his desk and Jessica would place the flowers in it. The sight of them as he worked there would remind him that she was near, and safe. Only when she had arranged them to her satisfaction – a lengthy process that he recognised as a tactic to delay bedtime – would he bring her back to Florence. There was no formal semi-official dinner tonight, no need for Veronique, her black Roscallan nurse, for putting her to bed. He did so with Florence and they remained until she had fallen asleep.

In a more comfortable bed than the blanket-lined ammunition box in which she had survived the journey down the Nile.

The recollection was bittersweet.

Because, in nineteen years, he must tell her the full story.

*

Florence, since her arrival, had visited a score of villages. She eschewed the use of an official coach and drove herself in a dog cart, the nursemaid holding Jessica and the groom, Hippolyte, borrowed from d'Erlanger, riding alongside as escort.

"You're a different sort of governor, Nicholas," she had said. "And I'll be a different sort of governor's lady. One who'll do as much as you will for the people here."

She liked them already, as much as he did for their resilience and cheerfulness in the face of poverty. He was not free to tell her the real purpose of his appointment and she had assumed that he was to follow on the work that had begun with *Scipio's* mission here.

The fund set up in London had released eight hundred pounds as a first instalment. Florence had gone to Saint Gérons to evaluate, with the aid of one of d'Erlanger's managers, the Reverend Gagneux and two other clergymen, how best to spend it. Grants were made for building or repair of homes damaged by the eruption and for purchase of essential items lost. Clothing was bought and distributed. A work-relief scheme for clearance of the ash provided wages for those who had been beggared. She had returned to the town several times since to oversee progress. Dawlish had stayed away – Saint Gérons was the least of his concerns at present and he disliked the possibility of public demonstrations of thanks. It was *Scipio's*, *Clyde's* and *Navigator's* crews, not him, who deserved them.

He had been apprehensive at first when Florence insisted on travelling without a police guard but he knew better than to argue. From what he had seen of the Roscallans, there was nothing for her to fear.

She had once brought a column of refugees to safety through a ferocious winter in Thrace, Bashi Bazooks and Cossacks notwithstanding, and had saved his life then too. She could cope here. The best protection in Roscal would be if the population knew and liked and trusted her.

And she proved invaluable.

He had ridden through all the same villages she had passed through, and others too, on first arrival, almost every one in the colony. He had dismounted in each, had talked to as many people as he could, regardless of station, but always the title of Governor stood like a wall between him and them. His predecessors, including Sir Clifford, had seldom ventured far from Escource and when they had it was in formal uniform and with a full entourage. That the new governor appeared in simple riding clothes and broad palmetto hat, accompanied by two mounted policemen, and asked questions of all he met, aroused reticence rather than trust.

Other than from insights from d'Erlanger, the Reverend Gagneux and Inspector Dorsette and a few others, and through his secretary Francis Blackford's relentless pursuit of statistics, he still had little appreciation of the real state of Roscal. That would change, be told himself, once Clemenger had established his intelligence network but, even then, he would lean on Florence's perceptions also.

She was a familiar figure in the countryside by now, breaking down barriers, as she always did, with humour and warmth, inviting confidences, listening in patience, viewing one-room schools, visiting sick and infirm, admiring babies and cradling them in her arms, accepting humble offers of food, letting women take Jessica by the hand to show her their homes.

And each time she came back to him with the same story.

Panama.

The French attempt to build a canal there demanded labour, not just men in their hundreds but in their thousands.

"Agents came recruiting," Florence said. "Not just here. All over the Caribbean. What they offered was tempting. A bonus of five pounds for signing on, about three shillings a day when they're working there, twelve hour a day, seven days a week. A fortune."

They both remembered the great steam dredger, first seen *en route* to the isthmus, which had played such a role in their lives six years before. It was one of several now attempting to gouge a ditch across fifty miles of swamp, forest and mountain to link two oceans. But steam power could only do so much. Men were needed also, to dig and blast and shovel and load. They had seen drawings of them in the illustrated papers, hordes labouring like ants in mud, rain and misery.

"I hear it in every village," Florence said. "In one it's three or four dead in Panama, as much as ten in another. A few come back, but they're broken. I talked to one of them in Orvault. Panama's rotten with Yellow Fever, he says. It comes and goes but spares nobody. Not the labourers, not the French supervisors. But those still there are hoping they'll be lucky and come home rich."

Dawlish had himself seen Roscal's widows and orphans somehow surviving on small vegetable patches, the older children leading tethered goats to graze along the roadsides. Pity had filled him at first. Now that he was familiar with the sight, he realised that he hardly noticed. He was hardening, he realised, and that troubled him. Perhaps it was only Florence who stood between him and callousness.

"They shouldn't have to leave, Nick," she had said, "though God knows it'll never be easy here. Even slaving in the cane fields would be better than Panama. They need work here."

But there was hope.

Limes.

And coffee.

*

Dawlish kept the Advisory Council's meetings shorter than in Sir Clifford's time. Armand Soulier had resigned on hearing of Dawlish's appointment, another member also. The three remaining councillors were cautious but not hostile, cooperative in small things, reluctant to voice opinions on anything of weight. They had not objected, not at least with any strength, to formation of the Rural Guard, but it was clear that they resented it. Small as it was, the existing police force kept the peace well enough, one had argued. There was little crime and two or three constables in each village were sufficient.

London was concerned by reports of seditious influences from Guimbi, Dawlish told them. He had heard the same concerns himself from prominent Roscallans when Maître Badeaux, the Guimbian envoy, had come with relief supplies. The concerns might or might not be justified but London preferred to take no chances. Deployment of the Rural Guard would prevent agitators slipping across from Guimbi into Roscal. He doubted if they believed him, even though they did not challenge the explanation.

At this latest meeting they moved quickly through the agenda – road maintenance, school repairs, night-soil collection in Escource – and noted with satisfaction that land-access to Saint Gérons had been re-established. A formal letter of thanks would be sent to Edmond d'Erlanger. He had paid for a replacement timber bridge across the now-solidified lava flow in the gully west of the town. Even before that, many residents who had been evacuated during the eruption had returned by sea. Now the remainder were following. The camps at Le Marigot and Thénac were almost empty and d'Erlanger had made his first shipment of lime juice since reopening Saint Gérons' port.

"Which brings us to economic matters," Dawlish said. "Mr. Blackford has some figures for us."

The secretary had been taking minutes. Now he distributed a single sheet to each member and began to talk them through it.

Sugar exports down 23% in the last five years, 41% in the last ten.

All other exports, except lime juice, down by 13% and 29% respectively.

Customs duties on imports – and they were few – down by 31% and 42%.

And then the statistics that told the saddest tale of all.

Poll-tax revenue down 19% in those last five years and 24% in ten.

The tax was the charge paid by each adult male, a pitifully small one at first glance, but an enormous burden for those who lived close to destitution. Dawlish had already written to the Colonial Office to request approval for a temporary reduction. The answer had been not just negative, but bordering on contemptuous, a subtle reminder that he was inexperienced in such matters.

"The men are leaving," Dawlish said. "They're going to Panama and the canal is killing them there." He paused. "They shouldn't have to leave. There should be work here for them."

One of the councillors, Marsac, a lawyer, was shifting in his chair.

"It's sad, Your Excellency," he said.

Dawlish found the mode of address ridiculous but he was used to it by now. An annoyance, nothing of which to make an issue.

"It's tragic," the councillor said. "We all regret it. But it's their decision to go to Panama. There's nothing we can do to stop them."

Dawlish ignored him. "Mr. Blackford has some last figures," he said.

And he had.

Lime-juice exports had increased 37% in five years and 61% in ten.

Blackford had another sheet to distribute. Three paragraphs only.

"It's a summary of a Board of Trade report that I requested from London," Dawlish said. "Perhaps you might like to take two minutes to read it, gentlemen."

He had absorbed the contents already. That the international market for lime juice was still increasing, that prices were high, were likely to go higher still. Were Roscal's exports to be quintupled, or more, they would still find a seller's market.

"That's easily said." The councillor who spoke was Verley, a sugar-planter. Barely surviving financially, he had told Dawlish. "It takes money and it'll years before the trees are grown enough to yield any substantial crop. I tried a half-acre of 'em and most died."

"But Mr. d'Erlanger's didn't," Dawlish said. "He ships nine tenths of the lime juice that leaves Roscal. I propose that –"

"He's the biggest landowner on this island." Verley, flushed, cut him off. "And he's got money, family money."

"But not enough even to start his lime business," Dawlish said. He had talked with d'Erlanger since return and had heard that even twice his wealth would not have sufficed. "So he borrowed what he needed."

A decade before, d'Erlanger had recognised the opportunity and had approached banks with meticulous plans. Unsentimental London financiers had been impressed because he was willing to bring in agricultural advisors and start on a small sale. Because he would experiment and import fertilisers. Because he had established links with major British and American importers. And because he was prepared to mortgage all his land and property to secure the necessary loans.

"He's a widower. He has no children," Verley said. The others were nodding agreement. "He could afford to take risks. We can't."

"There are two vacancies on this council. I'm appointing Mr. d'Erlanger to one of them." Dawlish let it sink in. Filling the vacancies was the governor's prerogative and he did not need their approval. He could see they didn't like it.

"He refused when he was invited before," one said. "We know that. Sir Clifford managed well enough without him."

The other two were nodding. Dawlish affected not to notice.

"He has accepted this time," he said. "He'll be joining us for our meeting next week. We'll need his advice. Bringing more land under lime cultivation may be the only way to save Roscal."

And perhaps save too the men still labouring, and dying, at Panama, and others still here and considering responding to the siren calls of the recruiters who so often came from there.

The meeting ended. They shook hands without warmth on parting.

*

Two days after the council meeting, Dawlish returned from an inspection ride of his own to find Florence jubilant.

"It was good that you let me drag you to that dinner in London, Nick." She was waving a letter, written on headed notepaper. "Read this. It arrived today."

The handwriting was clear and elegant. He looked to the signature – Neville Eversham, Chairman, Roscal Relief Fund.

"Another five hundred pounds, Florence!"

"It's only the start," she said. "That's as much as they're transferring for now. They've accepted the new plan I sent and –"

"What plan?"

"Mine, Nicholas, mine. My plan. Support for the Motherless Babies' Home here in Escource. And a new one in Orvault – I'll need to find a building for that, only a small one, three or four rooms, and a woman I can trust to run it and –"

"You said nothing to me about this, Florence."

"I don't need to, Nick. It's private business, not the government's, not yours. It's a charity." A hint of disappointment, even resentment, in her voice. "And I wanted to surprise you, Nicholas, to make you proud of me."

"I'm always proud of you, Florence. But you should have told me about this. No business is private for me while we're here, nor for you either."

Then he saw tears well in her eyes, her pride hurt, and he felt shamed. She had worked wonders with her friend Agnes Weston when setting up the Seaman's Rest in Portsmouth. She had tendered, awarded and overseen contracts for maintenance, extensions and catering supplies. She had hired responsible staff, had set and maintained standards. The expenditures there must have been well in excess of these five hundred pounds she had now received for Roscal.

"Let's go to my office, Florence. I want you to tell me your plans, everything, every detail." He tried to pass his arm around her waist but she drew away, then yielded.

"Let's go to my study instead, Nicholas. My paperwork is there."

Her judgement as to where to commence had been shrewd. Her cost estimates were methodical and her unwillingness to commit more until she had accumulated experience was impressive. It was easy to imagine Eversham and the other committee members in London being impressed as Dawlish was himself.

"A little goes a long way here," she said. "Not just the babies' homes. You've said yourself that half of the smaller villagers don't have schools. The fund will pay for three now, money for books and pay for teachers too. We'll see how it goes and build more if it goes well. And Agatha is looking for a British midwife. You know how many women die in childbed here?"

He didn't, but he realised that he should have enquired.

"Dozens per year, Nick, and most of them die when there are complications and friends and neighbours do more harm than good. I want a proper English midwife, a sensible older woman, a widow maybe, who'll go from village to village to train and teach. Agatha's looking for a woman like that already."

And there was more. An organisation to run it all, overseen by herself. Three wives or daughters of prominent citizens whom she'd liked when they'd come to the tea-parties she had held on arrival.

"But they're not the ones who'll really matter," she said. "It'll be women in the villages who're regarded as leaders, the sort who've scraped and toiled and fed their families no matter what and –"

Dawlish sat and listened, asked for clarifications, all of which satisfied and impressed. It was the Florence who had not flinched in Thrace or Cuba or, more recently, at Dieppe. The Florence whose compassion, no less than her courage, never failed. The Florence whom he had loved since he had first spoken to her on a chilly October morning off the coast of Troy.

His sheet anchor, his wife.

*

The *Falconet* yacht was in service now. She showed herself along the coastline and shuttled between Roscal and Antigua with despatches and telegrams. She circumnavigated the island several times and put in at Port Mazarin once with greetings from Dawlish to Guimbi's President Ravenel. She stopped numerous inter-island trading schooners and searched them, finding no arms or contraband. Under Sproul, her captain, her crew was striving for Royal Navy levels of efficiency.

Dawlish joined the yacht on one of the single-day circumnavigations. Ted came with him, thrilled to take the wheel under the direction of the bosun, to be initiated into the mysteries of the compound engine, to assist in practice-firing of the foredeck three-pounder. He was attending a school run by a retired Anglican clergyman and Dawlish recognised in him, to his satisfaction, much of himself at the same age. These were perhaps the last days, he realised, when the fraternal link, already stretched as it was by age-difference, would be easy. Even now, Ted was cautious about addressing him as Nicholas. In two years, the lad would enter the navy. Henceforth, awareness of rank would bring caution to their dealings with each other. But for now, as with Jessica, this time was to be savoured.

Falconet was creeping around the coast most days, close-inshore off Roscal, three miles out off Guimbi. When Dawlish accompanied her, he scanned the shoreline through a telescope. Much of it was rocky, especially where cliffs plunged into the water on both the north and south coasts where the central mountains met the sea. Dawlish jotted notes. The Guimbian coast was more open than Roscal's, long beaches unsuited to bringing even a small schooner close in, and Port Mazarin was the black republic's only significant harbour. If a small trader were slip in during darkness, offload an illicit cargo, and be gone by first light, it would most likely be at the small bays and inlets along the Roscal colony's northern and southern shores.

And *Falconet* could not be everywhere, not even where she might be needed.

Not until Clemenger could find his patterns.

Chapter 13

Dawlish loathed the white and gold-trimmed official governor's uniform, the ludicrous swan-feather bedecked helmet most of all. Today, long hours of enduring it still stretched ahead. Florence had just unveiled a plaque on the reconstructed crossing of the gully west of Saint Gérons that identified it as 'Scipio Bridge'. Dawlish had rejected d'Erlanger's proposal that it be named after himself but it made little difference, because it was him the crowd was cheering now. He half-recognised faces among them, some seen during the evacuation, others glimpsed during the construction of the camps or on that terrible night when the mob had attacked at Thénac. He might not know their names, but they knew his, and now they were cheering him as a saviour.

Others were lining the track to Saint Gérons, some waving green branches, all cheering, pressing close as the governor's landau passed. Florence – holding up Jessica, and encouraging her to wave back – sat with Dawlish in the rear and d'Erlanger, with Ted, sat facing them. Dawlish felt foolish and uncomfortable, forcing a smile and raising his hand in acknowledgement of the cheers. Nudges from Florence told him at intervals to do so with more enthusiasm. She herself was smiling and flushed with pleasure as she waved. Many of the onlookers were falling into a line behind the carriage, a cheerful, jostling throng following it towards the celebration in the town.

The crowd was denser as the landau moved along the harbour front. The buildings' walls were still dusted with grey but the roofs and streets had been cleared. No smoke drifted from the mountain slopes above and life, boisterous life, had returned. *Falconet*, moored in the centre of the bay, fired five blanks from her three-pounder and the crowd cheered.

Past the police station, the bank, the customs office, all remembered as once bathed in flickering crimson, and on past d'Erlanger's lime-press yard, now decked with bunting. d'Erlanger had pressed Dawlish to be here to celebrate Saint Gérons' resurrection but he had not prepared him for the extent to which gratitude would be focussed on him. Into the central square now, where the bells of the Catholic and Anglican churches there clanging in competition, only falling into silence when a choir, conducted by the Reverend Elijah Gagneux, launched into a hymn.

Across then to the scaffolding platform bedecked with Union flags and green foliage, a lectern at the front, a row of chairs behind. More cheering when Dawlish and his party mounted, silence again as Gagneux began an extended prayer that was punctuated by the crowd's 'amens'. Florence beamed when children came up to give her flowers and her lifting and kissing of the smallest brought roars of approval.

And then the endless speeches, beginning with d'Erlanger, followed by various worthies. Dawlish was touched as more humble speakers of patois followed them. They recalled incidents of their own deliverance as if he had been personally responsible for each. A woman in a bright head-tie pressed forward, holding up a baby, old enough to be bewildered by what was happening around him. He had been called Scipio, she said, for he had been born on the vessel's deck. Dawlish, embarrassed by the mother's flood of thanks, was moved close to tears.

He sat sweat-soaked for over an hour before it was his turn to speak. He had intended to say little more than emphasise that it was the warships' seamen, not himself, who deserved the credit, but the sight of the sea of upturned faces inspired him. It was they who had endured, who deserved this moment. He told them that in unrehearsed words that many could neither hear nor understand. He recalled men burrowing beneath rubble despite the lava flood's threat, digging the camps' ditches and latrines, building their huts. Women had sustained families through the ordeal, had cared for sick and weak other than their own, had organised makeshift schools, had created communities, had returned here in triumph. He ended by calling for three cheers for d'Erlanger, and three more for themselves, three more for Roscal itself and yet three more for Her Majesty. He sat down, felt Florence pressing his hand, and he was glad that he was here.

Renunciation of *Scipio's* command had been worthwhile.

Then Gagneux's closing prayer. The crowd dispersed, heading for the dozen locations where d'Erlanger had pigs roasting for sharing.

For Dawlish it was the opportunity to change out of the ridiculous uniform and into normal clothing for the return to Escource in *Falconet*. Back to budgets and accounts, to perusal of reports, to cajole support for expansion of lime production, to write again to contest the Colonial Office's refusal to consider reduction of the Poll Tax.

All burdens, but welcome when he remembered the sea of faces.

*

They were in the saloon of d'Erlanger's Saint Gérons house, enjoying the cool before departure. The sounds of celebrations were washing through the open windows. A servant entered, whispered to d'Erlanger.

"Ask the gentleman to wait in my study," he told the man. Then he said to Dawlish, "Your secretary's here. He says it's urgent."

Blackford, in riding clothes, had pounded from Escource with a message.

"There's a bad business, a riot, at Ganthier," he said. "The word came in two hours ago. From one of the village constables. Fleeing for his life, he said."

Dawlish's mind was racing. He had been there a week before. It was almost in the direct centre of the colony, a dusty, impoverished village surrounded by mostly abandoned sugar plantations. Florence had visited it too, had told him of the despair there.

"How bad is it?" Dawlish said.

"The women seem to have started it. They tried to drive off three officials – a collector and two clerks – who'd come from Escource to revise the list of who's liable for paying Poll Tax. It got out of hand and then many of the men joined in. They're holding the visitors hostage. And –" Blackford hesitated.

"There's worse?"

"There may be. There was a second constable. The last his friend saw of him was that he was being beaten. Very badly."

"Does Clemenger know?" Dawlish said.

"It was from him that I got the report. He set out at once for Ganthier with about a dozen men. He's probably there by now. He thinks it would help if you joined him."

It could not be more than six miles away by road. A half-hour's ride. Florence would return to Escource in *Falconet,* as planned.

"Ask Mr. d'Erlanger to join me."

Dawlish needed time to suppress the fear rising in him. An incident like this could spread, get out of control on a larger scale. Reaction must be measured, must not be such as to inflame further unrest. He could trust Clemenger's pragmatism for that until he could be there himself.

But that second constable. Murder might already have been done, and then . . .

d'Erlanger appeared.

"Can you mount me?" Dawlish did not try to explain. "Two horses. Mr. Blackford's must be blown."

"Hippolyte will see to it. I'll lend you boots."

Another thought struck Dawlish.

"Would you have the Reverend Elijah found? Good! Please ask him to join me at Ganthier. It might be a matter of life and death. Have you something light like a dog cart for bringing him?"

d'Erlanger could arrange it. He asked no questions and disappeared. A friend indeed.

Ten minutes later Darwish was drumming across Scipio Bridge on Bayard, the strong grey gelding he had borrowed during his first visit to the island. Blackford kept pace alongside.

The sun cast longer and longer shadows before them as they pounded eastwards.

It would be dark soon.

And that might make the situation more dangerous still.

*

If there had indeed been a riot in Ganthier, it was over now. Small groups of men and women were standing outside their shacks in the soft moonlight. There was a sense of resentment about them, of fear too perhaps, but no overt hostility. They drew back inside their homes as Dawlish and Blackford trotted past. A little further on a single figure was standing in the middle of the track and waving a lantern to halt them. It was one of Clemenger's Rural Guards, a black man, powerfully built, as they all were. He had fixed his bayonet on his Snider but he seemed in no fear of the few villagers hovering in the shadows.

"Major Clemenger? Where is he?"

"Up there, sir. At the school." He pointed towards the village centre. "It's quiet now, but be careful, sir."

The smell of lingering smoke as they rode on, then the charred remains, flames long extinguished, of what Dawlish recognised had been the two-room police station. His heart sunk. The three wretched officials must have had been surrounded there.

A low hubbub of voices ahead now. A corner tuned and there was a small crowd, blocking the track, shuffling, uncertain whether to move forward or draw back. Dawlish remembered that there was a two-room schoolhouse there and a small church, some local sect's.

It was good that he was not armed, he thought. However violent these people's earlier fury might have been, it must be spent by now and cooler heads among them might even be counselling restraint. It would be better to press on, he decided, to approach them with no outward sign of fear or anger.

"Follow close behind me, Mr. Blackford." He slowed his mount to a walk.

Faces were turning to him now and he sensed that some recognised him. Two men, bolder than the others, came to meet him. They looked prosperous by local standards, small traders perhaps, not field hands. And, like himself, unarmed.

He drew rein, forced a smile. "Bonsoi, mes amis. Je suis le gouverneur." He saw that they. recognised him. He leaned down and extended his hand.

One took it and said, voice trembling, "Bienvenue, Monsieur le Gouverneur," but the other hung back.

"Je suis désolé d'apprendre qu'il y a des problèmes ici," Dawlish was sorry to learn of trouble here. He could see others detaching themselves from the crowd and heading towards him.

"Une tragédie, monsieur, lamentablement," the man was shaking his head. He looked frightened.

More were crowding around now, desperation on many of their faces, some hostility too. But most of all, too-late realisation of the enormity of what had been unleashed and fear that retribution was inevitable and might perhaps be indiscriminate. No sign of machetes or clubs. These people had no desire to worsen an already bad situation. There must be long memories here of savage official reckonings.

"Y a-t-il eu des morts?" Dawlish hesitated before asking if there were deaths, dreaded the answer.

Two dead, the man had heard. He knew nothing more.

If he did know, had perhaps even seen the killings, he wasn't going to admit it, Dawlish thought. Others too would already be distancing themselves from the murders.

He shook his head, kept his voice calm. "Hélas, hélas. Mais retournez chez vous maintenant. Ce sera mieux de cette façon."

Most didn't seem to understand his formal French but the first man repeated the message in patois. That it was better to go home now. A few mumbled thanks, began to move away. From the crowd's outer fringe somebody called "Ennemi des pauvres!" but others close by hushed him and Dawlish pretended not to hear.

He urged his horse forward at a slow walk, did not look back and assumed that Blackford was following. The crowd opened before him and he heard the whisper going from mouth to mouth, "C'est le gouverneur."

He was through the thinning crowd now and could see the school and the church. A few lanterns winked there as men moved back and forth across them. Light glinted for an instant on a bayonet. Clemenger's people were there. A figure was coming towards him, leaning on a cane and unmistakable by his limping gait as the major himself. They met. No time for courtesies.

"Serious, I understand," Dawlish said. "Two dead, I've heard."

"Three now. A woman died a half-hour since." Clemenger paused before he said. "Gunshot. One of my men. Bloody unnecessary."

"And the others?"

"A clerk from Escource, here about the Poll Tax register. A poor fool, by the sounds of it. If he hadn't tried to make a break for it, he'd probably be alive now. But they caught him and some hothead stove his skull in. And one of the village constables too. He had it worse."

"What's happening now?"

"A half-dozen villagers – two of 'em women – have barricaded the school. They're holding the collector and the other clerk and threatening to cut their throats if they're not let go free. They probably know that that's impossible but they won't want to admit it to themselves yet. I've had the place surrounded and there's no sign of anybody hoping to rescue them. It's quiet otherwise."

Dawlish dismounted and handed his reins to Blackford. "I'll go forward on foot. Follow me." To Clemenger he said, "The Reverend Elijah is on his way here. Send two men up the track to meet him."

Now the full story. Avoidable, like so many tragedies, had the initial response been more measured.

The officials' visit had been announced days earlier, with all adult males ordered to come for registration. A collector and his clerks, all black Roscallans, had arrived from Escource that morning. They had sat with their lists and ledgers at a table under an awning outside the police-station, the constables herding all who turned up into a straggling line before them. The recording process had been slow – as slow as might satisfy the self-importance of any petty bureaucrat anywhere, Dawlish suspected. Tempers had frayed among those gathered without shade as the day's heat grew. Yet slow as it had gone, the last of the men who had presented themselves had been confirmed on the list by eleven o'clock.

"Over half of those on the previous list didn't turn up," Clemenger said. "The constables were sent to find them and bring 'em for registration. They couldn't, for the bloody good reason that most of the missing men had gone to Panama and not a few had died there on the canal digging. A few still here were damned if they were going to be registered and so they hid."

"And it angered the wives?" Dawlish found it easy to imagine women who were raising children on the edge of destitution resenting a search.

"Some woman, probably one of them inside the school now, gathered a group to come down to the station to protest. It seems to have been restrained at first. Then others came to join them, men also, and somebody threw a stone."

Then the inevitable. A constable grabbing a suspect and cudgelling him, a woman intervening, then struck down. General fury unleashed, the officials jostled and the wooden police building set ablaze. One constable – already unpopular apparently for his molesting of a recent widow – beaten to death while the other made his escape. Several who had come to protest, women as well as men, tried to protect the officials but one of the clerks broke free to follow the fleeing constable. He too was set upon and had his head beaten in.

"The killings sobered the mob," Clemenger said. "They knew they'd gone too far. Then some fool proposed holding the collector and surviving clerk as hostages. The school seemed a good place. A crowd was still gathered outside it when I arrived. Half of 'em dispersed at the sight of my men. The remainder stood their ground. I held my people back and went forward under a white flag."

Unwise, Dawlish thought. Clemenger should have waited for him. White flag or not, he represented armed force, threatened instant lethal response. Terrified people acted irrationally and often violently.

Clemenger must recognise that himself now, for his usual confidence seemed shaken as he continued.

"A man was coming out to meet me. He had his hand out to take mine. Then somebody threw a stone from the crowd. It struck me on the shoulder and –"

"One of your people lost his head?"

"My sergeant. He ordered a volley over the crowd's head. A bloody stupid decision. The chap who'd come to meet me turned and ran. One of my guards, I don't know who, fired too low and hit a woman. The crowd scattered. Only the few diehards retreated into the school."

"Where they're threatening to cut the throats of the collector and the clerk?"

Clemenger nodded in misery. He knew that his force had failed at its first test. "We did what we could for the woman," he said. "But it was in the head. It was hopeless."

"Where's the body?"

"Her neighbours came and asked for it. I thought it better to let them have it. They took it away."

"I trust the school's surrounded?"

"Nobody can get out. And, and I think –" Clemenger hesitated, as if afraid of optimism. "I think the hostages aren't in immediate danger. The murders at the police station were in the heat of the moment. There'll be no killing in cold blood now."

But the situation was still bad, pregnant with the potential for worse, not just in this wretched village, but elsewhere too when the news spread. The danger was not just at the school but in the whole community where anger and fear were even now festering.

"We'll do nothing more at the school until Elijah's here," Dawlish said. "He'll be our intermediary. But we can't risk another mob gathering."

An idea struck him. Wild perhaps, a gamble indeed. But if it succeeded then . . .

"Have you made arrests, major?"

"About twenty when the crowd broke and ran. They're locked in the church."

"Release them."

"Release them?" Incredulity in Clemenger's voice.

"They've been disarmed, haven't they?" The weapons would have been crude but deadly, probably cudgels and machetes. Nobody could afford firearms here. "Release them. Tell 'em there'll be no charge."

Clemenger hesitated, was then forcing himself against the discipline of a lifetime to challenge an order. "It wouldn't be wise, sir. If it goes badly then …" His voice trailed off.

Dawlish ignored the insubordination. He didn't want to tell the major that he did not yet trust all the members of Rural Guard. However well Clemenger had trained them, iron disciple could not yet be assumed. And subordinates eager to please superiors in circumstances like the present seldom hesitated to beat false confessions from innocent men. It was not uncommon even in British police stations.

And another measure might prove of value to reduce the tension.

"Where's the dead woman?" Dawlish said. "Could somebody bring me there? Not one of your people, major. Somebody who's been arrested. Preferably a woman."

"There might be someone in the church." The major didn't sound convinced but he wasn't going to argue.

"Bring me there then."

On the way he remembered that Florence had been to the school. The schoolteacher – the only one – had impressed her. He ransacked his memory for the name she had mentioned. It came to him.

"If a Madame Geneviève's been arrested, I want to see her."

She had been. When she was brought to him, he saw a large middle-aged black woman, her clothing dishevelled but of good quality by local standards. In other circumstances she would probably be jolly-looking. Now she looked defiant and with an air of indomitability. He introduced himself, addressed her politely as 'Madame'.

"I know who you are, Monsieur le Gouverneur. I saw you when you came here before. You didn't visit my school."

"But my wife did," he said. "She told me about it. Your name too, and that you did good work." He paused. "Hard though it is for you."

"What do you want of me?" Clear French, not patois.

He told her. She was as doubtful as Clemenger was about it, and said that it would be unwise, dangerous for him.

"And the other prisoners, monsieur? What do you want of them?"

"Only that they go home quietly. I'm ordering them released."

"Will they come before the court afterwards?"

"No, madame. Only those holding hostages in your school and threatening them with death. And threatening themselves also with death if they don't give those hostages up unharmed."

He looked to Clemenger and nodded. The instruction clear.

Release the prisoners in the church.

Madame Geneviève stood by him as they filed past, relief and bewilderment on their faces. He did not want to know what they had done, or not done There was more than that at stake now. She greeted some of them, reassured them that they were free, had nothing to fear.

When the last had trudged away he said to her, "Will you take me to the dead woman now, madame? Myself alone. You can see that I'm unarmed, no danger to anybody."

"But it'll be a danger to you, monsieur."

"I know. But I'm trusting you, madame. And all the village too. This gentleman," he gestured to Clemenger, "is ordering his guards not to follow us."

And so they went together, away from the lanterns and guards, away from assured safety, into the moonlit village, through narrow alleys with dark shadows and faces at open doorways that drew back as they passed.

His stomach was knotted, his mouth dry, and blood pounded in his head. He had seldom felt more frightened.

Chapter 14

It was bad, most of all in the first minute, as he pushed his way through a sullen crowd outside the shack where the dead woman lay. They offered no violence, but he could feel their anger, their resentment that had accumulated over two centuries of servitude, their bitterness about of the sham freedom brought by emancipation. Madame Geneviève opened a way before him, repeating "C'est le gouverneur," and answering queries in unintelligible patois. He saw, as he had hoped, that she was respected here, that her words had weight. But that they let him through was perhaps as much due to surprise that he was here, unarmed, unescorted, as to her reassurances.

Then into the candle-lit misery inside the cabin. A memory flashed of living in disguise in such a place himself, among such people, in Cuba, six years before, a reminder that they had not been stupid, had dignity and feelings, for all their poverty. Here now he saw a half-dozen adults, two generations, standing around a bed, one cradling a baby, two others holding sobbing children. The body had been laid out with dignity but blood had soaked through a cloth that covered the head. Dawlish feared that someone would strip it away, confront him with the full horror of the tragedy. The bare calloused feet protruding from beneath the tattered skirt-hem and the hands folded on the breast – a grey pallor already dulling their dark skin – were testimony enough of a life already brutally hard and now even more brutally cut off.

A man, grey-haired, skeleton-thin, old before his time, stepped forward, shouting, fist clenched. Dawlish tensed himself to receive a blow but he held his ground and hoped he would have the courage not to flinch or strike back. Madame Geneviève thrust herself ahead of him, spoke volubly and pointed back at him. That Monsieur le Gouverneur had come in regret, with sympathy, that he had not wanted this. A woman, perhaps a sister, rushed forward, shrieking accusations, reaching out to tear at Dawlish's face but the teacher blocked her, embraced her, somehow calmed her. And the man's belligerence was dying in hopeless recognition of his impotence in the face of authority, of the enormity of potential retribution.

Sudden pity impelled Dawlish to push past the two women and reach for the man's hand.

His words came involuntarily.

"Je suis désolé."

English could not have expressed it as powerfully. That he felt the loss as a fellow man, that differences of race or station meant nothing at this moment.

"C'était ma soeur. Ma plus jeune soeur," the man had taken Dawlish's hand. "Quatre enfants, et son mari morts au Panama." He was beginning to weep now.

My own tears too would be as despairing as these were this my sister. And four children, motherless, already robbed of their father by the canal diggings.

The murmuring in the crowd pressing in from outside slackened, died. Dawlish asked the woman's name.

Gilberte. Gilberte Thomonde.

No longer just a number, not just one of three dead. A person.

"Are these her children?"

They were. The youngest was two. Jessica was this age also and had experienced, unknowingly, the same tragic loss as this innocent.

Dawlish advanced to the bed, stood before it, head bowed, was lost in the silence broken only by the disconsolate children. The full burden of his office was heavy on him at this moment, heavier even than he had ever felt as captain of a ship. These people deserved all, and more, than he could do for them.

But first, resolve this night's crisis.

He made no speech – he could think of no words – but he touched the hand of each mourner lightly and met their eyes, then turned away. Madame Geneviève followed. The crowd outside parted, let them through.

And at the church he saw a dark face illuminated by a lantern held high by Clemenger.

The Reverend Elijah had arrived.

*

Dawn was breaking when two machetes and three knives were cast out from inside the school door. They fell in front of the preacher and the schoolmistress who had stood there for some five hours, pleading, cajoling, reasoning. Dawlish had decided that they alone should negotiate for him – the Reverend Elijah had been willing from the first but Madame Geneviève took more convincing. He himself had stayed well back in the shadows with Clemenger but specified the message to be conveyed to the hostage takers. It was uncompromising, a guarantee of fair trial but a reminder that murder of a hostage would result in a capital charge for all within the school.

Two hours had passed before the door opened and a single woman, pregnant, was allowed to leave, though nobody else showed themselves. Madame Geneviève met her, helped her to a nearby hut, listened to her story and then reported back to Dawlish. She had been caught up in the tumult, she claimed, had had no part in it, had pleaded with her captors to be let go free. There were four of them, she said, three older men and one just a boy. They were as frightened as the unharmed hostages. None of them were bad men, she said, none had participated in the killings at the police station. There was another woman there too, wife of a hostage taker and she had already pleaded with him to surrender.

The slow negotiations continued, the reverend and the schoolteacher taking it in turns to speak through a barricaded window. Listening from a distance, Dawlish could barely understand the patois, but could sense progress. His visit to the dead woman's family had impressed Madame Geneviève. He was *un homme de pitié, pas cruel*, she said, and could be trusted.

A full hour was occupied by answering fears that justice would be instant and merciless when the first captor would emerge with hands upraised. No, the Reverend Elijah said, le gouverneur was *un homme juste*, had given him his word that there would be a fair trial, but that even he could not save a cold-blooded murderer from the gallows. There was still time to avert that. And he reminded them, as he had through the night, that the collector and clerk being held were men like themselves, men with families, that they too were victims of the Poll Tax. This last, Dawlish had not authorised him to say but there was truth in it nonetheless.

And so, with sunrise, the door opened and the weapons were thrown out. Dawlish turned away, unwilling to see the faces of either hostages or captors.

"You see to them, major," he said to Clemenger. "You'll know who to arrest, what statements to be taken. And no ill treatment."

There would be a trial but a guilty verdict was inevitable. And he, as governor, must confirm the sentence and decide if there were grounds for partial remission. That power he had, for all sentences less than capital. When the necessary papers would come before him for signature, he did not want to remember those now emerging from the hut as individuals. Captors and hostages alike were victims. But justice must still to be done.

Time to remount and return to Escource.

The village he left behind was quiet with the calm of exhaustion. It could all have been much worse.

But a warning that he could not ignore

*

While riding back with Blackford to Escource Dawlish instructed him to call a meeting of the Advisory Council for that afternoon. The timing would allow d'Erlanger to ride down from Saint Gérons and a messenger was to be sent to alert him.

Ted came racing down the front steps when Dawlish dismounted at Government House. The boy threw his arms around his waist, buried his head against him.

"I'm glad you're back, Nicholas. I'm glad you're safe. Florence said you would be, no matter what."

My summons away must have frightened him. He's still a child, still innocent of the ways and evils of the world. And in five years, should he follow me into the navy, he may confront much worse. And he'll cope, won't break, will be a man before his time.

Dawlish laid his arm on his shoulder. "You've been looking after Florence and Jessica, have you, Ted? I knew I could rely on you for it." He could feel the boy's pride.

Florence joined them, Jessica in her arms and relief on her face. She was eager for details, was distressed when she heard them. She remembered Madame Geneviève from her visit to Ganthier, was not surprised by the role that she had played through the night.

"The worst of it is that things like this are inevitable, Nick," she said. "I've seen it. People are desperate. The men in Panama, the women trying to feed families from little vegetable plots. And the Poll Tax casting a shadow on them all."

"It's not being collected yet, Florence. It was just a revision of the tax register that sparked it all. Just a revision of the list." He knew that his words were hollow.

He was satisfied that, for now, Clemenger had the situation in hand in Ganthier. Several of his men would be sifting through the ashes of police station to find the remains of the murdered men. They must have decent funerals – they had died in the line of duty – and he would have to be present. And later today Clemenger would bring the prisoners back to Escource to be charged. It worried Dawlish that their trial, and sentences, might prove the trigger for further unrest.

It was time now to wash, snatch a breakfast, then lie down to sleep for two hours so as to think clearly afterwards before meeting the council. Jessica sat happily on his knee as he ate, laughing, melting his heart when she pulled his beard and he feigned surprise. Florence had stood up, had walked to the French window, was looking down in silence towards the town. Minutes passed before she turned to face him

"Nicholas."

"Yes, Florence."

He recognised the same quiet determination in her voice that he had first heard when she had decided to risk death, and worse, in Thrace to bring Bulgarian refugees to safety. He loved her for it.

"I'm going to Ganthier myself today," she said. "No – don't try to stop me, Nick. I'll visit the family of that woman who was shot. They've seen you, but you were an official. When they see me, they'll know we care. Not just me, but you too. That we'll do our best for them."

There was compassion in the suggestion, but logic and cold pragmatism too. He had always respected her for that combination.

"It could be dangerous, Florence." Even as he spoke, he knew that his words were futile, that her mind was made up.

She shook her head. "They're not that sort of people."

"You're not bringing Jessica, are you?"

"I'm bringing Jessica. And Ted too. I'll do him good to see poverty. He was very sheltered in Shrewsbury."

"I insist you'll take an escort."

"Not even Hippolyte, Nick, but I'll bring Veronique to look after Jessica. I'll take the dog cart and drive myself. I know the way to Ganthier. When I get there, I'll find Madame Geneviève. She'll help me. And the Roscal Relief Fund can cover the funeral expenses. A coffin at the least. It won't be government money."

The riot and its aftermath had haunted him on the ride back, so too the possibility of such disquiet spreading. If it did, suppression might be impossible with the forces he had available and, even if successful, would probably inflame resentment further. Florence had seen that too, was prepared, as always, to share his burden. What she proposed now could only help allay distrust.

And there would be no danger to herself or to the children.

Almost none.

When he rose from his brief rest, she was already long gone.

*

Sleep had brought no comfort, only an awareness on awakening that little he could do in in the coming months could alter the conditions breeding despair in Roscal. There was some hope for betterment, but he would be long gone by the time it might yield success. This was a long campaign, not a single battle. He must resign himself to that.

But a career administrator from the Colonial Office could deal with all this better than he could. He was here only because he fitted to face a threat that might never manifest itself.

The French.

*

Dawlish did not share his pessimism with the council. All other members, including d'Erlanger, had answered the summons. They were already aware, mainly through exaggerated rumours, of the events at Ganthier. Dawlish summarised what he had seen and done there, what Clemenger was still doing. They listened in silence and he sensed, from all except d'Erlanger, resentment against himself no less than fear. When he finished, he asked for questions.

"Why did you order the rioters released?" The councillor was a lawyer, Marsac. "There must have been murderers among them."

"And if they killed before, they won't hesitate to kill again." Verley, a planter, speaking. "It'll be the start of anarchy."

Dawlish had agonised whether the decision had been correct ever since taking it. And always he had come back to the conclusion that his rationale was sound.

"We could never have identified the real guilty parties," he said. "Terrified people – and they all terrified by then – would lie, would accuse each other to save themselves. On that sort of evidence, whoever we'd charge might well be innocent. Everybody in the village would know that and we'd have made martyrs. And the word would spread across the colony. There's discontent enough already. And damn good cause for it too, given the poverty. As it was, nobody else died."

"So nobody will pay for it?" The lawyer again.

"The hostage-takers will if they're found guilty."

"There won't be a capital charge, though. Just something worth eight or ten years' hard labour. What we need is a hanging or two to serve notice that we won't tolerate anarchy. It's all these people understand."

"These people?" Dawlish felt his anger rising, knew that he should quell it, but said anyway, "How long has your family been in Roscal?"

"Two hundred years."

"So might they be perhaps your people too by now?" The words slipped out, were instantly regretted.

The lawyer flushed, stood up, shaking, and stalked towards the door. The planter, Verley, was rising to follow him.

And I've made a fool of myself. This isn't a ship. These men aren't under my command, but I need them with me.

"Gentlemen!" d'Erlanger saved him. "I think there may have been a misunderstanding. We're all here for the same purpose. For the good of Roscal. The situation's serious. We need to hear His Excellency out and I've no doubt that he'll value our advice."

The two councillors had turned, were hovering by the door. The only course was one unimaginable in the navy, one that went against some thirty years immersion in unquestioning obedience, either from himself or from those he commanded

Dawlish stood up, moved towards the two men, held out his hand, forced himself to say, "I spoke too hastily. I apologise for any offence given. And Mr. d'Erlanger's correct. I need your advice."

Hesitation, then the lawyer taking his hand. "It's what we hope for, sir." He nodded to the planter, who reached out his hand too.

No warmth in either shake, no forgiveness in the eyes. But they returned to the table.

Have I weakened myself through apology?

d'Erlanger saved him again.

"With respect, Your Excellency, important as these matters are, there's one of special urgency. The burial of the victims of the riot."

A lifeline. Dawlish grabbed it.

"Both killed during exercise of their duties," he said. "They merit official funerals." And another idea struck him. He looked to the councillor who had remained sitting in silence throughout. Chevit, another planter, old, white-haired and unsmiling, a sense about him of self-importance masquerading as dignity.

"You're Colonel of the Militia, Councillor Chevit. You must have experience of such events. If the Militia were to render full honours . . ."

And the old man was nodding as Dawlish continued.

The Militia had once been a feared tool of the planter class. In the immediate aftermath of Emancipation, successive governors had called it out to repress the first signs of disaffection. Now it was little better than a drinking club for some two-dozen middle-aged and elderly planters and merchants, supported by twice that number of their employees. They turned out on ceremonial occasions in antiquated and shabby though ornate uniforms, the men carrying old Brunswick Pattern '36 rifles, the officers, swords. They had formed a guard of honour for Dawlish when he had arrived, and had bumbled through the simplest foot-drill. It had been hard to inspect them without a smile.

"Might you take charge of the funeral arrangements, Councillor – no, I should say Colonel – Chevit? Good. My secretary, Mr Blackford, to assist you as best he can. And I'll be present on the day of course."

Dawlish felt sudden guilt for his initial too-easy evaluation of the old man. Pompous, even ridiculous, Chevit might be, but he deserved respect. Clemenger's sources had discovered that the Soulier twins had approached him on the night of the attack on the refugee camp at Thénac and had demanded the militia's arms. The weapons would be returned by morning and nobody would know of it. Chevit had refused to hand over the armoury keys and his standing in the community precluded taking them by force.

And yet, out of loyalty to his class, he had never reported the incident to Dawlish.

"The dead men's families, Your Excellency?" d'Erlanger was speaking. "Pensions perhaps?"

They discussed it for five minutes, then agreed. Gratuities of ten pounds and pensions of one third of the salaries at death until the youngest children reached fourteen, the widows to receive one fifth thereafter.

"A wise decision." Marsac, the lawyer, was pleased that Dawlish had conceded that the initial proposal he had made was too high. "A generous settlement, especially with the Poll Tax yielding so little."

"Aah," said Dawlish. "The Poll Tax." He paused as if pondering whether to say more, then said. "Anything we say here, gentlemen, is confidential. I can trust you all for that."

Nods of agreement.

"Two items you should know. First that I'm ordering suspension – not cancellation, mind you – of Poll Tax registration for the time being."

More nods. The riot at Ganthier must have scared these men more than they admitted. They were in no doubt of what had triggered it and knew that the same could happen anywhere in Roscal.

"And my second point. I've written to the Colonial Office to suggest outright abolition of the tax."

"That's impossible, they'll never consent," Marsac said. "It's a tiny contribution to our revenues but we need every penny. They'll be damned before they increase the present grant."

That grant from London had been instituted a decade before in the aftermath of a hurricane that had wreaked havoc on Roscal. It had been intended to be temporary but, perhaps due to the inattention of some Whitehall bureaucrat, it had been renewed annually ever since.

"Let's wait for the reply," Dawlish said. "Even if it's a refusal I'll continue to press for it. I trust I'll have your support, gentlemen?"

Unanimous agreement.

I'll have an ally in Topcliffe, though I can't admit that here. He can't afford not to press for it, not with the threat he fears for Guimbi.

The atmosphere relaxed, however slightly.

"I've some news that might be of interest," d'Erlanger said, just before the meeting ended. "Perhaps of economic benefit, perhaps to help the general population. But perhaps just a vain hope."

"Perhaps that the European sugar-beet crop has failed?" Dawlish said, and they all laughed.

"Not that. But I've been in correspondence with a professor at Oxford University, a botanist and agronomist, highly thought of. He's had success with higher-yielding crop strains in West Africa, yams and the like. He's willing to send an assistant to conduct trials here if they can be provided with growing plots. I've agreed. If anybody else wants to do likewise then we can share the results, perhaps maybe join in propagating successful strains also."

Agatha's invitation to Professor Moncton to that dinner was paying dividends. It was a good note to end on.

And they day closed on a better still.

Florence was back safely from Ganthier, had been well received.

"Thar poor lady's burial's is to be tomorrow," she said. "Elijah's conducting their service. And I said you'd be there with me, Nick. You will be, won't you?"

He would.

It was cold pragmatism that demanded it, he told himself.

Chapter 15

The next three months proved busy but peaceful. The suspension of the Poll Tax registration, though not announced publicly, removed one source of unrest. Dawlish had found that the slowness of written communication with London could work to his advantage. Convoluted arguments that he sent for abolition of the tax elicited equally convoluted refutations that arrived a month later. He seized on some points in the answer, countered them and sent anther long screed back. In the meantime, no tax was collected. There was no need yet to call on Topcliffe's support. He found himself enjoying the process of bureaucratic delay and hoped he could maintain it indefinitely.

Florence was spending the Relief Fund's donation effectively and was tireless in inspecting the progress of her initiatives. The two Motherless Babies' Homes were open now and three one-room schools had been built in outlying villages. Madame Geneviève had found literate women whom she was now training as teachers. An English midwife had arrived, a Miss Giltrap, a grim but dedicated spinster of fifty, recruited through a missionary society. Allocated a donkey and cart for travelling about, she did not hesitate to sleep nights in the cabins of local families when she came to teach or intervene actively at births. Her presence had already saved several lives, Florence claimed.

A young protégée of Professor Moncton had arrived and was resident with d'Erlanger, who had taken to him. Trial seedling plots were established and, at Florence's suggestions, four were set up in villages elsewhere, providing some employment. To Dawlish's surprise, Councillor Verley had welcomed trial plots at his plantation also.

The trial of the Ganthier hostage-takers had provoked no protests, not least because the collector whom they had held hostage spoke up on their behalf and claimed that he never believed they would have killed him. Dawlish found the man's generosity of spirit inspirational. Only two men were convicted and their five-year sentences were light in comparison with what might have been.

Clemenger was not just forging the Rural Guard into an effective force, but building an intelligence network that gathered information from chance remarks, overheard comments, vague rumours and, most valuable of all, informers who were paid a monthly pittance. Little in itself was valuable or concrete but in aggregate, sifted, weighed, linkages found, it helped identify the currents underlying the apparent calm. A single incident could still unleash a storm.

"How active are the Soulier twins?" Dawlish asked Clemenger. He'd seen nothing of either since his arrival but memory of the attack on the Thénac camp still angered him. They were dangerous and malignant men.

"One of Armand Soulier's house servants is proving a good source," Clemenger said. "Soulier raped his daughter a few years ago – people like her father are expected to tolerate such things. Soulier paid some money to keep it quiet but the father still resents it even though he bows and scrapes as his work demands. He's been hungering to get even."

"So, what's he reporting?"

"Regular meetings with a few of the other planters. You'd recognise the names. Most were implicated in that Thénac riot and were acquitted afterwards. They're not happy that you're here, less happy still that many of their friends are starting to warm to you. And there's the usual talk about influences from Guimbi fuelling resentment here. At present, it's little more than an excuse to get drunk together and frighten each other with the prospect of uprisings and massacres. But they're worth watching."

Falconet had brought Dawlish for a single visit to Port Mazarin to meet President Ravenel again and to suggest cooperation wherever possible. The exchanges had been formal and polite but Ravenel looked five years older than when last seen. Maître Badeaux had suggested a separate meeting in his office. Guimbi's financial situation was the worst it had ever been, he told Dawlish. The French bankers had run out of patience and had refused further credit. The situation was desperate and he saw no way out of it. Dawlish reported as much to Topcliffe by enciphered telegrams sent through Antigua. The answers advised him only to hold course – and be alert.

But all still went well, or well enough, on Roscal.

Clemenger reported that Dawlish was apparently warmly thought of by the wider population – no previous governor had been seen so often outside Escource. Florence's good works were achieving respect out of all proportion to their scale. Many from the old planter families were viewing him more favourably. Other than a small coterie grouped around the Soulier twins, none of them ignored invitations to modest receptions in Government House.

It seemed too good to last.

And it didn't.

*

It was just before midday.

Dawlish was sitting alone at his deck, working through correspondence, looking out at intervals through the open French windows. The town far below looked pristine from here and the blue sea beyond extended rippleless to the horizon. Unexpected rain the day before had spurred growth and a slight zephyr was carrying in the sound of noonday insect chatter and a scent of bougainvillea in from the gardens. Work did not seem onerous at this moment.

A knock, then Blackford entered.

"It's urgent, for your eyes only, sir. A guard's just arrived with it from Orvault. He must have galloped all the way because –"

Dawlish wasn't listening, had recognised Clemenger's handwriting on the wax-sealed envelope. He tore it open and scanned the contents.

The major had written from the small village in the foothills of the mountain barrier that separated Roscal and Guimbi. He had been inspecting the garrison of the Rural Guard post there, by now well established.

It might be nothing, he wrote, but an informant had come forward, hoping for a reward. He had sworn that he had heard of unknown buyers paying abnormally high prices for mules in recent weeks. He hadn't been willing to sell his own beast but now he had been offered good money to be at a cove east of Muron, on the north coast, that night. Nothing else known.

It could be anything, or nothing, Clemenger said, but it had the hallmark of smuggling. And that was hard to imagine. Few in Roscal could afford imported luxuries. He suggested that whatever goods involved be allowed to land. The mention of mules indicated significant loads. He proposed an ambush with a Rural Guard force further inland, with only a few men posted at the coast to report any landing. Scanning the letter again Dawlish sensed the major's delight in again deploying skills early-learned and long-employed on India's North-West Frontier.

It was the moment that Dawlish had long anticipated. Concern in London about gunrunning into Guimbi had been a factor in sending him here. Each week he had anticipated some intimation of it in Clemenger's intelligence reports. But there had been none and he had begun to resign himself to his term on Roscal being wholly occupied with internal administration.

His mind was racing. Muron was on the edge of the mountains. A mule train could be lost among them within hours of the goods being landed – most likely rifles and ammunition. And Guimbi had never been more vulnerable. Clemenger's ambush, if successful, would not just scotch that danger but lay hands on whoever – most likely the Souliers – were complicit here in Roscal.

And another possibility, one that would round off the interception perfectly. He pondered it for a full minute. Then, decision made, he dictated a message to be carried back to Clemenger forthwith.

Proceed.

*

Clouds had been gathering ever since the *Falconet* steamed out from Escource soon after sunset. By now the moon was only breaking through at intervals, casting cold light on a lightly agitated sea, then lost again within minutes. The yacht was in darkness, her navigation lights extinguished and speed adjusted so that only the faintest glow shimmered above the funnel. The bosun, Bradbury, was standing by the three-pounder in the bows with Halligan, his loader, and a Roscallan deckhand. A half-dozen lookouts had been posted, one, an ex-Royal Navy seaman high in the on the foremast, equipped with a night glass, and the others on the bridge and superstructure.

Dawlish, on the open bridge with Sproul, *Falconet's* captain, could just make out the great hump of Mont Colbert, five miles distant on the starboard beam. Crawling eastwards, paralleling Roscal's northern coast, the yacht was keeping far enough offshore that any sighting by another vessel might suggest some tramp steamer plodding towards its next port of call. The objective was to intercept any smuggler on its way out, not in. It was best to allow its cargo to be landed and that Clemenger could swoop on it. *Falconet*'s capture of the escaping vessel would complete the job.

"Time to circle, sir?" Sproul asked.

"Dead slow," Dawlish said. "And a racetrack, not a circle."

A half-hour passed. A few bright pinpoints identified fishing hamlets along the coast. Muron must lie off the starboard bow, lost against the dark mass of the mountains beyond. No sign yet of any vessel, but that was no assurance that there was none. Gunrunners were unlikely to advertise their presence with lights and the darkness was almost absolute by now.

Silence reigned on *Falconet*, broken only by the slow swish along her flanks and the low panting of her engine as she steered one long oval after another. Dawlish could sense Sproul's unease – his fingers were tapping on a rail. He repressed his annoyance, felt sorry for the man, felt half-admiring, half-disgusted, by the disgraced lieutenant's eagerness to please. It was hard to imagine this balding, bitter man, aged-before-his-time, ever having attracted a brother officer's wife and leading her to their joint ignominy. This appointment to *Falconet* must be the latest of a series of tasks for Topcliffe which could never earn him public recognition or restoration of the reputation he had squandered. He must be longing even more for success this night than Dawlish did himself.

Two hours passed, four imagined sightings with them. The sun would rise in three hours' time and any self-respecting smuggler would have stood out well to sea by then. In this darkness, a small sailing schooner might even now be crossing *Falconet's* course, undetected, at a little as a mile's distance. A weary acceptance that this might be a fool's errand must be spreading among the crew. If it was, Dawlish tried to console himself, this night would at least have been a useful exercise, confirmation that Sproul had done well to forge British recruits and Roscal fishermen into an effective crew. But disappointing nonetheless, a warning that Clemenger's intelligence network might not be –

"You hear that, sir?" Sproul broke Dawlish's reverie.

He could hear nothing different than before.

"It's gone," Sproul said. "It must just have been my imagination."

But then it came, a remote, very remote, crackling for the shore, unmistakable as rifle-fire. Not as spaced shots but what might have been a rippling volley. Then brief silence, then firing again, irregular now, but sustained.

Clemenger had sprung his ambush.

Silence again, three, four minutes of ear-straining apprehension, then bursts of fire again that lapsed into individual reports.

This was no interception of a train of muleteers falling into panic at the first challenge. Whoever – whatever – Clemenger was facing was as well armed as his own force and was fighting back.

And then a cry out from the foremast lookout, all the more electrifying since he had reported no false sightings this night.

"Deck there! Off the port bow!"

Nothing to be seen from the bridge, no confirmation from the other lookouts. But *Falconet's* bows edged over and –

There it was, a fleeting glimpse when for two seconds a thinner patch in the clouds drifted across the moon and lightened the darkness a fraction. It was an outline only, a solid and irregular silhouette, no detail at this range but the impression of a vessel nonetheless.

And moving fast northwards, lost once more in the darkness.

"Overhaul her," Dawlish said.

The telegraph ringing for full speed, the bows swinging further over to a parallel course, Sproul calling to Bradbury at the three-pounder to stand by for a warning shot.

Darkness again, spasmodic gunfire still crackling from the coast astern. Unspoken fear that this was a mirage, that the increased revolutions were drawing *Falconet* into a stern chase of a will o' the wisp, that the actual smuggler might be slipping out elsewhere.

Now light, brief light, in the darkness again as clouds drifted. There was no doubt now that it was a ship, not a boat or schooner. She was all but dead ahead, view of her foreshortened and her outline obscured by black smoke spilling from a funnel. No sign as yet that she had sighted *Falconet* but she must do so soon, for the glow hovering over the yacht's smokestack was bright orange as she built up to full revolutions.

"We're gaining, sir," Sproul said. "We can't be making much less than fourteen knots now and that's near our limit. Should we challenge?"

"No." It was hard to be confident in these conditions but something about the vessel's lines worried Dawlish. There was a certain familiarity about them and –

The sky cleared again and now she was visible perhaps a mile ahead. She too must be building speed, for her smoke was thinner now and rolling upwards, partly lit by her funnel-glow. Like *Falconet*, she carried no lights. Seen from astern, she looked like a typical tramp, four or five hundred tons perhaps, barquentine-rigged to save coal on long passages, though no sails were set now. Encountered at any other time, properly lit, she would have aroused no suspicion, but she was forging, unlit, into the open sea and away from the coast, not running along it as any innocent trader might.

Five long minutes passed and there was no doubt now the *Falconet* was overtaking. She must have a knot, maybe two, advantage.

"Perhaps a nudge over to port." Dawlish was careful to make it sound like a suggestion rather than an order, though it was. Sproul was captain of this vessel. "And light the navigation lights." He regretted that *Falconet* had no searchlight.

"What separation?"

"A half-cable. And reduce speed to keep her on our beam."

The port and starboard lanterns had been lit and a white was being hoisted up the foremast. Even without them, the other vessel must have sighted the yacht by now but was betraying no sign of it as she forged ahead as a man might who scorned the yaps of a following dog.

Falconet drew further ahead until the stranger was off the starboard bow. Sproul reached for the steam whistle's line, pulled it twice, made two long blasts, the international signal to indicate intention to pass on the other's port side.

No acknowledgement.

And Dawlish had hardly heard it, for his horrified gaze was locked on the profile now more sharply defined against the slightly brighter darkness beyond. The bow had been revealed as *Falconet* drew level and Sproul ordered reduced revolutions to hold her there.

Not the usual clipper bow of a trader.

One sweeping ahead beneath the bowsprit, a curve that carried a ram and raised a wave that climbed up halfway along its length.

A bow design beloved of French naval architects.

He realised now why the vessel had seemed familiar, even at a distance.

This was *Le Déchaîné*, Guimbi's solitary warship.

Impossible to imagine that Ravenel or Badeaux could countenance this. Could it be that a disaffected general had suborned her crew and taken control? Had Ravenel already been deposed, murdered perhaps, the latest of a succession of Guimbian presidents whose tenures had been cut short?

Sproul too must have recognised her for what she was, for he too had seen her at Port Mazarin. There was bewilderment in his voice when he asked, "Hail now?"

Dawlish nodded. He could discern figures on the wing of the bridge ahead of the funnel, looking back and studying *Falconet*. They must have seen her during her visit to Port Mazarin. His brain was racing to identify explanations for their role in the night's gunrunning and –

"What ship?" Sproul bellowed through a speaking trumpet.

No acknowledgement.

"Again," Dawlish said.

And again no response. But the gunvessel's helm was over now and she was shearing away to starboard, presenting her stern to *Falconet* and thereby providing a glimpse of the protruding gun-sponsons. Dawlish remembered the condition he had seen of the pivot-mounted guns they carried when he been on board her. Unless they had been overhauled, *Falconet* had nothing to fear from them, he told himself, and the fact that she was turning away indicated that her captain had no stomach for confrontation. The advantage of resolution to press the issue lay with the armed yacht.

"A shot across her bows is in order, Mr. Sproul."

Orders shouted to Bradbury at the three-pounder, confirmation of a live shell in the breech and readiness to fire. Full revolutions again, speed gathering, arcing over to starboard to follow *Le Déchaîné*. Then pulling further out for a cable's separation, drawing ahead, then revolutions cut back slightly to match speed and hold position off the gunvessel's port bow.

"Your gun, Mr. Bradbury," Sproul called.

A bark, a red stab of flame, a long white plume of spray as the shell dropped and skipped and dropped again, three jumps more before it sank. Then Sproul yelling "Heave to! Heave to!" through the speaking trumpet.

The gunvessel still forged on in disdainful silence, turning away from *Falconet* and opening the separation further.

"Another shot?" Sproul said.

Dawlish nodded but the thought of what he could do next was perplexing. *Falconet* had the speed advantage, could follow *Déchaîné* all night and beyond, could fire repeated warning shots. But the legal and diplomatic implications of opening direct fire on the gunvessel worried him. *Falconet* was outside Roscal's territorial waters and he had no evidence that she had landed anything near Muron.

The three-pounder barked again. Her shell's foaming rip across the water's surface a half-cable ahead of the gunvessel's bows elicited as little response than before.

"They're not going to heave to, sir." Sproul was looking to Dawlish for orders.

I'm damned if I'll let them escape. Whatever has happened ashore, they've been part of it.

He made his decision.

Come what may.

"By your leave, Mr. Sproul, I'll speak to Bradbury."

No demur.

"Mr Bradbury!" Dawlish shouted down to the foredeck.

"Aye, aye, sir!"

"I want a round placed at her waterline, just abaft her bow. No higher, no further aft. Can you do it? If you're not confident, tell me now."

A pause, then Bradbury calling back.

"I'll manage it, sir."

"Only on my word, Mr. Bradbury!"

The gunvessel as was of composite construction, wooden planked, and probably thickly too at the point selected where nobody was likely to be killed. It would still be possible to explain with profuse apologies if there was indeed some misunderstanding.

An eternity as the breech clanged shut, *Falconet's* course steady, the gunvessel almost on her beam.

One last effort before firing.

"Hand me the speaking trumpet, Mr. Sproul."

Dawlish took it, raised it, shouted in the voice he had learned to use three decades before to be heard in Atlantic gales.

"*Déchaîné!* Prendre la cape! C'est le gouverneur de Roscal qui parle!"

And this time a single word shouted back, the filthy, defiant response of the commander of the Old Guard when called upon to surrender at Waterloo.

Disgust coursed through Dawlish.

You've asked for it, mon ami. You'll get it.

"Mr. Bradbury! Your gun!"

He could just make out the old bosun braced against the three-pounder's padded shoulder-rest, finger inside the trigger-guard beneath the breech, sighting down the barrel, swinging the weapon ever so slightly on its pivot to hold it steady on its target.

But Dawlish tore his eyes away, locked them on the black mass of the gunvessel's bow. And waited.

He heard the weapon's report and an instant later an orange flash and another crack confirmed the tiny projectile's hit. It was a mosquito-bit on an elephant, was unlikely to have done more that punch a shallow crater on the stout planking's surface.

And the gunvessel was still forging ahead unchecked.

Dawlish raised the speaking trumpet again.

"*Déchaîné!* Prendre la cape! Mettez-vous en panne, vous allez être arraisonné! C'est le gou –"

And then the unexpected, shocking, answer, stabbing tongues of flame from high on the gunvessel's foremast, their stuttering cutting off his words. Four, five, six blasts, not the chatter of a Gatling or a Gardner, not the ripple of a Nordenvelt, but slower paced, much slower, and more powerful sounding, larger, heavier, more deadly.

An explosion somewhere aft on *Falconet,* a crack weaker than her own hit on the gunvessel.

But a shell, a tiny one, not a solid round.

And Dawlish realised what it was high on that mast – a Hotchkiss one-pounder revolver cannon, as he had so often seen carried by French warships. A weapon intended to tear torpedo craft apart, one scarcely less lethal for *Falconet,* well capable of landing five or six shells for every hit that Bradbury might score with the three-pounder.

Sproul had realised it too, was already shouting orders to pull away to port and the wheel was spinning in the quartermaster's hands.

"Damn well done." Dawlish felt a tremor in his voice.

The right decision. There could be no contest. Flight was the only realistic tactic and *Falconet* had the speed advantage.

A seaman, ex-Navy, appeared, clearly shaken.

"It hit the bulwark just abaft the mizzen, sir. No serious damage, nobody wounded but –"

Poum! Poum! Poum! A second between them, a pause, then three following.

Dawlish forced himself not to turn his head when he heard the impacts – three at least – somewhere abaft the bridge. His eyes were locked on the gunvessel's foremast. Each brief lance of flame from there revealed two figures crouched behind the weapon mounted on a sturdy rail-surrounded foretop.

Déchaîné had carried no such feature, and even if she had it was impossible to imagine her crew firing with such accuracy.

This was not the Guimbian gunvessel.

And it was swinging over to port on a collision course with *Falconet,* not to shake her off, but to destroy her.

Sproul was shouting for Dawlish's attention, pointing aft. Smoke was jetting horizontally from a rent in the funnel just above the deck.

"We're losing draught!" Sproul yelled.

And furnace draught was vital now if *Falconet* were to maintain her slim speed advantage.

"Get wet canvas wrapped around it!" Dawlish said. Now into the darkness and counting on *Falconet's* turning circle being tighter than the gunvessel's.

The Hotchkiss was poum – poum – pouming again, but this time without scoring a hit. On *Falconet* a tarpaulin, the first to hand, was being bound around the lower funnel and a water hose was beginning to play on it. Smoke was still seeping above and below the patch, but the flow was reduced. With luck, close-to-normal draught could be maintained.

The separation between the vessels was increasing and the gunvessel was now scarcely discernible by the red shimmer above her funnel. *Falconet* was weaving now, seeking whatever seemed the deepest patch of shadow cast by the clouds above.

A half-hour passed and all sign of the gunvessel had disappeared. She might still be searching, but Dawlish doubted it. The sky was lightening in the east. Whatever that gunvessel was – and he was almost certain that she was French – her commander would not want exposure to identification in the clear light of day.

He went aft to inspect the damage, not just the funnel but a mangled ventilator cowl close by and a pulling boat reduced to matchwood. The only casualty was a deckhand, injured by a flying splinter, but the wound was minor and he'd survive.

The sun was up when he returned to the bridge, composing himself on the way, for he had been shaken. The sea was empty on all sides. The Roscal shoreline was hidden below the southern horizon but Mont Colbert's great mound rose above it to the south-west. The night's manoeuvrings had carried *Falconet* far to the north and east.

Sproul was looking to him for orders.

"Drop me at Muron," he said.

To learn about Clemenger's ambush.

He was already resigning himself to hearing bad news.

Chapter 16

Falconet's surviving boat put Dawlish ashore on the beach at Muron with two seamen, both armed with rifles. It was daylight and two cautious fishermen and a curious child came to investigate. He went forward alone to meet them. They shrank back at the sight of his holstered revolver and didn't recognise what looked like a common seaman as the governor who had visited there a few weeks before. One man, less timorous than the other, agreed to bring them to the Rural Guard post. *Falconet* was already departing for Escource – repairs must be completed quickly. She might well be needed soon.

The village's fear was palpable as they passed through the deserted alleyways and across the central square. No children playing, market stalls standing empty, doors and shutters closed, nervous heads exposed for an instant, then as quickly withdrawn.

It had been bad here last night – *terrible, très terrible* – his guide told him. But no, there had been no shooting in the town but over there – a finger pointed to the south-east – there had been a battle. And many, many dead, *un massacre énorme*. Or so he had heard, and so too everybody said, even though they'd spent the night cowering indoors.

A single Rural Guard remained at the Guard post, barricaded in, and he menaced Dawlish with a rifle until he was convinced of his identity. He too was frightened and could tell little more. He had been alone here since noon the previous day. A message from Major Clemenger at Orvault had ordered the post's sergeant and its other nine guards to join him. Why, he did not know. But the shots that had cracked to the east around midnight had surprised him. It was followed by heavier gunfire that had waxed and waned for two hours afterwards. Nobody from Clemenger's force had returned.

Dawlish felt exhausted but coffee brewed by the guard revived him a little. His first concern was to find Clemenger but with no horse available in the village he would have to set out on foot along the track that led here from Orvault. Somewhere along it, he must meet somebody who could tell him more.

Her Majesty's Governor of the Crown Colony of Roscal swallowed his pride. The two seamen would accompany him and the guard was to remain at the Muron post. The weary plod began. He wished that he had something better than canvas deck-shoes to walk in but at least he had his nautical cap to shield his head and water in the canteen borrowed from the guard. The sun was high now and the day's heat merciless.

And he dreaded what he might find.

*

They walked south for two miles, holding close the track's edge, ready to dive into cover at the first sign of danger. The nearby vegetable plots were deserted, even those close to shuttered huts. Fear reigned here as much as in the village. Dawlish gave up any attempt to find a pattern in the night's events. For now, it was essential to stay alert.

Then a track branching to the left, eastwards, towards the mountains. They turned into it. Somewhere further along would be a narrow pathway leading down to the cove where the landing had been expected, the only access, since high cliffs bordered the inlet to either side. The last huts and cultivation had been left behind and the terrain was more broken, scrub covered, rising towards the densely wooded mountain slopes above which towered Mont Henri's bare dead cone. The track itself was petering out, seldom trod, grassed over, almost blocked at intervals by bushes.

A little beyond the intersection with the cove path, a grey mound lay to one side of the track. They approached with caution, found that it was a dead mule, already swelling, head blasted open by gunfire, flies buzzing over wounds in its flank, the remaining eye locked open in uncomprehending reproach. Its panniers were still strapped in place, but empty. Further on they found a single sandal, such as a field hand might wear, and an already darkening trail of blood leading from it into the scrub. There might be a body there, or a wounded man, but there was no time to investigate.

The urge to retreat was strong. A cowardly, wheedling inner voice told Dawlish that this was no place for Roscal's governor, that he should manage this affair from a higher level, should take a wider view, that Clemenger probably had the matter in hand, could be relied on to –

No! Press on!

Two minutes later, they found a body half-hidden in scrub just off the track. It was, a dark Roscallan civilian lying on his side, fingers dug into the earth as he had clawed in his last agony, blood soaking his threadbare clothing. One of the seamen turned away and vomited. Dawlish affected not to notice – the first encounter with violent death took many like that. He pushed the body over with his foot, avoided looking in the face, found no weapon. This must be a muleteer tempted by a generous reward for a night's work.

They found three more bodies in the next two hundred yards. Two were poor sandal-wearing Roscallans, one of them shot in the back, but the third, propped up in a half-sitting position against a rock, was a white. His hair was grizzled and he looked about forty, sun-bronzed, solidly built. His clothing, of blue serge, had the cut of a military uniform, though it caried no badges. A bandolier crossed his chest just above the bloody crater torn in his stomach. He had been spared the slow death which that would have brought, for the powder-blackened edges of the wound in his left temple told that somebody had cared enough about him to administer a *coup-de-grace*. No revolver in the holster strapped to his waist. The bandolier's pouches had been emptied also. Dawlish searched in the jacket's patch pockets – they looked as if they had been ripped open in haste – but they held nothing but a pipe, matches and a leather tobacco pouch. There was nothing to identify the owner but the matchbox's paper label showed a smiling cat above the words *Le Chat Heureux - Toujours Fiable!*

On the track, and in the growth alongside, Dawlish found a scattering of brass cartridge cases. He picked up several, all of lower calibre than the Sniders carried by the Rural Guards.

Around the next bend were two more dead mules, both shot several times, crumpled as if they had bolted before collapsing, their panniers as empty as those of that animal found earlier. All indications were of an ambush by Clemenger's men, one that had inflicted casualties but that must have been beaten off. The repulse had gained enough time to strip the loads from the mules and give mercy to a dying comrade before hastening on.

Even as Dawlish was considering retreat again – and this time with better justification, he thought, for he was virtually defenceless – human voices sounded from further ahead. He motioned to the seamen to take cover with him in the scrub. The minutes passed slowly. What might have been brief exchanges, not conversation, were growing in loudness.

Then, coming into sight from around a bend, what might have been a model for a painting of the Good Samaritan. A plodding mule, a man alongside leading it and trying to keep a slumped figure upright on the beast's back. Both were Roscallans and both wore Rural Guard uniforms. Two other led-mules followed, another wounded man, supported on the first and a body slung across the second, head and arms dangling on one side, feet on the other.

Dawlish, waving his white handkerchief, went forward to meet them. They looked beaten.

And so too had been Clemenger's whole force, they told Dawlish in dead voices.

And where was the major?

Up ahead, two miles or more.

What was left of his men?

They could give no clear answer.

*

Clemenger offered no excuses when Dawlish found him in a slight bowl, ringed with rocks, that looked down on the track. The position was well chosen, easily defensible, and guards were posted around the perimeter, rifles at the ready. Several canvas pack-covers had been rigged together to form a small shelter and a cooking fire was smoking there. All but one of the mules that had carried his column's supplies had been sent back with the wounded.

He had failed, failed miserably, Clemenger admitted, failed most of all because he had relied too heavily on inadequate intelligence. His ambush had been well laid, adequate for capture of the mule train. There had been no armed guards with it and it had bolted onwards at first challenge. One of his own men had panicked, had opened fire and others had joined him, bringing down men and mules at the train's rear.

"That was when they hit us from behind."

"Who?"

"Who knows? But well-trained men, disciplined, cleverly commanded. We'd no hint of their approach. They flayed us, pushed us back down the track. I'm ashamed —" Clemenger stopped, had to force himself to continue. "I'm ashamed to say that some of my people broke and ran back. I managed to rally the remainder and drive forward again."

Advancing through the bush at either side of the track, they had seen that the mules they had killed had been stripped of their loads. They had been fired on again at intervals, had been outflanked once, so that this attack had come from behind. And they had taken casualties, four dead, five wounded, three too badly to be sent back by mule.

"It was a professional job," Clemenger said. "They'd no interest in destroying us, only in getting their mule train away. They harried us just enough to keep us at a distance. And they did it bloody well."

"But you didn't give up." Dawlish respected that.

Clemenger shook his head. "Not until we got this far. We'd no chance of catching them by then. I'd never be able to make anything of my people if we'd retreated. Some fled, but the majority stayed and did they best they could. Not bad for green troops. They'll do better next time."

Dawlish mentioned the dead stranger in the nondescript uniform.

"They must have had more wounded," Clemenger said, "but they left none of them behind. But look over here, see that we found."

The rifle's stock had been shattered by a bullet and the splintered remains were splashed with blood.

"It's a Gras," Clemenger said. "Standard for the French infantry, though others use it too. But I doubt if the Greeks or Abyssinians have sent them here."

Dawlish told him about *Falconet's* encounter with the gunvessel. All evidence now, the accurate Hotchkiss fire, *Le Chat Heureux,* the skilled harrying of the Rural Guard, the abandoned Gras, all led to one conclusion.

French involvement.

And it had been well planned. The landing of modern rifles, and no doubt ammunition too, and of a disciplined force which could train others in their use, would have gone undetected had it not been for the information that Clemenger had received from a Roscallan muleteer.

"They must be over the border by now." Clemenger gestured eastwards to the steep green-forested slopes. The unmarked frontier ran beyond. "Somebody must be waiting for them in Guimbi."

It would have made sense to have landed them in the black republic itself, Dawlish thought, would have avoided the arduous crossing of the mountains. Unless . . .

Unless there's no intention of storing or distributing them further east in settled Guimbian territory, not yet, at least. They would remain inaccessible, with the landed force, somewhere in the wooded mountain chain until other measures were in hand. And Guimbi's president would know nothing until . . .

"How many of your men can you rely on, major?" Dawlish said. "Rely on for your life? Not just willing men, but capable as well?"

The question took Clemenger by surprise.

"Right now? Today?" A pause, then, "Two. At the most three."

"I've heard that you'd shot tigers in India," Dawlish said. "You're a good a tracker, aren't you?"

"Are you thinking of following them, sir?"

"Tonight."

Having come this far, it was essential to know more if anything meaningful could be reported to Topcliffe. And a reconnaissance was unlikely to be expected yet, not after last night's disaster.

Clemenger looked down.

"You'll need boots, sir. One of the wounded men is probably your size. And may I suggest as much sleep as you can get?"

It was on bare earth beneath the shelter, next to a man coughing blood and slowly dying, but for Dawlish blissful oblivion nonetheless.

*

Clemenger led and Dawlish followed, both carrying Sniders – as did the two reliable guards behind them – in addition to their revolvers. They advanced not along the track but fifty or sixty yards parallel to one side, making long detours around dense brush, freezing for minutes on end when the major, alerted by some unexpected noise, raised his hand and dropped from sight and they followed suit. It was less cloudy than the previous night and the moonlight was at once both an aid and a hindrance. No rain had fallen for several days and the ground was firm underfoot but dry twigs, when trodden, seemed like pistol shots above the constant insect chatter.

Dawlish felt fear, the same hollow stomach and pounding heart as when he had crept through brush during other onshore night raids in his career. Seeing Clemenger in action convinced him that he had been an amateur lucky to have escaped detection before. Now he tried to copy the major's every movement. The man was an instinctive hunter, creeping forward with the patience and confidence of a panther stalking its prey. That he limped and needed the assistance of a walking stick, did not hamper him. At intervals he signalled to the others to remain under cover while he slipped towards the track. He waited several minutes each time to be sure that it was safe to move from the shadows, then sought for signs of movement along it, hoof or foot marks, mule droppings, discarded burnt-out matches. And always on return he motioned to them to follow.

They had set out when the last light died in the western sky. Progress was slow but sustained and Dawlish estimated that they were covering perhaps a single mile in each hour. Too dangerous to strike a light to read a watch, it was hard to estimate time. Only once did Clemenger beckon to Dawlish to join him after one of his investigations of the track.

"They never stopped for longer than a few minutes." He spoke in a whisper. "It's been at least twelve hours since they passed here."

"How do you know?"

"The mule-dung has dried. But we're near the crests now. Whoever's commanding might have posted an ambush there in case they're followed. I would."

"So what now?"

"Outflank them." Clemenger nodded south-eastwards. "Hook around that way. Try to get ahead of them. They're unlikely to expect it in this sort of terrain."

They set out. The crest above proved a false one, the edge of more gentle slope beyond, the tree-cover thinning as it ascended to another crest perhaps a mile distant. It lay like a dark, smooth, undulating line against the scarcely brighter sky with Mont Henri's inverted funnel over to the left.

Clemenger, crouching behind a bush, beckoned Dawlish to come forward. He pointed.

"There, you see it? It might just be a clump of trees but it looks too regular. What so you think, sir?"

Dawlish could see nothing.

"Look towards Mont Henri," Clemenger said. "Then shift your gaze slowly, ever so slowly, to the right."

It took two attempts before detecting the slight hump that barely rose above the dark undulation. Its top was level, an unbroken horizontal line, but the sides sloped at angles that seemed identical. It lay north-east, could not be far to the right or left of the track.

"We need to get closer," Clemenger said.

Onward, even more cautious now since there were small open patches here. They flitted across from shadow to shadow, each waiting until the next man joined him before moving forward again.

A half-hour passed, an hour, progress agonisingly slow, but that sharp-edged profile was rising higher above the ridgeline. There could be no doubt.

"It's a fort," Dawlish said.

A small structure, a pattern that had been common two centuries before, the sort built at hundreds of locations in their colonies by the French, Spanish, Dutch and British to guard small ports or anchorages. Probably polygonal or square, forty or fifty yards along each side, stone-built, embrasures for three or four cannons.

An obsession of one of Guimbi's first presidents, d'Erlanger had said. Built to guard the tracks across the mountains from Roscal in case the British ever decided to invade. And long abandoned, probably incomplete.

Even without artillery mounted there, it would be defensible, maybe impregnable, Clemenger said. A few dozen trained men armed with rifles could hold off anything that Guimbi's President Ravenel could throw against it. Rainwater would fill its cisterns, guarded mule-trains could carry food up from the cultivated plains beyond. A secure base, one that could afford shelter and training to Ravenel's enemies.

It might not be the only one manned. d'Erlanger had mentioned a second fort. What was happening here was not the work of some disaffected Guimbian general with aspirations to winning the presidency by a *coup d'état*. The groundwork was being laid for something much more ambitious, probably with French involvement, whether officially, but clandestinely, approved or as part of some conspiracy.

So many clues and yet, put together, providing no unarguable proof of such involvement. It was easy to imagine Farnsworth of the Foreign Office arranging a discreet meeting with some acolyte of the French ambassador in London to confront him with evidence of last night's doings. And being met with bland denials.

More information would be needed – Topcliffe would demand it – and this night's opportunity, however dangerous, might never come again.

"Bring me to the far side of the fort, major," Dawlish said.

There were still several hours to sunrise.

Every one of them worth gold.

*

Dawlish and Clemenger went forward, leaving the two guards under cover. They skirted further east, then north again, with the fort's sharp-angled profile occasionally visible to their left. On then for a half-mile further before turning west. The scrub was thick in places, with only the narrowest of passages through the thickets, but the major, though he carried no compass, seemed unerring in his judgement of position and progress. He spoke no word, signalling by hand alone whether to advance, hold back, crouch in cover or retreat from what proved some cul-de-sac in the brush.

They had reached the crest now. Ahead and below, they saw the outline of other ridges, dark valleys between, like waves breaking on a shore, hiding Guimbi beyond. Mont Henri loomed to the north, its sister Mont Sully to the south. This was the wilderness, one of rock and scrub at altitude, of dense luxurious growth in its gorges, of deep-shadowed defiles and gulleys, where an army of self-liberated slaves had held out for years and bled to death successive fever-plagued French armies.

And, at last, the fort.

It lay a half-mile to the west and now they could see that it stood above a narrow, winding, gap through which the track passed. A few tiny flames were flickering against the blackness of the wall behind. Dawlish could catch a slight whiff of woodsmoke – these must be campfires, outside, not inside. He had joined Clemenger, prone beneath a bush. He nudged him, jerked his head.

Closer.

Fear, close to terror, was strong within him as they crept forward, skirting south of those winking fires. It was madness to continue, the small craven voice within reminded him, as it so often had in times of danger, all there more insidious for its unchallengeable logic. Pride rather than courage was carrying him ahead, fear that Clemenger, still so assured and calm, would despise him. Such foolish pride killed, that cowardly, rational, voice whispered but he forced himself to ignore it.

The smell of woodsmoke was stronger now, and moving silhouettes were outlined against the campfire glimmers. He could hear the distant cadences of voices, the words indistinguishable, brief exchanges, not conversation. Then a sudden cry, loud and jarring, the braying of a mule, another joining in, and the sound of stamping hooves and human voices swearing in local patois as they quietened the beasts.

Clemenger was still edging forward from shadow to shadow and Dawlish followed. The strongest noise now was that of shuffling hooves and he could just make out the outlines of hobbled mules. Closer still and he could discern their shapes, twenty or thirty perhaps, a few lying down, most standing asleep. Around the fires, bodies were slumped in sleep. A dim glow hovered above the fort's interior. There must be fires there also.

Breath held now as a figure emerged from the darkness in a slow plod around what must be the perimeter of the encampment. He looked young, had slung his rifle on his shoulder and gave every indication of finding the duty burdensome and unnecessary. He passed on, was lost to sight. Dawlish slithered forward, found more cover, knew that the sentry would be back soon, retracing his steps. With luck something might be deduced from his appearance. Two minutes later, he returned, then halted suddenly, swinging the rifle from his shoulder.

"*Qui vive?*" The challenge came in a weary voice, as if a formality.

Dawlish froze, held his breath, felt his heart thumping, his mouth dry. With infinite caution, he slid his revolver from its holster but hesitated to cock it lest the click betray him.

"*Qui vive?*" again.

Then a voice from the right.

"Carette."

A figure emerging from the darkness, also with rifle slung. Another sentry.

"*Je déteste déjà cet endroit,*" the first one said. "*Nous étions fous de nous porter volontaires pour ça!*"

He was loathing the place already, was regretting volunteering.

Then Carette was suggesting a cigarette and dismissive of the first man's concerns. Le Sergent Debray would be sleeping soundly by now, Carette said. He was an old soldier, knew when there was danger, knew when there wasn't. Nothing to worry about for now. Just move over there into the shadows and we'll have a smoke.

And those shadows were ten feet from where Clemenger lay, closer still to Dawlish. Cigarettes produced, a match flared – possibly a *Chat Heureux* – and heads drooped close together to light off the single flame. In that moment two faces were revealed, one bearded, the other stubbled. The skin, though bronzed, was European, the features too, the accents such as Dawlish had remembered from youth, accents of Béarn or Gascony.

They smoked in silence until the younger asked how long these peasants with the mules – there was something of contempt in the term '*paysans*' – would be kept here.

Carette shrugged. Five or six days. They'd be let go home to Roscal in ones and twos. It was better that they'd find their separate ways and not by the way they had come. *L'anglais* would most surely be guarding the track.

And the mules?

They'd stay. They'll be needed.

But when?

Carette laughed. The colonel would keep that to himself until the right moment came. Desmarais was an old fox, *un vieux renard*.

A cigarette butt thrown down, a heel grinding it two feet from Dawlish's face. And another. The younger man grumbling again that he hated this place. He hadn't volunteered just to guard mules.

The other spoke with the wisdom of veteran. Be patient. There'll be money, women, even land. And it won't be difficult. Just a rabble of barefoot blacks pretending to be soldiers and scattering at the sound of the first shot.

Time to resume the patrol. The sentries trudged away in opposite direction. Time too for Dawlish and Clemenger to retreat, now with even greater caution than before.

Two words had justified the risk of the reconnaissance.

Colonel and Desmarais.

Chapter 17

Even condensed into telegraphese before enciphering, Dawlish's report to Topcliffe filled two foolscap pages. *Falconet*, hastily repaired, would carry Blackwell to Antigua to despatch it. A second, shorter version, would be sent separately to the Colonial Office, mentioning only detection of successful gunrunning and nothing of the short action at sea or of the name Desmarais. Topcliffe would prefer it that way. Dawlish expected answers and Blackwell would have to wait for them in Antigua. Taking account of likely Colonial Office delays, it was unlikely that he would return in less than five days.

Clemenger had placed watches at each of the few tracks leading across the mountains into Guimbi. Three returning Roscallan muleteers, less their animals, blundered into one of them, and there was hope of catching others. The prisoners detained so far had broken quickly under questioning. Still shocked by the ambush they had not expected, and by the death in it of four of their fellows, all had the same story to tell. Much of it was known already – high prices offered by some unknown person for one or two nights' work. They knew now – and swore that they hadn't in advance – that the loads brought ashore were rifles and ammunition, but they could tell little about the men who had landed with them. Only that they were not Roscallans, that they were soldiers, real soldiers, that they spoke French, had driven them like slaves, had answered no questions.

There was nothing more to be got from the prisoners, Clemenger advised. With the threat of prosecution hanging over them, and warned not to speak about their experiences, they could prove useful informants if released. Dawlish consented.

He had called an emergency meeting of the Advisory Council after returning to Escource. He was an old sea dog, he said, and enjoyed joining *Falconet's* patrols on occasion. It was fortuitous that he had been on board when she had encountered what appeared to be a smuggler. It had exchanged shots when challenged and had disappeared into the night. It was the sort of incident that crew members would inflate in the telling and exaggerated rumours would no doubt circulate. The same would apply to the Rural Guard's clash with smugglers ashore. And yes, in answer to a question posed by Councillor Marsac, the lawyer, it might well have been a case of gunrunning into Guimbi. Useful lessons had been learned for handling such matters in the future.

Dawlish doubted that any of the councillors were entirely convinced but he sensed that they realised that they'd get no more from him at present. d'Erlanger was the only one he trusted. Shared danger on the ridge above Saint Gérons, while Mont Colbert vomited above them, had forged that trust. Business interests, no less than personal repute, meant that d'Erlanger had contacts along the entire northern coast. He could be a good source of intelligence, but first he would have to know the full story, gunvessel and all. Dawlish would inform him separately in his study the next day.

It was otherwise essential to maintain an outward show of normality, meeting officials to discuss petty business, reviewing accounts, accompanying Florence to open a new village school and congratulate the new teacher trained by Madame Geneviève. Florence had seen that he was preoccupied – he had confided the barest outline of the events in the mountains – and she did all she could to put him at his ease.

And so, six, not five, long days passed in impatience before Blackford returned from Antigua.

With an encrypted, telegram from Topcliffe, shorter, far shorter, than Dawlish had expected and an even shorter one from the Colonial Office.

*

Dawlish left the Colonial Office transmission to Blackford – it used a simple code which he had heard Topcliffe describe as childish. He reserved the admiral's message for himself. Each sentence was Playfairenciphered with a different keyword. It had been agreed with Topcliffe that the words should be those of six-letters or longer occurring in sequence from the beginning of the sixth chapter onwards of *A Tale of Two Cities*. He decrypted quickly – he was long-familiar with the system that he had learned as a boy from his beloved uncle in Pau. Only at the end, with the full text *en clair* before him, did he allow himself to read it.

Topcliffe had supported his suggestions. Contact to be established with President Ravenel, in secrecy, through Maître Badeaux, and support offered as proposed. Expansion, doubling at the least, of the Rural Guard. A Royal Navy gunvessel, HMS *Chaffinch*, to make an ostentatious visit, not just to Roscal and Guimbi, but to French Caribbean possessions. She would bring two Gatlings for *Falconet* and the two cutters for her that Dawlish had asked for. And certain other resources that he had requested. The Colonial Office was still refusing to abolish the Poll Tax but, due to Topcliffe's appeal to a higher power, had agreed to its suspension for two years. It had also decided to an increase the annual grant, by forty-five percent. Half of this was to be spent on public works – roads, culverts, drainage – that would provide rural employment.

A surprise however in Topcliffe's message – no reference to a Colonel Desmarais.

But something that Dawlish had not suggested. Major MacQuaid would arrive separately and remain as an adviser. Ostensibly a private citizen, his identity would be that of a writer preparing a book on economic development in the West Indies. The subject would provide a plausible explanation for frequent visits to Government House and travel around both Roscal and Guimbi.

The Colonial Office's separate message was a masterpiece of non-commitment. It expressed general concern, made much of the grant increase, stressed the Poll Tax was suspended, not abolished, and reminded Dawlish of the importance of maintaining good relations with all classes in Roscal and with Guimbi.

And it recommended caution at all times and in all decisions.

Sir Cathcart Soames of the Colonial Office was ensuring that he would carry no blame should anything go awry.

That skill must have carried him far in his career.

*

Small as the island was, and in the absence of a telegraph connection, an entire continent might have separated Escource from Port Mazarin. Dawlish could not risk inviting Maître Badeaux to Roscal. If news of the meeting leaked – and secrecy measures could never be fully watertight – it would reignite outrage in the Souliers and their allies. Clemenger was already reporting rumours spreading about his failed ambush. Several members of the planter class were expressing sympathy for the gunrunners and for anybody else who might take down President Ravenel. Should Dawlish go to Port Mazarin himself in *Falconet*, so soon after his previous visit, it would arouse even greater suspicion.

He fretted over his options through a sleepless night. Just before dawn he decided that must draw on somebody else, somebody he could always trust.

"I've been busy," he said to Florence over breakfast. "You've been busy too. We could both benefit from a short holiday."

"When?" She looked surprised.

"Now, from today. I've no council meeting for the next five days and Blackwell can handle matters of routine."

"For how long, Nicholas?" She sounded as if she suspected that there was more to it.

"Just a few days, ourselves and Jessica. And Ted could come too. His studies wouldn't suffer too much if he loses a little schooling."

"We'd be 'not at home' here in Escource?"

"We've a standing invitation from Edmond d'Erlanger. He'll welcome our company – he's been pressing me for a while. And I could see how that young fellow from Oxford is doing with his experimental seedlings. And there's a new school near completion nearby that you'd like to see for yourself. And Ted would love to –"

She began to laugh "You can be so transparent at times, Nick. It's important for some other reason, isn't it? And yes, of course we'll go. We can be on our way within the hour."

Hippolyte rode ahead to announce their arrival. Dawlish and Ted would be ride also, escorting Florence in her dog cart with Jessica and her nurse.

No guards in attendance. It was better to be seen like that.

Just a family on a private excursion.

*

A dark night had settled on Saint Gérons and its streets were empty when a small skiff carried Dawlish and d'Erlanger out into the harbour towards the moored schooner *Eponine*. d'Erlanger, her owner, had sent a message ahead that afternoon for her captain to be ready for departure. Now he was coming to give him precise instructions. Dawlish's clothing was nondescript – an old linen suit that Florence crumpled up and rubbed on the verandah's floor to crease and grubby it. He wore no necktie and a frayed straw hat shaded his features. The black captain didn't query what sort of urgent business Mr. Page, d'Erlanger's friend, might have in Port Mazarin. Given fair winds and the blessing of the good God, he said, Mr. Page would be back in Escource the following night.

A handshake, a word of thanks, unspoken relief that d'Erlanger had agreed to help with no questions asked. Dawlish watched the skiff pull back towards the dockside as the schooner weighed anchor and caught the night breeze in her sails. d'Erlanger would be back at his mansion in two hours. Tomorrow he would conduct Florence and Ted on a tour of his plantation while His Excellency, incapacitated by a migraine brought on by overwork, would pass the day in a darkened bedroom.

Eastwards now along the northern coast, past Mont Colbert's menacing bulk, past the cove hidden in the darkness beyond Muron where the rifles had been landed. Then past the line of cliffs where the mountain belt ran down from Mont Henri and plunged into the sea.

Dawlish remained on deck, relished the soft breeze on his face, the unhurried, cheerful, efficiency of captain and crew, the creak of rigging, the gurgle of water alongside, the phosphorescent wake astern, the bitter coffee brough to him in a chipped mug. A quarter-century fell away. In West Indian waters like these, he had come to realise how much his profession would satisfy him. As it still did. As it always would.

The bows nudged over to the south-east to parallel the Guimbian shore. There were open beaches here, pale streaks in the darkness. The land behind stretched low and level, Dawlish knew. A place of squalid poverty, of near starvation on subsistence plots, of a promise of liberty betrayed, of corruption and endless struggle for brief occupancy of bankrupt government. A place mocked by those who quoted it as proof that blacks could never rule themselves. But a place too where an enslaved people had once risen up, had prevailed against all that France had sent against them, where men like Ravenel and Badeaux still tended a faint flickering flame of hope and dignity.

And because of that, this mission pleased him. Success on this island, in both Roscal and Guimbi, could be some atonement for what he helped bring about in Paraguay seven years before.

*

The schooner rounded Cap Louvois, the islands' eastern tip, soon after sunrise and by nine o'clock lay moored in Port Mazarin's crescent harbour, close to where *Déchaîné* swung at anchor. The captain himself, newly clad in his Sunday best, went ashore with a deckhand to locate Maître Badeaux's residence. He carried a note from Dawlish with him, a single sentence that announced his presence and requested an immediate meeting. The deckhand was back an hour later. Would eleven o'clock be convenient?

Two customs officials in tattered uniforms confronted Dawlish at the top of the landing steps. With all the officiousness of men hoping for a bribe, they asked his business and demanded papers. He was a trader, interested in finding sources of cheap rum, he said, and he bought them off with a silver Spanish dollar apiece. The deckhand had come with him to show the way. The schooner's captain would be otherwise busy in town until late afternoon, he said. From his leer, it seemed probable that women would be involved. At the gate of Badeaux's residence, a small mansion that must have once housed some senior French official, Dawlish dismissed the seaman with a dollar. He himself would be able to find his own way back to the quayside.

Badeaux, immaculately dressed, greeted him in a book-lined study, as meticulously clean and well-ordered as that of some wealthy savant of the *Ancien Régime*. It was clear that the visit did not surprise him. Exaggerated accounts of the battle on the mountains' western slopes had reached here, he said, rumours too of a force gathering there, reports of Guimbian peasants disappearing from their plots and soldiers deserting in ones and twos, taking their muskets with them.

"And the officers," Dawlish said, "the colonels, the generals?"

"No sign of involvement or of sympathy either." A pause, then Badeaux said, "Not yet."

He knew nothing of *Falconet's* encounter with the warship, had assumed that the guns landed that night had been from some inter-island trading schooner. Dawlish's account shook him.

"You're sure it was French?"

"Maybe not of the French Navy, but I can't even be sure of that." Dawlish was concerned that Topcliffe had offered no comment on that possibility.

"Could it come back?" An impossible question.

"A British vessel will be patrolling the area in the coming weeks. But not indefinitely."

Dawlish let the significance to sink in.

"It must be French," Badeaux said at last. "They're pressing harder than ever for loan repayments. The treasury's empty. We've nothing, not a sou, to give them."

"You have *Le Déchaîné*."

"Who'd want her? You've seen the shame of her condition yourself."

"Don't sell her. Arm her. Train up her crew. Patrol your coasts. Because if you don't there'll be yet more landings."

Badeaux stood up. "Thank you for your visit, Your Excellency." The urbane cosmopolitan had been replaced by an insulted patriot, trembling with fury. "Thank you for your advice, for your reminder of our poverty. I wish you Good Day."

"Hear me out, I beg," Dawlish had not risen.

"Two minutes then." Badeaux sat.

"I'm authorised by London to make a certain proposal and –"

"By London?" Suspicion in the voice. "You mean by Her Majesty's government?"

"By London."

There would be no record of official sanction, Topcliffe had indicated. Action, if discovered, that would be disowned as that of a rogue functionary taking decisions beyond his remit.

Myself.

Topcliffe's despatch had stressed that Britain could not afford to be seen as moving towards a protectorate over Guimbi. He did not need to tell Dawlish more. Since the Mexicans' eviction of the French two decades before, the United States was ever more dedicated to its Monroe Doctrine and suspicious of any European nation strengthening its position in the Western Hemisphere. Nor did Britain want a direct confrontation with France.

But I'll say nothing of this to Badeaux.

"You said that you had a proposal, Monsieur Dawlish. What is it?"

Not 'Your Excellency', not Her Britannic Majesty's proconsul. This man understands, recognises me for what I am here. An agent liable to disavowal.

Badeaux listened in silence to the details, then said, "Why do you come to me, Monsieur Dawlish? Why not go directly to President Ravenel himself."

"Because you're not a minister, Maître." Dawlish had anticipated the question and had rehearsed the answers. "Because I believe you have the president's ear. Because he can trust you and knows you have no personal ambition for power. And, lastly, because I don't want to be seen at the palace."

"You want me to carry the message?"

"Today if possible. I want to be back in Roscal tonight before I'm missed. I need general agreement only. There'll be further contact later regarding implementation."

"Tell me again, Monsieur Dawlish." Badeaux was reaching for a notebook, was already dipping a pen in an inkwell.

"No notes, if you please, Maître. Nothing in writing."

No objection.

Now the proposal again, step by step, Badeaux querying each point, searching for weaknesses. It was an interrogation, an impression too of facts and their implications being neatly stored in a mental card-index.

When it finished, Badeaux said, "It will take some time to explain this to President Ravenel. He'll have questions. How long can you remain here?"

"Until nightfall. I want to leave here unobserved. But I'll need an answer by then."

Badeaux rang for a servant, told him to fetch a cab, instructed him to make the visitor comfortable.

And Dawlish spent a long day in the study, sustained by a light lunch and coffee through the afternoon, occupied by a volume of Balzac that he found on the shelves. That it was from *La Comédie Humaine* seemed appropriate to the circumstances. For the Great Powers, the Republic of Guimbi was a joke.

And for men like Badeaux and Ravenel, an ideal.

One they probably thought worth dying for.

*

It was close to sundown when Badeaux returned. He looked weary but the president had agreed after long discussion.

"He recognised that we've no alternative," he said. "And it'll be hard to decide who to involve in this, who to trust. Some of the ministers —" Hands raised in an expression of near despair.

Dawlish was eager to leave but Badeaux asked him to stay a little longer and share a glass of wine. A brief discussion of practicalities, of means of maintaining contact. But no sense of elation on the maître's side, no optimism, only an impression of bleak acceptance that this was a last resort, that doom might have already fallen before any of this could be implemented. It was not surprising. Guimbian governments fell through insurrections or palace coups and this one had lasted longer than anyone could have expected.

Glass drained, Dawlish was moving towards the door that Badeaux was opening for him. And closing it again before he reached it.

"One thing you should know, Monsieur Dawlish." The words hesitant, spoken as if after long consideration of whether to utter them.

"Maître?"

"It's sensitive. About President Ravenel. You understand that he has borne much? Never more than in recent months. The demands for loan repayment, his distrust of so many about him, news of gunrunning, enemies gathering in the mountains. It preys on his mind and he hardly sleeps. Even the strongest bough can break."

"And then?"

"Only God knows. May he be merciful to Guimbi then."

The same thought haunted Dawlish as he returned to the quayside. Badeaux had insisted that one of his cudgel-armed watchmen escort him. The unlit streets felt threatening and the whole town seemed even more squalid by night, a place of misery and despair, of hopes and promises betrayed.

He was glad to find *Eponine's* skiff awaiting him. Should the night breezes hold, she might moor in Saint Gérons by sunrise.

And, even with Ravenel's consent gained, he wondered if his mission had achieved anything.

*

Within ten minutes of Dawlish's arrival in Saint Gérons in the early hours, Hippolyte, who had met him with d'Erlanger, was cantering towards Escource. He was carrying an order to Blackwell to go to Antigua with *Falconet* and telegraph an enciphered single-sentence message to London.

That Ravenel had agreed.

Then two days of true holiday at d'Erlanger's estate. A dog cart excursion with Florence and Jessica, a climb with Ted up the lower eastern slopes of Mont Colbert, discussions with the visiting Oxford botanist, long after-dinner talks on the verandah, d'Erlanger the perfect host.

Then back to Escource.

To hard reality again.

Chapter 18

Government House, windows open to catch the evening breeze, soft warm darkness outside, a faint aroma of bougainvillea drifting in.

"I can't eat." Florence pushed her dinner plate away. "Not tonight. It seems so –"

She could not find the words, was shaking her head, tears welling in her great brown eyes.

Dawlish jerked his head slightly to the waiting servant.

Leave.

He did not speak. He had seen her tired and dusty when she had returned from visiting an outlying village where Miss Giltrap, the midwife, was training women. She had bathed and changed since, and she seemed as beautiful to him as she always did. But her usual buoyancy was absent.

"We have so much, Nicholas."

He reached across the table, took her hand, said nothing.

"It weighs on me that we've so much and they so little." A catch in her voice. "The misery, the despair."

"In Thrace," he said, "in Cuba too, you saw worse, far worse, Florence. It never overwhelmed you there."

"There were enemies then, Nicholas. Bashi-Bazooks, Cossacks, that dreadful Major Fentiman. Flesh and blood enemies. We could stand against them. But this is different. And it's endless."

"What happened today, Florence?"

"Nothing much different than at any place I visit." The words came in a rush, angry rather than sad now. "Always the same story. Hungry children. Babies younger than Jessica wasting away. Mothers working themselves to death on little plots to feed them. Another young woman dead in childbed a week ago. A few old men doing their best. Most of the younger men gone to Panama and many of them dying there. And their remittances with them. Others, who recovered, too weak to work and without the funds to pay passage back here."

He squeezed her hand. "But you've achieved so much, Florence. The schools. Madame Geneviève's work. The new Motherless Babies' Home. And Miss Giltrap too, she's already saving lives, you've said." He was about to mention the Poll Tax's suspension and the seedling trials but thought better of it. They seemed such negligible victories.

"How much do you know what's happening in Panama?" he said.

A lot, it transpired. She had asked the Relief Committee to send her press and magazine reports. She'd also read accounts in the French newspapers that came here on occasion from Guadeloupe or Martinique. It impressed him that she hadn't mentioned any of this. She made her relations with the Committee her own business, not his.

There were two centres of work on the isthmus, she said, and workers were dying at both. Inland from the Caribbean coast, from near the port of Colón, huge dredgers were gouging a channel through miasmic swamps and thick forest. Rain was heavy and incessant, causing flooding by the Chagres River to hamper progress and often obliterate it. The other main activity was further inland, where steam shovels, complemented by an ant-like army of labourers, were attempting to cut a passage through the hills that ran parallel to the Pacific coast. Progress was slow and mudslides keep undoing the excavation. It seemed impossible, a labour of Sisyphus.

And month by month malaria, yellow fever and other tropical afflictions were scything workers down. Not only labourers but French engineers and supervisors also, and in large numbers. Some were gone within a month of arrival. Those who survived the fevers were weakened and, if they tried to resume work, the next bout was likely to kill them.

"If they can't work, they're almost as badly off," Florence said. "They're stranded. They might pick up a few dollars from light casual work but not enough to come home. Slowly starving. And they'll die."

"But how many Roscallans are still in Panama, Florence?" Dawlish should have known, in round numbers, and was ashamed that he'd never enquired.

"I don't know exactly. Probably three or four hundred, perhaps more. Many of them are ruined by fever and God knows how many dead already, or are too sick to work and without the money for passage home."

Only the strong and brave would have gone there. Some must still be healthy. And the others, however debilitated, could work the land here better than their wives.

"How much have you in hand from the Relief Fund's last donation, Florence?"

"Just over four hundred pounds. And Agatha has written that another seven hundred's been raised."

The contributions would dwindle month by month, he knew, would trail off to nothing as memory of the volcano's eruption faded in Britain.

"It might be possible to charter a ship," he said. "Not a steamer. A brig perhaps."

Large enough to carry a hundred or more, though in discomfort. But their ancestors had survived worse when brought in packed holds from Africa.

"How much would it cost, Nick?"

"I don't know. But d'Erlanger would. He charters such vessels for carrying lime juice to the United States."

"I'll go to see him tomorrow." Resolution in her voice.

The old, indomitable, Florence was back.

*

Now the wait for HMS *Chaffinch's* arrival from Bermuda. Worthy but dull administration. Work initiated on improving the road from Escource to Ganthier to provide employment for a few. Inspections of a hospital, schools, police stations. Scrutiny of accounts. Confirmation of appointments. Drawing up the next year's budget. Dawlish was regularly working twelve, sometimes fourteen, hours a day but had come to find it rewarding.

Clemenger was drilling his guards without let-up, not just the latest recruits but those older ones who had not performed well in the recent ambush. But his intelligence network was growing, even if half the information gathered was exaggerated or inaccurate. A means of passing informal messages to and from Maître Badeaux was established by a fishing craft owned by the brother of one of Clemenger's sergeants. Too humble to arouse suspicion, it could slip in and out of Port Mazarin without challenge.

Three times, Clemenger had gone into the mountains to the east with small patrols, once close enough to confirm that the fort there was now at the centre of a larger camp. Twice they intercepted Guimbian labourers who were trekking towards it from the plains beyond. Whatever means were used to gain their cooperation – and Dawlish did not ask the question – all told the same story. Inducement by strangers to join a group that would bring change, a golden age, to Guimbi soon. Good money paid in the meantime for just carrying a musket. One labourer had heard of a vessel landing men close to the village of Saint Symphorien, on Guimbi's northern coast. It was a large craft, he said, as big as the one he had seen at anchor at Port Mazarin and which carried huge guns. Clemenger had brought the captives back and they were now earning their keep as fettered labourers at guard posts. At least one of them, he thought, could be induced to return to Guimbi as an informant.

A pittance could buy a lot on this island.

*

Major MacQuaid – plain 'Mister', as he introduced himself to all others than Dawlish – arrived a week before HMS *Chaffinch*. He had travelled by mail steamer, via Jamaica, and had been brought immediately from the harbour to Government House. Though Florence already knew him, had indeed worked with him for Topcliffe, Dawlish noted a coolness when she welcomed him. Blackford would bring him later that afternoon to the small villa rented for him on the edge of town. Sitting now in

Dawlish's study, freshly changed into a white linen suit, the black leather on his artificial hand jarred against its brightness.

"From Topcliffe." He pushed a typewritten sheet across the desk.

Dawlish scanned it. He saw that he'd received what he'd asked for. An ex-Royal Navy commander, Sidwell, who had a French mother and had partly grown up in France. A promising officer, well talked of a few years before, though Dawlish had never met him. A great future had been expected of him. He would arrive with *Chaffinch* and bring three ex-petty officers to support him – a gunner, Sadler, a bosun, Aitken, and an engine-room artificer, Denison, all with experience on small warships.

"What was Sidwell's problem?" Dawlish said. Officers who left the service early usually had one. Especially one who'd commanded a gunvessel and had once had high hopes for promotion.

"Drink," MacQuaid said. "A pity, since he did well in *Ostrich* at Alexandria in '82. He followed Beresford in *Condor* close inshore to attack Fort Marabout."

Lord Charles Beresford, already well known for his friendship with the Prince of Wales, had become a national hero. The press had all but overlooked the less flamboyant Sidwell.

"He grounded *Ostrich* at Suda Bay a year later. A total loss. He was inebriated at the time, the court martial found. Dismissed from the service. He's done anything he can find since. But he took the teetotal pledge three years ago and he's stuck to it. We've had that checked."

"And the others?"

"Couldn't fit into civilian life. The grass wasn't as green on that side of the fence as they'd expected. And we're paying well. Topcliffe has the funds for it."

"We can talk to Clemenger later," Dawlish said. "He'll get the word to Badeaux and Ravenel. In her current state I expect that Sidwell won't find it easy to get *Déchaîné* to get ready for sea."

"You've identified a secure location?"

"Ideal."

Falconet had been busy, investigating a half-dozen small uninhabited islands to the north-west, dormant volcanic outcrops bordered by shallow reefs. But at one, Castries, the reef was broken at one side, giving entry to a tiny sheltered bay beyond.

"Topcliffe's reply said nothing about this Colonel Desmarais." Dawlish said. It rankled – he'd risked his life to learn the name.

"Aah, Desmarais." Smugness in MacQuaid's voice, that of a man who enjoyed knowing secrets that others didn't. "Topcliffe knew of him already. When your report mentioned him, it confirmed that Pelletier's ambitions were indeed focussing on Guimbi. Desmarais's been his right-hand man since the Prussian war. A damn good soldier."

"Who's Pelletier?"

"General Fernand Pelletier. A hero, even in defeat, in the war against the Prussians." Respect in MacQuaid's voice, admiration of one soldier for another. "He expanded Algeria, delivered Tunisia, snatched victory in Tonkin after others had failed. He was an army-reformer when he returned to a senior command in metropolitan France. Popular with brother officers. Adored by the rank and file. An advocate of *revanche* against Germany. Handsome, austere in his way of living, never an accusation of financial corruption. The very image of a leader, of a man of destiny."

"Is he still a serving officer?"

"No," MacQuaid said. "He resigned from the army to take up politics. He was clever enough not to identify with any one party, but he offers something to all of 'em. Radicals and Socialists. And the Monarchists – Bourbonists, Orleanists, Bonapartists. The Clericals and the Anti-Clericals. Veterans and workers. Peasants and bankers. He's a widower, devoted to his daughter. Women adore him and if he has a mistress, he doesn't flaunt her."

In the churn of short-lived coalition governments since foundation of France's latest republic, in the aftermath of humiliation by the new German Empire, different parties had courted this Pelletier. He had served as Minister of War in three governments and as Minister of

Colonies in another, had come close to forming one himself. A cabal of established politicians, the small circle among which power rotated, had united to stop him.

"It was then that he showed just how astute he is," MacQuaid said. "He resigned his seat in the National Assembly and let it be known that he has no further political ambitions. He makes only the odd public appearance, writes just an occasional article, but a powerful one when he does. Always the same themes – reform, *revanche*, an end to corruption. But when he appears in public, the event's always well chosen, and the journalists are alerted beforehand, and the veterans' organisations will be there *en masse*, and his speech will inspire an image of a France triumphant, virile, united, cleansed of fraud and peculation."

"So the crowds love him?"

"Yes – and each time he extends the network of supporters, with little in common with each other but himself, and it funds him. But before he makes his move, he wants something else to his name to show that he dares to get things done. It could be something like taking back Guimbi and wiping out the shame of its loss in the first place. And in the process, offering the hope to small French banks and investors of seizing enough to repay Guimbi's loans."

"There's nothing, absolutely nothing, there to seize," Dawlish said. "Nothing but the land and it's over-tilled and worn out. And the treasury's squeezed dry already."

"It won't matter. Nobody in France will want to believe that."

"If he takes Guimbi, will he stand for election again?"

"No. He'll stay his hand until yet another major financial scandal will tar the professional politicians. There'll be one sooner or later. There always is. Then, first the press and afterwards the country will call on him to clean out the Augean Stable. He won't need an election. He'll just seize power and the people will love it. *Napoleon redux*, France great and glorious again."

"Ready to take back Lorraine and Alsace from Germany?"

"Yes, Dawlish. Even if that launches a wider European war, with God knows what consequences. None of 'em good."

Falconet's night encounter off Roscal's north coast might be later seen as the first step to that disaster.

"The vessel that ran in the guns and landed Desmarais and his people," Dawlish said. "Was it from the French Navy?"

"No, though it used to be. It could be one of two gunvessels disposed of in the last year. *Hermine* and *Blairian*. Bought through an agent for Ecuador and Siam. Our consuls in Guayaquil and Bangkok can't confirm arrival of any such vessels in those parts."

If this Pelletier had a following of sympathetic naval officers, it would have been easy to have her declared outdated and surplus to French naval requirements, Dawlish thought. That was how HMS *Toad*, refitted first, had been purchased at scrap value by the Hyperion Consortium for service in Paraguay. And she had been deadly there . . .

"I only glimpsed her in darkness," he said. "What class are they?"

"*Belette* Class. Sisters of *Le Déchaîné*. Ironic, isn't it?"

"*Chaffinch* can't arrive too soon then," Dawlish said.

"She'll be carrying something else you asked for. Thirty thousand of 'em. They're from Topliffe's secret fund and the Colonial Office is to know nothing about them. To be spent at your discretion. He wants nothing on paper but he'll expect scrupulous accounting."

Gold sovereigns, to be used as I see fit.

To bribe and buy men.

Raison d'etat.

*

It pleased Dawlish that *Chaffinch* had been sent. There were three others of her class assigned to the North America and West Indies Station. Topcliffe must have had a hand in choosing her – it was hardly a coincidence that her captain was Commander Edward Purdon.

He came ashore at once to pay his respects at Government House. Dawlish felt a flush of emotion. Purdon had stood with him in Paraguay, in HMS *Leonidas* off Korea and East Africa, had been with him at Tamai in the Sudan when a spear-thrust had disfigured his face forever. A huge livid scar on Purdon's right cheek dragged his features over in a savage, leering grin and his diction was slurred, for the unseen tongue and gums had also been mangled. He had accepted it, made no effort to hide it. Promotion to Commander and appointment to *Chaffinch* seemed inadequate rewards, but Purdon would not have thought so.

Florence was no less pleased to see him – in Dawlish's absence, Purdon had helped her with a sensitive matter, even while still recovering from his wound. It was pleasing that Jessica too did not flinch from him when he took her in her arms and Ted approached him with something like awe.

A donkey cart, escorted by a heavily armed party of bluejackets passed through Escource's sleeping streets in the early hours. The four rope-handled wooden boxes it carried were locked in a cellar at Government House behind a newly installed iron grill. The only two keys would be held by Dawlish and Blackwell, hung around their necks beneath their clothing. From now on, the ten-thousand gold sovereigns they contained would be guarded night and day by three of Clemenger's men.

Chaffinch's arrival was an opportunity to invite the Advisory Council and various prominent citizens, to dine with her officers at Government House. There was another guest too, one who had arrived on the same mail-ship as MacQuaid. He had paid a courtesy call a few days earlier – Dawlish had kept it brief and formal. Tonight, the Hyperion Consortium's representative was introducing himself to planters and businessmen. It might lead to investment, and despite Dawlish's distaste for the Consortium, that could only be to Roscal's benefit.

The next day, Dawlish made his visit to *Chaffinch* seem more a social than an official occasion. Florence came with him to charm the officers and crew alike. Ted was entrusted to a young sub-lieutenant who would show him the five-inch breech-loaders and the engine room. It seemed natural that Dawlish would closet himself with Purdon in his quarters and that he should afterwards go below to inspect the stores and magazine. Not just to see the two Gatlings brought for *Falconet*. There was a third also. It was satisfactory to note that all stencilled markings on wooden crates there had been obliterated. It would have otherwise aroused suspicion when components and ammunition for French 138-millimeter breech-loaders had come in a vessel that could not use them.

But *Déchaîné* could.

That night a small fishing boat would be heading to Port Mazarin with a one-line message to Badeaux.

Rendezvous in three days at the bay of Castries.

*

Chaffinch twice circumnavigated the island on the day following Dawlish's inspection. She stayed just outside Guimbi's territorial waters, but close enough to be seen from shore, her ensign streaming bravely. She dropped anchor at Saint Gérons that evening and d'Erlanger entertained her officers in the town.

The next day was a triumph. Forewarned, crowds of townspeople gathered on the foreshore, close to where Mont Colbert's now-solid lava flood had spilled into the water. d'Erlanger had declared a holiday for his workers and they came with their families in their best attire. The Reverend Elijah Gagneux had organised three separate choirs to sing intermittent hymns of praise and thanksgiving. The mood was joyful, boisterous, as if for a carnival. At ten o'clock, *Chaffinch*, followed by a flotilla of small boats, steamed from the harbour, crept up to the location where *Scipio* had once moored, and dropped anchors fore and aft. A blast from her steam whistle at ten minutes to noon silenced the throng. Many were glancing up and back at the volcano's bare slopes. Nothing leaking now from its vents and fissures, no sinister glows in her gulleys, no smoke billowing above the summit.

And, at the stroke of noon, *Chaffinch* opened fire, her starboard weapons blasting flame towards the mountain. A half-dozen salvos, all blank, but defiance nonetheless and celebration of a town and people delivered and indomitable. Cheers erupted along the shore when the guns fell silent.

It would establish a tradition, Dawlish hoped. One to be followed by each Royal Navy vessel that would visit here in years to come. Until perhaps one day the mountain might come to life again and no earthy power could save Saint Gérons. But that would be in some indeterminate future and for now the townsfolk was pressing around the roasting pigs and other food that d'Erlanger had provided. *Chaffinch* had dropped boats and they were stroking towards the shore for crews to join the merriment. Each seaman would be a hero today.

Only when night had fallen, and the crowd had dispersed, did *Chaffinch* raise anchor again and head north-westwards.

*

Chaffinch was already moored in the centre of the bay at Castries when Dawlish arrived in *Falconet* next morning. There was no sign yet of *Le Déchaîné*. That was to the good. There was time to lay the yacht alongside *Chaffinch* and secure to her. The mountings for the new Gatlings were passed across. Work began to fix them in place, one on a raised platform abaft *Falconet's* bridge, the other on a similar one at far end of the superstructure, both with ready- use ammunition lockers at either side.

Dawlish was pleased to see that Sidwell, the ex-officer who had arrived with *Chaffinch*, and his three ex-petty officers were working well with *Falconet's* crew. The bustle and smooth efficiency of the activity aroused memories, even longing. This was the world in which he had grown up, in which he was most happy, to which he hoped to return. It must be torture for Sidwell to see it and to work with it, but know that he was no longer part of it, that honour in its service had slipped through his fingers.

The Gatlings were in place on the mountings, and test fired, by late afternoon. Bradbury, *Falconet's* gunner was familiar with the weapons from earlier service, but intensive training would be needed for their new crews. It would not just be a matter of firing, but of loading and reloading, jam-clearing, judging range. It must be learned first step-by-step and then at ever increasing tempo. Should *Falconet* encounter that gunrunning vessel and her vicious Hotchkiss again, her survival might well depend on such mastery.

A smudge of smoke against the lightening pre-dawn sky heralded *Le Déchaîné's* slow approach. Fearful lest she run aground on the nearby reefs, Dawlish despatched Sproul with *Falconet* to guide her into the bay.

"What do you think of her, Mr. Sidwell?" Dawlish was with him and Purdon on *Chaffinch's* bridge and watching the Guimbian's arrival.

"I'll have my work cut out, sir." Sidwell looked like a man who seldom smiled. He didn't this time either.

Déchaîné was a disgraceful sight, no less decrepit than when Dawlish had last seen her. Ample notice had been provided for preparing her but little had seemingly been done. Her erratic progress astern of *Falconet* confirmed his concern about her captain's and quartermasters' skills. He had agreed with Purdon that the risk of her coming alongside *Chaffinch* under her own steam would be too great. Instead, the gunvessel's launch and cutters were waiting to tow *Déchaîné* and lodge her, fendered, side by side against their mother's hull.

It was a slow process and only when it was completed did the Guimbian captain come across.

*

It would be hard for *Le Déchaîné's* captain to accept advice, perhaps harder still for Sidwell to proffer it and gain acceptance. The potential for offence taken, for bitterness and bad blood, was limitless. Badeaux had previously confided that Captain Maurice Queuille's experience, prior to the republic's acquisition of its one-ship navy, was of command of a small trading steamer. He had not only had no formal naval training but had never trusted his crew enough to exercise his ship's main weapons. Yet, at conference held in Purdon's quarters, this light skinned Guimbian seemed to strike an immediate rapport with Sidwell, who conversed easily with him in fluent French.

It was well that it would be so. Once *Chaffinch* had transferred the stores that she has brought, the real work would begin, her specialists in cooperation with Sadler, Aitken and Denison, who would be, de facto, *Le Déchaîné's* gunner, bosun and engineer.

The list of work needed was endless.

Overhaul of *Le Déchaîné's* boiler and engine. If necessary, fabrication of substitutes for damaged parts. Stripping and cleaning of the four 138 mm breech-loaders. Dumping of the munitions already on board which might well have deteriorated, and replacement by those brought by *Chaffinch*. Transfer and mounting on her foretop of a single Gatling that she had also brought. Checking and repair, or renewal, of both running and standing rigging. Hull repairs. Cleaning of decks, passageways and accommodation. And more, and more . . .

Dawlish looked back from *Falconet* as she left for Escource that evening. Hurricane lanterns were casting pools of yellow light on both gunvessels' decks. Work had commenced, work never to be admitted to officially, work to be dismissed by some Foreign Office bureaucrat as an unsubstantiated rumour should the French government come to know of it and seek explanation.

By the time *Déchaîné* would return to Port Mazarin two weeks from now, she would be all but a new vessel. She would be commanded by a Guimbian near-amateur, guided by British advisers whom he could ignore or overrule at any time. Sidwell's most difficult task of all would then commence, the training and welding her crew into an effective force.

But there would be other work to be done at Port Mazarin. *Déchaîné* was carrying with her spare parts and new munitions for the two 138s mounted at Fort Montmorency and originally bought, like her, as part of a corrupt bargain. It would be Sadler's task to oversee repair and training of gun crews for them.

With *Déchaîné's* overhaul complete, *Chaffinch* would conspicuously patrol the Roscal and Guimbian coasts for a full week. Then on to Guadeloupe and Martinique and a few smaller French possessions to show the flag and exchange salutes, courtesies, polite expressions of British friendship, before heading back to Bermuda.

Dawlish glanced astern one last time to see the pinpricks of light grow ever fainter. Tomorrow he would be at his desk in Government House again.

Chapter 19

Two months passed and with them the unrealised threats of the hurricane season. There had been no outbreak of cholera, yellow fever or typhoid, no rioting, no landing or detected gunrunning on Roscal's soil. Dawlish felt more comfortable now in his position, hopeful that measures in hand would be sufficient to cope with likely emergencies.

The Queen's Golden Jubilee also came and went. Dawlish had a proclamation issued identifying the actual day, June 21st, as a holiday. Florence, at her most charming, and most persistent, had elicited contributions in cash or kind from planters and businesses to supplement a grant from the Relief Committee to fund celebrations in the larger villages.

The Reverend Elijah and Madame Geneviève, and other humble but essential leaders like them, flung themselves into the preparations with an enthusiasm that Dawlish found surprising. The woman they were honouring probably knew little of Roscal, had few dealings with it other than to sign governors' appointments. She had personally donated a hundred pounds to the Relief Committee when it was formed – Agatha had prevailed on her father to suggest it to a senior court official. On the only occasion when Dawlish had met the Queen, she had radiated neither intelligence nor warmth. The brief audience had had an air about it of a tedious duty to be finished quickly. Yet for her he had seen men die and for her he had put his own life at risk. And in impoverished villages on this island, people who possessed almost nothing but a capacity to endure would honour her as they might some distant but benevolent goddess.

The day itself was onerous, made worse by the need to remain all day in the loathed governor's uniform and preposterous plumed helmet. *Falconet* fired a puny salute in Escource harbour that preceded a service of thanksgiving for the reign and an endless sermon in Escource's sole Anglican Church. Councillor Chevit, Colonel for the day, had done his best in parading the decrepit Militia. It was time then, in the official landau, to commence a route that passed through as many of the villages as possible. The sun beat down and Dawlish sweated and forced himself to smile, when appropriate. But Florence enjoyed every moment, waving and holding Jessica up, listening to choirs with rapt attention, admiring crude decorations, sampling meat from roasting pigs and goats, dispensing sweets to children. And for all his discomfort, Dawlish was touched. It took so little to make these people happy. They deserved more,

But he felt a pang when illustrated papers arrived later with detailed drawings of the Jubilee Naval Review held at Spithead. Some hundred and fifty warships had been drawn up in five lines that totalled thirty miles. The Queen had passed between them in the royal yacht and thousands of spectators had watched from civilian craft. HMS *Scipio*, under her new commander had lain in a place of honour, close to the head of one of the lines. He would have liked to have stood on her bridge himself at that moment, her crew lining her decks and yards, Saint Gerons' saviours. But he thrust the thought aside.

He had challenges here on Roscal perhaps greater, and certainly more perplexing, than those faced by any officer at that Review.

That was his consolation

*

MacQuaid's purported identity as an economist lent credibility for him visiting Guimbi. He had done so three times already, carried there, as if a private citizen, on a trading schooner and lodging in what passed for Port Mazarin's best hotel. The plausibility of his apparent reason for visiting was strengthened by Maître Badeaux, who arranged a meeting with the Minister of Finance and short tours outside the town to view rural life. On his second visit he met President Ravenel and agreed future communication with him through Badeaux. He had also rented a small house with a walled garden, where his comings and goings would be less conspicuous than at the hotel. He provided Dawlish with a sketch map of its location – it was close to the harbour.

"What do you think of Ravenel?" Dawlish had asked.

"Close to the end of his tether. Without Badeaux he'd break."

But slowly, from these contacts, an even more depressing picture emerged of Guimbi's prospects. Badeaux despaired not just for French banks' relentless clamour for repayment, but for fear of a coup that might happen at any time.

"The maître introduced me to a few of the generals," MacQuaid said. "I wouldn't put most of them in charge of a corporal's guard. But that doesn't matter. All it would take would be three or four determined men to get rid of Ravenel. And probably Badeaux with him."

"The Minister of Defence – what's his name?" Dawlish said. "Yes, Aubertin. I remember him. He looked dangerous."

"He is. And he's probably the only decent soldier in Guimbi. He served in Mexico with the French, and he claims to have been an officer there, though I doubt it. He's feared. He put down several minor insurrections without mercy over the years. It was a surprise that he threw his weight behind Ravenel, who trusts him. Badeaux thinks that he might already be in contact with Desmarais's group in the mountains. It seems that villagers are heading there in ones and twos to join them. Better than starvation, I imagine."

"How much is Ravenel concerned about Desmarais?"

"A lot. He'd send a force against him if he could. I advised against it. What few troops he has haven't been paid for months. They won't be either. They get by through intimidating and taking from anybody less poor than themselves. Ravenel's only hope is that Desmarais won't move before he's reinforced and that *Déchaîné* will deter that."

The gunvessel was now patrolling Guimbi's coast. Her captain and crew had responded well to the advice and training provided by Sidwell and his three ex-petty officers. She had returned to Port Mazarin from her transformation at the Castries anchorage as a vessel reborn. Aitkin had helped impose a regime of discipline and cleanliness. Denison had transformed her engine room – she was capable of eleven and a half knots under steam – fuelled by coal purchased by letters of credit brought to Ravenel by MacQuaid – and seven knots under sail. Sadler had familiarised her gunners with their weapons, even if they had not yet mastered them. She was a well-known sight from land by now, seen creeping along close inshore, bombarding cliffs on occasion to exercise her guns, stopping for inspection any vessels, including merchant steamers, that ventured inside Guimbi's three-mile territorial limit. Word of her presence and of her increased efficiency, must be spreading in this part of the Caribbean.

Roscal itself seemed secure, even if life for many was little better than in Guimbi.

Clemenger intelligence network had grown. It now included not just informants in the eastern villages and several among Escource's business community and even planters. There was evidence enough of discontent among these groups, but no worse than previously, and none of active opposition. Suspension of the Poll Tax had been popular at every level and payment for labour on new public works had brought a degree of quiet to the countryside. The Soulier twins' continued warnings of sedition by Guimbian agents, and of imminent uprising and slaughter by Roscal's poor, were confined to a small circle.

The Hyperion Consortium had advanced loans to three plantation owners for lime-planting and had contracted d'Erlanger for delivery of a full cargo of juice. The seedling trials by the Oxford botanist were proving promising – no immediate benefit but promise for the future.

Florence was spending the Relief Committee's funds wisely. Dawlish felt guilty that, though she always presented herself as plain Mrs. Dawlish rather than as the governor's wife, much of the credit went to himself. It didn't matter, she assured him, not as long as the simple schools and orphanages were busy, and Miss Giltrap was saving mothers' and babies' lives. And she had secured the Committee's agreement to charter a small steamer to bring labourers back from Panama. d'Erlanger had promised minimising costs by using a vessel soon due to ship produce from his estates.

Dawlish recognised in himself a temptation to complacency. One fact militated against it.

That all the time, just over the border, amid the valleys and canyons and forest-clad ridges that stretched from north coast to south across the island, a mercenary force, commanded by a competent French officer, was encamped.

Even without reinforcement, it might be capable of overthrowing Ravenel and installing a puppet. It could not just be concern for *Déchaîné* that was holding Desmarais back.

He was waiting for something else.

Something unguessable.

*

Dawlish was sitting down to dinner with Florence when a servant announced that Clemenger was asking to see him. Urgent, apparently. It must be, for it was unusual for him to come at such an hour.

"Bring him to my study."

It had been raining all afternoon and Clemenger's clothing was saturated, his riding boots mud-spattered. He'd come from Orvault.

"It may be nothing," he said. "We'd heard rumours like it before. But there's a ring of truth about this one."

"Why?"

"Remember those returning muleteers we grabbed some while ago? Whom we put the fear of God in, and then released on condition they'd feed us anything they'd hear. We've had only petty local stuff from two of 'em but the third took to the work like a duck to water. He knows the trails through the mountains and he's been crossing into Guimbi at intervals. He moves around the villages, reports back what he hears."

"Paid informers will say anything," Dawlish said.

"Yes, but a lot of what he's said has been confirmed by what MacQuaid has heard through Badeaux. About from which villages men have headed to the mountains. That sort of thing."

"And this time?"

"He'd heard rumours of a landing soon. Nothing exact, but much the same story in half-a-dozen villages where his reports had proved correct before."

It sounded thin, little worth delaying dinner for. But Clemenger, a veteran in intelligence work, had taken it seriously enough to drum fifteen miles over muddy roads to tell this.

"Any corroboration?" Dawlish said.

"No. But it all sounded strong enough for this chap to risk his neck to learn more. He knew we'd pay well for this if it's true."

"What did he do?"

"He'd met two Guimbian labourers who'd let slip that they had been approached by somebody who offered good money for going to the mountains. They'd been hesitating but he encouraged them. He'd go with them, he said – they'd assumed he was a Guimbian as poor and desperate as themselves. He could find the way of course and he'd accompanied me on a patrol when we scouted Desmarais's camp some time ago."

"Did they get there?"

"They were received with open arms. The camp's a lot bigger now, with many more men. They're being drilled not just by Frenchmen but by Guimbians too – probably army deserters, because they seem to have some basic familiarity with rifles. But they don't have enough of them and half the new recruits are training with wooden poles. There are more mules there too – they must be buying them one-by-one in Guimbi. Nobody suspected our man – he stayed only for two days drilling and he heard that the strongest mules had been selected for some coming task. They were corralled separately. And pack saddles being readied too. From hints and rumours, it sounded like it'd be a long trek."

"The south coast?" The north's was close to the camp.

Clemenger nodded. "My guess too. Our man had heard enough. So he slipped away last night – he cut a sentry's throat, he claims, but that's probably lying bravado. He reached Orvault this afternoon. I've talked to him myself."

"He could have been found out. He could have been made to talk," Dawlish said. "Or he could have declared himself to Desmarais and taken payment to come back here with a pack of lies."

"He could," Clemenger said. "But it's hard to see what Desmarais would gain from it. And there's nothing lost if we take it as true."

Possibilities, options and risks were already racing through Dawlish's mind.

"How long to get a mule train from the camp to the coast?" he said.

"Three days. Two at the least. Whatever tracks run north to south are small and tortuous. And Mont Sully's an obstacle to be got around."

Two nights from now. It could be a wild goose chase but . . .

"MacQuaid's with Badeaux in Port Mazarin just now," Dawlish said. "We need to get a message to him tonight,"

For there was an opportunity here, one enabled by *Le Déchaîné's* rebirth in the bay at Castries. A gamble, but one worth taking . . .

"I've checked that fishing boat that brings MacQuaid to and fro is in port," Clemenger said. "It can sail at a half-hour's notice."

Dawlish scribbled the message, sealed it in an envelope and handed it to Clemenger. "See that MacQuaid gets it." Then he sent a servant to summon Blackford.

"I'm unwell," he told him. "A touch of fever, serious perhaps. I'm taking to my bed for a few days." He winked. "So cancel all appointments. You can manage routine administration without me."

"I'm sorry to hear it, sir." Blackford was smiling. "I trust that you'll recover soon."

"And get a word down to Sproul at the harbour. Top up *Falconet's* bunkers, raise steam and be prepared to sail at midnight."

*

Early afternoon the following day and *Falconet* was steaming long racetracks at minimum revolutions. No breeze ruffled the dead calm and even Mont Sully's high cone lay hidden twenty miles beyond the northern horizon. Dawlish, had boarded just before sailing, riding down to the harbour with Hippolyte, whom he sent back with his horse to Government House.

"I'm a devoted wife, am I not?" Florence had forced a smile as he mounted. "One who'll insist on nursing her husband by herself, letting nobody else bring him his meals, dosing him with quinine and assuring everybody that his old malaria is back." She was suddenly silent and he saw tears welling. "Be careful, Nick, whatever it is."

He had slept only briefly in *Falconet's* saloon after poring with Sproul over the admiralty chart of the area. The island's south coast was rocky, with few beaches, and along much of its length cliffs fringed the water. Sproul had taken note of the few small inlets and coves in his circumnavigations of the island.

"I'd put my money on this one." Sproul pointed to a small semi-circular bay just west of the Guimbian village of Pressac. "I've seen a few huts there and fishing boats drawn up on a little beach. There must be a track leading inland." His finger stabbed the chart. "And there's another somewhat like it here at Corail."

Half-way between Pressac and Port Mazarin.

"Too far east," Dawlish said. "Desmarais would want to get whatever's landed into the mountains quickly. But Pressac does look promising."

His gaze shifted further west to where the mountains tumbled into the sea. He pointed to a narrow gash that reached in between steep cliffs.

"Did you have look at this?" he asked Sproul.

"I didn't come close enough inshore. It must be a dead end."

No place to land men or equipment. But a good one for sheltering out of sight. And three or four miles west of the possible landing point.

Dawlish fretted as the afternoon wore on. The message sent to MacQuaid might not have reached him yet. Even if it had, *Le Déchaîné's* furnace could have been cold, would need lengthy and careful stoking, leaving her unable to reach this rendezvous until the following day. An inspection had confirmed *Falconet* as fit for action, ready-use ammunition stacked by the three-pounder in her bows, the two Gatlings' barrel-stacks spinning freely, their Broadwell feed-hoppers full, reserves close to hand. Both Gatling-gunners were ex-Royal Navy seamen, already experienced with them, and the two Roscallan loaders had learned quickly. Dawlish regretted that insufficient ammunition was available for more extensive live-fire training – there could never be enough. But what nagged him more was that *Falconet* had no searchlight. The Very flare-pistols that *Chaffinch* had brought were a poor substitute, but they would have to do.

At last, a dark smudge above the blue horizon, then masts and yards and *Le Déchaîné's* dark hull growing above it as she ploughed on with a bone in her teeth. *Falconet* met her and both vessels hove to a cable apart. Dawlish went across with Sproul.

Captain Maurice Queuille received them at the entry port, Sidwell by his side. MacQuaid stood behind him. The message carried by the fishing boat had reached him. He had relayed the contents to Maître Badeaux, who had gone in turn to President Ravenel and had returned with the document he now presented to Dawlish.

An appeal from the President of the Republic of Guimbi to Her Britannic Majesty's Colony of Roscal for support against pirate activity.

A document to provide some protection against official wrath in London should all go badly.

Time to brief Queuille and Sidwell on his plan.

And then, after sunset, both vessels to head north.

*

A waning moon gave just enough light to identify the break in the cliffs. *Falconet* and *Déchaîné* had approached the island with double lookouts, alert for sight of another vessel's funnel glow.

Nothing seen, to Dawlish's relief. Not tonight, though he would welcome it in twenty-fours' time when he would be ready to spring his trap.

The entrance was tight, a half-cable's length at its narrowest, and *Falconet* crawled in at minimum revolutions, a leadsman at the bow calling soundings. There were never less than seven fathoms beneath the keel but the possibility of fallen rocks just hidden beneath the surface could not be discounted. *Déchaîné* followed astern.

Further in, the channel widened and doglegged towards the north-west so that the cliffs cut off direct view of the sea. Beyond lay a small bay, almost circular, about a quarter-mile across and fringed on its farthest shore by steep but not precipitations green-clad slopes. No lights to identify habitation, no beach on which fishermen might draw up their boats. A ship could shelter here for months without detection.

It was well past midnight when *Déchaîné* dropped an anchor buoy and secured to it, ready to slip the mooring and make for the sea at short notice. *Falconet* did not linger. She had come to reconnoitre the channel and Dawlish was content that the passage through was easier than he had feared. He was confident that, under Sidwell's direction, the gunvessel could leave as safely as she had come. He watched from *Falconet's* bridge wing until the channel bend hid her from view. She had already dropped a boat and it was stroking along the bays' eastern shore, seeking a landing place for MacQuaid, a British seaman detached from the yacht with him, and four from *Le Déchaîné's* crew. They had a gruelling climb before them, lugging a night-glass, a half-dozen lanterns and kerosene to light them, and enough provisions to last them four days. By sunrise, and with luck, they should have found a point high enough on a cliff top that would yield an unencumbered view not just out to sea but east and west along the coast.

Falconet emerged from the channel as cautiously as she had entered, her lookouts alert for any sign of another steamer. Only when satisfied that there was none did Dawlish order full speed southwards. Dawn found her ten miles directly south, once more steering slow racetracks.

Waiting.

And back in Government House an attentive wife would be barring access to all others than herself to her feverish husband's sick-chamber, perhaps sending Hippolyte to the town to buy more quinine. A young half-brother, recently orphaned of both parents and too young to be trusted to uphold the charade, would be haunted by fear of another loss. A little girl would be distressed that her father would not take her on his knee at the breakfast table.

All to the good.

Nobody would suspect that Roscal's governor was at sea.

And behind an impassive front, half-fearing, half-hoping for battle.

Chapter 20

The sun rose on *Falconet* steaming long slow racetracks parallel to the coast and twelve miles to its south. It was distant enough for any other vessel passing on innocent business to take her for some rich man's toy cruising for pleasure. From the island itself, or close inshore, *Falconet* was hull-down and her thin upper masts would be hard to spot. She carried no tops, no crow's nest, but seamen with telescopes had been drawn up by slings high on both masts to scan the coastline and watch for other shipping.

The sea was like a mirror, the sky blue, the sun merciless in its heat, blinding by its reflection. It was easy in such conditions for a torpor to descend on the crew but, small as the yacht was, Sproul had established a watch system and each man was either busy or resting. Dawlish, held aloof from the routine management of the vessel – that was Sproul's responsibility – and gave orders to be alerted only in case of a suspicious sighting. He watched the morning's gun drill but made no comment – Bradbury, the gunner, was a seasoned-enough hand to know that silence meant approval. It pleased Dawlish that Sproul, without prompting, had ordered clearing the deck as far as possible, running out firehoses and filling the two cutters carried amidships with water. He went to his cabin afterwards – he wanted to be well rested by evening – but slept only fitfully. It troubled him that his plan depended on so much guesswork, built perhaps not even on sand but on nothing at all.

The day dragged, with only ten sightings to break the monotony for the crew. Three schooners passed far to the south, interisland traders, and three more and a laden brig closer to the island but sailing unhurriedly from the east and disappearing over the western horizon. Sproul had Dawlish called to the bridge three times to alert him to lazy plumes of smoke, all to the south. It was best to take no chances. *Falconet* increased speed, closed, stood off at three miles range to inspect by telescope. One was the mail-steamer on the regular run from Grenada to Jamaica – she would put in briefly at Escource in late afternoon for passengers and post. The clipper bows of the other two, unlike the sweeping rams below the bowsprits of *Déchaîné* and the gunrunner that identified them as French-designed, told that they were merchantmen. They showed no interest in *Falconet* and passed from sight on their lawful errands.

Dawlish was eager for the sun's sinking, for the brief twilight, for the soft moonlit darkness. Here on the bridge with Sproul, he could feel the apprehension around him. This crew had experienced the shock of unexpected battle in the previous encounter with the gunrunner, had seen damage inflicted on *Falconet* that could well have killed some of them. They must be under no illusion that the next meeting – and by now most must guess that that was what Dawlish was now seeking – could prove yet more violent.

The unlit yacht's slow churn back and forth parallel to the shore was closer now, some eight miles. Mont Sully's great cone and the lower ranges to either side were stark black against the starlit northern sky.

"Seven-forty, sir." It was the fourth time that Sproul had crouched below the bridge screen and struck a match to read his watch.

"Very well."

Dawlish hoped that his tone did not convey his disappointment. The expected signal – a five-second flash from a red lantern on the heights above *Le Déchaîné's* haven, to be repeated three times at five-minute intervals – was already late. It would be confirmation that MacQuaid's group was in place and had the coast under observation, assurance too that the Guimbian gunvessel had steam up and was ready to slip her mooring if directed. But so much could have gone wrong – lanterns broken on the climb, kerosene spilled, a watch overwound and a spring broken . . .

"Deck there!" A call from the mast above. "Red light, sir!"

It was gone already but Sproul had lifted his glass, was ready for the next and Dawlish's eyes were locked on the dark profile to the right of, and below, Mont Sully.

The wait seemed endless before Sproul said, "I see it."

Dawlish had seen the pinprick too, had counted the seconds, one and two and three and –

"Five seconds, sir!" Relief in Sproul's voice as he handed the glass to Dawlish.

Five minutes, an eternity, until the light flashed three times more, mere winks in the dark circle of the lens.

"Acknowledge," Dawlish said.

A shutter on a red lantern high on the foremast raised and lowered three times.

Contact established and trap set.

*

Nothing happened through the long, frustrating, but clear night. With *Falconet* south of the island, and observers high on the coastal cliffs, and a half-dozen telescopes and night-glasses between them sweeping the shoreline and the inshore waters, Dawlish thought it likely that any vessel larger than a fishing craft could be detected.

Hour after hour passed, and still nothing seen other than a steamer, far to the south, passing eastwards and disappearing over the horizon. Doubts haunted Dawlish, concern that not only was this a wild goose chase but that at this moment reinforcements for Desmarais might be landing on the island's north coast. He kept the doubts to himself, exchanged only the briefest of neutral observations with Sproul, played the role of the imperturbable commander superior to all feelings of self-distrust and indecision. It was a pose that he had cultivated for years and, as always, felt himself an imposter for doing so.

Dawn came, the sky brightening, the rising sun's reflection blinding on the waveless sea.

Another day of watching, of hoping and of fearing, lay ahead.

*

If the gunrunner should indeed appear, it would be unlikely by daylight, Dawlish had decided. The intensive watch was however maintained through the day, all sightings as innocuous as before. But it pleased him to see how the crew went about its business – not just the few British seamen who had come with Sproul but the more recently recruited Roscallans. *Falconet* as not yet as efficient as a naval vessel – that would have been impossible in the time available – but training and drill, firm but fair discipline and a growing sense of shared pride would achieve it in time. Sproul's unwise dalliance with another man's wife had cost the Royal Navy a valuable officer.

Dawlish felt tension rise, no less throughout the ship than in himself, as the sun plunged. If nothing were to happen this night then Clemenger's original intelligence was probably wrong, worse than a rumour, mere gossip. This patrol could not be maintained indefinitely, nor could the charade that Florence was conducting to cloak his absence from Government House.

Falconet, again unlit, moved further north and hove to about six miles south of the possible landing site near Pressac. She needed brief bursts of slow revolutions to keep herself on station. The boiler was at full pressure, with only minimal stoking required to keep it there, and the shimmer above the funnel was so faint as to be undiscernible even from the bridge. This night was darker than that before, long cloud banks blotting out the moon for minutes at a time. It was hard to decide whether or not this might be an advantage. Bradbury and his crew were standing by the three-pounder on the foredeck, gunners and loaders by the Gatlings.

Dots of red light at the appointed time confirmed that MacQuaid was at his observation post and that *Déchaîné* was ready to emerge from her lair. Three brief flashes in return confirmed *Falconet* on station.

Four hours passed. Sproul ordered the mast-lookouts relieved at hourly intervals – eyes could tire – and others hoisted in their places. There were three false alarms, one to the east and two to the west, will o' the wisps that drew every glass aloft, and on the deck and bridge, to search.

Then the fourth "Deck there!" call.

No mirage this time, but a dark mass far to the east, distant enough offshore to stand out against moonlit water before drifting cloud-shadows hid it again. Only the sharpest eyes could discern it immediately after the lookout's alert. Dawlish's were not among them but he was taking no chances.

"Signal to Mr. MacQuaid," he said to Sproul. "Two flashes only."

The agreed notification of a sighting to the east – it would have been four had it been to the west.

Even before the shutter rose and fell on *Falconet's* lantern, two red dots showed and died on the island's silhouette. MacQuaid had sighted the vessel also.

"Five flashes," Dawlish said.

Not just acknowledgement but the agreed instruction to MacQuaid to signal down to *Déchaîné* to cast off from her mooring buoy and for her gunners to man their weapons.

Five minutes passed. Dawlish himself could spot the stranger through the glass now. She was coming on fast and must be south-west of Port Mazarin. If she was a sister of *Déchaîné* and making full speed – and it was likely that she was, for her captain would want his burdens landed so as to be gone by dawn – then she could be off the Pressac beach in half an hour.

Accustomed since boyhood to observing inverted images in wide-lensed night-glasses, Dawlish could just discern the pale ribbon that was the stranger's bow-wave. It was on the bow that his eye was locked, searching the wicked curve of the ram that would leave no doubt as to her identity. There was no indication yet that she had detected *Falconet*. He could sense that Sproul, by his side, was impatient for the order to move shorewards but it was better to wait, though that moment must soon come, and so too the signal to MacQuaid for *Déchaîné* to spring her surprise.

"It's her." Dawlish passed the glass to Sproul.

The ram was unmistakable and, so also, the three boats already swung out on the port side, ready for dropping. Behind the high bulwarks, the decks must be crowded. The success of the stealthy approach might have bred complacency in the vessel's officers, and their efforts now might concentrate on fast offloading and departure.

The few dim lights at Pressac were blotted out briefly by vessel's passing. She had reduced speed, was at a crawl, and it was obvious that she was headed towards the beach west of the village.

Dawlish's heart was thumping. Signalling too early to MacQuaid to unleash *Déchaîné* could bring her bearing down on the enemy gunvessel before it commenced discharging her loads. If he was a professional – and the earlier encounter had indicated that he was – the French captain would most certainly head seawards then. With *Déchaîné* between him and the shore, he would have the advantage of sea room for manoeuvre while his adversary would not. Yet signalling too late to MacQuaid might mean delayed arrival and the chance for the Frenchman to have landed his cargo and shown a clean pair of heels.

And timing was critical too for *Falconet's* advance. She was still hidden in the dark shadow of a cloudbank overhead, but that might drift by at any moment. It had already done so above the coast so that moonlight now illuminated the oncoming gunvessel. Dawlish was thinking of her as Pelletier's now, the key to General Fernand Pelletier's ascent to power as France's national saviour, as a new Bonaparte.

Dawlish weighed the options and decided. Patience was the best.

The gunvessel had hove to, was stern-on to *Falconet*. Intermittent revolutions must be holding her bows against the night's weak land-breeze. It was unlikely that an experienced captain would choose to anchor in such circumstances and would most likely remain a half-mile off the beach. The first boat had been lowered, was pulling towards the shore, probably carrying a dozen men or more to secure the landing point. Other craft were dropping on both sides and clustering against the hull. The davits could not have carried heavy loads and transferring these into the boats alongside would take time. That was when the gunvessel would be at her most vulnerable.

"Mr. Sproul, if you please. Six flashes."

It seemed impossible that the tiny winks would not be noticed by the gunboat. Dawlish held his breath, but there was no reaction from her. Then six tiny flashes in return from MacQuaid's eyrie.

The irrevocable decision.

Déchaîné would commence her crawl seawards through the narrow cliff-edged passage.

*

Falconet was underway now, creeping on a course that would bring her to a mile eastward of Pelletier's gunvessel. The cloud cover was still favouring her, but it was thinning, shredding to show patches of dark sky studded with starts. It could be only minutes before the enemy ship – for enemy she was – would sight her. The air carried intermittent scraps of sound, creaking blocks, shouted orders, even the thresh of oars, but nothing to suggest anything but unalarmed concentration on discharge of men and cargo.

A lookout from the port bridge-wing approached Sproul, whispered and handed him the glass. He took it, steadied himself against the rail, focussed westwards astern of the gunvessel. Long moments passed before he said to Dawlish, "*Déchaîné's* out."

She must be some three miles beyond the enemy gunvessel. According to their orders, Sidwell and the Guimbian captain, Queuille, would be driving her at full speed, sweeping just south of east to place the Frenchman between her and shore.

Now to buy her time.

"Full speed, Mr. Sproul."

The plan had been fixed two days before and Dawlish had accepted its risks. But now, as the screw bit and the yacht gathered speed, the small cowardly, wheedling inner voice that he had heard so often before was whispering again. This was madness, it told him. At least one of the gunvessel's 138 mm weapons on the starboard side must be manned and a single shell, driving down the lightly built *Falconet's* central axis from bow to stern, could rip her apart. And there was that terrifying Hotchkiss revolver in the enemy's foretop, longer ranged than the Gatlings, even if vulnerable to them at close quarters . . .

Yet, as always had at such moments. Dawlish's nerve held – somehow – and Sproul beside him was holding his also. At his command, the quartermaster was spinning the wheel over, then centring it and *Falconet* was driving straight towards the enemy.

"On my word, open fire on the boats alongside," Dawlish said. "Then keep firing until I order it to stop."

Sproul relayed the order to Bradbury, who was manning the weapon himself. The gunvessel had previously shown herself invulnerable to the three-pounder, but the now-laden boats alongside, and that one straining towards the beach, were defenceless against it. Surprise would be a weapon in itself, shells dropping in rapid succession from the darkness shocking the enemy into long seconds of inaction before responding. Each minute was bringing *Falconet* almost two cables nearer to the gunvessel and the three-pounder's likely accuracy was increasing as the range closed. But at any moment some lookout might sight the foreshortened yacht and advantage would be lost.

Dawlish glanced skywards. There were still clouds above but so thin that the moon was showing through as a fuzzy blur of light. He was counting off the seconds and estimating the range – four cables now. Comfortable for the three-pounder, just possible for the Gatlings.

He could wait no longer.

"Open fire, Mr. Sproul."

"Rapid fire, Mr. Bradbury!"

Now the sharp bark, the stabbing tongue of flame that briefly lit the entire foreship, the whiff of burned powder wafting back. Then the white plume that raced towards the target as the shell dropped before dying just short of the boats. Bradbury had already stepped aside, and the smoking breech was open and the hot shell-casing was ejecting to the deck and the loader was pushing in the next. The breech closed and Bradbury was throwing himself against the shoulder-rest again, was reaching for the trigger, was taking aim.

And firing.

The shell exploded squarely in a boat already stacked with long wooden crates, another dangling on a sling above it.

"Gatlings!"

Their target was not the boats but the gunvessel's foretop where that deadly Hotchkiss was mounted – that had been impressed on the gunners beforehand. Only the Gatling on the platform abaft *Falconet's* bridge could yet bear and Dawlish flinched as it stuttered into life above him, five rounds, pause, another five, pause, and then again and again, the spaced stutter of the experienced gunner grinding the barrel-stack around in short increments to avoid jamming. There were figures at that foretop – they must be swinging the revolver-cannon around. The chance of finding them at this range was low but the Gatling chatter and rapid muzzle-flashes might well distract them.

Bradbury was firing again, three rounds in quick succession – the endless hours of drill were paying off. Two more had blasted into the second boat caught while loading and the other had smashed into the gunvessel's flank, hurling splintered planking into the boats below.

Two cables separation now and luck could not hold much longer. It was close enough to see that the first boat hit – a large one, a cutter probably – was sinking by the stern and the other was heeling over, one crate already sliding from it. Men were throwing themselves into the water or scrambling up the vessel's side. The bulwarks were lined with heads and shoulders now, and bright stabs identified rifle-fire.

"Port, Mr. Sproul! Sixteen points!"

Helm over, bow swinging across, Bradbury landing one last round among the boats. *Falconet's* after-Gatling was unmasked now and was opening with its fellow forward, hosing towards the gunvessel's foretop. An instant later the Hotchkiss there opened fire, four rounds that threw up spray fountains off the starboard quarter. Then, sudden silence, as if one of the Gatlings had found its mark.

Now a long flame reaching out from somewhere forward on the gunvessel. The almost simultaneous crash of sound confirmed it as from a sponson-mounted 138 mm. The aim was off, the shell tearing a racing streak of spray a half-cable off *Falconet's* starboard quarter. The yacht was well into her half-turn and Bradbury could bring his three-pounder into play again. He had shifted his aim, was dropping shells close to the first boat launched by the Frenchman. It was pulling hard, had almost reached the shore, and at this range Bradbury's shells were plunging at a steep angle. Three threw up small geysers close to the boat but the fourth dropped into it. A flash as it hit and then, a second later, one larger, much larger, a glowing orange hemisphere the burst up and out and carried debris – part of it human perhaps – with it. A second eruption followed, dynamite or gunpowder, then only darkness.

"Cease firing!"

Falconet's half-circle was complete and she was running eastwards, parallel to the coast, on a sinuous track to the throw off the French 138 gunners' aims. Both the starboard-side weapons were in action now, over or under-firing, and never dropping shells nearer than fifty yards. The Hotchkiss had coughed into life again – too late – for the range was now too great for any accuracy.

Cloud cast a darker shadow on the waters off the starboard bow and *Falconet* was swinging over towards its shelter. She was unscathed – surprise had been a shield no less than a killing weapon.

On the enemy gunvessel her officers might be consoling themselves that, though it had inflicted loss, the yacht they had encountered previously was fleeing again, would be unlikely to return this night. There had been damage enough, but other boats still lay tethered, undamaged, on the gunvessel's port side, and there were still men and guns to land.

And, somewhere to the south-west, the cloak of darkness shrouded the nearing Guimbian gunvessel. *Falconet* had provided the diversion.

Le Déchaîné's moment was at hand.

Chapter 21

The enemy 138s had fallen silent as *Falconet* lost herself in shadow. But she must return, for only another attack on the gunvessel could distract her lookouts and allow more time for the still undetected *Déchaîné* to close the range.

Falconet was coming around now in another half-circle turn. Dawlish felt fear, stomach-knotting, heart-pounding fear, and the entire crew must feel it too. They had done well in this night's first attack and would have felt relief as the yacht retreated without injury. But this time surprise would be minimal and the enemy's manned 138s were likely to respond to the first flash of Bradbury's puny three-pounder.

Straightening out now, a sheet of waveless moonlit water ahead and the Frenchman's hull dark against it. The minutes of hiding had given time for barrels to cool and for replenishing the Gatlings' Broadwell magazines. Sproul relayed Dawlish's orders to the gunners, no different than before.

A muzzle-flash ahead, another two seconds later, bathing the enemy's mast and yards in brief red light, and then the sounds of discharge washing over *Falconet*. An agony of delay that seemed like centuries, then grey fountains of spray climbing off the starboard bow. Dawlish glanced back and up and saw the intense glow hovering above the funnel. The French gunners had seen it too, were responding, had done well with this first salvo. The situation was good, could not be better, a cold logical voice told him in his brain. Enemy attention would be focussed on *Falconet* again, reducing the chance of noticing *Déchaîné's* furtive advance. But the diversion might come at high cost . . .

Falconet was weaving as she burst from the shadow into the moonlit water. The gunvessel was still a half-mile distant, still out of range for the three-pounder but that did not matter. Diversion was everything . . .

"Mr. Bradbury!"

"Aye, aye, sir." Even in that experienced voice was a note of fear, awareness that this was suicidal.

"Open fire. On the hull, mind you, and keep firing!"

An enemy 138 blasted again. Its twin was silent for now, must be holding fire to observe the other's fall of shot and then correct. Long seconds, then climbing spray to starboard – and close.

Falconet sheered to port on a course that would bring her seawards of the gunvessel and the three-pounder was hurling its first shell as the enemy's second 138 opened.

Another miss.

Bradbury and his crew were back in their practised rhythm, their fire dropping ever closer to the enemy. The short flames spitting from *Falconet's* bow added to the funnel-glow as aiming marks for the Frenchman. Again and again the helm was thrown over but the yacht was no torpedo boat designed to dart and slew in tight turns. The French gunners' professionalism was showing now, sometimes anticipating the *Falconet's* manoeuvrings and dropping shells close enough to shower spray on her bridge and decks.

A flash against the dark profile of the gunvessel's hull, the first three-pounder round scoring. The Hotchkiss in the enemy's foretop was opening slow and steady fire but not yet hitting.

The range had closed too much, and the advantage was now the gunvessel's. *Falconet's* luck could not endure. Time to turn and run.

"Port, Mr. Sproul, twelve points!" Enough to reach the shadowed water again.

Turning away now. The three-pounder fell silent as the yacht arced over and blocked its line of fire. The gunvessel was falling astern, her weapons were still reaching out and –

An explosion, ear-splitting, a red flash lighting *Falconet* for an instant. Then a searing blast of hot air made Dawlish spin about. Dark as it was, he could see a large gap torn in the port bulwark amidships and hear blood-chilling, inhuman screams.

And at that instant came a flash from seaward, a mile or less astern of the Frenchman. Then a second – it must be from the weapon in port sponson forward, for the long curve of *Le Déchaîné's* ram stood dark against its brightness. On her current heading she could bring both her forward 138s firing towards the enemy gunvessel's stern.

A long white plume raced parallel to Frenchman's flank – Sadler, *Le Déchaîné's* gunnery officer in all but name, was aiming low. The second shell fell closer still. Another salvo and this time a hit, a very palpable hit, a detonation high on the Frenchman's counter. A few feet lower and the steering might have been wrecked and the gunvessel left incapable of manoeuvre. Only her port guns could reply at this moment and they were mounted ahead of the hit. The slightest angle of the hull to the line of *Le Déchaîné's* onrush would mean that its flank would mask them.

Another salvo falling close and as the spray collapsed a red streak of flame was reaching out from the Frenchman's side. But the aim was well off.

"She's moving," Sproul yelled.

Dawlish could see it too, the gunvessel nudging away from the beach, the boats she had been loading cast off and left behind. She gathered speed, was coming about now. She was still vulnerable, her sea room restricted by the nearby coast, but if she could reach open water, she could meet *Déchaîné* on equal terms.

The Frenchman was heeling in the tight turn and in this long moment it was impossible for her gunners to aim with any accuracy. It was *Le Déchaîné's* chance. Her bows edged over, straightened, brought both her forward 138s to bear. They blasted simultaneously. A column of foam rose just ahead of her target's bows and the other shell detonated on the foreship – it looked as if where the bows curved down towards the ram.

Déchaîné was coming about as well – she was already too close inshore and she also needed sea room. She and her adversary would soon be on parallel courses, broadside to broadside.

On *Falconet's* bridge, a seaman was reporting to Sproul that the bulwark had taken the brunt of the detonation amidships. Splinters had killed two men and seriously wounded a third. But no damage to her propulsion machinery.

Dawlish heard it as if from a great distance for he was thinking himself into the mind of the captain of that French vessel. He had two choices now – to fight it out with *Le Déchaîné,* Guimbi's one-ship navy, or to run for whatever base from which he was operating. The second option seemed more plausible – this gunvessel was a one-ship navy also, Fernand Pelletier's navy – but it still needed to engage *Le Déchaîné,* even if only to disable her to prevent pursuit. Tonight's landing had been frustrated but that could not be the end of it. Given the man that Pelletier was, he would still want to reinforce Desmarais with more men and weapons, and for that he would need this gunvessel.

The temptation to join *Le Déchaîné,* give whatever support was possible, was strong. But there was an important enemy closer to hand.

"Mr. Sproul!" Dawlish pointed to the boats abandoned by the Frenchman. Three remained, those that had been loading on her port side and now, oars flashing in the moonlight, they were pulling hard for the beach.

"We'll sink them. No fire until we're nearly on top of 'em. Then the three-pounder and the Gatlings also."

Falconet pulled into a turn and as she straightened Sproul ordered four flares launched from a Very pistol. Four cartridges in succession – some ten seconds between them as they had to be loaded into a single barrel. They left no trail, their presence announced only when they burst into light at the apex of their trajectories. They fell quickly, falling stars reflected in the sea, bathing the escaping boats in icy light.

Falconet was driving towards the craft nearest shore. It was a cutter, piled with crates, men standing packed between them, hampering the oarsmen, and so deep-laden that the gunwale must be but inches above the water's surface. Winking dots of flame indicated occupants firing back with rifles, pistols, anything they had. Another, smaller, boat was following at a crawl, it too at the limit of its capacity and one more, seemingly half-empty was pulling faster towards the beach. Dawlish could see movement there – probably the men and mules that had come to carry landed loads back to Desmarais' mountain camp. But they could be dealt with later. The immediate concern was the boats.

There were bobbing heads, floating debris, shouts of terror and of anger as *Falconet* ploughed through the remnants of the craft that she had destroyed earlier. Then Bradbury's three-pounder spat, missing the leading boat with his first shot but smashing his second into it. Its bow was down at once, its stern rising and whatever occupants that had not been stunned or killed were casting themselves into the water.

Two more flares were falling, illuminating the doomed boat and men in hideous light. Bradbury fired again, smashed the craft into two separate parts that were gone in seconds. *Falconet's* twin Gatlings were stuttering too, their target the laden boat that had been following in the first's wake and was now trying to turn away. In the light of another falling flare Dawlish saw bodies jerking under the leaden hail, chunks of wood leaping from the hull and crates, despairing and wounded men jumping overboard.

This was slaughter, butcher's work, repellent, yet Dawlish hardened his heart. It was not just the men, the reinforcements, that must not reach the beach but the rifles in those crates now plunging from the shattered boats. *Falconet* was driving through the gap between the wreckage, close enough to hear cries from the water during the brief intervals between firing. Bradbury was swinging the three-pounder over, pumping two rounds in succession into the craft already scourged by Gatling fire and finishing it.

"Where's the third boat, Mr. Sproul?"

It had been last seen thrashing towards the shoreline and now was lost in the darkness. Dawlish was determined to have it also.

"Flares! Two of 'em!" Sproul called to the seaman with the Very pistol and pointed shorewards.

The same ghastly light as before found the boat. Terror-driven oars were speeding it towards the beach and it was close before the Gatlings lashed it. The light died before Bradbury could sweep the three-pounder to bear but the Gatling ripples continued. Now another flare was bursting and seconds later Bradbury's shell was throwing up a fountain close to the boat. His next destroyed it. Time now to lash the dark beach with Gatling and three-pounder fire. Exploding shells illuminated running men, stampeding mules, the column that Desmarais had sent here to meet the landing now in headlong, panicked retreat.

But Dawlish was no longer watching. He was looking seawards, could see both the Frenchman and *Le Déchaîné* lit up for seconds by their broadsides. They looked as if they were on a parallel south-easterly course, and upwards of a mile separated them. Both were trailing long plumes of funnel smoke and must be churning at maximum revolutions. If either was damaged, then it could not be serious. Their firing was slow and deliberate, but it was impossible to see how close the shells were falling.

And then a single flash against the enemy's hull – it looked somewhere amidships – told of *Déchaîné* landing a round. She might already have been hit herself while Dawlish's attention had been focussed on destroying the boats but there was no obvious sign of it.

Falconet could do little, but that little had provided distraction before. And the two gunvessels, sisters of the same class, were evenly matched. Even a modicum of support might tip the balance.

"Take us about, Mr. Sproul."

The Frenchman's 138s blasted simultaneously, long enough to wash her hull in scarlet light. Dawlish pointed.

"Put us off her starboard quarter."

He was sure now that the Frenchman had chosen flight, and preservation for another day, over *Le Déchaîné's* destruction. It was uncertain how long both vessels could maintain maximum speed and even a single knot's advantage could ensure the enemy's escape. *Falconet* might be making a knot or more than either, but at the gunvessel's current distance from her – Dawlish estimated three miles – it would take a quarter-hour before she could close enough to play any useful role.

So, *Falconet* followed, a spectator for now, parched gun crews slurping water from buckets, and a messenger from aft announcing that the wounded man had died. The distant gunfire was less frequent, still disciplined, but with no indication of further hits. The sky above the eastern horizon was faint pink now and lightening by the minute. The masts and yards of both gunvessels stood out as silhouettes against it and the sun would soon soar up as an incandescent ball. It was clear now that the enemy had drawn ahead and that *Déchaîné* lay off her stern quarter.

"He's turning!" Sproul pointed.

The Frenchman was edging to port, was holding the helm over, was straightening to run due east. *Déchaîné* was slow in following the turn and the gap between was growing. Then she too nudged over.

This was a stern chase now.

As long as the range did not open yet further, this was to *Déchaîné's* advantage. Her sponsoned 138s forward could now fire straight ahead. The smoke billowing from the enemy's funnel was drifting aft and down, impeding the aims of her two 138s aft. *Déchaîné's* view, by contrast was unhampered by her smoke.

This was her opportunity. Both forward guns fired. One shell fell close off the enemy's port beam but the other was a hit – not on the hull, but somewhere on deck aft, the flash rising above a bulwark. The vessel lurched, wavered from its course, straightened again, kept running, speed apparently undiminished. The sun was climbing over the horizon now – bad, that, for *Le Déchaîné's* gunners had it in their eyes.

Dawlish had laid his night-glass aside, had grabbed a telescope, had the enemy vessel in sharp focus. His heart leapt. He could see smoke, lighter, thinner than that from the funnel, rising from somewhere abaft it. And then, flickering above the bulwark line, flames rising, falling back from sight, then rising again. Something was burning there, nothing that affected propulsion, but a deckhouse perhaps or stowed cordage or more crates. It did not matter what – it was a fire and this, despite her iron framing, was a wooden ship. Her captain and her crew must know that this danger was deadly, that if the hungry flames could reach a magazine, or even ready-use lockers, an explosion could blow the vessel apart. And all on board must be aware that they had no boats now . . .

Yet she was still fighting. Her 138s aft, now with a momentarily smoke-free line of sight, were firing again, two rounds in quick succession.

Both hit – a detonation high on *Le Déchaîné's* foremast, another far aft along the flank. Dawlish saw the port shrouds snapping, whipping like writhing snakes, then the mast itself lurching to starboard and the upper yard tearing free. It crashed down, impacted on the foretop and mainyard below, carried them with it to the foredeck. The wreckage landed just ahead of the forward-sponsoned guns – the gun crew was leaping back from that visible on the port side. The mainyard struck the bulwark there, broke and fell, dropped into the water, was dragged along by a tangle of rigging. The lower mast still stood, but was tottering.

Déchaîné was slowing – the right decision – and her survival now depended on cutting that trailing wreckage free and staying the foremast. It must be done quickly but even a well-trained Royal Navy crew could not manage it in less than twenty minutes. This crew had no such training and should the French gunvessel turn and circle . . .

But there was still hope.

Shifting his focus back to the enemy vessel, Dawlish saw that she had not changed course nor had her speed diminished. The fire hidden behind her bulwarks was still burning but no flames rose above them. Smoke still drifted up, but less dense than before, and white clouds – steam – swirled within it. Water hoses must be playing there, might still have a long battle ahead to find and quench the last embers. Survival clearly his objective, the French captain had no intention to curve back to pummel *Le Déchaîné*. *Falconet* might draw close enough to have hurled a few three-pound shells towards it, but that was not needed now.

"Take us alongside *Déchaîné*," Dawlish said.

She was dead in the water. Sidwell had decided not to risk trailing cordage snaring her screw. She would need any men whom *Falconet* could spare to help clear the wreckage and dump it overboard.

The enemy fired two Parthian shots. They fell short, yet there was something of menace about them, a reminder that this contest had not ended, that she would return another day. Her smoke thinned as she headed for the eastern horizon and dropped from sight, destination unknown.

But by then Dawlish had crossed to *Déchaîné* and most of *Falconet's* men were hacking and heaving with the Guimbian crew. The lower foremast still stood and Sidwell was directing its re-staying. The falling yards had killed three men, another looked close to death and two more were lightly wounded. But all four 138 were unharmed, and their gunners with them.

It could have been worse, much worse.

Guimbi's one-ship navy had done her proud.

*

It was early afternoon before *Falconet,* her borrowed crewmen now back on board, left *Déchaîné,* which would return to Port Mazarin. MacQuaid went with her to report the action to Ravenel and Badeaux. It might not have been an outright victory but it was at least a stay of execution.

Falconet hove to off the beach where the landing had been frustrated. Shattered boat-sections drifted there, splintered planking, broken oars. A few bodies still clung to them, lifeless, faces dropped in the water, rising and falling with the small breeze-driven ripples. Most were clothed in the same blue serge badgeless uniforms seen previously on Desmarais's men. Dawlish repressed his nausea and had one turned over with a boat hook. The skin might have been bronzed until the previous night but it was a pallid white now and the eyes were locked open above the dark moustache.

There were more bodies in the shallows and others on the sand beyond. Figures – villagers, ragged and straw-hatted – turned and ran from them at *Falconet's* appearance but they had drifted back when they saw no hostile move and resumed their looting of the corpses. Dead mules lay among them, bones white against dark red in the sun's glare, half-skeletons already, their flesh stripped away. Meat was a luxury in

Guimbi. The few three-pounder shells that had landed here had brought unexpected feasting for a nearby village tonight. Nothing more remained.

Dawlish turned away. He had known success as well as failure before, had won what counted as victory. And the feeling afterwards had always been the same as now, an emptiness, a vast sadness and a tinge of self-disgust, however much he assured himself that there had been no alternative.

Time now for *Falconet* to steam back to Escource.

Carrying her own dead.

Chapter 22

Dawlish directed that *Falconet* stand off until darkness before docking at Escource. He went straight to Government House, well muffled to avoid recognition since the fiction that he still lay ill there must be maintained. It was essential to write the necessary reports to Topcliffe and the Colonial Office immediately. The yacht, though damaged, was seaworthy enough to carry Blackford to Antigua. He would see there to transmission of Dawlish's brief enciphered telegraph accounts and bring also the more extensive written reports that would follow, locked in the captain's safe, on the next Royal Mail steamer to depart. Florence, woken from sleep, insisted on bringing coffee and food herself as Dawlish worked with Blackford in his study. He saw that she guessed from his clothing and fatigue that there had been action, and she was relieved to see him whole. They embraced with passion but she did not query him. She had accepted his profession and was proud of it. Had he not come back, she would have borne the loss with a fortitude no less than her sorrow. He loved her for that indomitability, as for so much else.

Falconet departed in the early hours. Only after Blackford had left with her did Dawlish bathe, allow himself an hour's sleep and then dress in clean clothing. He gave himself a half-hour afterwards with Jessica and Ted. They seemed even more precious now because a day before he had accepted that he might never see them again. Jessica was unwilling to leave him when her nurse returned for her. She had merely missed him, had not guessed anything. But Ted had been told by Florence that Dawlish was seriously ill and could not leave his room. It must have frightened him badly, so soon after his parents' deaths, and he had struggled to hold back his tears when he saw Dawlish hale again.

"It was only a touch of malaria, Ted." He hated lying to this boy. But questions might be asked at school and the subterfuge must be played out. "Remember I told you about Ashanti? Malaria followed me from there and it hits again at times. It's unpleasant, but it won't kill me."

"And you take quinine for it, don't you, Nicholas?" Ted was still not comfortable about addressing a man thirty-two years his senior by his name, even though he was his half-brother.

"That's it, Ted. Quinine helps. So whatever will kill me, it won't be malaria."

"But that won't be for a long time, will it, Nicholas?" A tremor in the boy's voice.

"Maybe a long time. But, whenever it is, I'll rely on you to look after Florence and Jessica for me when I'm gone, won't you? That's a bargain, isn't it?" Dawlish held out his hand.

Ted shook it with solemnity.

Another step towards him being the man I hope he will be.

*

Falconet's dead had been brought ashore before she departed for Antigua. Labourers and others at the harbour had seen this – and her damage – and must have guessed that she had engaged some enemy. Half of Escource would know of it by now and rumours would be spreading. Let them, Dawlish thought. What only mattered was that any talk of Roscal's governor's presence on board would seem an unlikely fabrication.

He sent Hippolyte to summon the Advisory Council members for an emergency meeting at noon. It pleased him to learn that d'Erlanger was in town and that he could rely on at least one supporter. Beforehand, he met Clemenger and briefed him on what had happened.

"It's a setback," the major said. "Damn well done, but only a setback. They'll be back. But, until then, Desmarais is weak. He'll be short of the rifles and men he expected. Morale will be low after the debacle at the beach."

"You're going to recommend attacking him soon, aren't you?" Dawlish could see it coming.

"There'll never be a better time. The Rural Guard's up to strength. It's well trained. If MacQuaid can persuade Ravenel to send a Guimbian force west against Desmarais, we can catch him between us."

Dawlish shook his head. He already considered and dismissed it. Ravenel could hardly rely even on the troops in Port Mazarin, much less their commanders. Better for him not to test their loyalty. *Le Déchaîné's* recent success would strengthen his standing. Her crew had done well, could do as much again. Without reinforcements, the Desmarais threat would weaken by the day.

And there was another consideration. Dawlish had stuck his neck out very far already. He would prefer a degree of approval from London before committing himself further.

"We'll keep this matter in review, major," he said. "I think that's all for now."

Clemenger looked crestfallen as he left. An ageing man, with an admirable career behind him, but still hankering for larger glory while there was still time.

A man such as I too may become if all here fails.

*

None of the four councillors appeared to suspect that Dawlish's indisposition had been a fake – he still looked fatigued enough to make it credible – but there was warmth only in d'Erlanger's congratulations. All were aware of *Falconet's* arrival and fast departure, of the landing of the bodies. None appeared to suspect that he had been on board and they accepted at face value that the yacht, on regular patrol, had encountered an apparent smuggler and had been fired on when she challenged. Only the fortuitous arrival of *Déchaîné* had saved *Falconet* from worse damage. The yacht's captain had been wise indeed to retreat and leave it to the Guimbian gunvessel to deal with the intruder. Councillor Marsac, the lawyer, seemed the only one less than convinced by the story but he did not challenge it.

"There'll be alarm in the community, Your Excellency," Verley, the planter, said. "Will you make a public announcement?"

"An excellent suggestion," Dawlish said. "Perhaps a message from myself to the editor of the *Escource Courier*?"

It was Roscal's sole newspaper, published twice weekly. It had a small circulation, only among businessmen and planters. Few others, even if literate, could afford a copy. It had been grudging in its praise for Dawlish's recent initiatives. Its constant themes were distrust of Guimbi and the reminder the black republic represented of rebellion and dispossession.

"An announcement would be welcomed," Marsac said. "There are already so many rumours about and causing unrest."

"The editor will have it in early afternoon," Dawlish said.

It would be concise, a few sentences only, would say no more than he had told the councillors. In time the full story would emerge but he'd manage that when it happened. A lot might have changed by then.

"The burials, Yor Excellency," Chevit said. "An occasion perhaps for the Militia to pay full honours to the fallen?"

As colonel, he had gloried in turning out in uniform at the funeral of the riot victims. So too had a dozen other officers, all overweight and ailing amateurs like himself.

"I'd be pleased to take full charge of the funeral arrangements," he said. "My brother officers would be equally happy."

Dawlish would have preferred to indulge the old man – his liking for him had grown – but the less attention drawn to this matter the better. "I'm informed that the families want private arrangements, colonel," he said. "But I suggest the same compensation as on the previous sad occasion."

"Appropriate, most appropriate," d'Erlanger said. "I've no doubt my fellow councillors are in agreement."

Nobody demurred.

"I'll wish you 'Good Day' then, gentlemen." Dawlish drew a hand across his face and sighed. "I'm still a little indisposed. We can defer other business to a later meeting."

He sensed amusement and understanding on d'Erlanger's face as they shook hands.

It had gone better that he expected.

*

d'Erlanger was at Government House again the following day, though to meet Florence, not Dawlish. He did not stay for lunch because he had business back in Saint Gérons.

"What was it about, Florence?"

She had not mentioned the meeting to him beforehand.

"About a ship to bring workers home from Panama. We'd hoped for maybe a brig. But this is better still. A small steamer. Mr. d'Erlanger told me that it'll be coming here next month. And there's even better news. He said he'd cover the cost himself – though he doesn't want anybody to know. Just an anonymous donor. I'm not to tell the Relief Committee his name."

The shadow of his family's past still lies heavy on him. This is expiation.

Florence was rushing on. "He'll go with it himself to find Roscallans who want to come back. He has the patois and the standing to convince them. And I suggested that he brings Madame Geneviève with him. I know she'll be glad to go. She'll have to get names from families here – I can help her travel about – and she can bring messages from them with her to convince them to come back. And –"

She stopped suddenly, voice trembling, tears glistening in those eyes he loved so well. He understood.

"You wanted to go yourself, did you, Florence?"

"Yes. Not just because I'm responsible for spending the Relief Committee's money wisely, though that's no longer the case, but because there'd be officials to deal with, paperwork, permissions, probably demands for bribes and the like, and I've experience managing that sort of thing."

He listened, but he guessed there was yet more to it than that.

"I'd have gone as Mrs. Dawlish," she said. "Mrs Nicholas Dawlish – I'm always proud of that – but I wouldn't have disguised the fact that I'm wife of Roscal's governor. Because that would have carried some weight. But Mr. d'Erlanger can manage as well, or better, I know that."

"I can give him a letter of introduction to the British consul," Dawlish said. "There'll be no abuse of my position in doing that. It'll ensure assistance and lead to other introductions."

"You could have done that for me too, Nicholas."

She had hungered for Panama as an adventure, he realised. She had never flinched from danger or responsibility, either by his side, or when she had undertaken tasks for Topcliffe while he himself was overseas. She carried responsibility here on Roscal too. But only because she could do so despite a constraint that she hadn't had before.

"You were concerned about Jessica, weren't you, Florence?" He drew her to him as he said it. "You couldn't have brought her with you because Panama's a death trap. And you knew that you might die of fever there yourself. Jessica has already lost one mother. You didn't want her to lose another."

Mentioning Jessica's real mother hurt him. He had never told Florence the full story of that unknown woman's death. Better to tell even himself that he had just found her lying in the desert with the baby in her arms.

"I was worried about Ted too, Nicholas. He's lost both his mother and his father so recently."

"And you've been afraid that you might come someday to resent Jessica for denying you the opportunity?" Hard as it was, better to say it. "As you would not, had you given her birth yourself?"

He couldn't see her face as it was pressed against his shoulder. But he felt her nodding.

"You'd never have resented Jessica for that, Florence. You're not that sort of woman nor that sort of mother. It was a foolish fear but you took the right decision about Panama. And anyway –" he tried to speak with the mock severity that often amused her, "I could have forbidden you."

"You could have, Nick, but you're not that sort of husband. But you could have talked me out of it."

He kissed her, then pushed her gently away.

"You've a lot of work to do with Madame Geneviève before that steamer leaves, Mrs Dawlish. You had better get started."

"Aye, aye, sir," she said.

And smiled.

*

MacQuaid arrived from Port Mazarin later that week by the fishing boat that he used regularly.

"*Déchaîné* and her crew are the heroes of the hour," he said. "People heard the firing in the night and when the word spread that she was limping into port, half the town came out to see her. Captain Queuille and his people were boasting – God knows they deserved to – when they came ashore."

"What did they say about the enemy gunvessel?" Dawlish asked.

"That she was French, no doubt of it. That brought out all the hatred, all the memories, all the resentment, and the crowd went wild."

It was understandable, apparently the first victory since independence of a humiliated nation over the oppressor that had held it to ransom. But a dangerous assumption, very dangerous. There had been no French government backing.

"You spoke to President Ravenel?"

"I went to see him directly. He'd already heard confused reports. He listened to me and then –" MacQuaid paused. "I hadn't expected his reaction. He'd always seemed so rational and dignified. So courtly. But now he was furious and his venom shocked me. He was on his feet, swearing, gloating. It would mark the start of a new era, a new Guimbi, he said, one that could no longer be ignored or intimidated. He'd show France who was master here."

"You emphasised that the enemy gunvessel had almost certainly no French government sanction?"

"I tried, but he didn't want to hear. He wouldn't have listened to the Archangel Gabriel himself at that moment."

Ravenel had been at the end of his tether, Maître Badeaux had warned weeks before. Now it had snapped.

"Are there loan repayment instalments due soon?" Dawlish said.

"Next month."

They could not be worse timed, not with Ravenel in this mood.

"Did you see Maître Badeaux?"

"I went straight to him after I left the presidential palace. There was nothing to be gained from talking any further to Ravenel while he was damn nearly frothing at the mouth. And Badeaux was alarmed. He could see that no good could come from precipitate action against France. He'd talk to Ravenel himself later and try to calm him down, though he wasn't hopeful. But in the meantime, he was worried by the mood in town. And he was right to be."

"The crowd?"

"The mob, rather, by nightfall. They'd gone beyond triumph and were out for blood. Any blood. There're a few French businessmen still living in Port Mazarin. Chandlers and importers and the like, many of 'em there for years and married to black women. Most saw what was coming and they left town early for properties outside. But two didn't. They were long established, good employers, and they probably thought they were well accepted. But they were dragged out anyway, beaten and hanged off trees. Their houses burned too. God knows what happened to their wives and children."

"Calm now?"

"Calmer, but feeling's still running high."

"And Ravenel?"

"He didn't help. He spoke to a crowd – raved rather – from the palace balcony yesterday. They loved it. But he spoke alone, none of the ministers with him and notably not General Aubertin."

It was easy to imagine that Minister of Defence watching a descent into hysteria, even madness, and biding his time. And he would not be alone . . .

"Wasn't there a French consul?" Dawlish remembered mention of a mulatto lawyer, a Guimbian, who'd held that position. "What became of him?"

"He kept his head. He brought his family to Badeaux's residence before his house and office were set alight. They were safe there."

"There still?"

"No," MacQuaid said. "He chartered a schooner to take himself and his family and a half-dozen others to Guadeloupe. They boarded quietly last night and were gone by dawn."

Silence, a sickening awareness that there was a telegraph link from Guadeloupe. French newspapers were probably already publishing inflated accounts of massacre of French citizens in Guimbi. There would be calls from the opposition parties for immediate action, attempts to calm the outrage by the cautious government – for however much longer it might stay in power. And that could mean just months, maybe even weeks, in France's volatile Third Republic.

All welcome, all full of promise, to a would-be Man of Destiny.

General Fernand Pelletier.

And all enough to cancel the repulse of the gunvessel a few nights since.

Wounded, not killed then, it would most certainly return.

*

Blackford did not return from Antigua for a full week. In reply to the telegraphed battle reports, Topcliffe had ordered the secretary to wait for further instructions. In the meantime, the damage to *Falconet* was to be repaired in a local boatyard. Now Blackford was back with a long enciphered telegram from Topcliffe and a curt one from the Colonial Office. It was no more specific than recommending taking all considerations into account and proceeding with caution.

Topcliffe's reply had been delayed until answers had arrived to telegraphed queries sent to British consuls and attachés around the world. Other than the two *Belette*-class gunvessels allegedly sold to Siam and Ecuador, all French units of the type were located in the Mediterranean or at Tonkin. None was undergoing repair. But the embassy in Bangkok had confirmed that the ex-French *Blaireau* had indeed entered Siamese service. The consul at Guayaquil indicated that no such vessel had arrived in Ecuador. It was safe then to assume that the gunvessel encountered off Guimbi was the ex-*Hermine*. Not that the name mattered. Repaired, she would be as dangerous as before.

Dawlish had shared with nobody the vain hope that General Pelletier might have been on board during that battle, might have died in it. But vain indeed the hope had been. Topcliffe indicated that he was still in France, was addressing large rallies, had never been more popular.

And Topcliffe's advice?

Little better than the Colonial Office's.

Wait for further developments and take all appropriate measures accordingly.

The admiral too was distancing himself from possible failure.

Chapter 23

Falconet was almost constantly at sea now. Between patrols along the Roscallan and Guimbian coasts, Dawlish sent her on fast runs to Antigua for telegraphed messages to and from London. He also sent her twice to French-held Guadeloupe to buy Paris newspapers. They were three or four weeks out of date but all, regardless of political affiliation, were united in indignation against Guimbi. It wasn't just the exaggerated numbers of French citizens killed in the rioting that fuelled the anger but the rising anxiety about loan repayments. General Pelletier was not alone in his concern for the widows and orphans who had invested in Guimbian bonds through banks and agents but he was the most eloquent. He was constantly on the move around provincial France, speaking as often in small villages as in large towns. His message was clear. The great enemy that had robbed *Le Patrie* of two provinces now menaced its eastern border and could only be faced by a strong, united, country. But the greatest immediate enemy was internal, the rotten, bickering, self-serving political class that let even a tiny, black, so-called nation threaten the savings of ordinary, thrifty, French citizens. He never mentioned his own ambitions. He didn't need to. The crowds loved him.

Topcliffe's messages confirmed Pelletier's soaring popularity. He had never once made direct mention of recovering Guimbi and that was significant. If he acted, he would want it to be as a bolt from the blue, news that would electrify France, that would line the docks at Cherbourg or Le Havre with cheering hordes when he returned, that would carry him within weeks to the presidency. But in the meantime, Pelletier was still in France, ready for his ideal moment.

And that moment would demand more than some new financial scandal bringing down yet another government. It needed the *Hermine*, the gunvessel repulsed by *Déchaîné* and *Falconet*. It was impossible to know how badly she'd been damaged in that action – remembering seeing her burning was sweet – but Dawlish guessed that she had needed extensive repairs. But where? Topcliffe's network of consuls and informants still reported nothing of her.

Dawlish had suggested to Topcliffe that a Royal Navy patrol be established around the island, far enough over the horizon to arouse no suspicion. Working together, two vessels like *Chaffinch* would be more than a match for *Hermine*. But Topcliffe dismissed the proposal. In a direct confrontation, Pelletier – who might well be on board this time – would run up the French tricolour. Authorised or not by the government in Paris, his gesture would evoke massive support in France. Exchange of fire with a British vessel would serve him better still and bring both nations to the brink of war, or beyond.

No, Topcliffe said, Guimbi must save herself without overt support. It was good that *Le Déchaîné's* toppled mast had been replaced and other damage repaired under Sidwell's direction. She was again patrolling the coast and he was drilling her crew relentlessly. The men had taken well to it, their pride and morale boosted by their previous success.

And while that one-ship navy kept its lonely vigil, President Ravenel was proving himself Guimbi's worst enemy.

*

Dawlish loved the time before sunrise, rising to spend a quiet hour on his papers before breakfast, enjoying the birdsong and scent of flowers entering though the study's open windows. This time there had been a storm in the night, with heavy rain and thunder, so that the succeeding calm had especial freshness, a sense of the world reborn.

A tap on his door and then it opened to show MacQuaid pushing past the servant who had ushered him here. His clothes were soaked and he looked exhausted. There had been no plans for him to come so soon from Port Mazarin. Whatever had brought him was urgent enough for him to make a night's stormy passage in an open fishing boat. Dawlish gestured to him to sit and dismissed the servant.

"I couldn't wait," MacQuaid said. "You need to know immediately."

"News of Desmarais? Another landing?"

"Ravenel. He'll be making a proclamation this morning. Maître Badeaux came to me about it last night and he was distraught."

"What sort of proclamation?"

"Ravenel's renouncing all loan-repayment obligations. The proclamation's already printed. It'll be distributed this morning. There's already word out that he'll be talking from the palace balcony at eleven o'clock. The crowds are probably gathering even now. Nobody knows more yet except that it'll be important."

Dawlish felt chilled. Guimbi was plunging into a trap more dangerous than any Pelletier could have dreamed of. It could unite all France in outrage.

"Badeaux tried to talk him out of it but it was impossible," MacQuaid said. "A delegation had arrived from France a few days ago, three of 'em representatives of banks and the fourth from the Finance Ministry. They'd already feared renunciation and wanted to forestall it. They were quite reasonable, Badeaux said. They were ready to accept rescheduling of repayments, offer better terms, anything to avoid default. Badeaux worked out a schedule with them, a better one than he could have hoped for. But when he presented it to Ravenel –"

"– he went berserk." Dawlish completed the sentence.

It was probably inevitable, judging by reports of the president's increasing instability. He'd become ever more addicted to long rambling and hysterical speeches from his balcony. Each time, yet larger mobs listened and cheered and looted rum shops afterwards.

MacQuaid's voice was weary. "Badeaux said that Ravenel was damn-near apoplectic. He was even raving about having the French delegation arrested and charging them with God knows what. If he had, they'd probably have been dragged out of gaol by a mob and torn limb from limb. Badeaux spirited them out to his own house under cover of darkness before he came to see me. He's hoping to get them off to Guadeloupe in a schooner once things quieten."

Dawlish's first impulse was to think of sending *Falconet* – she was in in Escource harbour at present – to their aid. Regardless of mob feeling, a small landing party under a Union flag would not be challenged. Once on the yacht, the four French delegates could be brought within hours to safety in Guadeloupe.

But then . . .

The news would be flashing to Paris by cable, enough not only to stoke outrage further but to precipitate bank-failures, panic-selling on the bourse.

Better that Topcliffe should know before that. Discreet warnings to British financial institutions could limit damage to their interests, perhaps offer opportunities to capitalise on French weakness . . .

"But the French gentlemen are safe for now?" he said.

"As long as nobody knows they're with Badeaux."

Dawlish pressed the button on his desk to summon Blackford. He appeared two minutes later in his dressing gown, still bleary eyed.

"Inform *Falconet* that she's to be ready for departure within the hour," Dawlish said. "You'll be taking a message to Antigua. I'll draft and encipher it myself while you're getting dressed."

He noticed that MacQuaid was smiling, as if over a secret shared, one never to be acknowledged, even to a colleague.

Those four Frenchmen would have to take their chances.

They too would understand *Raison d'etat*.

*

MacQuaid returned to Port Mazarin and sent back reports in the following two days. Ravenel's madness had triggered massive celebrations. The French delegates were still in hiding in Badeaux's house. Dawlish decided that he would send *Falconet* to carry then to Guadeloupe once she had returned from Antigua. She had not done so yet, an indication that there might be differences of opinion in London on how to react and what instructions to send back.

Clemenger's agents deep in Guimbi reported that Ravenel's proclamation had become of item of awe in the villages, a sacred text tacked on doors and market stalls. The wording and the content were incomprehensible to the vast majority but that did not matter – it had a sanctity about it, a magic even, proud confirmation that Guimbi was at last wholly free, that the millennium was at hand, that the republic would flow with milk and honey. But the higher the expectations were raised, the more violent would be the reaction when they were not fulfilled. Even without the threat posed by Pelletier and Desmarais, Ravenel's days might well be numbered.

And all this while the mundane but necessary administration of Roscal took up much of Dawlish's days. He approved or queried expenditures, contracts, appointments of officials. He spent long days in the saddle visiting villages to inspect progress of school and road construction. He listened to appeals and complaints and found that as his popularity had grown – and Florence was in no small way responsible for that – his decisions were being accepted with little demur. Time-consuming this work might be, but it offered a relief from the nagging worry about Guimbi.

But one responsibility he had not thought much about until the chief justice of Roscal asked for an appointment. Dawlish had kept his contact with him only to the unavoidable – it was impossible to respect a man who had acquitted the Souliers and other planters involved in the riot at Thénac.

"It's a mere formality, Your Excellency." The judge laid a crested sheet of the paper on the desk. "Your signature's needed on this letter to the Colonial Office."

Dawlish scanned it, then read it again with greater care.

"It requests confirmation of a death sentence," he said.

"It's unfortunately beyond your authority, Your Excellency." The judge looked as if he enjoyed saying it. "A court in London must confirm it – it's never a problem – and the Colonial Offices manages the procedure for us."

"What was the charge?"

"Murder."

"When was the man sentenced?"

"Yesterday. He committed the crime two days before. It's better to get these things out of the way quickly."

"You want me to sign immediately?"

"It's a formality, Your Excellency, the merest formality."

And Dawlish remembered that his predecessor, Sir Clifford, had told him that nobody had been hanged on Roscal during his tenure. There had been two death sentences but, in each case, after reviewing the trial transcripts, he had recommended clemency when he forwarded the Roscal court's verdict to London. And both times the sentence had been reduced to life imprisonment.

"Have you brought me anything other than this letter?" Dawlish said. "Transcripts, police reports, that sort of thing."

"You would find them very tedious, Your Excellency. It's a simple case, premeditated murder, a man hacked to death before reliable witnesses. The trial was over in an hour."

"So you've brought me nothing? Then I trust the court transcript could be delivered to me here this afternoon."

It could, though the judge assented with bad grace.

"And three fair copies in addition," Dawlish said. "Two for my records and London will get the other."

Dawlish wondered if he'd have been so insistent if he hadn't already disliked the Chief Justice. In any case, he'd study the transcript at his leisure this evening.

*

It was indeed a simple case and the was no doubt that Jean-Baptiste Marignan was guilty of premeditated murder.

He was thirty-four years old, married with four children, a road-maintenance labourer. He'd had a dispute about wages with the foreman of the contractor who employed him. Resentment had been building for weeks until, emboldened with rum, he had sworn to three friends that he'd kill the foreman. All had been called as witnesses and had confirmed that, though with reluctance. They had tried to restrain him but to no avail. He'd gone to the wretched foreman's house, taking a machete with him, and had split his skull in the presence of his wife and children. He had made no attempt to escape or to deny his guilt, nor had he expressed remorse. Permitted to speak before sentence was passed, he said he'd do it over again if he had the chance.

Dawlish sat up late after he finished the transcripts, unwilling to accept yet that there was no justification for clemency. The man had known what he was doing and justice must be seen to be done.

And yet . . .

The idea of cold-blooded execution repelled him. He had killed himself before now, but they had been men who had been just as ready to kill him. Once, once only, he had killed out of mercy. But cold-blooded execution seemed somehow more repellent. It would be months perhaps before London's approval would be forthcoming, and weeks more before the professional hangman could come from Jamaica. The long anticipation would be almost as terrible for the condemned man as the actual execution . . .

He pushed that concern aside – it wasn't easy – and told himself that he could allow himself no emotion in this matter. There had been murder done and he could see no extenuating circumstances. He was about to sign the letter as it stood when Florence entered the study, candle in hand.

"You're working later than's good for you, Nick," she said. "It's time to –" She stopped, must have noticed strain on his face. "Are you feeling well, Nicholas?"

"It's nothing," he said. "Just tiredness. It's been a long day."

And better to wait until the morrow to sign.

Dawlish slept badly, woke several times, felt uneasy about the letter and resolved to find out more before signing. He rose even earlier than usual, went to his study and read through the transcript again. The accused man had had no counsel to represent him, and so he had spoken for himself. In doing so he had confirmed his guilt. The trial had been a fair one and it was impossible to find a reason for recommending clemency.

And yet he hesitated to sign.

There were other matters to concern him in the morning but just before noon the butler announced that the Reverend Elijah Gagneux had arrived without warning and was requesting a meeting. Should he send him away?

"Send him in." Whatever it was about, Dawlish could spare ten minutes. He liked and respected the black clergyman.

Gagneux was formally attired, so uncomfortable in his clothing's stiffness as to make it obvious that he'd dressed specially for the occasion. He looked ill at ease while Dawlish had him seated and asked to have coffee brought for him. Few black men must have ever entered Government House, fewer still to receive hospitality.

Several minutes of inconsequential chat, enquiries about health and families, long intervals of embarrassed silence. In the end, patience lost, Dawlish asked outright if there was a special reason for the meeting.

There was.

Jean-Baptiste Marignan, sentenced to die. And did not deserve to, guilty though he might be.

Dawlish said nothing, waited.

An uncomfortable silence that Gagneux broke.

Did his Excellency know the full story?

Yes. He had read the trial's transcript.

Gagneux said that there had been no lawyer to represent Marignan. If Mr. d'Erlanger had not been away in Panama he would have paid for one. He had done that before in a serious case. A lawyer could have revealed the full wickedness of the murder victim. That might have influenced the verdict. This foreman had been withholding half of the wages due to the men under him, had been doing to for months. The contractor who employed him had been unwilling to listen to complaints about him.

Nothing of this had been touched on during the trial. Only that there had been a dispute about wages. But there could have been other ways of getting the matter resolved – such as contacting the Reverend Elijah – than butchering a man before his family.

When did the Reverend Elijah hear about this?

Only yesterday. He hadn't known Marignan. The labourer had lived several miles from Orvault and his wife and brothers had come last night to ask Gagneux for help. Marignan had four children and another had died recently. If the foreman been honest, there might have been money to save her.

It makes no difference. With or without counsel, Marignan was convicted, fairly, on his own confession.

Was His Excellency aware that Sir Clifford had twice intervened to have sentences like this reduced?

The appeals for clemency would have been confidential. Some clerk, some member of Gagneux's church perhaps, must have passed him that information. Nothing can stay confidential here for long.

And yes, His Excellency was aware. But each case must be judged on its own merits.

Gagneux said that he understood.

Dawlish assured him that he'd give the matter serious thought.

Gagneux said that he's pray for the Lord to guide him.

And Dawlish thanked him, stood up, rang for the butler and guided Gagneux to the door, where they shook hands and parted.

He felt depressed when he was alone again, almost overwhelmed by the tragedy and the pity of it, not just for the two families but for the murderer and for his victim too.

But he knew now what he must do.

He had sworn an oath to govern Roscal.

He would do so without fear or favour, would uphold its law, regardless of personal feeling.

The letter lay on the table before him.

He added nothing to it, just signed. Then he dripped hot wax beneath his signature and pressed the governor's official seal into it.

That it was the right thing to do, was no comfort.

*

He had a second visitor that day, another urgent and unexpected request.

"Tell me the name again," he said to the butler. It struck no bell.

"Gilman, sir. Young Mr. William Gilman." Said as if Dawlish should know old Mr. William Gilman also. "About a serious matter, he said."

"Send him in."

He recognised him as soon as he saw him, the young man who had been so frightened when captured after the attack on the Thénac camp. A fool inveigled into it by the Souliers, he had wept and had wet himself. He had been abject in his thanks when dismissed with contempt but without charge. He looked little less frightened now.

Dawlish sat down, left Gilman standing before his desk.

"What's brought you here?"

No welcome, no small talk, no offer of coffee

"I've been asked, Your Excellency, to –" Gilman stopped, tongue flickering over his lips, eyes avoiding contact.

Dawlish had seen young midshipmen like this when held to task for some misdemeanour.

"Some gentlemen, Your Excellency . . . some important gentlemen asked me to come to you and –"

"Some gentlemen like the brothers Soulier and their ilk, perhaps?"

"Mr. Etienne and Mr. Armand Soulier. And my father also and some other gentlemen. Important people."

"And you're their lackey?"

A miserable nod. Dawlish suddenly felt sorry for him.

"At least you've the courage to meet me face to face even if they haven't. What did they tell you to say?"

"That responsible property owners and businessmen are worried about news from Guimbi." The words came in a rush, as if memorised. "They say that the blacks are slaughtering whites there. That it'll encourage our own blacks to do the same if they're not kept in place."

"They've been saying that since before you were born. It hasn't happened yet. Has it?"

A slow, reluctant, headshake.

"You don't believe it yourself, do you?"

"No, but my father said ..." Gilman' voice trailed off.

"They didn't send you to tell me just that, did they, Mr. Gilman? It's something else that they'd prefer not to say to my face, isn't it? Something they could deny later, something they could explain as a misguided young man's own foolish intervention if things didn't go their way?"

Had he not realised it before, Gilman must now. His head was bowed and he would not meet Dawlish's gaze.

"So what exactly do they want you to tell me, Mr. Gilman? More than just general concern about Guimbi, I imagine."

"It's about a murderer, Your Excellency. Yesterday he was sentenced to hang. If he doesn't, they say, every other black in Roscal will think he can get away with murder too. None of us will be safe."

"The court passed sentence," Dawlish said. "Isn't that enough for them?"

"Mr. Armand says you might ask the government in London for the sentence to be reduced. They say you're already too friendly with the blacks. The others think the same and they don't like it. And when Sir Clifford was here, he recommended two reprieves and got them. They don't want that to happen a third time."

Some other official has been passing confidential information. Maybe even the chief justice himself. But ...

The decision not to recommend clemency would be regarded as compliance, as a surrender to the Souliers' clique, acceptance of reassertion of a power that had slipped from them. The story of this meeting would not stay inside that group, would be spread with glee outside it. The governor's authority would be compromised and the hanging celebrated as a victory.

Dawlish stood up.

"You're a young man, Gilman. You could still be something better than a lackey." Cold fury in his voice, contempt also. "And I suggest that you get out of here immediately. If you don't, I'll kick you down the front steps myself."

After Gilman had scurried away, Dawlish sat for a long time contemplating the implications. He had wrestled with his conscience before signing the letter without recommending a reprieve. That the Souliers wished for that same outcome did not invalidate the decision's moral basis. If it had been justified before the contemptible Gilman's appearance, it was still justified now.

But a small voice within reminded him of Gagneux's story. Of provocation, despair, two families' happiness devastated. The squalid legal killing of a single man could not change that fact. A reprieve would be an assertion that the power of the Souliers and their like had had its day. But London was unlikely to review the case for clemency if Roscal's governor did not recommend it.

He read the letter one more time, then locked it in his safe. No need yet to seal it in an envelope for transmission.

It couldn't leave anyway until after *Falconet* returned.

He still had time to think about it.

Chapter 24

Falconet arrived from Antigua that evening and Dawlish ordered that she steam to Port Mazarin at first light. Sproul, her captain, was to contact MacQuaid and find a way to spirit the four French delegates from Badeaux's house and bring them to Guadeloupe.

Dawlish worked far into the night with Blackford to decipher Topcliffe's and the Colonial Office's telegrams. As ever, those of the CO were anodyne, deploring developments in Guimbi and recommending caution when considering response.

It was Topcliffe's messages that mattered. The news of President Ravenel's repudiation of the French debts had been discreetly communicated in certain quarters, both private and official, in London. Appropriate actions taken thereafter had been to the advantage of British interests – banking and commercial, Dawlish guessed. Coming out of the blue, for the French government had as yet no notification from Guimbi of the repudiation, unexplained British activity had triggered a small panic in French banking and investment circles. The situation could only worsen after *Falconet* landed the four Frenchmen in Guadeloupe. They would wire the full story to Paris and fear would ripple through bourgeois France – bonds worthless, banks failing, investments evaporating, widows and orphans facing beggary.

It could be Pelletier's opportunity.

Which meant Guimbi.

But only if he could get there.

And the whereabouts of the gunvessel *Hermine* were still unknown.

*

Dawlish was in his office in mid-morning when the butler arrived to say that Monsieur d' Erlanger had arrived and had asked to see him. It was the first indication that he had returned from Panama.

"Bring him to the drawing room and inform my wife," Dawlish said. "She'll want to see him. I'll join them later."

Florence had been looking forward this moment with mixed hope and apprehension. The Panama initiative had been hers and it was she who should hear first of its outcome.

"The gentleman indicated that it was you whom he wanted to see, Your Excellency," the butler said. "Alone. He was emphatic about that."

The words cut sharper than any knife.

It can only be failure then, failure so abject that d'Erlanger thinks it better that I break the news to Florence myself. And she had pinned so much on it . . .

"I'll meet him here."

When d'Erlanger collapsed into the chair before Dawlish's desk he was sweat-soaked and hollow-cheeked. He looked half the man he had been before he'd left. He had ridden hard from Saint Gérons after the steamer had arrived there just after dawn.

"Success?" Dawlish said.

"Better than we hoped. We've brought two hundred and sixty-seven back. Some of them would have been dead by now if we hadn't. But I need to talk first about something else –"

Whatever it was, it must be important to bring an ill man hastening here. Dawlish felt fear mounting in himself.

If these people have brought yellow fever back with them then ...

"You don't look well." He hesitated to ask outright.

d'Erlanger must have guessed his fear.

"Malaria," he said. "I'm lucky. It laid me low for a few days but the worst's over. It's the real killer on the isthmus, month by month right through the year, they say. The other –" he too seemed reluctant to utter the name, "hasn't struck yet this year."

He was rummaging in a saddle bag he'd brought.

"You should see this before we discuss anything else."

He took out a leather-covered folder and flipped it open. It was full of pencil sketches on individual sheets of thick drawing paper. Dawlish glimpsed river and forest scenes, low hills under a threatening sky, as d'Erlanger riffled through them. Three were watercolours. They must have been his diversion in Panama. He found what he sought, laid one on the desktop, said nothing, just gave Dawlish time to study it in silence.

Shocked silence. Then Dawlish said, "How did you make this?"

"From memory, but as soon as I could after stumbling on it. In a backwater near Colón."

The port on the Caribbean side of the isthmus. The point of entry for everything needed for canal construction.

There's no mistaking the sweep of the ram, and that draped tarpaulin doesn't hide well the sponson close to the bow ...

"When?" Dawlish said.

"Six days ago. We departed next morning. I guessed you'd want to see it. It looked so like what you described meeting north of Muron."

"How did you find it?"

It had been by the merest chance. On advice from the British consul at Colón, d'Erlanger had begun his search for destitute Roscallans at the range of hills that lay athwart the isthmus. It was marginally healthier on the higher ground there, where a vast cutting was being hacked through the mountain barrier. But, even there, disease and death were common. With Madame Geneviève's assistance, he had found sick and penniless Roscallans and sent them back by rail to the coast. The consul had recommended keeping the search around Colón – a death-trap of contagion – until the end. It should be as short as possible. And later, at Colón, d'Erlanger had found few Roscallans in the town itself. Most stranded victims of the canal's construction were eking an existence in makeshift slums outside.

The worst, and most remote, encampment was on swampland flanking an inlet several miles away. Men came there to die, just as did the worn-out, abandoned, half-sunken dredgers and barges and machinery that clogged the creek.

d'Erlanger pointed to the sketch. "I wouldn't have noticed it hadn't been for the masts."

There were three, but lower masts only, nothing above the tops, scarcely higher than the bucket-ladders of two listing dredgers beyond. No top masts, no yards, no crosstrees to draw attention from a distance. And a barge was moored alongside, no derelict but one carrying what might be a workshop or store at one end and a stiff-leg crane at the other. Another barge, smaller, moored close to the bow, was not high enough to mask the sinuous curve that dropped from the prow towards the ram.

"The camp was a foul place. It was a quagmire – it rained all the time we were there. Filth everywhere. You could feel the air heavy with malaria." d'Erlanger's voice was weary, every word an effort. He mopped the sweat running down his face. "We went from one wretched hut to another, asking for Roscallans. The word spread that we were there and a crowd gathered – not just Roscallans, but Jamaicans, Barbadians, others, wretches all, clamouring to be brought away. It was that noise that attracted two Frenchmen."

"From the ship?"

"No doubt of it. They were dressed like seamen, smartly too, and armed with pistols and cutlasses. The crowd cleared on seeing them coming. They demanded to know what we were doing there. Just charity, I said, from a church group in Colón. Geneviève backed me – it's lucky that she'd brough a basket of provisions with her for distribution, though it was empty by then. Maybe they believed us."

"Did they explain who they were?"

"Just company employees. They didn't say which company. They were patrolling the foreshore to dissuade pilferers because they'd had much trouble from the camp. It wasn't safe for us to be there, they said. They'd escort us to safety. They were courteous enough but there was no doubt that they intended us to comply. We had rented a cart and driver in Colón and it was waiting nearby. They brought us to it. We thanked them for their help and returned to the city."

"What became of the Roscallans at the camp?"

"The consul – he's a good fellow – procured a few guards for us and we rented three more carts. We went back that night, late. No sign of the Frenchmen. We collected forty-three Roscallans. Seven of them had to be carried and one died in a cart on the way back to town. I'd never been able to manage it so quietly without Geneviève. They listened to her and never argued. We had them loaded on the steamer – it had remained anchored off the harbour to catch clean air. The others we'd found previously were already on board. We left at dawn."

d'Erlanger looked on the point of collapse. It seemed cruel to push him further, but Dawlish did.

"Those Frenchmen, did they have a sense of confidence and discipline about them? Something more than you'd expect from merchant service?"

"Something like the men crewing your yacht? Yes. Just like them."

Dawlish felt a flush of anger.

d'Erlanger might judge the Colón consul a good fellow, but he'd reported nothing about this vessel. If he had, Topcliffe would have known it. That it was hidden in what amounted to a scrapyard was no excuse. A more thorough search might have identified it. Colón would have been ideal for sheltering Pelletier's gunboat – most assuredly the *Hermine*. There were repair facilities there and it was probable that many French business interests associated with the canal construction would have been sympathetic and cooperative. In this busy port, arrival of men and crated supplies for Pelletier's enterprise would pass unnoticed.

By now repair of battle damage inflicted by *Déchaîné* could be complete and she might already have departed. Steam would carry her seawards and a good crew could have topmasts and yards raised and secured while under way.

Pelletier's one-ship navy.

It was time to brief d'Erlanger on the full nature of the threat. Of the entire Advisory Council, he was the only member that could be fully trusted.

And perhaps needed for more than advice.

*

d'Erlanger was unwilling to meet Florence while he was still travel-soiled and he left immediately for his Escource house. He would bathe and sleep and, at Dawlish's suggestion, come back next morning to report his success to her and discuss measures for getting the returnees to their villages.

But the immediate concern was to inform Topcliffe of the *Hermine's* finding as soon as possible. For that, *Falconet* must first return from Guadeloupe to carry Blackford to Antigua to send yet another enciphered telegram.

And, in the meantime, think.

*

Clemenger's contacts in Guimbi, and the few cautious patrols he sent across the border at intervals, all reported the same. Desmarais' force was still in place, but dwindling in numbers, more recent recruits drifting away as the prospect of action faded. The losses of supplies as well as weapons when the landing near Pressac was frustrated were biting now. Without replenishment, without reinforcements, without more weapons – and probably without Pelletier's inspirational presence – President Ravenel had nothing to fear for the time being.

Except himself, did he but recognise it.

For MacQuaid's reports were telling now of an ever-quickening descent into madness at Port Mazarin. Ravenel was leading it, entranced by the popularity of his oratory – he was speechifying from his balcony every day now, sometimes for hours. He was following a path that previous presidents had treaded also, like them convinced of his infallibility, inspiring random violence, more suspicious by the day of those around him, more vengeful towards any who had ever opposed him. Three ministers of a previous regime, that which had tortured and maimed and imprisoned him – old men now, almost forgotten – had been lynched by mobs enraged by one of his harangues. Houses and businesses had been looted and burned. A colonel and two army captains had been accused of conspiracy, tried and condemned within the day, stood against a wall and shot next morning to the delight of a cheering mob.

Even Maître Jacques Badeaux, that rock of wisdom and restraint, and until now Ravenel's conscience and best adviser, was avoiding him. Badeaux was fearful, MacQuaid wrote, that he too would dangle from a lamp post were it be known that he had hidden the French delegates before *Falconet* could carry them away. During the terror-filled days of waiting, he had had tried to convince them that disaster might yet be retrieved, that in time the loan-repudiation could be reversed. They had heard him with respect because of what he'd risked for them but, when they left, they carried with them knowledge of the growing anarchy.

Falconet brought Dawlish the thanks of the Governor of Guadeloupe for their deliverance. She also brought local newspapers from there – the telegraph link to France fed recent news. Frequent and admiring reports told that Pelletier was still been travelling the country, still drawing crowds that were not yet enraged by news of the default and the ruin of banks and savers. But they would be by now.

Taking no longer in Escource than to recoal, *Falconet* headed to Antigua with Blackford bearing Dawlish's enciphered reports to London. It was three anxious days before she returned. Topcliffe's reply stated that the consul at Colón had been instructed by telegraph to check if the gunvessel was still hidden among the abandoned derelicts. He took two days to reply.

No sign of her – she had departed under her own steam a week before, while d'Erlanger was still at sea.

She might be anywhere by now, skulking perhaps in a remote bay at some obscure West Indian Island, perhaps with the connivance of a French governor who saw a national saviour in Pelletier.

And Topcliffe had one piece of advice only. Shuttling *Falconet* to and from Antigua for reports and instructions was taking too much time in the circumstance. It would be better in the coming period to send her to

Guadeloupe for newspapers. All Dawlish would need to know was whether Pelletier was still in France and decide action accordingly.

Guimbi would the honeytrap for the aspirant president of France.

The loan default, and the widespread bourgeois losses and despair that would follow, would bring him his moment. Retrieving Guimbi would carry him to the Elysée Palace.

He could not but play that card.

The question was only "When?"

*

Dawlish didn't send *Falconet* immediately to Guadeloupe. He wanted time, culminating in a whole restless night sitting in his study, to agonise over recommending clemency for Jean-Baptiste Marignan. If the letter – for or against – was to catch the monthly Royal Mail steamer to Britain, then Blackwell, in *Falconet*, must bring it to Antigua.

The Reverend Elijah's petition had the merit of compassion and it had touched Dawlish. But there must be justice, he told himself, not just for the dead man, but for his family too, for the wider community. And the murderer had acted with deliberation, had known what he was doing, would have known the consequences and accepted the risk of conviction. The chaos into which Guimbi was descending was warning of what could happen when the cold impartiality of law and justice failed. His oath of office as governor had bound Dawlish to uphold such law.

And yet a cold voice within his mind reminded him of a night on the Thames Embankment, a decade since, when he himself had done what would have earned him the gallows had it come to a court of law.

Determined to kill, regardless of consequences, he had tracked a man through London streets and pounded him to death. He had shown no mercy then, nor had he felt remorse afterwards. The man had earned it for his mistreatment and deaths of defenceless prisoners, Dawlish had thought then, and he still believed it. But any British Court would have called it murder nonetheless. Had it not been for Topcliffe covering up the incident, he would have stood in a dock, would most certainly have seen a judge call for a black cap before pronouncing sentence. Topcliffe had never referred to it afterwards, nor would he himself, but it had created a link and mutual recognition that they were two of a kind, apart from other men.

And so, that icy voice within asked him, if he, a murderer in law himself, could withhold mercy from a man no more or no less guilty than himself. But there was another voice too, somehow contemptible for all that it urged reprieve. Clemency would gall the Souliers and their cabal, withholding it would be taken by them as a victory, a confession of submission to their residual power in this colony.

He weighed and reweighed the arguments through the early hours and came, just before dawn, to a decision.

The letter that would leave with *Falconet* was that which now lay, signed and sealed, in his study's safe.

Without a recommendation for reprieve.

*

"You didn't come to bed," Florence said at breakfast. "You were up all night, Nick. You look terrible."

He tried to brush her concern away. It was just that he'd found it hard to sleep and that he had sat up reading instead.

"You'll never be a good liar, Nicholas. There's something more than usual troubling you, isn't there?"

It was impossible to deny it. They were too close for that, had shared so much, good and bad, had loved each other for a decade.

"If it isn't an official secret, you can tell me, Nick. If it is, just let me know and I'll hold my tongue."

"There's nothing secret about it, Florence. It was all in open court."

"Tell me, then."

She had heard already of the case – all Roscal had. She knew too that the sentence must be confirmed in London, had suspected that the governor had the power to recommend a reprieve. But she had never raised the issue with Dawlish. He guessed that she had regarded it as being for his conscience alone.

He told her now of the meetings with Gagneux and Gilman and all their implications. And of his final decision. She didn't interrupt or comment.

They sat in silence for several minutes after he finished. Telling her had brought him no relief.

"Is there a transcript of the trial?" she said at last.

"Of course. One's going to London."

"Are there any other copies?"

"Two here. I need to retain one of them."

He saw the faintest smile. And the glint of determination that he knew so well.

"Would there be any objection to Agatha's cousin seeing it, Nick?"

Neville Eversham, Chairman of the Roscal Relief Committee.

And Queen's Counsel.

"I don't see why not, Florence."

"Thank you, Nicholas. I'll send it by the regular mail."

Enough had been said.

*

He had seldom seen Florence happier than when she set out for Saint Gérons for the ceremony of welcoming the returnees from Panama. They had been held in quarantine in one of d'Erlanger's warehouses – no yellow fever, no cholera, thank God, though malaria had already weakened some to close to death. Wives and children had walked from villages to call to them from the far side of a police cordon and now they could go, or be returned, home.

d'Erlanger had organised a public celebration similar to that when the *Scipio* Bridge had been opened. There would be green branches and bunting, bells clamouring, the Reverend Elijah conducting a choir, prayers, speeches, thanksgiving and roasting pigs. d'Erlanger would provide wagons to bring those too ill to walk back to their homes. Florence would make a speech, which Elijah would translate into patois. She had worked long over the draft, and had refused to let d'Erlanger see it beforehand since she was attributing all credit for success to him and Madame Geneviève.

It was not an official occasion and Dawlish would not attend. The achievement belonged to others, including Florence. She refused to borrow the governor's landau and would drive herself in her beloved dog cart, the nurse, Veronique, carrying Jessica on her knee beside her. Ted, bursting with pride at the responsibility, and mounted on a borrowed pony, would ride as escort alongside Hippolyte.

Dawlish stood on the front steps and watched them depart in the first cool hour of daylight, his heart soaring, flushed with love for them. And he thought then of the returnees. Some would be useful supports to their families, others burdens, due to broken health. But however hard it might be, most would be loved and respected by their families and village communities. Better death here than as just another statistic in the disaster unfolding in Panama.

He felt gratitude that he had accepted the governorship.

There was still poverty and resentment and despair in Roscal but the colony was marginally better than before he – and Florence – had come. There had been a start, even if significant improvement would take long years, far beyond the term of his own appointment.

However long that might be.

He wondered whether he would depart from here as a success or as a failure in London's eyes. And that would depend on events in Guimbi, where he had little influence and no authority, and on decisions by a man he had never seen.

Fernand Pelletier.

Chapter 25

Dawlish was now receiving newspapers from Guadeloupe once a week, and sometimes twice, their collection a task that was by now as routine for *Falconet* as her patrols. The cost of telegraph transmission meant that the despatches of Paris news agencies were probably necessarily brief, but imagination, indignation and skill in flowery prose enabled local journalists to amplify. But even allowing for exaggeration, France was in turmoil. The news of the Guimbi debt repudiation had brought about the failure of a dozen small banks and the ruin of thousands of small investors. The newspapers relished in stories of solid bourgeoisie reduced to penury, of despairing widows and starving orphans, of suicides, of a banker who murdered his wife and children before cutting his own throat.

Yet this could just be the beginning, the papers screamed. Unending difficulties had repeatedly, year by year, pushed back the estimated date for opening of the Panama Canal. Expenditure so far was a multiple of the original estimate for completion. Worst of all, eminent engineers were now challenging the feasibility of a sea-level waterway. The prestige of its promotor, Ferdinand de Lesseps, who had driven construction of the Suez Canal, had, from the outset, convinced investors to pour in ever more money to sustain the effort. But now, even his reputation was not enough to reassure the doubters and the latest calls for further investment were not being met. Collapse of the entire project was now a possibility. If it came, it would make the losses from Guimbi seem miniscule by comparison and would take with it the savings of hundreds of thousands.

Fernand Pelletier was still crisscrossing France, speaking to ever-larger crowds, deploring the inability of the present government, the third in as many years, to take decisive action. He had evidence of contracts awarded through bribery, he said. Bankers and foreign interests had corrupted the political class. It was time for change.

And then, an announcement that Dawlish knew must be inevitable.

That problems with an old wound, sustained in Algeria in *La Patrie's* service, necessitated General Pelletier's temporary withdrawal from public life. There was nothing to be concerned about, his doctors had said. A minor medial intervention and six weeks' convalescence at an unidentified friend's estate would restore him to full health.

Ready to save France.

*

Given Guadeloupe's telegraph link to France, it was likely that Pelletier had already dropped from sight. He might already be at sea – he had enough wealthy backers that a fast steam yacht might be at his disposal. If so, he could be in the Caribbean in about two weeks to rendezvous with *Hermine* at some remote location. A few days more could bring him with her to Guimbi.

Everything would depend on intercepting *Hermine* before Pelletier could land. *Déchaîné* was better prepared now, for her Guimbian captain had thrown his authority behind Sidwell's relentless gun drills. But she alone could not keep the entire coastline under constant observation. *Falconet's* deployment must complement hers, one patrolling along the northern coast, the other along the southern.

But which vessel for which coast?

The decision would be a fraught one, for with her present whereabouts unknown, *Hermine* might appear on either. *Falconet*, alone, had survived engagement with her twice before. She might not be so lucky a third time.

Dawlish pondered his options in his study well into the late evening. He wanted other perspectives before deciding. He would speak to Clemenger in the morning. Pelletier's success would depend on allies already in Guimbi. With Desmarais weakened by a slow but steady trickle of desertions, and complacent perhaps after being left unmolested for weeks, now might be the time to reconsider the idea of using the Rural Guard to attack him in his camp. And it would be essential also to summon MacQuaid from Port Mazarin for an evaluation of the situation inside Guimbi. Ravenel's growing insanity and the slide into anarchy there would be a complication and –

A knock on the door.

He looked up, expecting to see Florence coming to urge him to come to bed. But it was Blackford, his face serious.

"There's news from town, sir. Very bad," he said. "A police inspector brought it post-haste just now. He's outside."

And what the man told outraged Dawlish. He had never expected anything like this, not against a victim so harmless and well meaning.

"Have my horse saddled," he said. "We'll leave in five minutes."

He reached into the desk-drawer and took out his Enfield revolver, always kept close and always loaded.

Be ready for anything.

*

The plantation was two miles outside the town, the fields untilled and overgrown. Even in moonlight, the mansion looked decrepit. The owner's wife had died several years before and his daughters were married elsewhere, Dawlish had heard. For an old man, on the edge of senility, the once-splendid surroundings meant little. All that was left to him was pride in his membership of the Advisory Council and his role as Colonel of the Militia.

Clemenger met Dawlish on the entrance steps. He too had been alerted by the Escource police and had come with Inspector Dorsette and a half-dozen Rural Guards.

"He's still breathing," Clemenger said. "A doctor's been fetched. He's doing what he can for him."

"Conscious?" Dawlish said.

"No."

"I want to see him."

Councillor Chevit lay on a shabby sofa in a corner of a neglected drawing room lit by two ornamental kerosene lamps. The doctor, a white Roscallan, shook his head and held a finger to his lips as he gestured for Dawlish and Clemenger to come forward. The old man's face was black with bruises. Great swellings hid his eyes. Blood saturated the white hair on one side of his head. Only a slight wheezing confirmed that he was still breathing.

Dawlish felt a stab of mixed anger and pity. Shame too that he had once regarded this stricken man as vain and pompous, almost a joke, until he had learned more and had come to like him.

"He was found in there." Clemenger pointed.

It must once have been a combined office and study. A musty smell indicated that it might have been closed for months. A guttering candle on the desk cast flickering shadows. Desk drawers hung open, their contents strewn on the floor, chairs lay overturned and splintered cabinet doors looked to have been prised open.

And in one corner, a small metal safe, its thick metal door, with inbuilt combination dial, was open. It was empty, though a few rolled documents and bulging envelopes that must have filled it had been trodden underfoot outside.

"Whoever they were, they must have demanded that he open that safe," Clemenger said. "He must have refused, but they must have beaten him until he did."

Dawlish had not heard of a single case of violent robbery since he had come to Roscal. And in his straitened circumstances, Chevit would have been unlikely to have kept much cash here.

"What happened exactly?" he said.

"Dorsette will know by now. He's been talking to all the servants, other than one poor wretch who was killed."

Dawlish, on entering, had walked past that body without noticing it. It lay half-hidden below the stairway that rose from the entrance hall. Another frail old man, but this one black, in frayed and faded livery, blood soaking the back of his grizzled head, more on a shattered hand that some heel had ground into the floor.

"Chevit's major-domo," Clemenger said. "He must have tried to keep them out."

Inspector Dorsette had gathered the servants – three women and four men – in the kitchen. He had already questioned them. Most spoke only patois and several, some as old as Chevit or the dead man, were still mute with shock. A younger man had blood on his face but seemed little the worse for it. It was he who had run to alert the police after the intruders had left on horseback. Everybody's experiences and accounts had been slightly different, but a coherent reconstruction had nonetheless emerged.

Councillor Chevit – he seemed so proud of the title that it had been used even in his own home – had, as usual, dined alone. He had gone afterwards to the drawing room to drink a glass of wine and read for half an hour. His custom was to retire at nine o'clock.

A few minutes before that, a maid who was laying out the master's nightshirt on his bed, had heard knocking on the hall door. She had thought nothing of it and she had only gone to investigate when she had heard shouting. Looking down the stairs, she saw Monsieur Dufaure, the major-domo, throwing his weight against the door to close it against pushing from outside. Frightened, she began to scream to attract help. As she did, Monsieur Dufaure – such a good, kind man, she said – had fallen backwards and three men burst in.

Dorsette had been summarising in English but now the bloodied young man interrupted in patois that, other than the word 'blanc', Dawlish could not follow.

"What's he saying, inspector?" he said

"That they were white men. He'd seen them himself when he arrived in the hall. One beat him down with a pistol butt."

"Did he recognise them?"

The man must have understood for he looked down, shook his head. No, he didn't.

Even if he had, he won't say it. It's still dangerous for blacks to accuse whites here.

The maid had seen the poor Monsieur Dufaure struggling to his feet. The intruders – and yes, she confirmed, they were white – knocked him down and kicked him in the head and stomach as he scurried for safety on hands and knees. One of the devils had followed him under the stairs. She'd heard his pleas for mercy cut off abruptly. The commotion brought the other servants hurrying to the hall and Councillor Chevit came to the drawing room's door. The intruders had pistols in their hands and one held the servants – other than the maid, who'd hidden upstairs – at gunpoint in the hallway, on their knees and facing the wall, hands clasped on their heads. They heard the other two whites bundling the protesting councillor into his study and slamming the door.

Then shouting and the sound of ransacking within, Chevit crying out, first in indignation and then in pain. Ever louder and angry voices yelling what might have been demands.

Was it possible to distinguish any words?

Several were sure that they had heard the councillor crying out, "Non, Non, Non," in an ever-weakening voice.

And afterwards, his silence.

"Monsieur le Gouverneur . . ." A young maid, hesitant, as if frightened by her own temerity in addressing so august a personage.

"N'ayez pas peur, mam'zelle," Dawlish softened his tone. "Dis-moi. Prends ton temps." She shouldn't be afraid, should take her time in telling him.

Relieved, she unleashed a torrent of patois, stopped, began to weep, struggled to continue.

Dawlish didn't wait for Dorsette's translation He had distinguished two words, and they were enough.

Les clés.

The keys.

And at once it seemed so obvious. The only keys in Roscal worth battering an inoffensive old man to get.

"The keys of the Militia's armoury," Dawlish said to Clemenger.

Where eighty Brunswick Pattern '36 rifles and their ammunition, with officers' side arms in addition, were stored. They were outdated muzzle-loading percussion weapons, used for years in ceremonies only, but could still kill in the hands of trained men. Weapons that Dawlish had afterwards learned Chevit had refused to hand over to the Souliers on the night of the riot at the Thénac camp. There had been no trained men among their sympathisers then and probably none now either.

But Desmarais needed weapons and was well capable of training even the most unpromising of recruits to use them . . .

The truth had dawned on Clemenger also.

"To the Armoury, sir?"

"Immediately. Dorsette to leave a man here and follow us with the rest. And send somebody to muster all your other people in town and meet us there."

*

They were too late.

The nightwatchman who had been on duty inside the Armoury must have opened the entrance door – the only one for which he had keys – without suspicion. There'd been no need to force his cooperation but one intruder had knocked his teeth out with a revolver butt anyway before he gagging him, trussing him up and dumping him in a corner. The iron grill leading to a passageway hung open and another like it further on, also open, led into the windowless storage rooms. The racks were empty, the hinged bars that had closed on the muzzles and butts hung loose and the chains that had passed through the trigger guards lay on the floor like dead snakes. The grill leading to the ammunition store was also open and all the shelving there was empty.

Three men alone could not have spirited so much away.

The effort would have demanded several mule or horse-drawn wagons. It would have been easy enough to have brought them here and have loaded them without arousing suspicion. The armoury stood at one corner of the Militia's seldom-used parade ground on the edge of town with no dwellings nearby. The individual wagons could have reached there by different routes.

"Block all roads leading from Escource," Dawlish told Clemenger.

"And close the harbour?"

"Yes. Nothing to leave."

It wouldn't be easy to enforce. *Falconet* was cruising off the northern coast.

"One thing more," Dawlish said. "Arrest the Soulier twins. I'll want to speak them myself."

Another thought struck him.

"And William Gilman too."

"The father?"

"No, the son."

The Souliers would be hard nuts to crack but that feeble lackey would surely talk if he knew anything of value.

*

The weapons were gone, brought to the port by four wagons. A policeman patrolling the wharves claimed that he'd challenged them but was satisfied that they were on legitimate business. He said that it hadn't occurred to him that there was anything strange about crates of lemons being loaded on the harbour's single tug that had stream raised already at three o'clock in the morning.

"I've had him arrested," Clemenger said. "He's been paid off, no doubt of it. But he'll talk, I'll see to that, though I doubt it'll be worth much."

For the tug had chugged out of port to be lost in the darkness. Visits to the captain's, mate's and engineer's homes confirmed that they were still in bed and knew nothing of it

"Damn well planned," Clemenger said. "Three capable seamen at the least brought in to steal the tug."

"In from Martinique or Guadeloupe perhaps?" It would have been so easy to do, Dawlish thought. Small sailing traders often went there.

"Almost certainly."

It was dawn now. The tug could by now be lying off that beach near Pressac where the *Hermine's* attempted landing of men and supplies had been frustrated before. Desmarais's people would have been waiting with mules. Within hours they would be losing themselves and the laden beasts in the forested valleys below Mont Sully.

An entire island lay between that beach and *Falconet's* present cruising ground off the north coast. The chance that *Déchaîné* had been close enough to detect the landing would have been slim.

Raids on the houses of the Soulier twins confirmed that they too were gone. Where to, their sullen wives claimed not to know. But William Gilman had been found at home. He looked as if he hadn't been to bed, and he was frightened. He made no protest on being arrested, hadn't indeed said anything.

"Take him to Councillor Chevit's house," Dawlish said. "I'll see him there."

*

Two Rural Guards were standing over Gilman. Smelling of brandy, he was wearing riding breeches, but not boots, and his feet were enclosed in incongruous bedroom slippers. He was slumped on a chair, head in hands, in the hallway. The old major-domo's body, now covered with a bedsheet – blotched with red – lay two yards away.

Gilman heard Dawlish's footsteps, looked up for a moment, then looked down again – there might even have been a trace of shame on his face. He said nothing.

I guessed correctly. He's involved somehow.

"Has he seen it?" Dawlish pointed to the corpse. "No? Then bring him over."

Clemenger ordered the Guards to drag Gilman to his feet. Though apparently uninjured, he moaned. Like a soul in despair.

Dawlish knelt and drew back the sheet. He found it hard himself to see the battered head. "Don't look away, Gilman," he said. "Look closely."

Gilman had been turning his face away but Clemenger caught him by the hair and forced him to contemplate the body.

The wretch was shaking now and had to be supported.

"It takes a lot of courage to kill an old man, doesn't it?" Dawlish said after a long minute. "Or Councillor Chevit too. Remember him? A kindly old man. He's not likely to live, I'm told." He paused. "Then that'll be a second hanging matter."

Gilman was weeping and mumbling something incoherent.

"Is there a cellar here?" Dawlish said "Good. Bring him down. And a chair too. He looks as if he can't stand by himself." He could see that Gilman was expecting a beating and that was all to the good.

They brought down a single candle to light the cellar's cool darkness. Its swaying flame cast vast shadows on the racks of bottles there. It might have been an illustration of a Spanish Inquisition dungeon, Dawlish thought. Perhaps Gilman was thinking that too, for he was shaking when he was forced on to the chair. At a nod from Clemenger, the two Guards left.

"Just the three of us now," Dawlish said. "We can talk man-to-man, Gilman, and I think you've a lot to tell me."

"I've nothing to say. I wasn't here." Voice almost inaudible.

"It's a hanging charge already. And I can assure you that there's no chance of the governor making a recommendation for clemency."

Dawlish paused. "You might just swing on the same day as that Jean-Baptiste Marignan whom you came to talk to me about."

Clemenger pointed to Gilman's riding breeches. One leg was soaked. "You hadn't changed yet. Your servants will tell when you reached home – they'll talk, believe me. And you started drinking. Maybe because you didn't like what happened here. You didn't want to go on with the others after that, did you?"

"That's something in his favour," Dawlish said. "The court might take note of that. But it would need more."

"They didn't say that anybody would be hurt," Gilman whined. "They thought Chevit would hand them the keys if they threatened him."

"And 'they' were the Souliers, weren't they?"

Gilman nodded. "And Gaston Delbos too."

The name was familiar. Another planter.

"You see how easy it is," Clemenger said. "If you keep talking, you might just save your neck."

"I was only holding the horses," Gilman said. "I was frightened when they came out. They were angry about Chevit. He was too old to be a hero, Etienne Soulier said, and if he'd been sensible, it wouldn't have been necessary to . . . to . . . to persuade him."

"And you realised that you'd been a fool to have been there at all, did you?" Dawlish said.

A miserable nod.

"I said I wouldn't go on with them. Not after that. And when they'd gone, I went inside and I saw that . . . that body in the hall."

"Just that? You didn't search for Councillor Chevit?"

"No. I didn't want to go in any further. And nobody had seen me there. So I rode back home."

"And threw off your boots and got drunk there."

"Yes," Barely audible.

Dawlish waited a full minute before speaking.

"In the eyes of the law you're as guilty as the others. They may be gone but you'll stand trial for murder."

"But I didn't —"

"You're an accessory. That'll be enough to hang you."

"There'll be another capital charge too," Clemenger said. "High treason. Too serious for a Roscal court. It'll have to be tried in London. No chance of having friends of your father on the bench there."

Gilman lurched forward and vomited on to his knees.

Dawlish said nothing.

Let him stew.

"You might go Queen's Evidence, of course." Dawlish broke the silence. "That might just help you."

"Only if you tell all you know, Gilman," Clemenger said. "Start now. Name names — there are more in it than just the Souliers, aren't there? And where the Militia rifles were to go, and who'd go with 'em. To Guimbi, isn't it? And what was to happen there then?"

And Gilman talked.

*

It had been planned for months and the Souliers had been at the heart of it. Gilman had only been drawn in in recent weeks. He'd been told that forces were at work in Guimbi that would bring down the Ravenel government. Not just the usual disaffected generals and politicians who led coups with regularity and were themselves deposed in turn., but others too, powerful outsiders ready to deal with such people as long as necessary. The Souliers had already established contacts with them.

There would be a new regime, one that would enforce order, tolerate no resistance, restore property rights lost when Guimbi had achieved independence. Many families here in Roscal had such claims. They'd found it hard here to make their plantations profitable while the black population was so cosseted under British rule. But estates that would revert to rightful ownership in Guimbi could be profitable if a new government was prepared to rule with a stern hand. It would be a regime with protection from an external power, one adept at managing colonies more ruthlessly than Britain.

It would come soon.

For when a force, one professionally led and already established just over the Guimbian frontier, would march on Port Mazarin to join their allies there, the Soulier twins and a dozen of their adherents would be marching with it. The arms they had brought from the Militia armoury would buy them the right to reclaim their own lost inheritances.

And Dawlish cursed himself for his own short-sightedness.

The Militia's weapons should have been long-since confiscated and some pretext found for arresting the Souliers.

He had only himself to blame.

Chapter 26

The wretched Gilman had been charged with murder. Of all his revelations, that which concerned Dawlish most was mention of Desmarais having confederates in Port Mazarin. There were no old French families left in the republic, so the implication was that those allies must be Guimbians. They might be politicians or soldiers who had dreamed for years of seizing power, but some might be ostensible supporters of President Ravenel. They might perhaps even be ministers in his government, who feared his suspicions and his vengeance.

Yet, though Ravenel might be a madman, any replacement would be a puppet of Pelletier's and Pelletier would be on the path towards a presidency of his own elsewhere. There was no option – for Britain or for Dawlish – but to maintain Ravenel in power.

There was no doubt now that the Roscal Militia's rifles had reached Desmarais. Two of Clemenger's people had reconnoitred his camp and had seen men drilling there. One, observing through glasses from a distance, was confident that he had recognised Etienne Soulier with them. And Sproul, sent with *Falconet* to investigate the suspected landing point, had dropped three men on the beach there by a small boat, under cover of darkness. Foot and hoof-prints, tracks of heavy objects dragged across the sand, mule droppings, all confirmed that the weapons had been brought ashore there. There was no sign of the stolen tug.

Dawlish had sent instructions to MacQuaid in Port Mazarin to inform Maître Badeaux. It was better that it was he who should tell the news to Ravenel – he seemed to be one of the few whom he still trusted.

But there was something Badeaux should not know, something to be arranged between MacQuaid, Sidwell and *Déchaîné's* captain. A hundred gold sovereigns per week, from the secret fund that Topcliffe had provided, would buy more than the captain's loyalty. It would ensure that the gunvessel would remain at sea as much as possible, patrolling under sail to minimise coal consumption. Ready for action.

For Pelletier must be close now, and might perhaps have even rendezvoused with *Hermine*, and could appear at any time. Some unknown ally or allies in Port Mazarin might be on the brink of launching a coup and Desmarais, his force well-armed, ready to march to support him.

*

Dawlish was accustomed to the loneliness of command in a warship but he had seldom felt more alone than now. With *Falconet* no longer available to come and go between Roscal and Antigua, the only regular contact with London was via the mail steamer that passed to and fro monthly on the Jamaica to Grenada run. Communications did still come by mail from the Colonial Office, all related to routine administrative affairs. Nothing worth the effort of coding, nothing about Guimbi, no reference to the problems unleashed on French lenders by Ravenel's debt repudiation.

And no message at all from Topcliffe.

He had given Dawlish all the tools he could for dealing with the Pelletier threat. It would be his decision how to use them. A decision that could easily be condemned should it lead to failure or embarrassment, one to be portrayed as the rash action of the governor of a tiny colony who had exceeded his authority.

And the end of my career.

Only with MacQuaid could he discuss the decision, but MacQuaid was in Guimbi and he too was Topcliffe's man, assigned to advise and support but not commit. He too would be adept in sidestepping responsibility should all go awry.

Florence had noticed Dawlish's preoccupation but knew better than to question him. She also had worked for Topcliffe and probably sensed that it was he who had arranged this governorship for his own purposes. Dawlish had never explained and she had never asked – she understood the necessity of watertight compartments. All she could do was divert him in his brief leisure hours, encourage play with Jessica and Ted, share news of her work for the Relief Committee. And try as she did, it was never enough to lighten his worry and foreboding.

Time was running out, confrontation was imminent, Pelletier was being drawn towards Guimbi like a fly to a honeytrap.

The key to countering him was Ravenel.

And for his personal no less than political survival, Guimbi's president must face facts.

Time to make him a proposition.

*

Roscal's governor's recurring malaria had struck him down again. His devoted spouse had once more insisted on nursing him herself and was adamant that nobody else would see him. She said that he'd had many bouts like this before – that much was true – and he'd be himself in a day or too. Mr. Blackwell, the governor's secretary, would handle routine matters until his recovery.

Next morning, shortly after dawn., the fishing boat that usually carried MacQuaid and his messages from and to Port Mazarin, slipped into the harbour there after a fast passage from Escource. Dawlish, clad in stained and threadbare clothing borrowed from the skipper, was the only passenger. Even had there been comfort to allow it, he could not have slept for his mind had been visualising all he remembered of the harbour from previous visits. He had dismissed bringing binoculars, for they would have drawn attention. Now he must rely on his own eyes to study every detail of the headland dominating the eastern side of the Port Mazarin's harbour entrance.

High above, the bastions of the old Fort Montmorency looked out on all seaward approaches and, on the inner side, over the town itself. Abandoned and now useless cannon of an earlier age still jutted from a few embrasures. Two weapons only mattered there now, and they were out of sight. But the military engineers of two centuries before had chosen well. Near-vertical cliffs comprised the headland's seaward sides. Only at a cleft, hidden from view from the town, did a narrow zigzag path, of dozens of steps, lead down from a small gate in the bastion above to a short stone wharf at the water's edge. No sign of life or activity there now but, in France's interminable wars with Britain for control of the Caribbean, that path would have provided a route to resupply the fort were the town itself be taken by an enemy attacking from landward. The last French governor might have left from there, knowing all was lost, when the bloody slave revolt had triumphed in 1791, beginning two decades of hell.

The fishing boat moored amid a cluster of similar craft at a rickety jetty at the western edge of the harbour. No customs officials to demand bribes. All here were focused only on landing the night's catch. Dawlish told the skipper to be ready for departure at sundown. Then he pulled the frayed brim of his straw hat down to his eyebrows and drifted through the thronged fish market. He didn't hasten or push and he paused a few times to feign interest in haggling at stalls. The Roscallan sun had darkened his complexion. Many Guimbians, of mixed heritage, were lighter skinned. It was unlikely that anybody would question him. The heat was growing and despite his unhurried pace he was sweating heavily. That was all to the good – it made him one with the crowd.

His gaze kept returning to the landward face of the headland as he strolled. It rose less steeply there. MacQuaid had previously told him that a reconnaissance of his own had revealed that, in classic Vauban tradition, a deep ditch lay before the bastions. A drawbridge, probably unraised for decades, crossed the obstacle to access the fort's main entrance. An enemy without modern heavy artillery would find Fort Montmorency still impregnable were it to be manned by a few dozen determined men.

Dawlish found it easy to pass around the edges of the harbour and locate the main wharf where he had landed previously. With that as a reference point, he was confident that he could locate MacQuaid's house from memory of a sketch map he'd provided.

The streets were a labyrinth and none were paved. He realised twice that he had lost his way and retraced his steps rather than ask directions in his formal French that differed so much from the patois. The poverty, worse by far than in Roscal, oppressed him no less than the heat and dust and smell of human waste. Pasted on many walls, he saw posters of Ravenel's debt-repudiation proclamation. Most hung in strips by now and many has been defaced by smeared filth. It was dawning on the population that the gesture had not brought a golden day and that Ravenel's promises, like those of all presidents before him, were hollow. In the small groups of idle men gathered at corners he sensed no resignation, only angry sullenness that might all too easily flash into violence. The women had a look of desperation and even the barefoot, half-naked, children had no air of fun about them. The thought struck him that direct rule by France could be no worse than this. Yet, for a higher purpose, it was his duty to prevent it.

Raison d'etat.

He turned into what must be MacQuaid's street. Several poorly stocked vegetable stalls, few customers, unwilling goats being herded towards their deaths, a single donkey cart plodding in their wake with barrels of water that sloped from the open tops with each lurch.

The sun was in his eyes so that it was only when he was almost underneath it that he was aware of a dark object dangling from a balcony. The passers-by below it were taking no notice of it. He stood out in the centre of the street to look up. It was a body, the neck drawn out to twice its normal length, head canted to one side, mouth open, tongue protruding, black flies buzzing around it. It wore remnants of a uniform still ornamented with gilt braid. The feet were bare. A wooden sign over his chest proclaimed him, in straggling white letters, to be *ennemi du peuple*. The house behind him – a substantial if not opulent one – looked to have been looted, the front door missing, every window smashed.

It took much gesturing, and a coin, to convince MacQuaid's single servant – selected because he was a deaf-mute – to admit the apparent beggar at the door.

"It must be something damn serious to bring you here like this," MacQuaid said. "It's a tinderbox. Another riot yesterday, a small one. Did you see that poor devil down the street? An army colonel, no worse than any of the others."

"Who killed him? Ravenel supporters?"

"Maybe. Or perhaps just some settling of a private score. There's a lot of that nowadays."

Dawlish told him what he wanted.

"It'll do no good," MacQuaid said. "Ravenel will rant nonsense at you just like he does at everybody else. And he doesn't listen to anybody either."

"Including Maître Badeaux?"

"Maybe not. But I wouldn't bank on it."

"I'll see him first then. Take me to him."

*

Speed was everything now. Dawlish refused MacQuaid's offer of a change of clothes and elected instead to follow him at a distance to Badeaux's house. They entered through a back entrance. The servants knew MacQuaid, though they looked askance at Dawlish, as they were guided to Le Maître's study. He must have been as surprised by Dawlish's appearance, no less than by the fact that he was here at all, but he made no reference to it, just welcomed him with his usual antiquated courtesy.

"Both you, Maître Badeaux, and President Ravenel could be dead in days." Dawlish had decided on bluntness. "The Republic with you. And Guimbi a French colony once more."

Badeaux nodded, showed no emotion. French men and women of the *Ancien Régime* had gone to the guillotine with similar dignity.

For all his life he's had a vision of what Guimbi could be, has held faithful to it through thick and thin. Ravenel was his last hope. Now he's lost even that.

"Has Major MacQuaid alerted you to recent running of guns from Roscal to Desmarais?"

Another nod.

"There's worse," Dawlish said. "We've every indication that a coup against Ravenel is imminent. You can guess better than we do who might lead it. And when it happens Desmarais and his force will sweep into Port Mazarin to consolidate the change." He paused, then said, "Not that you nor Ravenel will be alive to care by then."

Badeaux said nothing.

He's already resigned to it.

"But that's just the start of it for the end of your republic," MacQuaid said. "It's almost certain that the warship that was driven off before is on its way. This time, it'll carry General Pelletier with it. You know of him, don't you?"

"Yet another man of destiny," Badeaux's voice was weary. "France has had so many of them. They all fail in the end. And so many others die because of them."

"With Desmarais' help he'll dispose of whatever fool will have led the coup. He'll hold this city and the countryside in an iron grip," MacQuaid said. "In another week he'll have proclaimed Guimbi a French colony again."

"It'll make him President of France in two months," Dawlish had forced sympathy from his voice. "He'll meet no opposition to sending troops to garrison the colony then."

"We have *Le Déchaîné*," Badeaux said, but did not sound convinced.

"Only because British gold is buying her captain's loyalty. And allegiances change quickly after successful coups."

According to her current schedule, the gunvessel was watching the northern coast. She could not be everywhere at once.

"But catastrophe isn't inevitable," Dawlish said. "Not if President Ravenel sees reason and cooperates with us without question. I have a proposal for him. It gives a chance – the only chance – for saving him, and you with him. It's the only hope for preserving Guimbi's independence. No argument, no negotiation, exactly as I dictate."

"I?" Badeaux said. "I? Not Her Majesty's Government?"

"At this moment, I am Her Majesty's Government," Dawlish said. "The offer will run out at sundown if I haven't Ravenel's signature by then."

"You want to put it to the president immediately?" Badeaux said. "He won't –"

"– listen to me." Dawlish completed the sentence. "I know that. But he may just listen to you, Maître."

A minute of silence before Badeaux said, "It would be hopeless." Another pause, then, "What are your terms, Your Excellency?"

"We'll get to them shortly," Dawlish said. "I'll dictate – no argument – and you'll put them into suitably diplomatic language. I'll need Ravenel to sign it, you to witness. But first, who would be most likely to lead a coup? Who's likely to be in contact with Desmarais already?"

Badeaux shrugged. "Pierre Aubertin, Minister of Defence. Perhaps two or three more besides. Mostly generals."

"The presidential guard is fifty or sixty strong," MacQuaid said. "How many of them can Ravenel rely on if he's attacked?"

"Maybe half. They still worship him. There was a time when they all did. He was that sort of man. Before he … before he became ill."

"Would money make a difference?"

Badeaux held up his hands in a gesture of despair. "The treasury's empty. Paper's worth less and less each day."

"We can offer gold," Dawlish said. "Gold coin. It's buying *Le Déchaîné's* captain already. Twice as much again can buy the whole guard's loyalty. They could have the first payment in their hands in a day's time."

"But how long could they defend the presidential palace?" MacQuaid addressed himself to Badeaux, not Dawlish.

"I'm a lawyer, not a soldier."

"I'll tell you," MacQuaid said. "Ten minutes at most. The palace isn't walled. The guard will run, depend on that, gold or no gold. These things always go the same way. Coup leaders will drag Ravenel – and yourself – into the courtyard and stand you against a wall. Or hand you over to the mob that'll already be rampaging through the palace."

As two thirds of Guimbi's presidents have ended.

"If Desmarais's there then he'll just stand back and smile and swear later that he couldn't control the fury," Dawlish said. "He'll smile even more as some fool proclaims himself the next president, one who won't last a month."

"You wouldn't be here, Your Excellency, if you thought all this inevitable." Badeaux's voice betrayed no emotion. "I asked before for your terms. What are they?"

"Ravenel will sign and seal a formal request for Her Majesty's Government's assistance. I'll have it before I leave tonight."

The document that may just save me in London should all fail.

"Is that all?"

"Just the beginning. I'll specify the measures needed from Ravenel's side. If there's any failure to comply with my decisions at any stage, the agreement's voided. But if he signs, and if there's no coup in the next thirty-six hours, he may just save Guimbi."

Badeaux was silent, eyes fixed on the clock on the opposite wall. No sound but its pendulum's swish and click counting lost minutes.

And then he sighed and said, "Let's begin."

The voice of a man devoid of hope but honour-bound not to yield.

*

Badeaux drafted the appeal for assistance in French and he didn't argue about the few modifications that Dawlish requested. It took longer to set out Dawlish's conditions and demands but, even so, Badeaux could leave for the presidential palace before eleven. That gave him little over six hours to convince Ravenel and gain his signature.

The wait after he had left for the palace seemed interminable, broken only by food brought to the study and two hours' sleep on settees in the adjoining salon. On wakening, Dawlish turned again to *La Comédie Humaine* but, try as he might, he could not concentrate. MacQuaid produced a deck of cards and buried himself in games of Patience.

Neither spoke. It was all too easy to imagine Badeaux now pleading a hopeless case, enduring rejection and ridicule and tantrums from the man in whom he had placed so much trust. Yet easy too to imagine him, after each brutal dismissal, returning with new and patient arguments, hoping that perseverance might in the end break down a hysterical will. If, at this moment, any man could save Guimbi, then it was Badeaux.

Shadows lengthened. Even behind these thick walls the temperature lessened. Both men's eyes drifted towards the ticking clock, away again in embarrassment as the other caught him doing so. The sound of a servant passing outside or closing some distant door raised hopes that were instantly dashed. Six o'clock passed, six-thirty, and apprehension grew. Badeaux might be dead by now, latest victim of Ravenel's delusions.

The sun had set, soft darkness filling the study.

And, at last, a voice outside, the door thrown open.

Badeaux.

Who smiled as he showed Ravenel's signature, witnessed by himself.

Time to return to the harbour.

*

His recovery hastened by copious doses of quinine, Roscal's governor was at his desk at nine next morning and discussing improved sanitation for Escource with its mayor. The skipper had driven his fishing craft hard through the night and Dawlish had stepped ashore as the sky lightened in the east. There had been time enough to transform the nondescript near-beggar who had slouched through Port Mazarin's streets the previous day into Her Majesty's elegantly tailored viceroy.

In the harbour far below, *Falconet* was coaling and revictualling. She did so on a monthly basis and, though this was now early by a few days, it was unlikely that anybody would see anything of significance in it. But the most important stores would be brought on board after darkness fell. The two small wooden boxes, heavier than might be guessed by their dimensions, were closely guarded by six of Clemenger's men. He would follow with another twenty, all fully armed.

By then, the work that Hobson, *Falconet's* engineer, was supervising in a dockside forge would be finished. Bolted to a hastily purchased handcart, the iron frame would provide a mounting usable on land for the Gatling removed from the vessel's after-mounting. Getting it, in pieces, up those zigzag steps at Fort Montmorency would be a nightmare but Clemenger was the man to see it done.

The headland would hide *Falconet* from any observer in the town when she moored at the wharf below those steps to set the greater part of Roscal's Rural Guard ashore. Though the Gatling would follow, the first loads lugged up them would be the rope-handled wooden boxes. MacQuaid would be there to meet them. He would have accompanied Ravenel and Badeaux as they slipped from the palace under cover of darkness and headed for the fort with twenty of the presidential guards who were considered trustworthy. The first distributions of gold sovereigns from the boxes would consolidate their loyalty.

Down at the wharf, *Falconet* would land ammunition, cooking utensils, blankets and a fortnight's frugal rations for ninety men would follow. One of her crew, an ex-Royal Navy seaman with experience of such matters, would supervise rigging of a shear legs for a block and tackle system for hoisting loads to the fort above. Bradbury, *Falconet's* bosun and gunner, would join the garrison. He was unfamiliar with the recently refurbished 138s there, but he was experienced enough to learn quickly.

By daylight, Fort Montmorency would be a manned fortress again, with MacQuaid its commander, Clemenger his deputy, and the president of Guimbi its virtual prisoner.

For his own and his country's good.

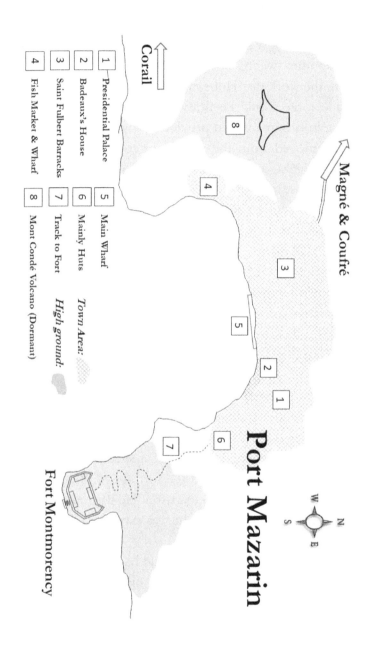

Chapter 27

One of the cutters carried by *Falconet* arrived under sail at Escource an hour after sunset next evening. The despatch it carried from MacQuaid confirmed that occupation of the fort had gone as planned. At the last moment Ravenel had refused to leave the palace and a degree of persuasion, not specified, had been required to change his mind. The only access to the fort from the land side was across the drawbridge over the outer ditch. Unraised for years, it had proved impossible to lift. That had been expected and Clemenger had brought explosive charges that were now in place beneath it. Issue of two gold sovereigns to each man of the garrison – Guimbian troops and Roscallan Rural Guards alike – and the promise of more, had been enthusiastically received. Lookouts were in place, sentries now patrolled the bastions and the Gatling had been reunited with its wheeled mounting. Bradbury was familiarising himself with the two 138s, had chosen crews to man them and was about to begin training. *Falconet* had landed the stores, and the completed ropeway had begun hauling them up from the wharf. She had then headed to the north coast in search of *Déchaîné*. She was bringing new orders and from now on they would work in close concert.

The town of Port Mazarin was quiet as of time of MacQuaid's writing – soon after noon – and Ravenel's retreat to the fort was probably not yet widely known.

And that could not last.

Dawlish reread the dispatch, then spent an hour ploughing through legal documents before concluding that the step he intended might – just – be considered lawful within the limits of a governor's remit. He'd argue his case afterwards, if he had to, with the help of a certain prominent QC. At worst he might not even be alive to do so. He summoned Hippolyte. Riding under faint moonlight, he could be at d'Erlanger's estate in two hours and carrying a request.

To be at Government House at nine next morning.

*

"I'd assumed that you'd called an emergency council meeting," d'Erlanger said when Blackford ushered him into Dawlish's study.

"It's an emergency," Dawlish said, "and there'll be a meeting later. I haven't called it yet. I want to speak to you first."

He told him of Ravenel's withdrawal into Fort Montmorency and that Badeaux was with him. The fort was now sealed and under command of MacQuaid, ready to withstand a siege to defend the lawful president of Guimbi. It was unlikely, Dawlish said, that anybody outside the fort had realised the extent to which its defences had been reinforced.

d'Erlanger was surprised. "While he's inside there, one of Ravenel's associates will see it as an opportunity," he said. "There'll be a coup."

"That's what I want."

"What?" Incredulity.

"It'll force Desmarais' hand. He can't keep his brigands lurking in the mountains if there's a coup in Port Mazarin. He'll have to march there, ostensibly to support it. He'll need to secure the town and depose and probably kill Ravenel before he can install some puppet in his place. But first he'll need to get his hands on Ravenel. He'll need to do this sooner than he and Pelletier had planned. Desmarais won't realise it, but he'll be acting in my time, at my convenience, not his, and before Pelletier's arrives."

"Arrives in that ship I saw at Panama?"

"I don't intend it to arrive. That's why I called you here, Councillor d'Erlanger. It's why I need you."

"Me?"

"I must be absent for a few days," Dawlish said. "If possible, from tonight." He paused. "I need you as my temporary replacement."

"As what?"

"As governor."

d'Erlanger looked stunned. "It's impossible. I'm a councillor, nothing more. I can't –"

"You're the only man here I'd trust to do it. You have respect throughout Roscal, you've courage, you've a conscience and you're a pragmatic businessman who isn't afraid to take difficult decisions."

"But, constitutionally, it's surely –"

"– a Colonial Office appointment," Dawlish completed the sentence. "But the Antigua telegraph office is far away, and London's a damn sight further. I couldn't expect confirmation within a week, if ever. But I need to act today."

"It sounds treasonous. A coup of your own."

"Not quite," Dawlish said. "I've consulted the terms of my appointment. They give me a wide degree of autonomy in a crisis. Which this now is. The wording is complex, even opaque. But I think there's enough ambiguity that a good lawyer could argue a sound case for me handing you temporary responsibility."

"Why must you leave here? What do you want to do?"

He told him.

"You'll do it anyway if I refuse?" d'Erlanger said.

"Yes. I've nobody but Mr. Blackford, my secretary, to turn to. He's a good man but he lacks experience. But I'll appoint him if I have to."

d'Erlanger said nothing, walked to the window, looked down towards the harbour. He didn't turn to face Dawlish.

"You don't leave me much choice, do you?" He sounded burdened, troubled.

"You'll have Blackford. He'll handle most routine matters and guide you on regulations. And you can rely on Inspector Dorsette. He's here with some of the Rural Guards. With the Militia weapons gone, any hostile planters are unlikely to cause trouble. It's put the fear of God in them that Gilman's under lock and key and that warrants for murder out for the Souliers. And your brother councillors will have no sympathy with any of them after what happened to poor Chevit."

"When will you tell the council?" d'Erlanger had turned around.

"That's why I'm calling a meeting this afternoon. The invitations are already out."

d'Erlanger was silent

"And the Chief Justice will attend as well. He'll swear you in the same duties I swore to myself. Agreed?"

A long pause.

"Agreed."

Dawlish sensed the same resolution that d'Erlanger had shown when they had stood side by side on the ridge above the seething lake threatening Saint Gérons.

"I'll sail in the evening," Dawlish said. "We'll have time enough before then to discuss specifics. I'll bring in Blackford and Dorsette too."

"Have you told Mrs. Dawlish?"

"I will now."

She'll accept it and send me away as she did often before, when a parting might have been final. She would have made a good Spartan wife and mother.

It'll be harder to part from Jessica and Ted. I can't tell them even if they could understand. But they will someday.

If they're the people that Florence and I want them to be.

*

Falconet's cutter caried him through the night and met her three miles south-east of Port Mazarin two hours after dawn. *Déchaîné* was visible on the northern horizon, off Cap Louvois, Guimbi's eastern tip. Both vessels would cruise back and forth here on short racecourses, Dawlish had decided.

Waiting for Pelletier and his *Hermine*.

Heavily armed twin sisters would meet, as they had done before, but this time the fight must be to the death. *Falconet* could distract. That humble contribution – that and superior tactics – might just be enough.

Falconet's bows swung over towards *Le Déchaîné*.

Time for a conference with the officers of both vessels.

*

"You see the fires, sir?" Sproul was pointing north-westwards.

Falconet's captain had sent a messenger to awaken Dawlish and ask him to come to the bridge. It was two hours after midnight. A glance told that the yacht must be due south of Port Mazarin, at the western extremity of her cruising area. Orange pinpricks were flickering against the island's dark mass.

It has started.

"Bring us closer in," Dawlish said.

He took the night-glass that Sproul proffered, adjusted it to his eye. The inverted image showed that the fires were in the town itself, two larger than the half-dozen others and probably growing. The waning moon lighted the sky enough for writhing smoke columns to stand out against it. No lights, no sign of life at Fort Montmorency atop the headland. MacQuaid, as agreed, was standing aloof from whatever was happening in the town.

Falconet advanced to a mile outside the harbour and, at minimum revolutions, crawled back and forth to keep the town in view. There were sounds of small-arms fire now, individual shots, nothing for minutes at a time, then brief rattles that died as suddenly as they had erupted. In the breaks between, angry shouting, at times a roar, carried across the water. The impression was of chaos, of a riot beyond control rather than of any well-ordered attempt to seize power. Many of the fires had petered out but others had replaced them. At one point, an inferno was consuming a large building – Dawlish guessed that it was the presidential palace – and reaching out to engulf others close-by.

"We've seen enough, Mr. Sproul," Dawlish said. "Stand further out but keep it under observation. I'm returning to my bed. Have me woken if there's any change."

When he came of deck again it was in full sunlight. The town seemed quieter now, no sounds of tumult, fires burned out but lazy threads of smoke still drifting from blackened ruins. A few people were moving around the harbour-front and even a few fishing boats were putting out to sea, though giving *Falconet* a wide berth. It was impossible to know if the quiet was that of exhaustion or of some new form of order imposed.

It was time for *Falconet* to resume her station to the south-east and remain in sight of *Déchaîné* on her patrol eight miles to the north. Passing south of Fort Montmorency, she dropped a boat to bring Dawlish to the wharf at the bottom of the zigzag steps. MacQuaid met him.

"You've seen what's happened in the town?" he said.

"It looked bad. Do you think some new strongman's in control?"

"Impossible to say. Too early, I think."

They began the laborious climb. By halfway up, Dawlish found his breath shortening but he disguised it and persevered.

I'm nearly forty-two. Time was when I'd have run up.

They entered the fort through the small gate set into the bastion. Clemenger was waiting there with a six-man Roscallan guard of honour.

"I'll pay my respects to President Ravenel first," Dawlish said.

"It's better that Badeaux brings you in," MacQuaid said. "Ravenel's bloody nearly cataleptic. Seeing the palace burnt was too much for him."

Maître Badeaux looked in shock too, but he was at least coherent and grateful to have been spared the madness that had raged through the town. But Ravenel, installed now in a guardroom with a makeshift bed and little more, did not look up when they entered. His already pitifully contorted body was slumped in a chair, eyes locked open and fixed on the opposite wall. He did not respond when either Badeaux or Dawlish spoke.

Yet, at this moment, this wreck who had dedicated his life to the ideal of a better Guimbi, and had suffered grievously for it, was still the embodiment of the nation. Dawlish, moved, reached and touched his hand but got no response. He caught Badeaux's eye and nodded to the door. It was better to talk outside.

"I'm regarding you as acting president, Maître," he said.

"But constitutionally –"

"Constitution be damned. All you've got to do is to sit tight here, Maître. Keep out of sight. Leave it to us. There's worse to come but we'll weather it. And you'll be needed afterwards."

MacQuaid brought him to the bastion at one side of the main entrance gate and handed him his binoculars. Far below he saw the town pockmarked with the aftermath of fires. Little but roofless blackened walls remained of the palace and surrounding buildings. Here and there, tiny figures were picking through what must still be hot ash in search of something valuable.

"Badeaux's house went up also," MacQuaid said. "He took it well, poor devil. It all started when somebody must have learned that Ravenel had come here. Maybe some minister or officer seizing his chance. If he did, he miscalculated. Mobs gathered at two or three places, maybe in opposition, maybe some remaining Ravenel loyalists. Whichever it was, there was massive rioting. You can see that it's quiet enough now. Many dead I hear, but God knows who killed who."

"How do you know?"

"A small crowd came up here to beg protection. Terrified families, men carrying bundles, women with children, old people supported on donkeys. Twice I've had to order warning shots to stop them trying to cross the drawbridge."

As always during conflict, the burden is falling on the innocent.

"It'd take a heart of stone not to pity them," MacQuaid said. "Some stayed pleading through the night – some had already lost all they had and most were sure that there was yet worse to come. They gave up this morning and went back down. God knows to what."

They stood in silence for a moment, conscious of shared understanding.

Raison d'etat.

"I want to see Bradbury. Have him meet me at the 138s."

MacQuaid turned to an accompanying guard and sent him on the errand. Then he conducted Dawlish along the ramparts. *Falconet's* Gatling stood by an embrasure that commanded the track leading up from the town and the open ground to either side. Several of the Rural Guards who were patrolling the bastions recognised him. They flashed broad smiles when they saluted. He stopped several times and inspected rifles. All were spotless. Clemenger had trained them well.

From the seaward ramparts, Dawlish saw *Déchaîné* and *Falconet* on their patient vigils. But his attention was focussed on the two modern 138 breech-loaders, kin of the weapons carried by *Déchaîné* and *Hermine*. Purchased by a venal president in the same corrupt bargain that had also purchased the Guimbian gunvessel, the two weapons had nevertheless been properly mounted. Standing fifteen yards apart on a protruding bastion, well anchored on stone platforms, they commanded an arc that extended from north of east to west south-west.

Responsibility for *Falconet's* puny three-pounder must have seemed a demotion to Bradbury, who had some twenty years as a Royal Navy gunner. Now, with the 138s, he again had weapons worthy of him. He stood by the nearer, a hastily trained three-man crew at attention behind him. A similar crew was standing by the second gun, led by the same seaman who had rigged the cables to bring supplies up from the wharf. No experience as a gunner, Dawlish remembered, but a handy man nonetheless who'd learn fast.

"Satisfied, Mr Bradbury?" he said.

"Aye, sir."

Dawlish walked to the nearer 138. Though of a little smaller calibre, it was not unlike the six-inch Armstrongs that had served him so well when he was captain of the cruiser *Leonidas*. He spun the gleaming brass handwheels. No great force needed – the gears were well greased. Elevating and bearing gave equal satisfaction. He pulled the handle of the breech's interrupted screw and swung it open, then crouched to look up the barrel. The muzzle's disc of sky gave light enough to see the rifling spiralling up the well-cleaned bore. Last of all, he examined the sights, marked in meters, not yards. Here was the one weakness. He had no idea how well these had been calibrated. Bradbury would be too busy to calculate corrections should it come to action.

"Consider the meters as yards," Dawlish told him "It'll be good enough for ranging fire. After that it'll be up to your judgement for correction."

"Aye, aye, sir."

"Now show me the munitions."

Bradbury had stacked five ready-use shells by each weapon, their charges still in boxes lined with oiled-paper.

"The rest are in that bomb-proof over there, sir." He pointed to an iron-doored shelter built into the rampart's rear.

Dawlish inspected them too.

And was satisfied.

*

Dawlish was about to descend the zigzag to *Falconet's* cutter. He wanted to be back on board the yacht by mid-afternoon. *Hermine* could appear at any time.

"Listen!" MacQuaid had accompanied him to see him off.

The sound of distant rifle shots, single at first, then growing in number. By the time that they arrived in haste together at the parapet of the high gatehouse, the noise was almost continuous. Clemenger was there already. He passed Dawlish his field glasses.

"There!" He pointed down towards the town. "Do you see that church tower? Then to the left a little. You see 'em?"

Ant-like figures on rooftops, brief billows of grey gunsmoke rising above them, glimpses of other scurrying though streets. And a walled compound, a three-storey building within, a Guimbian tricolour drooping from a pole, rifle-smoke rolling from the parapets.

"It's the Saint Fulbert barracks," MacQuaid said. "Whoever's in there can't hold out. Not with the sort of troops I saw there. I was able walk in and out without challenge."

"Bloody fools, inside or out," Clemenger said. "They could spend a week taking pot-shots at each other and wasting ammunition like that."

Smoke was rising from somewhere over to the right. Shooting there too, though spasmodic. Then the flicker of growing flames.

"I think it's the Treasury," MacQuaid said. "It's beyond me who'd want either to take it or to defend it. It's bare."

But there must be two separate factions down there now, Dawlish thought. However amateurish, there were attempts at organised attack and organised defence. This was no riot, for the streets were empty of crowds, but it was a conflict for dominance and was growing in intensity.

A half-hour passed, the gunfire dying away at intervals.

"Somebody's realised that they can't keep wasting ammunition," Clemenger said each time – but always it returned and grew, then died again.

One thought dominated Dawlish now. Had Desmarais and his force arrived? It was unlikely, he thought. It was even more unlikely that a battle-hardened soldier would have allowed himself to be bottled up in that dilapidated barracks. And, given his reputation, he would have been inside it by now had he been attacking. He might be on his way, but for now two opposing Guimbian groups were contesting control of the town without outside help.

Then a larger cloud of smoke rising beyond houses that blocked sight of the barrack's wall. Seconds later, the deep boom washed over the fort.

"It's artillery!" Clemenger said. "An old field piece by the sounds of it. A muzzle loader, a six or seven pounder."

The team serving it was inexpert, for five minutes passed before it spoke again. It hardly mattered. The range must be point blank and whether the target was to blast a breach in a flimsy wall, or batter down a gate, the outcome was inevitable.

The small-arms fire had died, as if in expectation. The gun crew was settling into an irregular four to five-minute rhythm, then pausing, as if waiting for more shells and charges to be brought up, then starting again. There were fewer men on the rooftops now and, in one of the streets sheltered from the barracks' rifle fire, a dark mass of men was gathering.

"It can't be long now." Clemenger voiced what all were thinking.

More smoke swirling up from the unseen cannon, more delayed booms. Then silence that seemed to last an age until broken by rippling rifle-fire and the sound of cheering. A breach must have been blasted and the attackers were surging into it. The wave of small arms fire died quickly. Defenders were disappearing from the barrack parapets, probably throwing down weapons, raising arms, descending with hopes of quarter.

And of that, there was none.

There were no single shots now, no long irregular rattles. The sound was of eight or ten rifles crashing together at three or four-minute intervals.

"Poor devils," Clemenger said.

It was easy to imagine what was happening there. Small groups of despairing men babbling for mercy as they were herded against a blood-spattered wall. Though rifles were already levelled towards them, some still disbelieving that this could be happening. Then weapons blasting, bodies jerking as they fell. More pockmarks on the wall, more blood. Then the next group, shocked and terrified, dragging the corpses aside and, almost paralysed with dread, taking their own places before the wall.

It happened seven times, a roar of triumph and of hatred after each, ending with several individual shots. Then figures were moving away from the barracks, through the streets, in groups. There seemed to be no intention of heading towards the fort, their goal instead what MacQuaid identified as the hated tax offices. The closer they came, the easier it was to see through glasses that most were troops in ragged Guimbian uniforms. But there many civilians among them and more were joining from houses as they passed.

Some new power now controlled Port Mazarin.

For however long it would last after Desmarais's arrival.

*

Shadows were lengthening and there was nothing more to do but observe a town in torment. Dawlish was again ready to depart for *Falconet*. He was sitting with MacQuaid and a very melancholy Badeaux when a messenger from Clemenger summoned them to the gatehouse parapet.

A horseman was spurring up the track leading to the fort, dust boiling around his mount's hooves. Further back, a crowd – a mob rather – had emerged from the cluster of huts at the town's edge. A few had run on up the track in hopeless pursuit of the rider but they were falling breathless to the side as the incline increased. Shots were sounding from further back, no less useless.

Clemenger handed his field glasses to Badeaux.

"D'ye recognise him, Maître?"

Dawlish was already using MacQuaid's glasses. He caught horse and rider in them and adjusted focus. The beast was winded and slowed to a trot to negotiate a sharp bend. Only brutal flogging got it moving again, and then only at a fraction of its earlier pace. The rider was wearing uniform – his braided tunic was flapping open and he had no hat. The face, a dark one, set in desperate resolve, seemed familiar but Dawlish could not put a name to it or remember where or when he'd seen it.

"He's being followed!" Clemenger pointed.

Further down the track were four or other horsemen, threshing their mounts onwards in obvious pursuit. All in uniforms, one waving a sabre as he drew ahead.

Badeaux, unaccustomed to glasses, had the fugitive finally in focus.

"It's Aubertin," he said. "Defence Minister."

The man he had suspected as the greatest threat to Ravenel. And now a fugitive himself. One who had gambled and lost.

If nothing else, he can tell what's happened in town.

Dawlish didn't drop his glasses and to MacQuaid he said, "Let him in. Whoever's after him, take 'em down."

Even as he spoke, he saw Aubertin's wretched mount stumble, sink on buckling legs, fail to rise. Its rider was not thrown and he leaped free to run in a spurt that was impossible maintain against the slope, hobbled as he was by riding boots. It was still over a hundred yards to the drawbridge. The nearest of his pursuers was as much again behind him and, exhausted as that horseman's mount was, it could not be outrun.

Clemenger was leaning forward, right elbow resting on the parapet as he sighted down his Snider's barrel. Dawlish had never seen a man so intent on any task. Time was standing still for the old *shikari*, his whole being concentrated on choosing the exact moment to squeeze against his trigger's second pressure.

Aubertin's pace had dropped to a fast stumble and the nearing drumming of hooves must be telling him that he could never reach the fort in time. His hunter was fifty yards behind him now, arm raised, sabre poised for a downward slice.

Then the *shikari's* shot.

The heavy slug caught the horseman in the chest – Dawlish saw blood fountaining from it – and hurled him to the ground. Clemenger was reloading already, his face expressionless, that of a killing automaton rather than a man's. His aim was shifting towards the three remaining pursuers. Two had drawn rein and were hesitating, but the third, a very foolish man, was breaking from them and coming on fast. Clemenger dropped him just short of his fallen colleague.

By then Aubertin had plodded across the drawbridge and was pounding for admission on the iron-studded gate.

*

General Pierre Aubertin made no excuse for what he had done. As far as he was concerned, he told them, Guimbi's presidency had been there for the taking once Ravenel had disappeared into the fort. There had been bewilderment in the town when his retreat became public knowledge, then rioting, looting, settling of private scores before it burned itself out. Aubertin had enough troops loyal to himself to impose a degree of control, establish himself in the Saint Fulbert barracks and set a printer to producing a proclamation of him as president.

"With Desmarais's support?" Badeaux spoke with bitter contempt.

"I wouldn't be here if I had it," Aubertin said. "Not that I didn't try. That *salopard* drives a hard bargain. And Fontaine outbid me. I know that now. He's calling himself president now."

"Fontaine?" The name was new to Dawlish.

"Another general," Badeaux said. "A previous Minister of Defence. Even more corrupt than that one." He nodded towards Aubertin.

And General Fontaine was president now. He had mustered support enough to take the barracks. Aubertin had managed to slip out by a back entrance while his supporters were being slaughtered in the courtyard. He had found a horse, had nearly escaped the town when he was recognised and the chase began. He expressed no thanks for his deliverance by Clemenger.

"Any Frenchmen among the attackers?" Dawlish said.

Aubertin was confident that he had seen three or four directing the assault – his description of their blue serge uniforms matched what had been seen on Desmarais' people.

"Only four?" Dawlish said.

"The rest are on the way. As many as two hundred marching from the hills. We'd taken a prisoner before the attack. He didn't take much persuasion to talk. Desmarais' force had probably reached Coufré already, he said. They'll be in Port Mazarin tomorrow or the next day."

Desmarais would impose an iron grip, with this General Fontaine as puppet president, as Dawlish had foreseen. Until Pelletier arrived, when that wretched dupe would then be pleading for restoration of Guimbi's rightful status as a French colony. Whether he'd do so willingly or not was immaterial. Desmarais would see to it that he did anyway.

But Ravenel, cataleptic or not, is still the legal president, still recognised by Her Britannic Majesty's government and still promised its support. And he's safe for now within this fort. And they'll have to come here to do away with him if Fontaine is to have any shred of credibility as president . . .

"I've still got supporters I can count on," Aubertin said.

"Like those you abandoned in the barracks?" Contempt in Dawlish's tone.

"In Lafiteau. My hometown. I'm well thought of there. I've been good to it. I can raise two hundred men or more."

Dawlish had memorised the map. Lafiteau was a fishing village a few miles north of Magné, the last town on Desmarais' likely line of march before reaching Port Mazarin.

"Are they armed?" he said.

Aubertin smiled. "Enough of them will be. I've a hundred and fifty rifles stored. I've been making preparations for some time."

"Preparations to oust Ravenel?" Badeaux said.

"You must have suspected that before now, maître," Aubertin said. "But things happened so quickly that I didn't have them here."

"So you're proposing a deal, are you?" Dawlish said.

"You have a ship. You can land me at Lafiteau. Desmarais will never expect me to arrive in his rear."

"And your price?"

"Fontaine." Cold hatred in his voice. "Fontaine alive. For me myself to deal with."

Dawlish turned to Clemenger. "Have him taken out. Give him a meal. We've things to discuss."

They talked the options for a half-hour. Badeaux, shaking with anger, was alone unwilling to countenance any bargain. Benign and wise and courteous as he'd always been, now he wanted nothing other than Aubertin stood against a wall and shot. But his objections counted for nothing.

Dawlish listened to MacQuaid's and Clemenger's advice also but the final decision was his. There would be conditions of course, unlikely as it was that Aubertin would ever keep to them. But that did not matter. He would be a thorn in Desmarais' flesh now – and disposed of later.

Aubertin would accompany Dawlish back to *Falconet*. In a few hours a boat would drop him on the beach at Lafiteau.

Chapter 28

Dawlish watched from *Falconet's* bridge as her dinghy stroked back across the level moonlight sea after dropping Aubertin east of Lafiteau. He was alone, armed only with the revolver he had been wearing when he had reached the fort, but that didn't seem to bother him. He'd have an armed force mustered by evening, he said. Bitterness at his overthrow after a single day as Guimbi's self-proclaimed president would be a powerful driver, Dawlish thought. Aubertin would be at best a menace to Desmarais and at worst a distraction. Either way, he could not be ignored.

Le Déchaîné's dark profile close to Cap Louvois confirmed that she was still on station, far enough out east to detect the approach of another vessel from any direction. *Falconet*, returning to Port Mazarin, exchanged only a few pre-agreed light signals with her, enough to confirm that there was no sign of the *Hermine* yet.

A cutter, left behind at Fort Montmorency's jetty, pulled out as *Falconet* approached just after dawn. It carried a report from MacQuaid. Dawlish, half-fearful, half-hopeful of its contents, took it to his cabin to read. A degree of calm had returned to the town, with only a few isolated instances of shooting flaring up, then dying quickly, through the night. Several fishing boats had left the harbour and had already returned – whoever might be president, people must still eat. But a single trading schooner had left as well and had ghosted southwards on light airs.

MacQuaid had made no attempt to stop her, though Bradbury had been itching to open on her with the 138s. It was better not to draw attention of their readiness, better too if the schooner was headed to Guadeloupe, or even Martinique, with news of the coup. If Pelletier and the *Hermine* were lurking in some secluded cove on either island, with the connivance of a governor or administrator, the news would draw them here. It should be soon, Dawlish hoped. *Le Déchaîné's* crew and the fort's garrison were at a hight state of readiness, but morale and effectiveness would decrease with time.

Falconet stood a mile off the harbour entrance and Dawlish studied the town through his glasses. People were moving about again, women clustering around re-opened market stalls, children playing in the streets. Minute by minute, the community was coming to life again. So, Dawlish thought, must have normality reasserted itself after countless previous coups. Bloodshed and destruction had been accepted with weary resignation and without hope of betterment.

The morning passed with painful slowness. Dawlish retired to his cabin but his slumber was so fitful and unrefreshing that he was glad to come on deck at intervals. Each time he found the town still quiet and the Guimbian flag still flying, unchallenged, above Fort Montmorency.

He had lapsed into uneasy sleep when a request from Sproul brought him to the bridge.

"There's something happening there." Sproul pointed and handed him his glasses.

There was movement at the eastern edge of town, a ragged column shambling out on to the track leading to the fort. At most, there might be two or three hundred men, the uniformed troops among them outnumbered by what looked like armed civilians. At the rear came mules dragging three field guns and limbers, probably those had breached the Saint Fulbert Barracks' wall. A wagon followed, most likely carrying more ammunition.

"Hold station and give me a telescope," Dawlish said. "The most powerful you have."

He heaved himself up to the foremast shrouds and arrived breathless, then braced himself and focussed. The image sharpened and he fancied that he saw three men in blue serge, ranging back and forth along the column to keep it moving towards the open scrub-dotted slope below Fort Montmorency. Halfway along the straggling line, a horseman was holding a Guimbian flag aloft. Three riders followed, two black men in gorgeous uniforms and the third, a white, in unadorned dark blue. Only one explanation possible.

The rider in the middle is President Fontaine and he's coming to demand his predecessor's surrender. And one of Desmarais' people is with him.

They halted where the track was beginning to wind to reduce its incline. The range from the fort was about five hundred yards, out of effective rifle range. A confused process of forming platoon-sized groups began under the direction of the men in blue serge. Two guns were meanwhile dragged over to the right, the other to the left of the track, then spun about to face the fort. Men – they seemed to be mostly townspeople – were set to throwing up earthen breastworks before them. The limbers and the ammunition wagon were placed behind the guns. The platoons, formed up at last, moved into a fold of ground that hid them from Fort Montmorency.

Dawlish swung his glass towards the fort. He could discern a few heads above the parapet – a half-dozen, not more. Flashes of sunlight on lenses indicated that MacQuaid and Clemenger must be among them, observing, perhaps with something like amusement, the charade on the slope below. For it was a show, one that might have intimidated the fort's meagre garrison had it not been reinforced. There was a good chance that its strengthening had not been suspected. Hidden from direct sight from the town, the wharf and zigzag steps on Montmorency's seaward side had seen to that. Even now, MacQuaid was keeping the extra defenders out of sight and the Gatling was still in cover to one side of its embrasure.

Falconet's three-pounder was a puny weapon but its brass-case rounds and its breech loading allowed rapid fire. Its maximum range was just over five thousand yards.

More than enough.

Dawlish descended to the bridge again and called for Halligan, the ex-Royal Navy seaman who had previously been the weapon's loader. He had neither flinched nor faltered in the earlier engagements and had ensured that Bradbury, the gunner, had maintained rapid fire. But Bradbury had been able to give him only the brief instruction in aiming before he himself went up into the fort to command the 138s there.

"You see those guns?" Dawlish pointed shorewards

Halligan raised his hand to shield his eyes. "Aye, sir."

"Are you confident enough to take them under fire?"

The seaman hesitated. "May I speak, sir?"

"Go ahead."

"I've never fired it, sir. There was only time for Mr. Bradbury to teach me about ranges and aiming and the like. But I've never hit nothin' with it."

"We'll come in closer," Dawlish said. "You'd have two thousand yards at the most, Halligan. I'm not hoping to hit any of those guns. Dropping bursting shells close will be enough. And rapid fire, that's important. You can manage that?"

"My loader's a good bloke, sir. A black, called Ambroise. We'll do our best, sir."

"Very well. Stand to your gun. And you'll fire on my word only."

Dawlish turned to Sproul. "Take us closer in. Dead slow. And hold position two cables from shore."

He took up the telescope again and saw that the four horsemen he had seen before were advancing up the track at walking pace. The rider out in front had exchanged his Guimbian flag for a white one.

It was a gesture calculated to impress. President Fontaine, anxious to avert spillage of his countrymen's blood, reluctant to unleash his forces, was risking his life to negotiate a peaceful settlement. Ahead of him, the Guimbian flag still drooped above the fort.

Further up the slope now, the horses' pace slowing with the ever-steeper incline. The riders were well within in rifle range – Clemenger probably had one in his sights already. The rider out in front with the white flag was glancing back over his shoulder. The man at the centre of the trio behind him – it must be Fontaine – was waving to him, in obvious irritation, to keep advancing.

Still no response from the fort, not even heads visible, no flashes from binoculars. Dawlish felt grudging respect. All four men must be fighting fear now, conscious that they were well within rifle-range. They emerged from the track's last tight twist on to the plateau on which the fort was built. At its edge, Fontaine called a halt, then rode forward alone, urging his beast into a canter, not drawing rein until he had reached the drawbridge.

MacQuaid had him at his mercy now. At his word, Clemenger could smash him from his saddle or detonate the explosives beneath the bridge.

And make him die a hero.

But MacQuaid did worse.

He ignored him.

Fontaine was standing in his stirrups, was calling up and getting no response. In the end he turned his beast away, rode back beyond the bridge, wheeled about again to shout in what must be increasing anger and frustration. It was his luck that the rounding of the slope masked his humiliation from the greater part of his force below. But a few could see it, and the word would spread, and when he returned to them it would be in abject defeat.

He was raging now, was waving his fist towards the fort. His mount had caught something of his fury and was stamping and trying to turn away and perhaps throw him. He must have realised the futility of it and pride alone was keeping him there.

Falconet was stationary. She was now well inside the harbour, its waters unruffled by the slightest breeze. It needed only a few slow revolutions ahead or astern at intervals to hold position. The rise of land masked the third field gun from the three-pounder on the foredeck but the nearer two were exposed to view. Halligan, his loader Ambroise, and a seaman-helper were at their stations. Dawlish estimated the range as fifteen hundred yards. Halligan had elevated the barrel in accordance with the range-table and had braced himself against the shoulder rest and was holding the nearer field gun in his sights.

"At the fort! He's turning back!" Sproul said.

For Fontaine had spun around and was spurring towards the other horsemen, waving to them to ride on down ahead of him. He turned one last time to shake his fist, then followed. Dawlish swung his lens back towards the fort and could see MacQuaid standing on a parapet, observing through binoculars, then dropping out of sight.

Fontaine reached his field guns and did not dismount, shouting to underlings who went scurrying to relay his commands. Soon the troops hidden in the fold of ground were emerging, trudging forward in an unwilling, straggling line towards the fort.

Towards the unsuspected Gatling that MacQuaid had ordered to be pulled into its embrasure. Should the men toiling up the slope get much closer, only a massacre could follow.

Dawlish's mind recoiled from it.

Panic, not death, would be enough.

"Halligan!" he shouted. "Shift your aim! A hundred yards ahead of that line of men! Three rounds, rapid fire!"

A full minute before the three-pounder barked – Halligan had been painstaking in aiming. The explosive round fell closer to the advancing line than Dawlish had wished, but that was perhaps all to the good. Its detonation and its flash and the shower of rock shards it rained down on the leaders were enough to halt them and for a few to turn and run back.

Halligan's next shell was in the air when a louder boom announced the nearest of Fontaine's field guns opening fire. It was shooting at a high target – difficult even for experienced artillerymen, and there were none there today. Three successive spurts of dust marked the solid shot's bounce as it landed far short of the fort. Even had it struck, the effect on the ten-foot thick ramparts would have been negligible.

Worse than a gesture. A pantomime. One in which unwilling conscripts could die by the dozen. Men for whom Ravenel and Badeaux had dreamed of a better future.

But none of Halligan's three shells did more than terrify. The line had broken, had gone to ground behind illusory shelter at some points, was streaming back down the slope at others. But the second and third field guns were firing now, one round as useless as the first's but the other just visible as a black dot soaring above the fort's parapets and dropping somewhere behind. It was a ball, not bursting shell, but were it to impact on either of the two 138s the consequences could be devastating.

"Halligan!" Dawlish shouted. "Range on the field guns. One round only!"

Handwheels spinning as Halligan swept the three-pounder across to the new bearing and dropping the barrel ever so slightly. Ambroise thrust a round into the smoking breech and closed its sliding block. Then Halligan was squinting down the sights, making a half-turn handwheel adjustment, leaning into the shoulder rest, squeezing the trigger.

Then the impact, short of the nearest gun and fifty yards ahead.

"Up a degree!" Dawlish called. "And correct your aim."

The barrel rising and edging leftwards. Ambroise pulling the breechblock open, the hot, spent, brass casing falling on the deck, his helper passing him a fresh one. Halligan immobile, eye locked on the target as the breechblock closed on the new round.

"Ready, sir!"

"Four rounds!" Dawlish called. "Rapid fire."

Four small flashes on impact, four small spatters of shell fragments and earth and pebbles close enough to drive gunners fleering from the nearer weapon.

"Elevation up a degree! Four rounds, rapid."

Halligan's shells fell just beyond the second gun, perhaps even close enough to menace the third, unseen, weapon. The cannoneers there must be unpractised, if ever trained at all, men hastily set to manning antique artillery unused for years. The three-pounder's threat was minimal and experienced gunners would have seen that and would now be hauling trails about to bear on *Falconet*. But instead, they were falling back, abandoning guns, limbers and tethered mules. Fontaine was raging among them, slashing down with his sabre, incapable of stemming the increasing flood of fugitives. The crack of individual pistol shots told of desperate officers losing authority and perhaps their lives with it.

Time now to complete the rout.

The three-pounder was swinging around, raising elevation, bearing now beyond the troops further up the slope who had sought cover and had not yet fled. Three rounds saw to it that they did. The slopes were dotted now with retreating men, some alone, some clustered, some throwing rifles away, diving for cover as each next shell landed above and behind them.

Fontaine and his mounted companions were trying to bar the track between the guns, still gesticulating, still threatening, still exhorting, but the fugitives were streamed past them on both sides. His cause was not theirs, was one for which they would not give their lives.

"Halligan! Shift aim to the guns again. Three rounds! Rapid!"

They fell just short of the track.

Close enough even for Fontaine himself to join the retreat.

Humiliated.

*

MacQuaid sent Clemenger with some twenty men down from the fort to capture the abandoned guns and munitions. A crackle of rifle fire opened on them from buildings at the outskirts of the town. Fontaine must have rallied sufficient men to muster a rear-guard there. The range was long, but wild shots could still kill so *Falconet* dropped a half-dozen rounds on the shacks above which gunsmoke drifted.

Many of the tethered mules had been cut loose during the panicked retreat but enough remained to tow two guns and limbers up the track to the fort. While they toiled up the slope, Clemenger swung the remaining weapon about and blasted solid rounds towards the shacks. They did more damage than the three-pounder's had, collapsing one of the flimsy structures in clouds of dust. The rifle-fire died. It stammered into life again, ten minutes later, but a few more solid rounds silenced it.

A mule-team returned from the fort to collect the remaining gun and limber. Clemenger's men followed it up the slope, picking up discarded rifles on the way. They crossed back over the fort's mined drawbridge and the great double gates closed behind them.

Falconet stood outside the harbour entrance again, time for her crew to rest. They had done well, Dawlish reflected, and Halligan best of all. The town seemed deserted, even dead, again. Residents were cowering in their houses, fearful that the horrors of recent days were not yet over. Men who had cast weapons and uniforms away, and had clad themselves in any civilian garb they could find, must be hiding too, unwilling to serve Fontaine further but fearful of his retribution.

The sun dropped. No rocket soared from Fort Montmorency to relay a signal from *Déchaîné* that would warn that Pelletier's *Hermine* had been sighted. Dawlish considered whether he should bring *Falconet* to share the night's patrol with her – Pelletier could surely not be long delayed. He decided against. The Guimbian gunvessel would have to look after herself for now. Port Mazarin was the greater concern. When darkness had fallen, a light-signal to the fort had requested MacQuaid to send a written report on the repulse of Fontaine's stupid, botched, but welcome, attack. It arrived by cutter a half-hour later.

Three six-pounder cannon and some eighty rounds captured.

Seventy-two rifles recovered, half of them Chassepots. Little ammunition for them – few fugitives had cast away their cartridge pouches.

Two dozen ancient muskets also.

The 138s were untouched by the single ball that had plunged down inside the fort and done no damage.

Despite efforts to inform him, Ravenel, sunk in a near coma, was oblivious of his deliverance. But he was legitimate president of Guimbi still, his would-be usurper repulsed and shamed.

MacQuaid ended his report with a request for further instructions. Dawlish scrawled a two-word reply.

Hold fast.

When the cutter had departed with it, he began to estimate numbers of rifles and muskets.

How many could Fontaine now have?

Before the coup, the entire Guimbian army had some two hundred and fifty men, officers included. It was impossible to know how many had been killed inside the St Fulbert barracks. About a hundred rifles and muskets had been abandoned on the slope before Fort Montmorency.

How many Chassepots had Desmarais brought ashore on the night of *Falconet's* first encounter with the *Hermine?* Fifty? Sixty? There hadn't been mules enough to carry more.

The Soulier brothers had brought eighty slow muzzle-loading Brunswick '36s.

It meant that Desmarais might have, in total, little over two hundred rifles.

The balance was shifting.

For General Aubertin claimed to be able to field almost as many. And there was MacQuaid's force in the fort and –

"Sir. Captain Sproul's compliments." It was an ex-Royal Navy seaman, still observing correct etiquette. "He requests your presence on the bridge."

No need for Sproul to hand him his glasses. The sounds of cheering and the winking of a line burning torches, now seen through gaps between the town's buildings, then obscured, seen again a block further on, all told the same story.

Desmarais had arrived to join Fontaine.

The force that Aubertin had claimed he could raise at Lafiteau had not stopped him.

Chapter 29

Dawlish kept *Falconet* loitering outside the harbour through the day, going up the foremast several times to study the town more closely. Life of a sort had returned, individual figures scurrying out to find food and then back home quickly. Flags had been raised at several points and armed men, mostly not in uniform, appeared along the wharves at intervals. No further cheering, no sounds or signs of riot either. The town might well be under martial law. Sun flashes from a knot of men on a rooftop indicated that *Falconet* was under observation through glasses. Dawlish fancied that he saw blue serge among them but could not be sure.

But there was no movement towards the fort.

If Desmarais was indeed here, he would not repeat Fontaine's mistake. He would initiate no action and needed only to hold Port Mazarin until the *Hermine* arrived with more men – trained men in badgeless blue serge – and more weapons. And with Pelletier, Guimbi's saviour, soon to be recipient of President Fontaine's plea for establishment of a French protectorate.

But Pelletier would have to land here first...

Soon after noon, a lookout sighted a single fishing boat paralleling the coast to the west and heading towards Port Mazarin. No boats had entered or left the harbour for the last day and a half.

"Should we allow her to enter?" Sproul asked.

Dawlish felt uneasy. She should be initiating her turn towards the port by now, but her course was directly towards *Falconet*.

"Let her get closer. Have a man with a rifle ready to put a shot across her bows if necessary."

She kept coming on and now somebody at the bow was trying to maintain balance while waving a white rag on a stick. Closer still, and Dawlish saw a black man in a shabby uniform, with tarnished epaulettes, crouched beside the skipper by the tiller. If he was an envoy from

Fontaine and Desmarais, about to suggest a deal, he would have come out from the town, not from somewhere to the west.

The boat drew alongside and the uniformed man came on deck, lithe, perhaps thirty, and addressed Dawlish in perfect French. He looked tired, exhausted even, but he still gave an impression of determination. Something too of supressed dislike, even hostility, heritage of centuries of subjugation. He was Colonel Eugène Robillard, he said, nephew of General Aubertin.

"Where's your uncle now?" Dawlish said.

"He reached Corail this morning." A gesture westwards.

Dawlish had seen the place when cruising past it previously, a village – little more than a collection of huts – above a small beach on the southern coast, five or six four miles from here. It seemed an unlikely location for a man who claimed to have his supporters on the north coast.

"Does the general have men with him, colonel?" Dawlish said.

"Over two hundred."

"Armed?"

"Just as he promised you, Monsieur le Gouverneur. A man of his word. And most with Chassepots."

The general's preparations for a coup of his own against Ravenel had indeed been thorough.

"Did you encounter Desmarais' force?"

Robillard shook his head. "My uncle hoped to reach Coufré first and occupy it. If we had, we'd have beaten them there, but they'd already passed through when we reached it. They were probably in Port Mazarin by then."

"Why did your uncle decide not to follow them?" Dawlish was mystified. The agreement with General Aubertin was that he'd halt Desmarais' advance, or if not, then dog it and bring it to battle.

"Follow him, Monsieur le Gouverneur?" Something of contempt, even condescension in Robillard's tone. "And arrive exhausted at Port Mazarin? Where Fontaine and Desmarais would have heard by then that we were coming and be ready for us? No, Monsieur. My uncle is too wise a soldier for that."

"So why is he at Corail then?"

"Because he values surprise, Monsieur le Gouverneur. Because he knows a better way to take Port Mazarin than attack it head-on. But for that he will need your support."

"Tell me," Dawlish said.

Five minutes later he was in the fishing boat with the colonel and heading for the wharf at the base of Fort Montmorency's zigzag steps.

*

"This map isn't worth a tinker's curse."

Clemenger was looking at the creased and stained sheet that Colonel Robillard had laid on the table.

Dawlish was more diplomatic in his translation into French. MacQuaid and Badeaux were present also in the fort's old guardhouse.

The colonel must have understood some English for he said, "Inform your officer, Monsieur, that Guimbi can't afford triangulation. It's been paying France too much interest for that."

The map was sketched in pencil, not inexpertly, the coastline from Corail to Port Mazarin at the base. The slopes rising towards the cone of the extinct Mont Condé volcano were lightly hatched. On its eastern side it reached almost to the town's outskirts and blocked direct access to it from the west.

But one feature stood out when seen on the map, even though Dawlish had paid it no attention – he should have, he realised – when he had viewed the mountain when he had steamed past previously. The stream of lava that had run down to the sea, long before the first European sighted the island, had formed a narrow ridge that ran southwards. From there, the flow had dropped and widened into a fan.

"How wide is this?" MacQuaid was pointing to the ridge.

"Little over a kilometre," Robillard said. "I've been to the top last night. My uncle sent me to judge if it's possible to get guns across. It's steep on both sides, but it can be done."

"In darkness?"

"Difficult. But yes, in darkness."

Dawlish sensed the others recognising the opportunity. If Robillard was correct, then a force could be advancing, unexpected, into Port Mazarin's south-west corner as dawn broke. Surprise would be a powerful weapon. But stronger still if supported by artillery.

"Colonel Robillard has brought me General Aubertin's request that we provide him cannon," Dawlish told the others.

"The six-pounders. Those you captured," Robillard said. "He needs your Gatling too."

"If you're given them, have you mules enough to get them across that ridge?" MacQuaid said.

"Only a few. But we'll have men enough for hauling also."

"Two guns," Dawlish said. "Not more. But not tonight."

It would take at least twenty-four hours to get the weapons to Aubertin. Hauling the Gatling and its carriage up into the fort in pieces had taken over an hour, even after the ropeway had been put in place. Lowering it to the wharf again wouldn't take much less. The cannon and their carriages would be heavier still.

"Not two. Three six-pounders," Robillard said. "They're Guimbian property. And the Gatling." His eyes had gleamed, just as his uncle's had done, when he had seen it outside. "The Gatling will make all the difference."

Dawlish looked towards MacQuaid and lifted an eyebrow in query.

"He's correct," MacQuaid said. "But our people must man it. But one gun to remain here. For diversionary fire if nothing else."

"Three guns and the Gatling," Robillard said.

"Your uncle will damn well welcome what we give him. Montmorency can't be left defenceless." Dawlish felt his temper rising and his voice betraying it.

Robillard must have noticed it

"Very well, Monsieur le Gouverneur." He was forcing a smile. "Two guns. But with the Gatling."

A half-hour to agree all measures needed to ensure that Aubertin's force, and the landed weapons, should start crossing in the ridge not later than midnight next day. They should be at its base on the far side an hour before dawn, ready to drive into Port Mazarin at first light.

It was essential that all activity at the zigzag remain unobserved. *Falconet* would see to that, standing close in off the harbour, ready to warn back by a rifle-shot any fishing boat that might try to emerge.

The ropeway, the weakest link, must be checked immediately, in view of the heavier loads, and its supports reinforced where necessary. Dawlish would see to that himself. At the same time, Clemenger would direct disassembly of the field guns to barrels, carriages and wheels. A single limber would be swung down, empty, the shells and charges to follow.

Once Dawlish was satisfied with the ropeway, the lowering to the wharf would commence, the Gatling first. The system had carried it safely before and even if a cable snapped, or a support collapsed, under the weight of a cannon barrel, there would at least be the Gatling to ship to Aubertin.

MacQuaid would remain in command of Fort Montmorency – and the priceless 138s there. Clemenger would accompany the Gatling, with one of *Falconet's* ex-Navy seamen to man it and three Rural Guards to assist. He would also oversee aiming and firing of the cannon. It hardly mattered that he was not an artilleryman – the ranges would probably be point blank – and Robillard admitted that his uncle had nobody with him capable of even that much.

Falconet's two cutters would carry the cannon, one apiece, and with the limber in the first craft and the munitions in the other. With the Gatling components added, freeboard would be minimal and, even if the sea remained calm, the cutters could only be towed at slow speed. That would be in darkness early the following evening.

The most difficult part of the transfer would begin on arrival at Corail. There the cutters should be run as far as possible into the shallows under oars and the separate weapons-components manhandled on to the beach for reassembly.

It was a gamble, Dawlish knew. He was risking all on the judgement of this Guimbian colonel. But the man had an air of resolution about him that impressed.

He'd take the chance and rely on this Robillard and his uncle, just as he was relying on *Le Déchaîné*.

Off to the east.

Waiting for Pelletier.

*

Robillard returned after dark to Corail in the fishing boat that had brought him. He carried Dawlish's request to Aubertin to have the larger part of his force gathered at the beach next evening. A smaller group should advance to the ridge crest and remain in cover there to watch the town.

The ropeway operations continued slowly through the night and on into the hours of daylight. The Gatling sections passed down smoothly, the six-pounders' wheels, in pairs, also. The first guncarriage, the heaviest item yet attempted, followed without incident but the second got stuck half-way when a block jammed. It took well over an hour, a nerve-racking hour, to clear it. The second carriage arrived at the wharf without incident. Time now for the exhausted men who had hauled on the ropes to rest for half-hour before the greatest labour of all, the lowering of the heavy gun barrels. While they did, Dawlish inspected the ropeway again. He was reassured.

And wrong.

Men straining on the cable, pulleys squeaking inside the blocks, the first barrel lifted from the ground and swung beneath the shear legs mounted on the fort's parapet. Step by cautious step the men edged forward under Dawlish's own command and the load began its slow descent. A quarter of the way down, then a half and –

A loud sharp crack, and then the pulling team collapsing backwards as the tension disappeared instantly and a length of parted cable lashed back over the parapet like a whip. It dragged the shear legs with it to collapse inside the fort. A crash told of the barrel's impact somewhere below.

Dawlish rushed for the gate leading to the zigzag, Clemenger following. They paused there but could not see the fallen barrel. Now down the steps, turn after turn, Clemenger lagging with his lame leg. Men were coming up from the wharf to meet them.

"It's somewhere there, sir!" The seaman who had overseen construction of the ropeway was pointing down into the cleft.

Half-hidden by bushes, it had landed muzzle first and was buried for a third of its length in scree.

They climbed down. What could be seen of it looked intact.

"We can take a chance on it if the muzzle's not damaged." Hope rather than conviction in Clemenger's voice. "If the ropeway's repaired it should be possible to –"

Dawlish cut him off. "No time for that."

But a memory was stirring.

Ten years ago, the crews of the Ottoman flotilla he commanded had lifted huge shore-mounted Armstrongs from their emplacements at Batumi. They had dragged them on improvised sleds down to the harbour over muddy tracks and rain-washed cobbles. It had been brutal labour but it had been accomplished.

The six-pounder barrels weigh a fraction of those Armstrongs. But this zigzag's steeper than any track at Batumi and the steps are narrow and the turns are tight and –

He stopped himself. Obstacles existed to be overcome.

"Have this one dug out," he said to Clemenger. "We'll begin with the other barrel." He turned to the seaman. "Follow me. I need you up above."

To scour the fort's interior to identify substantial balks of timber, roof beams and supports in the long-abandoned barrack huts. There were men enough to drag them free but only a few axes available to trim their lengths. But there was cable enough to lash a sled together.

It was possible.

Just.

*

The eight-feet long sled was crude and the bindings that held it together were likely to fray and need replacing. But there was rope enough for that and an examination at each sharp turn of the steps would identify need for repair. It lay now on the stone platform at the top of the zigzag, secured by a block and tackle anchored by the entry door. A dozen men, supervised by the seaman who had constructed the original ropeway, were holding the cable that ran through the block to restrain the descent. Others were standing by with lengths of timber to use as levers to keep the ungainly load on the steps as it bumped down.

Dawlish was standing on the edge of the platform. The wharf seemed impossibly far and almost vertically below. At each tight turn the sled must be heaved around and an anchorage found to restrain it on the next zig or zag. Another failed rope, men losing their footing, the sled plunging free, and smashing as it careered down, seemed all too likely. But he turned and nodded to Clemenger.

Go ahead.

Shoulders, including Dawlish's, heaved the sled forward to the edge of the platform, half-on, half-off, rocking gently as the tackle held it there. Then, inch by inch, the hauling crew eased the restraint until the sled tipped over and lay over four step edges. Further easing and it lurched towards the next step below. And again, and again, and again. Half-way, it lurched to the left and jammed. Pulled back up a foot to free it, levers forced it back to the centre of the steps before lowering recommenced. It reached the hairpin at last. Securing a new anchorage for the block and tackle gave respite to the men whose rag-wrapped hands where already red with blood. Dawlish looked at his watch. It had taken eighteen minutes to get this far and there were six more flights of steps and five more turns until the wharf below. Allowing for further jamming it was unlikely to get the barrel there in less than two hours. And the other barrel, which had by now been dug free, had yet to be manhandled back to the steps, secured on the sled, and lowered. It was past noon now and he had been too long away from *Falconet*. Clemenger must oversee the barrel's lowering from now. Down at the jetty, the loading of the cutters there was well advanced.

Time to signal to *Falconet* to send her dinghy to collect him.

*

Before he left the fort, Dawlish climbed to the easternmost bastion. Through glasses be saw *Déchaîné* maintaining her vigil five or six miles distant, off Cap Louvois, under just enough sail to ghost with the light winds and conserve her precious coal. But a thin thread of smoke drifted from her funnel also. Her boiler was warm, ready to be brought to full pressure by fast stoking should the need arise. Dawlish was worried that the gunvessel had been cleared for action for days now. The crew must know that action was expected, if not imminent. There was only so long that morale could remain high during such waiting. But there was no alternative . . .

He crossed to the fort's town side. There was some activity in the streets but the same ominous quiet reigned as on the previous day. Brief glimpses of armed men moving about in small groups told that Desmarais had control and would sit tight there until Pelletier arrived.

Dawlish swept his glasses towards the town's western edge. The jumble of shanties there was bounded on one side by Mont Condé's southern slopes and on the other by the harbour. It was there that daily life had returned to something like normality – women hanging out washing, children playing, fishermen unable to put to sea gathered in small groups to smoke and chat. And it was through there that Aubertin would be driving his force little more than twelve hours from now.

If all went well . . .

Sproul, on *Falconet*, had nothing to report. Dawlish briefed him on her role that evening and then went to his cabin to sleep. He needed it.

*

Light faded on the western horizon but *Falconet* remained on station outside the harbour, her navigation lights unlit, until full darkness fell. There was no moon this night and only a light land breeze ruffled the water. Guided by a lantern at the zigzag's wharf, *Falconet* crept towards it at revolutions low enough to cause no noticeable bow wave or send sparks spilling from her funnel. She stood off from the wharf while the laden cutters were rowed out to her and tows passed. Clemenger came on board and reported that both six-pounder barrels had completed the descent unharmed. They had been the last items loaded.

Falconet's bows swung south south-east. Blocked from sight from the town by the headland on which Fort Montmorency stood, she would maintain this course until three miles offshore. Only then would she turn west by north towards the beach at Corail. With the cutters in tow, and in anger of swamping, she could risk no more than four knots.

Time was the enemy now.

Chapter 30

Three lanterns, pre-agreed markers that were barely visible from a mile out, identified the beach at Corail. Dawlish would not risk bringing *Falconet* in any closer. He was unwilling also to send the laden cutters in until he was sure the dark groups just discernible were indeed Aubertin's people. Clemenger undertook to confirm it. The dinghy was dropped and he took his place in it. A seaman pulled it shorewards and it was soon lost in the darkness.

Five minutes later a lantern's shutter at the beach opened and closed five times, then did so twice again at twenty second intervals.

Confirmation that Aubertin was there.

Land the guns.

The cutters cast off and stroked into the night. Most of *Falconet's* crew were pulling them. Until they returned, Dawlish could not move from this location. There was nothing more he could do for now to aid Clemenger and Aubertin, nothing but smother and disguise the fears and doubts that nagged him.

The seaman who had brought Clemenger ashore returned in the dinghy and handed Dawlish a pencilled note.

173 here with Aubertin. 30 on ridge with Robillard.

The ridge crest was just visible against the sky to the north-east. It was nearly ten o'clock. In two hours, at most, the reassembled cannons should be starting up the slope towards it.

One of the cutters returned an hour later. It had been unloaded quickly. By the time it pushed off, the Gatling that it had brought was ready for action. The first field guncarriage was ashore, and on its wheels, and the barrel was ready for mounting. The second cutter arrived back fifteen minutes later with an equally satisfactory news. Clemenger had sent a note with it – the Gatling had started up the slope towards the ridge crest and the field guns were following.

Once both cutters had been hoisted back on *Falconet*, Dawlish sent their exhausted crews to sleep until dawn.

Still unlit, the yacht turned east again, headed for Port Mazarin. The darkness was profound. With luck, her absence from her station off the harbour mouth might have gone unnoticed.

*

Dawlish was on the bridge as the eastern sky brightened. He did not see the sun burst above the horizon for Fort Montmorency hid it and cast long shadows across the mirror-smooth harbour. The town was quiet and only a few figures drifted along its frontage with no sense of haste. No activity at the fishing wharf either – boats clustered along it, their yards bare of sails, held there by *Falconet's* blockade. He swung his glasses further west towards the shacks on the western outskirts. Quiet there too, nothing but cooking-smoke drifting above, no indication that Aubertin's force, obscured from sight by the lava ridge's last plunge into the sea, might be in position. Dawlish fought down the fear that the advance had stalled, that Robillard had been too sanguine about getting the guns across. Without them –

And then the first rifle shots, individual, a half-dozen only, then silence. His heart was pounding, fear of failure gnawing within, awareness that catastrophe now would end his career, destroy his reputation. This was the moment to feign calm that he did not feel just as generations of officers before him had feigned it on roundshot-lashed decks. He turned to Sproul.

"A good start, I think." He spoke loud enough for the quartermaster at the helm, and the messenger by him, to hear.

"There doesn't seem to be much opposition yet, sir." Sproul too was affecting calm. "But we're ready if there is."

Down on the foredeck, Halligan had ranged the three-pounder on the huts, a round in the breech, another ready in his loader's hands, his assistant with an open crate of shells beside him. If it came to a serious battle in the town, the weapon could add little.

But a little is often just enough . . .

Movement among the shacks now, brief glimpses of scurrying figures that might be residents seeking cover or Aubertin's force advancing. The squalid hutments were too close together to give a clearer view and it was impossible to know if the field guns and the Gatling were trundling forward somewhere in that labyrinth of narrow lanes. Now came more rifle-fire, irregular but still separate shots. More likely, some unfortunate dwellers there were being mistaken for threats and dealt with without question.

"There, sir! By the fishing pier!" Sproul was pointing.

Men were bursting into the open from the shacks and hutments and through the more open, and deserted, fish-market, driving towards the old town. Twenty or thirty with rifles, some with bayonets flashing back the rays of the climbing sun. Somebody charging ahead before them, sword upraised, not turning to see if he was being followed. Unmistakable as Robillard.

And no defensive volleys crashing out to halt them.

Desmarais must have been alerted by now, might be disconcerted by the attack from this unlikely quarter. But, professional that he was, that would not last. He would soon be judging whether this was a feint, a diversion for a larger attack from the north-west, where Aubertin's force was likely to be. He would be cautious about throwing too many men forward, would hold his most in reserve in more defensible positions.

Robillard and his men had disappeared among the buildings beyond the fish-market, substantial stone-built houses from the earliest French colonial days. But others were streaming across the market and the Gatling too, lurching forward on its wheeled mount, ten men heaving on tow ropes. Clemenger, urging by their side, was unmistakable by his limp.

Now the first sustained crackle of rifle-fire, then a brief pause – that might mean the advance slowed or halted – before it began again. This time it did not die down. Somewhere in the streets, hidden from *Falconet's* view, Robillard and Clemenger would be probing, seeking to outflank Desmarais' hardening opposition.

The two field guns, the first mule-drawn and with the limber attached, the second pulled by men on tow-ropes, were moving across the market now. No defensive fire was harassing their advance and that must be General Aubertin himself with them, urging with sword brandished high.

A crash, the unmistakable bark of a six-pounder. But not from inside the town. Dawlish swept his glasses towards Fort Montmorency. There. on the plateau before the drawbridge, smoke was still drifting above the field gun that MacQuaid had retained. It had been trundled across the drawbridge and sited to menace the town. A cloud of dust was rising, as it had before, among the huts at the base of the slope.

The crew was ramming another ball home, standing back before a figure that might be MacQuaid himself jerked the lanyard. A stab of flame, rolling smoke, a moment later the report reaching *Falconet*, and then a roof collapsing in a billow of dust. Desmarais might not have many men there but, with luck, the bombardment might be mistaken as the prelude to an attack from the fort. Any diversion of resources from resistance to Aubertin's advance was worth diamonds at this moment.

The fish-market was deserted now and the six-pounders had disappeared into the streets beyond it. The unseen Gatling there, its reports louder than the rifle-fire, was stuttering into intermittent five or six-round bursts. Flame-shot smoke was rising from some house there, a blaze perhaps initiated to flush defenders out.

And now another crash, a six-pounder's, though not MacQuaid's. Smoke was churning up from a narrow thoroughfare. Before it could fire again Aubertin's second gun was blasting in some adjacent street to the west of the Saint Fulbert Barracks. Desmarais might well have established his headquarters there but it had fallen once before to cannon fire and could do so again. Trapping the usurping President Fontaine there would be sweet revenge for Aubertin.

The six-pounders were firing again and then twice more. A silence of moments only before the rifle-fire grew again, a ragged volley followed by intermittent firing that rose and fell in intensity but never died completely. Dawlish fancied that he heard distant shouts and cheering, perhaps some small defensive position being stormed. The sound of rifle-fire dwindled and died.

It was tempting to imagine Aubertin's force driving onwards towards whatever new point of resistance that Desmarais might have improvised and Clemenger's field guns following the advance. But in these streets a house at every corner might become an instant petty fortress that only artillery could reduce if the attackers were not to incur murderous casualties. Dawlish's mind retuned to the estimate of men and rifles he had made previously. The forces were well balanced but Desmarais's experience and expertise might be worth another fifty men. The battle for Port Mazarin might still go either way. Neither the popgun on *Falconet's* foredeck, nor the rounds that MacQuaid was still dropping from Montmorency, could have any effect now on that bitter street-to-street battle.

"Sir! Over the fort, sir!" Sproul was pointing.

A signal rocket was still rising as Dawlish turned. It exploded in a scarlet flash and, as it did, another was rising behind it, and another.

The agreed signal.

Something of importance sighted.

Perhaps directly from the fort or it could be a signal relayed from *Le Déchaîné*.

It could the thing for which he had both longed for and feared.

The struggle for Port Mazarin was out of his hands now and *Falconet* was needed to the east.

*

Falconet had built up to full speed by the time she forged past Fort Montmorency. Only now, as she cleared the headland, did masts and yards and a streak of smoke identify a hull-down vessel on the eastern horizon. Dawlish raised his glasses towards the figure standing still on the parapet above the zigzag. It was Bradbury, pointing towards the newcomer and then waving something that seemed like confirmation. From his higher vantage point, he must be able to see the entire vessel and was sure that it was the *Hermine*. Dawlish waved back and felt reassured – Bradbury's 138s would already be in readiness.

He searched the horizon for another ship and saw none. *Déchaîné* must be somewhere to the north-east, hidden from view by the strip of coast that ran towards Cap Louvois, the island's easternmost tip. She might, or might not, have already detected the drifting smoke to her south and might, or might not, have already started on an interception course.

The stranger was hull-up now and coming straight on. She was some ten miles distant and if she was at full speed, and if *Falconet* maintained hers, they would meet in about twenty minutes.

Dawlish pointed to her. "Hold course on her," he said to Sproul.

In a telescope's disc he caught the white foam climbing far back and high from the ram bow, and the sponsons extending from either side of the hull. No doubt of it – *Le Déchaîné*' twin.

Hermine.

Pelletier must be there, his eye also glued to a telescope. He must hear the irregular and distant boom of cannon fire from the west, must guess that there was fighting in Port Mazarin. He would be feeling mixed hope and trepidation, knowing that his hour of triumph – or of failure – was at hand.

And he had one great weakness. His gunvessel wasn't just a warship. She was a transport as well. She was most likely packed with serge-clad volunteers like Desmarais – how many? a hundred at the least? – and as many arms and supplies as she had failed to land successfully at Pressac. Laden as she was, Pelletier would not want to engage *Le Déchaîné*, would be intent on landing his force at Port Mazarin before she could arrive.

And until she did, there was no option but for *Falconet* to provide a diversion.

With her single three-pounder, and her single Gatling, and at the risk, maybe the cost, of her own destruction.

*

The separation was little over three miles now, less, much less, than the effective range of *Hermine's* 138s. She was just beyond the maximum range of *Falconet's* puny three-pounder. Both weapons on *Hermine's* forward sponsons could bear on *Falconet* and could dismember her with a single round. That *Hermine* had not yet opened fire did not surprise Dawlish – calculating range on head-on courses was more a matter of luck than expertise. But fire she would – and soon.

He was standing with Sproul to either side of the quartermaster. They must be as terrified as he was, he thought, but they were holding fast, just as were Halligan and his men by the three-pounder forward and the gunner and loader on the Gatling's exposed platform abaft and above the bridge. He had ordered both teams to keep the oncoming gunvessel in their sights.

Closer still, close into the range of the Hotchkiss revolver cannon in *Hermine's* foretop that he feared as much as the 138s. Holding the present course was more deadly by the second.

"Two points to starboard." He heard a tremor in his voice.

The bows were swinging over as *Hermine's* forward guns opened fire. An eternity of terror ended with two splashes a cable's length off the port quarter. Pelletier's gunnery officer had misjudged *Falconet's* speed.

And our speed's critical, gives us an advantage of two knots or more.

The vessels were still closing but due the slight deviation from the head-on course, *Hermine's* starboard bow-sponson was slipping from view while the port-after sponson was still masked by that ahead of it. It was a fleeting opportunity while the forward 138 was reloading and that aft could not yet be brought to bear.

"Halligan!" Dawlish shouted. "Three rounds rapid!" And to the quartermaster, "Four points starboard."

Ten seconds between the three-pounder's barks. Two harmless splashes off the gunvessel's port flank but the third round struck the hull just ahead of the forward sponson on that side. The shell's detonation could have done little more than blast a shallow crater in the thick planking, and its flying fragments might not have cut down any gunner in the sponson, but it must have interrupted loading.

And have served notice that, weak as she was, *Falconet* could sting and could not be ignored.

Her new course had unmasked the 138 in *Hermine's* port sponson aft. Flame blasted from it and the aim was good, but the elevation too high. The shell must have shaved only feet above *Falconet* for it dropped a cable's length off her starboard beam.

Now came what Dawlish had most feared, the slow but steady pounding of the Hotchkiss in the enemy's foretop, a half dozen rounds, each falling closer in *Falconet's* wake. But the range was opening and its fie died. Now off *Hermine's* port beam, her course was generally south-east and, at Dawlish's commands, was weaving to upset the 138s' gunners' aims. They fired twice more, dropping shells close, but not close enough, then fell silent as *Falconet* drew away.

"Sir!"

The Gatling gunner was calling from his perch and pointing northwards towards Cap Louvois. Smoke was drifting eastward from behind it. Dawlish's heart leapt. He grabbed the telescope and focussed.

A vessel was emerging from behind the high, rocky, extremity and turning to sweep around it, with white foam climbing far back and high up her ram bow. *Déchaîné* was on her way and less than five miles distant. *Hermine* was sufficiently far to the west that the cape still blocked the Guimbian gunvessel from her sight.

Hermine was off *Falconet's* port quarter now and the range was opening. It was time to bring *Falconet* sweeping around on to a parallel course and draw level off her port beam. He moved to the telegraph, drew the handle fully back to ring for attention, then ground it forward again to the full-ahead position. He bent close over the voice tube, and above the thrashing of the pistons heard Hobson, the engineer, acknowledging.

"I want more speed," Dawlish said.

Hobson hesitated before replying. "We're at maximum revolutions, sir. The safety-valve's close to lifting and –"

"Turn it down, Mr. Hobson. Just enough for five pounds more."

It was asking a lot. The boiler's maximum operating pressure was a hundred pounds per square inch and its seams must be straining already. Were it to rupture, Hobson and his strokers would die in scalding agony. But those five pounds might push *Falconet's* speed advantage a fraction higher and hold it there. It was her only protection.

Hobson hesitated again, then said, "Aye, aye, sir." A pause. "But better not go higher, sir."

Hermine was off *Falconet's* starboard bow now and they were running westwards in parallel, outside effective 138 range. At any time now, *Hermine* must sight *Déchaîné* sweeping around the cape and ploughing towards her on an interception course.

Dawlish fancied the deck beneath his feet was throbbing faster now and that *Falconet's* speed had built such that the gap was closing more rapidly than before. Pelletier's gunnery officer had noted it too. A flash at *Hermine's* port quarter, then smoke trailing astern from the after sponson and an instant later came the 138's report. Then a column of spray climbed a half-cable off *Falconet's* starboard bow.

A sane captain would be pulling away to port, out of range. Dawlish sensed both Sproul and the quartermaster glancing towards him, wondering, praying, when he would give the order.

"Halligan! Hold her in your sights! Fire on my word."

And at his word too, the quartermaster was spinning the wheel over and back, weaving *Falconet* towards the gunvessel, closing the range yet further. The line of approach had one benefit – the masts abaft the Hotchkiss on *Hermine's* foretop were blocking its fire.

Two more 138 shells dropped close, one close enough to shower water on the foredeck.

"Halligan! One round!"

It landed fifty yards short in the gunvessel's wake.

"Up elevation! At your discretion, three rounds!"

Two out of the three hit, one on the transom just above the screw and the other blowing splinters from atop the bulwark just above it. Neither were serious in themselves, but they were warnings that a lucky shot might wreak devastation on the gun crews exposed in the sponsons.

It was as if Pelletier's patience was at an end and he was determined to destroy this stinging nuisance. *Hermine* was turning to starboard to expose *Falconet* to an unhindered broadside from the 138s fore and aft.

"Eight points port!" Dawlish was determined to draw out of range astern of the gunvessel. And to Halligan he shouted, "Five rounds rapid."

To torment, even if not to damage.

Hermine's turn was tight and she was heeling from it, spoiling the aim of her 138s as she did. Her bows were directed northward now, still sweeping around, and she must turn further still if she was to have *Falconet*, now escaping north-westwards, at her mercy.

Then, suddenly, as *Hermine's* bows were headed eastwards, she was turning again, this time to port, to drive north.

Hermine had sighted *Le Déchaîné*.

Chapter 31

Falconet's helm was over, carrying her into a tight turn that would position her off *Hermine's* port quarter as they both rushed north. She straightened into the new course and Dawlish could see *Déchaîné* off the starboard bow, running parallel to the coast and perhaps four miles distant. Within minutes, the twin sisters would meet in mortal combat and *Falconet* was, for now, the least of Pelletier's concerns. The five extra pounds of pressure were telling and she was overtaking *Hermine*. Dawlish intended to draw slightly behind her port beam and slacken speed to remain there, ready to dart in and harass with the three-pounder once the gunvessels engaged each other.

It was Sidwell's moment now, the chance for clearing the shame of his dismissal from the Royal Navy. With him alone in command, Dawlish would have felt less apprehensive but his control of *Déchaîné* was dependent on her Guimbian Captain Queuille accepting his advice, indeed his direction. They had cooperated well together in the engagement with *Hermine* off Pressac but it might be too much to hope for the same in the heat of today's battle.

A flash from far forward on *Le Déchaîné*, smoke billowing and thinning as she charged on through it. The shell was still in flight when the boom reached *Falconet* and seconds later it was throwing up a column of foam a cable ahead of *Hermine*.

Not bad for an opening shot.

Return fire, two shells dropping close in *Le Déchaîné's* wake. The range was closing steadily, and with it must come increased accuracy. *Hermine* was holding fire for now but the Guimbian gunvessel, dead ahead of her, was blasting with both portside weapons.

Two more misses.

Le Déchaîné's helm was over and she was swinging to port to put herself between the enemy and Port Mazarin.

Dawlish's glasses were trained on *Hermine*. He saw four men, one the helmsman, on the exposed bridge that spanned the high port and starboard bulwarks. One stood apart from the others, his binoculars locked on *Déchaîné,* ramrod straight, as assured as if he had been watching a military review at Longchamps. Even had he not been in full uniform – the red breeches and gold-striped red kepi contrasting with the black tunic and riding boots – it would have been impossible not to recognise General Fernand Pelletier. He was dressed for arrival in Port Mazarin as a conquering hero. One of the others – in naval uniform, though without insignia – was approaching him and pointing towards *Falconet.*

Pelletier turned, medals glittering on his left chest. For a moment he and Dawlish were studying each other. Then he lowered his glasses. It was easy to sense why men followed him and women adored him, why millions saw him as their hope. His face was not just handsome but strong too, his iron-grey beard as closely cropped as Dawlish's own, and even at this distance, the deep-set eyes conveyed courage and resolution. Smiling slightly, he raised his hand in salute. No mockery about it, nothing of personal animosity, something of courtesy even, one professional acknowledging another in mutual respect.

He must know of me already and guess now who I am.

Dawlish returned the salute and saw Pelletier smile before he turned back again towards the main enemy, the Guimbian gunvessel.

Kill him and it will all end.

"Halligan!" Dawlish shouted and pointed. "We'll close with that vessel presently! Hold the bridge in your sights! On my word, four rounds rapid!"

The chance of a direct hit was minimal but fragments from a close impact might just cut down Pelletier.

Hermine was bow-on towards *Déchaîné* and both her forward 138s blasted as one. The aim was good but the elevation was misjudged, for both shells dropped short of their target's flank.

Déchaîné was firing now with both portside 138s.

And one achieving a hit.

A flame-shot detonation below *Hermine's* port-forward sponson. A momentary glimpse of a jagged hole punched in the hull's planking where the sponson's metal supporting-brackets were anchored. Derived of their support, the sponson hovered in position for an instant, and then it was collapsing, tearing from the vessel, spilling the gun crew into the water.

Taking the 138 with them.

This was *Falconet's* chance.

At Dawlish's command she drove towards the stricken gunvessel, which was now lurching to port as if out of control. Nearer and nearer and *Hermine's* turn was tightening, enough to unmask the Hotchkiss revolver in her foretop. It opened now, flame stabbing at three-second intervals, each shell dropping closer as the range closed.

"Halligan! Open fire!"

The three-pounder barking. One of the four shells found *Hermine*. A hail of splinters exploded from its impact on the foremast twelve or fifteen feet above the bridge abaft it. The stout mast shuddered but did not fall, though the Hotchkiss in her top was instantly silent. Three of the four figures on the bridge had fallen. Two were struggling to their feet, one of them the quartermaster, who was taking the wheel again, but the third lay crumpled. The fourth man, Pelletier, had not flinched from his ramrod stance.

Hermine was wounded, but not mortally, for there was no sign of fire within that ragged pit in her side. The helmsman had regained control and she was swinging away from *Falconet*, to carry her on a course parallel to *Déchaîné*. As long as she could maintain the Guimbian to starboard she could still bring two 138s to bear on her.

Falconet ploughed on, passed astern of *Hermine*, outside the arc of the remaining portside 138. Only when the range had opened did Dawlish order a course change to parallel *Hermine* and again hang off her starboard quarter. While her two starboard weapons were engaging *Déchaîné,* she posed little risk to *Falconet*.

All three vessels were now on parallel courses, south of west, towards Port Mazarin. Both gunvessels were equally matched for now, even despite *Hermine's* lost 138, for each could bring two guns to bear on the other. Dawlish guessed that the captains of both ships were reluctant to close the range. Neither vessel had been designed for ship-to-ship combat – their role was bombardment to support shore operations, most likely in colonial conflicts. Closer engagement would mean inevitable mutual destruction. The 138s' flat trajectories would make multiple hits a certainty, but survival was unlikely if even as few as three or four shells smashed through the wooden flanks to explode within. Sidwell on *Déchaîné* and his counterpart on *Hermine*, were accepting the lower likelihood of hits but hoping for the few lucky ones that could doom the other. As the damage inflicted on *Hermine* must have come close to doing.

Both gunvessels were firing at longer intervals now but with greater deliberation, single shots to test range, ready to follow immediately with the second weapon should the first score a hit. The accuracy was improving and each splash – short, straddle, too far ahead or too far astern – was closer than before but still not close enough.

Falconet alone had decreased the range, nearing sufficiently to land a four-shell three-pounder salvo on *Hermine*. But not on her starboard sponsons and the crews of their 138s. Halligan's aim had been too high, two shells ripping through standing rigging and another detonating against a spar that did not fall. But the other might have caused significant damage, for it hit the top of the belching funnel and smoke was suddenly jetting horizontally from a hole in its side.

It was probably not enough to reduce draught much, but even the slightest drop could lessen *Hermine's* speed by a fraction of a knot. And that might matter. *Falconet* fell back, turned in a tight full circle, resumed her former position off the enemy's starboard quarter, ready to pounce again.

"*Déchaîné's* hit!" Sproul shouted.

Dawlish had already seen the explosion above the bulwarks, just aft of the port forward sponson. Grey smoke churned there but the gunvessel was still ploughing forward, leaving it in long wisps behind. His spirit howled in silent despair as he saw that the entire bridge had disappeared and with it the men there – Sidwell and Queuille and the helmsman, perhaps more. The ship that had had two captains now had none and she was slewing over to starboard – a severed steering cable must have jammed somewhere and was holding the rudder over.

Time stood still for Dawlish as his mind raced through a half-dozen options. A flash of insight told him that only one had merit.

"Lay us alongside her, Mr. Sproul."

It might already be too late. *Déchaîné* was heading towards the coast now and at any moment some uncharted rock might rip her bottom out. Her guns were silent, their crews probably shocked into confusion. *Hermine*, course unaltered, was drawing away but her starboard 138s were dropping shells close. *Falconet* was racing towards *Déchaîné* now with a mile still to cover.

Who else died in the explosion, who remains to take command?

Sadler, the gunner, had impressed by his training of the Guimbian gun crews and would most likely have the initiative to act, but he might have been on the bridge at the moment of impact. The engineer, Denison, had also worked wonders with his people but, with the telegraph and voice-pipe connections from the bridge severed, he might not yet understand the situation.

But *Déchaîné* was still turning, was curving away from the coast, was drawing out seawards again. With her rudder locked she would continue circling until *Hermine* turned back to kill her.

"I'll board her myself, Mr. Sproul," Dawlish said. "I'll take command."

"We can't come alongside," Sproul said. "Not with those sponsons protruding."

"Come close in to one of 'em aft and try to hold there. I'll jump across."

It'll need fine timing, and superb ship control. And the danger of the two vessels entangling, perhaps tearing the sponson away. And my necessary leap . . .

But no alternative.

"When I've crossed, Mr. Sproul, harass *Hermine* to the limit."

Impossible to be more specific, but Sproul was pragmatic. He'd grab opportunities on the basis of calculated risk. Everything depended on how badly *Déchaîné* was crippled. She had almost completed a full circle but now she was lurching out of it, bows headed south. Her course was sinuous but there was an impression of some limited control. She had no after steering position but somebody must have freed the jammed rudder cables and set men to dragging on them manually. She had slowed to perhaps half her previous speed – did that imply damage, or had Dennison deliberately reduced it? A flash from the 138 on her after starboard sponson announced that she still had fight in her though the shell fell far short of *Hermine*, which was now coming about to finish her.

Sproul was bringing *Falconet* curving around, to take her aft of *Déchaîné*, then straightening to draw parallel to her port side where she would be shielded from fire. Dawlish left the bridge, taking a speaking trumpet with him, and set deckhands to dragging any fendering material they could find to drape over the starboard side. The yacht's steam whistle was blasting short shrieks to draw attention. The gunners in *Déchaîné's* sponsons had seen her and were waving. One disappeared, was back a moment after on the portside aft sponson with a grizzle-haired figure that, even at this distance, Dawlish could recognise as Aitken, the adviser-bosun.

Falconet was close off the gunvessel's port quarter and gaining on her. He could see that *Hermine*, some two miles distant, was drawing over in a wide arc towards the north. Her captain's intent was obvious. With only one 138 available on her port side, he would soon swing eastwards, drive aft of *Déchaîné* and unleash a broadside on her stern with his two starboard weapons before steaming parallel with her to administer further pummelling.

But he must be assuming, wrongly, that *Déchaîné* was still wholly out of control, as her wandering southerly course suggested.

Falconet was level with *Déchaîné* now. Sproul was edging the yacht over to a half-cable's separation and cutting back revolutions to match her speed.

Dawlish had raised the trumpet. "Mr. Aitken!" he bellowed. He saw that the bosun had one also. "Where's Captain Queuille? And Mr, Sidwell?"

"Dead, sir! Both of 'em! I've taken over!"

"Can you steer?"

"I've men on the cables. We can turn. But not tight and not at full speed."

Enough perhaps – a big perhaps – to facilitate escape but not to fight a battle that relied on clever manoeuvring.

"Damage to the boiler or engine?"

"Mr, Denison says there's none, sir!"

"Where's Sadler?"

"With the starboard guns, sir!"

"Hold her steady as she goes! We're drawing in on your sponson." It looked higher than *Falconet's* bulwark. "I'm coming across to take command. Have a man ready with a bowline to cast to me before I jump. A man you're sure can do it. You understand?"

"It's better I do it myself, sir!" Aitken must be close to forty but he was strong and hulking, with enormous biceps.

Hermine was lost to view now, hidden by *Déchaîné's* hull, but she must be drawing ever closer, at full speed, while these two vessels crawled. Keeping her at a distance was critical.

"Send word to Mr. Sadler!" Dawlish called. "Engage with starboard guns. Continuous fire!"

A man disappeared and another brought Aitken a coil of rope. He was knotting a bowline at the running end.

Falconet was edging closer now, closer than anything possible in a sea any less calm than this. Dawlish had stuffed his binoculars inside his shirt and mounted the bulwark abreast the foremast, his left hand grasping a shroud to steady himself. Fear had gripped him – the sponson's deck was at least two feet higher than the bulwark. He forced himself not to look down into the frothing wash between the hulls.

O'Harney, one of the ex-navy seamen, was braced in the shrouds to his left to assist him.

Closer now, ten or twelve feet between bulwark and sponson. A lurch to starboard could bring *Falconet* smashing into the gunvessel.

Dawlish's eyes were locked on Aitken. He had advanced to the edge of the sponson deck – the stanchion rails had been hinged down – and was swinging the bowline, ready to cast. Two men were standing close behind to hold him if he stumbled. He waited until *Déchaîné's* unseen starboard weapons blasted towards *Hermine*.

"Ready, sir?" Aitken called.

Dawlish only nodded lest his voice betray fear.

The line flew towards him, the knot too far to his right. He reached, missed, saw it drop.

The yacht was lurching to port, the gap widening again. Sproul held off a half-minute – an aeon of fear – before he was satisfied that he could safely draw close again.

"Again, sir!" Aitken had drawn the line in, had coiled it, was beginning to swing.

Droplets showered from the line as it flew across.

"I've got it, sir!" O'Harney had caught it.

Dawlish took it, pulled the bowline over his head and shoulders to settle it under his armpits. He saw Aitken's men securing the line's far end to the sponson's 138, then grasping it, prepared to haul.

"Inform Mr. Sproul that I'm ready."

He did not glance back to the bridge as O'Harney called.

Falconet edged closer, six feet separation, five, four, almost three . . .

The foaming chasm could only widen again.

"Now, Aitken!"

Dawlish jumped, fell short, legs kicking in the air, his body impacting again the sponson edge. Pain stabbed from what must be broken ribs. But the bowline was tight and holding him suspended, legs kicking in the air.

"We've got you, sir!"

Hands had grabbed under his arms, were hauling him upwards to land on all fours on the deck. He was shaking, and in pain, but he caught Aitken's hand and drew himself to his feet. He looked back and saw that *Falconet* was pulling away to port.

He crossed the deck and saw a half-dozen Guimbian seamen on each side grasping the rudder cables that ran though eye-bolts let into the scuppers to guide them aft towards the steering flat. A British seaman was calling to the groups, port and starboard, alternately tautening or loosening the cables in response to the shouted corrections of another, far aft, at the open hatch above the steering flat, to hold the rudder midships. A third seaman stood by the engine room companionway and Dawlish glimpsed another at its bottom.

Aitken, thrust into a role he had never anticipated, had done well to set up relays to transmit orders for both steering and speed.

The 138s barked as Dawlish reached the starboard sponson aft and found Sadler, the gunner, there. Eyes stinging as the sulphurous smoke cleared, he saw two fountains climbing ahead of *Hermine*. She was a mile off *Déchaîné's* starboard bow and running northwards. Even allowing for *Déchaîné's* reduced revolutions, the relative speed must be close to twenty-five knots, making aiming difficult. The French captain had recognised this and was holding his fire.

But *Déchaîné* must not. Hitting or not, her salvos could distract.

And might just be lucky . . .

"Keep firing, Mr. Sadler."

Dawlish could see the bridge's twisted wreckage ahead of the funnel. No sense of positioning himself atop it.

"Orders, sir?" Aitken had joined him.

"I'll command from up there." Dawlish pointed to the mizzen shrouds. "You'll stay on deck. Keep your relays standing by for my orders. Get a message to Mr. Denison, that I'll be calling for full speed soon. And get your teams busy on the rudder cables. We're turning to starboard."

Even with a seaman's help, his ribs made it agony to gain the top of the bulwark and stand there, one arm hooked around a shroud, the speaking trumpet in his other hand. A searing gale of acrid smoke lashed past him as the 138s opened again. His eyes streamed – he was too close to the after sponson, but there was no help for it. This was his optimal position.

Down on the deck Aitken was urging the men on the starboard steering cables to haul, those on port to slacken. *Déchaîné's* bows began nudging over, slowly, ever so slowly, then quickened, easing into a broad turn. *Hermine*, to the north-west now, was heeling in a tight turn that would carry her aft of *Déchaîné*. She must fire soon. Dawlish tore his eyes away from her, concentrated on his own vessel's continuing turn, gauging the moment when she should pull out of it.

Aitken had shifted men across from the port steering cable to throw their weight behind those hauling on the opposite side. Inch by inch, bare feet slipping on the smooth deck-planking, heaving like a tug-of-war team, they dragged the line's end another full foot further back. Human muscles could do no more than hold it there but the turn to starboard continued.

And *Déchaîné's* bows were headed south of west now.

Towards Port Mazarin.

"Rudder amidships!" Dawlish shouted to Aitken.

The relay-man above the steering flat was shouting that the rudder was already creeping back. Within a minute, two at most, the vessel would be on a straight course.

"Aitken! Message to Mr. Denison. Full revolutions!"

A half-minute later, *Déchaîné* was surging ahead and gathering speed.

Dawlish glanced towards *Hermine*, just ahead of the starboard beam and on an opposite course. An instant later Sadler's 138s blasted again.

Unlucky shots, their aim thrown off by the relative passing speed of over twenty knots, their splashes rising a half-cable aft of *Hermine*.

"Rudder amidships, sir!" Aitken relayed the confirmation from the man above the steering flat.

"Steady as she goes!" Dawlish shouted back.

Then Aitken was calling for the cable teams to balance themselves again in equal numbers port and starboard. Speed was close to maximum but Dawlish saw that the course was wandering slightly, but brought back each time by commands to heave or slacken.

Towards the headland outside Port Mazarin, and Fort Montmorency atop it, four miles ahead.

Then *Hermine* fired.

Her 138s' reports reached *Déchaîné* a moment before one of their shells smashed into her starboard flank. An expanding hemisphere of chips and splinters blasted out from the point of impact.

And then the shell exploded.

Inside the hull.

Chapter 32

"She's holed, sir! About level with the foremast," Sadler shouted.

He was hanging out as far as he could from the after sponson and looking along the flank.

Dawlish could see nothing from his vantage point.

"At the waterline?"

"Looks like it's just above. A bloody great gap, six or eight feet!"

"Any sign of fire?"

"No, sir."

The denial was no guarantee. Sadler couldn't see inside. The crew's mess compartment was there and just ahead, two decks below, was the magazine for the forward 138s.

Dawlish shouted to Aitken. "I want a damage report. And a hose playing in there, fire or no fire! Buckets until then!"

He looked astern. *Hermine* had come about and was following. Only one 138, that at the starboard bow, could be brought safely to bear. In this stern chase those in her after sponsons were useless. But *Déchaîné's* corresponding pair were not. A mile and half separated the vessels and their speeds were well matched. The range would not change significantly and would favour accuracy. And with only marginal steering ability, Dawlish was unwilling to weave or zigzag.

Sadler had brought his aftermost 138s to bear on *Hermine*. Both ships were dropping shells ever closer, along each others' flanks, ahead of one's foaming bow wave, astern in the other's white wake. Neither's luck could hold much longer.

"There's a fire forward, a small one, sir!" Aiken was back. "They're quenching it, it won't spread. But the damage's close above the waterline. At this speed water's washing into it."

"A lot?"

"Knee deep already."

I'll take my chance. No slackening of speed. And Montmorency's a mile closer.

"Damage to the foreward guns?"

"None, sir, but a man killed by a splinter. Two wounded. Badly."

A column of white water rose just feet below the starboard sponson aft, drenching the 138 crew and Dawlish himself. The weapon on the opposite side had just fired. He looked towards *Hermine*, saw a flash high above her funnel. The main-topmast was arcing over to port, topsail-yard with it, parted rigging whipping, a spar breaking free, then dropping in a tangle of debris towards the ventilator cowls and funnel.

Déchaîné's gunners were cheering but Sadler was shouting for silence, to resume fire, then for the crews in the sponsons forward to carry shells and charges aft. Dawlish hadn't kept count – he knew he should have and felt angry with himself – and the gunvessel's munition stocks must be close to exhausted. His eyes were locked on *Hermine*. She was lurching out of her straight course, guns silent, then coming about again, unhandily, speed unchecked.

But the distraction was *Falconet's* opportunity. She had been following on *Hermine's* port quarter. Now Sproul was driving her towards the gunvessel, pumping shells from her three-pounder – a tiny spark against the hull marked a hit. She was in the blind spot of the enemy's Hotchkiss revolver and in a break between shots the rattle of her Gatling was unmistakable – she must be close enough to rake the gun crew in *Hermine's* port-aft sponson. Then she was pulling away to circle back to stalk again.

Hermine had recovered her course and was bow-on to *Déchaîné* but, in her brief moments of deviation, the range had opened. Dawlish tore his eyes from her, looked forward. Above the wreckage of what had been the bridge, and to the right of the foremast, the headland's bulk was looming massive.

Under three miles.

The maximum effective range of a 138.

And positioned in a fort two hundred feet above the sea, the maximum range would be longer still.

Has the security surrounding the refurbishment of the two weapons mounted there been effective?

Has Desmarais come to learn of it and, if so, had the information reached Pelletier?

Because at this moment *Hermine's* onward rush, and her determination to overhaul and destroy, *Déchaîné*, indicated that it had not.

Falconet was charging towards *Hermine* again with such disregard for the 138 in the port-aft sponson that earlier Gatling fire must have cut down its crew. Sproul was keeping his approach inside the blind spot of the enemy's foretop-Hotchkiss. Halligan's three-pounder was pop, pop, popping steadily at twelve second intervals and, at Sproul's orders, probably aiming for the funnel to destroy furnace draught.

Tormented beyond endurance, *Hermine* was swinging her bows to port to unmask her Hotchkiss. It burst into its slow poum, poum, poum but *Falconet's* helm was also over and she was in the blind spot again and drawing away to safety.

Hermine curved back into her previous course astern of *Déchaîné* but the range had opened yet further and the next shell she hurled dropped short.

Dawlish glanced towards Fort Montmorency. Under two miles now. *Hermine* was entering an unsuspected zone of danger and it was critical to keep her attention focussed on *Déchaîné* to the exclusion of all else.

"Sadler!" Dawlish shouted. "Up your rate of fire!"

The gunners must be close to exhaustion but the intervals between the next three salvos were nevertheless shorter than before. White splashes climbed and fell ahead of *Hermine's* ram. Her starboard forward 138 was replying, its shells dropping close, but never close enough, in *Déchaîné's* wake or off each quarter.

Fort Montmorency was closer now, a mile and a half, and up on the bastion MacQuaid must be observing the three vessels' remorseless advance, calling range estimates and judging the moment for open fire. Bradbury would be at one of the 138s, edging the handwheels over to adjust aim and elevation, and shouting his corrections to the crew of the second weapon. And still waiting for MacQuaid's word.

Minutes, even seconds, were eternities now.

MacQuaid's a soldier, has no experience of naval weapons. He's being too cautious.

For God's sake, don't hesitate further!

A flash, a detonation, at the port extremity of *Déchaîné's* mainyard, splinters and shell fragments showering from it, but no collapse.

Hermine's gunners were well on target now and the next salvo must surely wreak greater devastation. Dawlish braced himself for it, flinched as the 138 nearest him barked again, was enveloped for a moment in the chokings gunsmoke billowing from its muzzle. He was watching for the shell's fall when report of the first 138 to open from Montmorency washed past him. His heart sang as a column of water climbed just off *Hermine's* starboard bow.

A superb opening shot, fired from a rock-steady mounting – not an unsteady ship. An instant later the fort's second 138 spoke also, dropping its shell closer still.

And then more salvos. Safe from return fire, Bradbury's fresh and unfatigued loaders were working like automatons. The rate of fire was faster than any achieved by either gunvessel that day and both weapons were firing in sequence, each correcting aim and elevation on the basis of the other's fall of shot.

Then the first hit, a detonation far aft on *Hermine*. The steering might have been damaged for she was slewing over to starboard, presenting a wider target than before. Montmorency's 138s had settled into a steady rhythm, straddling the wounded gunvessel. *Déchaîné* fired another salvo, scored a hit on the enemy's flank – a flash, sundered wood blasting from it, though no sight of a satisfying glow within.

"Three rounds left in starboard sponson, sir!" Sadler shouted up to Dawlish. "Four in the port!"

"Very well! Hold fire for now!" Then Dawlish called to Aitken. "Get hauling on the port rudder cables. We'll bring her about, sixteen points. Hold the rudder hard over until I call for straightening the course!"

To bring *Déchaîné* around to maul her persecutor.

The was a fire somewhere aft on *Hermine* now, flames flickering above a shattered bulwark and strengthening. No gun crew visible in the sponson there and, with the weapon in the forward sponson long gone, her port flank was defenceless. Her steering must indeed be damaged for her bows was edging slowly to starboard in what must be an intent to draw from range.

Two more hits from the fort, successive explosions, one on the hull amidships and the funnel ripped away by the second. Black furnace smoke was rolling up around the mainmast and carrying sternwards in what must be an eyes-searing and throat-rasping cloud.

Yet she was still a living ship, with a disciplined crew and still-defiant officers. The fort's next rounds straddled harmlessly but the fire aft was the greatest enemy now. Flames were roaring high above the bulwarks. *Falconet*, ever persistent, came curving around, four cables ahead of *Hermine's* bows, Halligan's three-pounder and the Gatling blasting towards the hated Hotchkiss.

Aitken had brought *Déchaîné* well into her turn and was calling corrections to his cable-hauling crews to maintain it.

Then the explosion that almost blew *Hermine's* entire stern away. The flames had reached the after magazine. Wreckage was blasting up and out and smashing down to create a foaming pool from which the maimed ship sought to drag herself. For she still had some forward motion, though it was dying quickly, and what remained of the aftership was sinking. The bows had risen and the ram's vicious point had just broken surface, but they climbed no further and the tortured ship was dead in the water, wallowing and defenceless.

But no colours to strike – none had been flown – and no halyard was whipping a white flag up a mast. Dawlish could just make out figures on the bridge – Pelletier must be there, *Hermine's* resolute captain too, but there were no others. Amidships, another fire was taking hold, fed by the flames roaring from the unseen furnace. It had reached the mainmast's standing rigging and the tarred ropework was itself ablaze and soon the unbraced mast must topple. Small splashes indicated despairing men casting overboard anything that might float and following themselves while others were swinging a boat out on its davits.

Yet still no surrender.

Another round from the fort punched into *Hermine's* flank and detonated within. A second later steam erupted from the rent as the boiler burst. The mainmast was toppling to port, its surviving shrouds snapping and whipping as it swept over into the sea, heeling the wreck so that Dawlish could see that much of her deck was a lake of flame. Men were cascading over the bulwarks into the water, many flailing and disappearing, others striking out for any piece of wreckage that might support them.

Another hit by Montmorency gunners, the shell dropping on the boat now half-suspended from *Hermine's* davits, blowing it and its occupants to fragments.

This is murder.

And still those two figures had not moved from the bridge, holding the rails to avoid sliding down the slope but making no effort to abandon ship.

Pelletier won't surrender. The legend he wants won't allow it.

Déchaîné's ungainly course reversal was complete and *Hermine* lay now a mile off her port quarter. Another salvo from the fort straddled – *Harmlessly, Thank God!* – the dying gunvessel. There was no way to signal to MacQuaid to cease firing. Nothing but to lay *Déchaîné* across the line of fire of his 138s.

"Mr. Aitken! Eight points to port!" And then "Message to the engine room! Half speed!"

The bows crept over sluggishly, for the men on the steering cables were at the limits of exhaustion. It would take two or three minutes more to complete the turn and run parallel to the blazing hulk. But MacQuaid must have seen the significance of the manoeuvre and Bradbury and his 138s were holding fire. Sproul, in *Falconet,* must have recognised that also and she was moving in closer to the burning wreck, one of her cutters swung out for lowering.

Dawlish called a seaman to help him down from the starboard bulwark, across the deck and climb to a similar position on the opposite side. His injured ribs made every movement, and every breath, an agony. He felt so unsteady as he hooked his left arm around a shroud that he asked the man to stay with him, ready to catch him should he lose his grip. He gestured to another to come up to hold the speaking trumpet and groped inside his shirt to extract his binoculars.

"Mr. Aitken! Message to the engine room. Dead Slow!"

It was too dangerous to pass closer than four cables, for *Hermine's* forward magazine might blow at any moment. That was perhaps what Pelletier was hoping for.

Dawlish had him sharp in his glasses now, still proud, even magnificent, his uniform now smoke-darkened but the double row of medals still bright upon his breast. He was looking down towards the men struggling in the water, clinging to wreckage, trying to swim towards *Déchaîné*. His face seemed infinitely sad, that of a man who had gambled and had failed but who asked for no pity in defeat.

Though he did for the men. whom he'd brought to this.

He turned, lifted his eyes towards Dawlish, saluted as he had done before, was saluted in return. Then he swept his hand towards the men in the water in a gesture that said, *Rescue them*.

Dawlish waved in acknowledgment, was glad to see that *Falconet's* cutter was by now stroking towards them.

I should hate this Pelletier for all the misery he has caused, for the bondage he aspired to impose once more on Guimbi, for the ambition that might have carried him to the Elysée Palace and all Europe into war. But I see a man whom I'd have valued as ally, might even have welcomed as a friend, in some other time or place.

Pelletier had turned to the man – surely *Hermine's* captain – still standing by him. They shook hands and then Pelletier was pointing to the water, as if urging the other that it was time to save himself. The captain was shaking his head – he too would remain. They stood in silence, grasping the rail before them for support as the gunvessel heeled further, looking towards the island that had drawn them like a fatal lodestone.

And two minutes later *Hermine* rolled over and disappeared in a cloud of hissing steam. She left nothing but a carpet of debris and struggling men behind.

France had lost her Man of Destiny.

*

A green rocket rising from Fort Montmorency confirmed that it was safe to enter harbour. *Déchaîné* crawled past and Dawlish could see MacQuaid and Bradbury high on the rampart above, Badeaux with him, the 138s' gun crews lined up to either side, all others than Le Maître cheering and waving. Dawlish would have sent a boat to the jetty to fetch MacQuaid, but *Déchaîné's* two were trailing on tows astern, laden with fifty-seven exhausted or wounded or dying survivors from *Hermine*. *Falconet* was still standing off the wreckage field, her boats searching for the last living bodies amid the floating debris.

Around the headland now – and the town of Port Mazarin was revealing itself. Smoke still rose from a few dying fires but there was no sound of cannon fire or rifle volleys. At the sight of *Déchaîné*, figures at the main wharf ahead scurried back into the town behind to spread the word. Soon a crowd was gathering there and growing. Some were cheering. Then a small commotion, men with rifles pushing the throng back to create a space at the landing steps. Dawlish focussed his glasses, saw Aubertin arriving – he was in full uniform now, feather-trimmed cocked hat and gold braid aplenty, a savage joy in his face. His nephew, Robillard, was on his right, Clemenger on his left.

Port Mazarin had fallen and Guimbi had a new master.

Déchaîné dropped her anchor and a small boat cast off from the jetty and stroked towards her.

*

"It was somewhat of a damp squib," Clemenger said. "Fontaine's people had no heart for it. They broke inside an hour."

He was sitting with Dawlish in one of the offices inside the Saint Fulbert Barracks. MacQuaid had come down from the fort to join them.

"And Desmarais?" Dawlish knew that he had been captured.

"A bloody fine soldier," Clemenger said. "Made a warehouse into a little fortress. Without the six-pounders we'd be there still. He surrendered to save his men, what was left of 'em, when their ammunition ran out." He paused, then spoke with a trace of disgust in his voice. "Aubertin wanted him shot then and there. I wasn't having that. Nor his people either. Damn fine fellows, even if they're Frenchmen."

Fontaine, the short-lived usurping president, had been less lucky after he'd been found hiding under sacks in one of the barracks' cellars. During the hour-long session that Dawlish and MacQuaid had just had with Aubertin and his nephew, the general had recounted with wolfish delight how he'd personally pounded his rival's head to pulp with a rifle butt.

Dawlish hadn't commented on that. What had mattered was to impress on Aubertin that it was not in his interest to supplant the ailing President Ravenel immediately. Restoring rather than replacing the existing government after what had amounted to an attempted coup would give an impression of stability. It might even impress Guimbi's numerous creditors, the more so if Maître Badeaux be formally appointed Minister of Finance. Aubertin would serve as Minister of Defence for five or six months and succeed then as president, with Ravenel's failing health an excuse. There would be a semblance of order restored and, as so often before and as so often betrayed, of hope that Guimbi might settle its debts someday.

It had been more difficult to persuade Aubertin that Desmarais, and the seventy or so Frenchmen who were *Hermine's* survivors, should not be shot. Robillard, less vengeful than his uncle, had suggested keeping them as forced labourers – it would be good for Frenchmen to have a taste of slavery in Guimbi. But there would be resentment enough in France, Dawlish said, when news of Pelletier's heroic failure reached there. Shooting his supporters would evoke outrage and probably prompt demands for an official punitive expedition that the French government could not resist. Better to ship the prisoners, including Desmarais, to Guadeloupe, where they would be the responsibility of the French authorities. The argument went back and forth for a half-hour before Aubertin agreed with reluctance. What would become of the Guimbian prisoners was not discussed but Dawlish suspected that, for many, justice would be summary.

The callous but necessary business of negotiation with lives as currency disgusted him. He wanted to be gone as quickly as possible now. *Falconet* could have himself, MacQuaid, Clemenger and the Rural Guards back in Escource by nightfall.

But before leaving, he would have two short meetings.

*

Desmarais was detained, alone, in a malodorous cell in the barracks' guardhouse. He was as Dawlish had imagined him, lean and sinewy, face leathery from years' exposure to the sun, hair and beard both grey. The right sleeve of his badgeless blue serge uniform had been ripped away to allow bandaging of his upper arm. Somebody had taken his boots and left him barefoot. That made him look no less uncowed when he rose from his plank bed when Dawlish entered.

"Monsieur le Gouverneur? L'Anglais? Capitaine Dawlish?" he said.

Dawlish confirmed it, speaking French.

"Colonel Gustave Desmarais. Late of the Forty-Third Regiment of Infantry." He extended his hand.

There were limits to chivalry. Dawlish didn't take it.

"I presume there's to be a firing squad." Desmarais said it calmly.

"It won't come to that."

"So then?"

"My yacht will return tomorrow," Dawlish said. "She'll ship you and your people in Guadeloupe. I imagine you've friends and influence there. What they do about you is none of my business. I'll expect your word of honour that there'll be no effort to take over the yacht. Her crew will be armed and with orders to shoot to kill if anything's attempted."

"D'accord," Desmarais said. "And the wounded?"

"I've seen to it that they'll get as good treatment as is possible here."

Which meant almost none. It had taken hard arguing to get Aubertin to agree even to that. Given the hideous wounds and burns of so many of *Hermine's* survivors it was likely that there would be fewer of them by morning.

"Thank you, Capitaine," Desmarais said. "And may I ask for two favours more?"

"Within reason."

"Tell me how the General died." For Desmarais there could be only one general. Pelletier.

"He died well," "Dawlish said. "As I think he'd have wished. At the end of a long battle. Beaten, but not defeated." That had to be admitted.

Then he told the details and, as he did, he felt increasing hostility to the dead man, though he strove to keep it from his voice. It had all been so unnecessary, this squalid little war and untold misery brought about by one man's messianic vision and iron will. There were tears in Desmarais' eyes as he listened and he looked away lest Dawlish notice them.

"He was the best man I've ever known," he said when the account of the battle finished. "I'd have been honoured to die by his side."

His voice had been trembling before he fell into silence.

Dawlish said, "You mentioned a second favour."

"Give me a revolver and a single round. Then leave me alone here for ten minutes."

It might be an act of kindness. But there's been enough death already. I won't be party to more.

Dawlish shook his head.

"Your men will need an advocate in Guadeloupe. In France too. That's your duty now." He hesitated before adding. "And the general's memory will need a witness."

For Pelletier had indeed had something of greatness about him.

No further words were exchanged and Dawlish left.

*

The second visit brought bitter satisfaction.

The Soulier twins had been crammed in a tiny cell with a dozen or so of their Roscallan associates. They had been stripped to little more than underwear and all were barefoot. Most were badly bruised about their head and torsos but Dawlish saw no open or bandaged wounds. He recognised faces he'd first seen indignant on the Escource quay when Badeaux and *Déchaîné* had arrived with relief supplies for the refugees from the volcano's ire. He saw others who had joined the attack on the camp at Thénac. They'd been sullen in defeat afterwards and all of those detained that night had been later judged innocent by a sympathetic Roscallan judiciary. But today there was despair on their faces and terror in their pleading to be returned to Escource. None of them had distinguished themselves in the fighting in Port Mazarin's streets and most had run, Clemenger said. His Rural Guards had enjoyed rounding them up.

Dawlish had the two Souliers dragged out and brought to an empty cell. Both were hobbling. One – Armand probably, though facial bruising had made it hard to distinguish between them – seemed to be finding it as painful to draw breath as Dawlish did himself, even though his ribs were by now bound for support.

"You can't leave us here," Etienne said. "Not with these savages."

"We're British citizens." Pleading in Armand's voice. "We've a right to decent treatment."

"Where?" Dawlish said.

Neither answered.

"Where would you prefer? Here in Guimbi, where you're no more than bandits, and bloody ineffective ones at that? Or in Roscal where there's a charge of murder waiting for you?"

"We don't know anything about any murder." Etienne wouldn't look Dawlish in the eye.

"Not the killing of Councillor Chevit's old major-domo? He had a name – Mathieu Dufaure – not that it would mean anything to you. And there's the attempted murder of the councillor himself. He barely survived but he'll never talk again."

"You've no witnesses. No white ones," Etienne said. "No black's testimony is going to count in a Roscal court."

"But it would have to listen to your lackey William Gilman. He's ready to go Queen's evidence. He's sworn an affidavit. Against you both and against your crony Gaston Delbos who broke into Chevit's house with you. I've noticed that he's been sharing a cell with you. I don't think he'll hesitate to swear like Gilman if it'll save his neck."

"I told you we shouldn't involve him," Etienne snarled at Armand.

"But there'd be another charge too," Dawlish said. "Theft of eighty Brunswick rifles, and other arms and ammunition besides, from a Roscal government armoury. Delivering them to rebels in a friendly country and waging war against a legitimate government there. That counts as treason. Something too serious to be tried in Roscal. It would have to be in London."

A pause to let the words sink in, to enjoy their terror. The image was strong in his mind of two inoffensive old men, one black, one white, both beaten mercilessly, one to death, the other to just short of it.

"I understand that they don't draw and quarter for treason anymore," Dawlish said. "But they still hang."

He turned away, ignored their babbles, wanted to see no more of them. He turned to Clemenger.

"Have them put back with the rest of 'em," he said.

Etienne's knees were giving away and a Rural Guard had to half-carry him. Armand was weeping.

And afterwards, when they had been locked in again, Clemenger said to Dawlish, "What's to happen to them now?"

"They came of their own free will," Dawlish said. "They're welcome to rot here."

*

Just off the deep cliff-bound inlet where *Déchaîné* had once lurked, *Falconet* passed from Guimbian into Roscallan waters.

The mundane concerns of governorship seemed very attractive to Dawlish now. Before addressing them however, he must write his reports to London, long and frank for Topcliffe, shorter, and with much unsaid, for the Colonial Office. But then the business of doing what he could for Roscal would begin again. He would be immersed in the always-inadequate revenue allocations, the to-and fro communications with London over grants, the encouragement of new crops and fostering of new trade opportunities. And the schools and roads, employment for the returnees from Panama, finding others like Madame Geneviève and the Reverend Elijah to bring hope to communities, supporting the initiatives that d'Erlanger had commenced and that others of his class were now starting to take heed of. And Florence and the Relief Committee's funds would make some difference too.

What he could do here would never be enough and he didn't know how much longer he'd remain as governor, but he'd do his damnedest. The people of the whole island, Roscal and Guimbi alike, deserved better of history.

One man and one woman could only do so much.

But it was better than doing nothing.

Chapter 33

Birds were singing in the trees of Waterloo Gardens as Dawlish walked past the monument to Sir John Franklin and the crews of *Erebus* and *Terror* on his way to Pall Mall. It was ten minutes to eight on a glorious late spring morning, bringing 1888 the promise of an even better summer. He had left Florence, with Jessica and Ted, behind at the Charing Cross Hotel. Agatha was to collect them later to take them on a tour of London to show the children the sights. Ted was hungry to visit the Tower and Jessica was now just old enough to want to see the queen and the princesses. They weren't at home today, Dawlish had told her, but she would see the palace where they lived. The RMS *Eudoxia,* which had brought them from Jamaica, on the last stage of their return from Roscal, had docked the previous day. He had telegraphed Topcliffe to confirm his arrival and they had come directly to London. He found an unsigned note signed waiting at the hotel.

Eight o'clock in the club in Pall Mall.

Topcliffe was sitting in the familiar library, in civilian attire, like Dawlish. Handshakes, pleasantries, a servant bringing coffee and closing the doors when he retreated.

"We'll be talking to the Colonial Office – Sir Cathcart Soames and his people – at eleven," Topcliffe said. "And Farnsworth at the Foreign Office at two. Best to get the meetings with them over. They won't be easy and it's better we're prepared."

Dawlish hadn't expected that they would be easy. He had guessed as much from a few remarks made by his successor when responsibility for Roscal had been passed. Sir Robert Gibson, previously governor of some fly-speck island in the Pacific, had been especially disapproving of efforts to get the Poll Tax abolished. His wife had turned down Florence's offer of a tour of schools. Suggestions for meeting Miss Giltrap, the midwife-trainer, and Madame Geneviève – "She's black, is she?" the new governor's lady had asked – had been declined with ill-concealed scorn.

"Naïve benevolence gets you nowhere with such people." Sir Robert told Dawlish. "Like that suspension of the Poll Tax. It only creates expectations that can't be met." His only regret was that now-disarmed *Falconet's* chartering had been terminated. Had it not been, Dawlish suspected, the accommodation on board would have been renovated with considerable luxury.

"So, Soames and Farnsworth aren't pleased about the outcome?" Dawlish said to Topcliffe.

"Oh, they're delighted with the outcome. But they'll question if there wasn't any other way of dealing with Pelletier and Desmarais."

"Was there?" Dawlish felt his temper rising and repressed it.

"Of course not. It was well done, couldn't have been better. They know that just as well as you and I do, though they'll never admit it." Topcliffe said. "But I understand that Farnsworth had some difficulty in keeping the full story of your involvement from the French ambassador and he won't forgive you for that. And as far as Soames and the CO are concerned, you aren't one of theirs and never will be."

"He's correct in that, sir," Dawlish said.

"If it's any comfort, they don't think anything better of me, Dawlish. One gets used to it in my position."

The position never exactly defined.

Topcliffe smiled. Dawlish had seldom seen him do so. "D'ye know your worst offence in Soames's view?"

"No, sir."

"You recommended that man d'Erlanger as your successor."

"He did a good job in my absence, sir."

"That was the worst of it, as far as they're concerned. And the fact that he isn't one of theirs."

Topcliffe had drafted a list of questions that were likely to be asked and had already prepared outline answers as *aides-memoire*.

"If you can't remember any, just clear your throat, Dawlish," he said. "I'll wade in to emphasise the good news."

Good it indeed was. Guimbi quiet, for now at least. Revocation of the repudiation of all debts. Ravenel still president in name. Aubertin biding his time as Minister of Defence. Maître Badeaux, as Finance Minister, currently in Paris, negotiating yet another loan to pay part at least of outstanding interest. Order in Port Mazarin, calm in the countryside, the calm of resignation rather than of content.

And in France a growing scandal about corruption in the finances of the Panama Canal venture, accusations and counter accusations, resignations, threats of prosecution and even of duels, and investors ruined in vastly greater numbers than had ever been ensnared in loans to Guimbi. Pelletier had been forgotten already and Desmarais, never prosecuted, had attached himself to yet another would-be man of destiny.

"Business as usual for the French," Topcliffe said. "And no taste for *revanche* or for recovering lost provinces when there are more immediate problems at home. Long may it be so."

It was doubtful that anybody would be concerned about conditions in Roscal. With Guimbi restored to its traditional state, Dawlish's successor would manage the Crown Colony as it had been before. Out of sight and out of mind in Britain.

"It's a splendid day out there," Topcliffe said at the end. "Too fine to take a cab. Let's walk to the CO together."

He was more affable than Dawlish had ever known him. And a sense that the relationship had changed and that something was yet to be said.

They passed the Franklin memorial. Topcliffe nodded towards it.

"It broke my heart as a lieutenant when my application to join his expedition was refused," he said. "But men like you and me survive disappointments." He paused and when he spoke again there was something like sympathy in his voice. "You've probably guessed there'll be no K for you, haven't you?"

Dawlish nodded. He had. Being dubbed Sir Nicholas had never been an ambition for himself, but he'd wanted it for what it would mean to Florence.

Lady Florence.

He was glad that he had never mentioned the possibility to her.

"Is there another appointment in the offing, sir?" he said.

"A ship?" Topcliffe said. "There'll be one of course. But better not immediately. I'd prefer to have you in my office for a few months to learn the ropes. Nothing promised, you understand. But I can't live forever."

And as with all Topcliffe's suggestions, impossible to refuse.

*

Agatha was still with Florence and the children when he arrived back at the hotel that evening. Both women were smiling. Agatha fished in her enormous handbag and produced an envelope. It was addressed to him.

"From my cousin," she said. "He sends his regards and he thinks you'll like the contents."

He tore it open, scanned it. One name immediately caught his eye.

Jean-Baptiste Marignan.

Who, in despair, had split his exploiter's skull with a machete.

Over whose sentence Dawlish had agonised and for whom he had decided in the end that, honour bound by his oath as governor, he could not recommend clemency.

But Neville Eversham, Queen's Counsel, could.

He had taken up the case, had appealed, had found irregularities in the handling of the original trial and evidence, had argued it and won a reprieve with his golden tongue.

Marignan would live out his life in hard labour but it was better than the noose.

Thank God.

The End

A message from Antoine Vanner and Historical Notes

If you've enjoyed this book, I'd be most grateful if you were to submit a brief review to Amazon.com, to Amazon.co.uk or to Amazon.com.au. If you're reading on Kindle, you'll be asked to rate the book by clicking on up to five stars. Such feedback is of incalculable importance to an author and will encourage me to keep chronicling the lives of Nicholas and Florence Dawlish.

If you'd like to leave a review, whether reading in paperback or in Kindle, then please go to the *"Britannia's Rule"* page on Amazon. Scroll down from the top and under the heading of "Customer Reviews" you'll see a big button that says "Write a customer review" – click that and you're ready to go into action. A sentence or two is enough, essentially what you'd tell a friend or family member about the book, but you may of course want to write more (and I'd be happy if you did since readers' feedback is of immense value to me!).

You can learn more about Nicholas Dawlish and his world on my website www.dawlishchronicles.com. You can read about his life, and how the individual books relate to events and actions during it, via www.dawlishchronicles.com/dawlish/

 You may like to follow my weekly (sometimes twice-weekly) blog on www.dawlishchronicles.com/dawlish-blog in which articles appear that are based on my researches, but not used directly in my books. They range through the 1700 to 1930 period.

By subscribing to my mailing list, you will receive updates on my continuing writing as well as occasional free short stories about the life of Nicholas Dawlish. Click on: www.bit.ly/2iaLzL7

Historical Notes – *Britannia's Rule*

France's Third Republic was born during the disastrous Franco-Prussian War of 1870-71 and died in an even more humiliating defeat in 1940. During its lifetime it saw loss of territory to Germany, vicious civil war, unstable governments that often endured only for months, massive corruption, frequent scandals, social unrest, and bitter political and religious feuding. The nation came together heroically during World War 1 but, though the lost provinces were recovered, that unity ended thereafter and two decades of decline followed. The period up to 1914 was however of great scientific, industrial, artistic and literary achievement.

Dreams of revenge against Germany, and of recovery of the lost provinces of Alsace and Lorraine, were strong influences on politics in the Third Republic's first four decades. More realistic leaders recognised however that France alone did not have the industrial strength, or population, to defeat the military and industrial superpower that the new German Empire had become. The alternative was to rebuild confidence and prestige by winning a French colonial empire overseas. Vast territories were conquered in North, West and Central Africa, in Madagascar and in Indo-China (latter known as Vietnam). The ease of success against weak local forces may have engendered the overconfidence that led to the massive French defeats in the first month of war in 1914.

Widespread disgust and anger about the corruption and weaknesses of the political class caused many to hope for a new "Man of Destiny" who, like Napoleon I, would impose order, discipline and unity. Many found him in General Ernest Boulanger (1837-1891), a national hero who went into politics and gained wide following from a range of disparate interest groups. He lost his nerve however when his opportunity to seize power came in 1888 and he failed to grasp it. Charged with conspiracy and treason, he fled from France and died by suicide on his beloved mistress's grave three years later.

France's most ambitious undertaking of the late nineteenth century was the attempt to build a sea-level canal across the Isthmus of Panama. If successful, the profits from passage-tolls would be enormous. The technical challenges and the costs were underestimated from the outset. Vast numbers of institutional and private investors poured money into the venture because of confidence in the promotor, Ferdinand de Lesseps (1805-1894), who had previously overseen construction of the successful Suez Canal. The feasibility of a sea-level waterway at Panama was not questioned, nor was account taken of endemic Malaria and Yellow Fever that made the isthmus a killing ground. Construction lurched ahead from 1882, losing thousands to disease and making ever-greater demands for further investment as setbacks mounted. The crisis came in 1888, when failure could no longer be disguised. Massive financial irregularities were exposed, including widespread bribery of parliamentary deputies to gain continuing support. Thousands were ruined, de Lesseps died in disgrace and respect for the political class plunged even deeper than before.

The Spanish-American War of 1898 emphasised the strategic necessity of such a canal to the United States to allow fast transfer of naval units from the Atlantic to the Pacific. When the United States committed to the project in 1904, it was for an above sea-level waterway with locks at both ends. The first step was however the all-but-total elimination of the Malaria and Yellow Fever hazard. This was through a "War on Mosquitoes", which were by then recognised as the vectors for infection transmission. A further American measure was supporting secession of Panama, then a province, from Colombia and recognising it as an independent nation that would support the project on mutually agreeable terms. There have been few more effective examples of ruthless application of the idea of *Raison d'etat*.

The debt problem that dominates Guimbi in this book mirrors that which crippled Haiti – still today the poorest nation in the Western Hemisphere. Originally the French colony of Saint-Domingue, it was, like other European colonies in the West Indies, of immense value in the eighteenth century for its sugar-growing capacity. Abominably treated slave labour underpinned this. When the slaves did revolt in 1791, it was the prelude to a quarter-century of massacre, attempted reconquest by the French, civil war and, finally, establishment of an independent nation. The price of France's acceptance was that Haiti would take out vast loans from French banks to pay compensation to the previous slave owners. Haiti's slaves were thus required to pay for their own emancipation.

The hated plantation system had been destroyed however and it was now impossible to produce sugar on a scale sufficient to underpin payback of interest on the loans, much less the principals. Compound interest meant that the debts soared by the year and yet further loans were needed to continue repayment, thereby incurring more debt – and so on, and so on. The inevitable consequence was a perpetually failed state, lacking the wherewithal for development and mired in corruption, instability, ignorance, poverty and violence. Many interests internationally, which did not want to see a "black republic" ever succeed, took malicious pleasure in Haiti's plight, holding it up as evidence to support concepts of inherent white racial supremacy.

Britain took a different approach when it abolished slaveholding in all its territories in 1834. It paid compensation to the slaveowners, taking out a loan to do so that amounted to some 40% of the national budget of the time. The debt was not paid off finally – by the British taxpayer – until 2015. It should be noted that Spain did not abolish slavery in Cuba until 1886, nor did Brazil do so until 1888, a form of compensation being paid to owners in both cases. In different and disguised forms, slavery is still with us today in many countries, including developed ones, to the eternal shame of Humanity.

The Eastern Caribbean is an area of significant volcanic activity. As of the time of writing, some nineteen volcanos are considered active there, even if not in eruption The fact that most are located on tiny and relatively densely populated islands, with limited flight opportunities, makes each one a potential catastrophe. The eruption of Mont Pelée on

Martinique in 1902 was especially devastating, killing some 19,000 people and destroying the town of Saint Pierre so completely as to leave only one survivor. A more recent eruption was that of the Soufrière Hills volcano on the small (10 miles long, five miles wide) teardrop-shaped island of Monserrat in 1995. It continued intermittently until 2010. Over half the island was made uninhabitable and some two-thirds of the approximately 7,000 population were forced to emigrate. A gripping account of the residents' resilience in the face of this disaster is provided in *The Volcano, Monserrat and Me* by Lally Brown, who was there at the time of the initial explosion and for a long period thereafter. Her book is a paean to the ability of "ordinary people" to rise to extraordinary levels of courage, resolution and endurance in the face of disaster.

Warship design was in a state of flux in the 1880s, reflecting arrival of new technologies and uncertainty as to how best to incorporate them in individual vessel types. This applied especially to battleships. It was not until 1891 that the Royal Navy's *Royal Sovereign* class established the "Pre-Dreadnought" paradigm that was copied in other major navies for over fifteen years. Prior to that, small-number classes of widely differing configuration predominated. One such design approach was concentration of the main armament in staggered turrets amidships, located on opposite sides of the centre line. The Royal Navy built five such ships in the *Inflexible*, *Ajax* and *Colossus* classes. HMS *Scipio* in this book belongs to the last of these. Similar ships were built in the United States – notably the ill-fated USS *Maine* – and in Italy and in Germany (for the Chinese Navy). The configuration was superficially attractive since, in theory, it allowed all the main armament to fire on almost all bearings, while grouping it amidships to allow concentration of armour there. It took, however, little account of the blast implications of cross-deck fire. The idea had a limited revival later in several Royal Navy Post-Dreadnought battleships and battlecruisers.

Our Authors

Rick Spilman is the founder and manager of Old Salt Press, an independent publishing company that provides the umbrella for a number of authors who write nautical fiction. As well as keeping up a hugely popular blog, "Old Salt Blog", Rick has published three very successful nautical books — *Hell Around the Horn*, *The Shantyman*, and *Evening Gray, Morning Red*, plus a novella, *Bloody Rain*. *The Shantyman* won a Kirkus Reviews Indie Book of the Year award, and deservedly so. All four are absolutely first-class reading.

Alaric Bond, an English Old Salt Press author, is the producer of the hugely popular "Fighting Sail" series, set in the Napoleonic Era, the latest of which is *The Barbary War*, the fifteenth book in the series. He has also produced three stand-alone books, *The Guinea Boat, Turn a Blind Eye,* and *Hellfire Corner*, the latter being set in WW2.

Joan Druett became a maritime historian by accident. While exploring the tropical island of Rarotonga in the South Pacific, she slipped into the hole left by the roots of a fallen tree, and at the bottom discovered the centuries-old grave of a whaling wife. Because of this, Joan became a noted expert in the history of women at sea, leading to ten novels and seventeen works of nonfiction, including the bestselling *Island of the Lost*.

Linda Collison is American and has written the Patricia Macpherson nautical adventures series, the first being *Barbados Bound*, the next two books being *Surgeon's Mate* and *Rhode Island Rendezvous*. Linda has also published other works independently, including biting satires under the *'Knife and Gun Club'* banner, and *Redfeather*, which was a finalist in Foreword's Book of the Year Award. A fourth book published with Old

Salt Press is *Water Ghosts*, a haunting tale that was a number one Amazon bestseller in the Young Adult category.

Seymour Hamilton is Canadian and the author of The *Astreya Trilogy*. His work, though maritime, is very reminiscent of Tolkien's carefully wrought fantasy worlds. He also set *Angel's Share*, which was beautifully illustrated by Shirley MacKenzie, in the *Astreya* world.

The list also features V. E. Ulett, the nom-de-plume of a very successful Californian writer who normally specializes in steampunk adventures. Her three maritime novels, are published under the Old Salt Press colophon: *Captain Blackwell's Prize, Blackwell's Paradise,* and *Blackwell's Homecoming.*

And there is also Antoine Vanner – author of the *Dawlish Chronicles* series of historical naval adventures set in the late 19th Century. Eleven books in the series so far, and still counting!

Visit: oldsaltpress.com/about-old-salt-press

Made in United States
Orlando, FL
19 December 2023